ANNAPOLIS

THE MAKING OF A NAVAL OFFICER

A NOVEL

CARL A. NELSON

Copyright © 2012 by Carl A. Nelson

ISBN 978-0-7414-7645-6 Paperback
ISBN 978-0-7414-7646-3 eBook

Printed in the United States of America

Published July 2012

INFINITY PUBLISHING
1094 New DeHaven Street, Suite 100
West Conshohocken, PA 19428-2713
Toll-free (877) BUY BOOK
Local Phone (610) 941-9999
Fax (610) 941-9959
Info@buybooksontheweb.com
www.buybooksontheweb

DEDICATION

To the Annapolis Class of 1956

And all the men and women of the blue and gold, who
for a century and a half have trained to defend their
country from the sea.

"One ship drives East, one ship drives West

By the self-same winds that blow;

But it is the set of the sails and not gales

That determines the way that they go.

And so it is with the ways of Fate

As we journey along through life;

It is the set of the soul that determines the goal

And not the strain and the stress."

Ella Wheeler Wilcox

ACKNOWLEDGMENTS

A work of this kind is a fictionalized patchwork of things that actually happen during life at the service academies, particularly Annapolis and West Point. To my recollection it is the only novel that reveals for the reader the total four-years at the academy. I am grateful to those who gave freely of their time to read and critique and otherwise make this a more interesting story. My thanks also goes to those classmates and other Annapolis graduates who passed-on their recollections of the academy experience. They include: Barbara Nelson, Ralph Harms, Roger Box, '56; Paul Fournier,'56; Don Scovel,'56; Gerry Fulk,'56; Dan Harington, '38; Mike McBride, '56; Mal Malloy, '56; Brian 'Spider' Havey, '62; and Katie Edwards, '92. I can't forget the Seven Come Eleven read & critique group of: Keith Taylor, Paul Darby, and Gene Elmore; as well as Marsh Cassady's critique group. They all gave me excellent criticism.

Of course my wonderful wife Dolores did a masterful editing job and gave me several important ideas to improve the work.

PREFACE

When I started this work, my perspective was that this book would write itself. After all, much of my life had been spent in the yard at Annapolis as a midshipman and later as Company Officer. I even served a year as Tactical Officer (equivalent to Company Officer) at West Point. I know a lot about the making of a military officer. But as the characters took form, I began to think more about what the story was really about. It could not be another non-fiction book explaining the structured hardships of academy life. More than anything else it had to capture the essence of the experience, i.e. how core values are introduced and where the training leads the graduate, that is, how the Academy turns teenagers into naval officers. It also had to capture the youthful virility, drive, action, conflict, and enthusiasm of the entire scope of training experience. Not every midshipman becomes an admiral in the Navy. Not everyone who completes the course lives his life like a Boy Scout. Yet they all carry with them more than an engineering degree and a stripe pinned on their collar that shows they passed through the gate. For the boys (and girls) who might be interested, the alumni who will remember, and citizens who have foot the bill, my hope is that this book adequately captures the essence of the culture that is planted during those years in the yard – upon which the navy's tree of life continues to grow.

To be sure there will be those who read this book, set in the 1960's and say, "But the Academy has changed. For one thing there are women in the service."

My answer is that the message imprinted while in Bancroft Hall will live with the graduate no matter their gender, race, or religion.

CONTENTS

Read Carl Nelson's other books by placing your order at his website: www.carlanelson.us.

CHAPTER 1

THE BEGINNING

They came to Annapolis from every valley, mountain, plain, and surrounding islands. They came from towns named Cave Springs, Georgia; Sausalito, California; and Loa, Utah. They were the sons of farmers, gas station operators, bread makers, ditch diggers, doctors, and professors.

All but one wanted to become a naval officer and even he, Seaman Blake Lawrence III took a deep breath, held it, and silently questioned, *yes? Or no?* The words came in an indifferent mumble that reluctantly sealed the contract. "So help me, God!"

He breathed normally.

"Welcome midshipmen! You are now officially plebes," said Commandant Robert O'Brian. Then he added, "One last announcement. After you're dismissed, would Midshipman Blake Lawrence please come forward? All right, you may break ranks and join your families."

"Me? What's up?" Blake felt embarrassed at being singled out in front of his new classmates, but they didn't notice. They just ran in every direction, weaving their way toward the crowd of onlookers who had witnessed the swearing in.

Blake made his way through the mass of moving classmates until he stood in front of the commandant who was talking to another officer whose body language seemed familiar. Blake saluted Captain O'Brian. "Midshipman Lawrence reporting as ordered, sir."

"So you're Lawrence," O'Brian said turning away from the other man. "Well, another Blake Lawrence joins the brigade. Someone's here to see you, son."

"Thanks, Bob." The other man shook the commandant's hand and turned.

It was too late to walk away. Blake found himself standing in front of Captain Blake Lawrence II, the man he hated.

He couldn't walk away; instead he remained at attention and saluted again, this time to his father.

"You two probably want some privacy. Use my office, Blake."

"Thanks again, Bob."

"Least I can do for an old grad. Take care." The commandant turned and walked toward other parents and friends.

"You look good, son," Blake's father said. "Gained a bit of weight since I last saw you. You look smart in your uniform."

"What do you expect after five years?" Blake said sarcastically. Then he added, "I have things to do." He began to walk away.

"Now hold on, son. I came up from Norfolk to congratulate you. You could have told me you wanted to be a midshipman. But, I'm proud of the way you did it: enlisting in the Navy and all."

Blake stopped and faced his father. "You didn't come all this way to see me. That's B.S. You were at the Pentagon on business. That your next job?"

"Well, I'm here. And I'm glad to see you."

"After five years. You're glad? No way." Blake didn't want to be any more disrespectful than he'd been already. He turned and started down the steps from the Rotunda, intending to get back to his new room and away from the man who abandoned his mother and children for a younger woman, a flag wife.

"Trey, come back here! That's an order!"

Blake stopped and turned.

"Aye aye, sir!"

Pilot wings glittered in the light. Four gold stripes lay across the shoulders of the white uniform that provided background for his father's face, now red with anger. "It's about me and your mother, isn't it?"

Silence.

"Well, is it?"

"I have things to do, sir," Blake said. "Request permission to shove off, s*ir*?"

"Trey, you don't have to *sir* me. Damn it, I'm your father. Tell me; is it about your mother and me? Why are you acting this way?"

It was the face everyone said Blake resembled, blue eyes and the fair complexion of their Swedish heritage. Unlike his father's hair, once blond but now dark brown, Blake's was still only lightly tarnished. The two had the same protruding brow, high angular cheekbones, and sturdy cleft chin. His father's lips surrounded bright teeth, which, when he wanted, gave a charmingly easy smile. It was the face that resembled Blake's grandmother, a loving woman, one of his heroes. *Not like this person who I stand before, who I dislike more than any other.*

Midshipman Blake Lawrence III looked Captain Blake Lawrence II directly in the eyes and with a defiant expression saluted and walked away.

CHAPTER 2

RISE AND SHINE

Light. Morning. Quiet. Much like a Pennsylvania trout stream on a Monday after the weekend fishermen had gone home. Blake's eyes opened slowly. He heard birds on the windowsill and the quiet breathing of his roommates. He scanned the room like a submarine periscope circles the horizon for enemy ships. His two roommates were still asleep in their bunks against the opposite wall.

Emerald Groler, already nicknamed "Stone," had a face like a beautiful woman -- too pretty for a man. He had delicate features with big round eyes as if he were from the West Indies. Tall and thin, his walk and graceful balance give the impression he was better suited to be a ballet dancer than a naval officer. Stone's hands were slender and bony like those of a piano player, and he looked very young, no more than sixteen or seventeen at the most. But he also looked strong. His muscles were long and hard, no fat. Everything seemed to surprise him, like when plebes were told they had to change their underwear every day. Stone said, "I've never seen this much underwear before, let alone change it every day."

Brandell Sikes, the other roommate, looked like the lineman he claimed to be. His body showed a plump middle, probably beer-fat. His shoulders were so wide they stretched the seams of his white work blouses. He had flat cheeks and a blunt nose with a neck like a Sumo wrestler.

The two looked as if they were at peace with the place. Blake was not. He rolled on to his back and stared at the ceiling. His feelings and thoughts spun out of control. *So, I'm here -- the place of Nimitz, Porter; and my grandfather.*

His life in the Navy stretched back to the time when he first visited his grandfather. The first Blake Lawrence. was class of 1904. His grandmother still spoke with a Swedish accent. Granddad married her during a tour of duty as attaché in Stockholm. As a "Tombstone Admiral," he and Grandma lived in retirement in San Diego until he died. She still lived there. Granddad said all he got out of the Tombstone promotion was a little better parking spot. But when Blake was a kid, his grandparents lived in Washington, D.C. So did Blake's parents. His dad was an aviator, Class of 1938. It was during that time that he learned the most about the Navy. He even went with his granddad to visit the Academy.

"Let's go into Memorial Hall," his grandfather had said. Blake remembered that they had passed through the massive doors of Bancroft Hall, through the rotunda, then up another flight into a large, round room. Pursing his lips, his grandfather said, "Shhhhh... Shhhhh... Quiet. Be quiet and listen." He whispered, "Quiet. Listen. Do you hear them? Listen. Look around. Listen hard. You can hear them -- the voices of those who came before – listen! Noble men: Bull Halsey, Farragut, Dewey, Arleigh Burke, Perry, Dan Gallery, Nimitz, King, John Paul Jones. They're just a few of the heroes of the Navy. You may wish to join them. You could come here, you know, and complete the course of instruction. You could take your place among those heroes."

His granddad told him a lot of other things about the Navy, about World War I and about going to sea in the North Atlantic and about the old four-piper destroyers. That was when Blake fell in love with the Navy.

Of course, all that happened before the divorce.

So far, being at the Academy is like the three days I spent in the brig when I was a sailor. Instead of Marine guards, I'm surrounded by the mausoleum called "Mother B" - – six wings of concrete and granite. It will be four years with no life. Boring khaki, white, and blue uniforms. No radios, stereos, coffee, TV, cars, or marriage, and... worst of all, no beer. Plebe summer was only eight weeks, but it amounted to a repeat of boot camp. Hell, I could do that standing on my head. It couldn't be too much harder than boot training. That wasn't too bad, except for Chief Beliechechovich. It was old Belly Checker who tried to keep Erie and me out of the Academy. BC was an SOB. But this will be different, an entire year of hazing by upper-class pricks.

They say there isn't hazing, but everyone knows there is, at least there used to be -- when Dad and Granddad went here. But it's different than boot camp -- on top of the hazing there's the schoolwork -- engineering stuff -- math and science. What did Diogenes say? "I'm looking for an honest man." The founders of this place also had virtue in mind. Especially honor -- the Navy believes honor is everything.

Wonder if we'll all make it through plebe summer? So far it's a lot of running -- run, run everywhere. Get uniforms, haircuts, learn to march. So far so good, for me... but not for the other two. They may not make it.

Well, they're my roommates for the summer, until the academic year begins, when the brigade comes back from summer leave. It's not the same as the real Navy, but I may as well make the most of it. It is an honorable place and the education is more than just naval training -- it's a good school -- among the best, so people say. My granddad, in his pep talks, quoted someone -- I guess one of the old geezers of the past, "'The Academy,' he said, 'It's a fine place to train naval officers and eliminate the unfit.'"

Where would I get a better education? Penn? Pitt? I doubted it. No better nor worse than what this school does. But this is about giving your life – maybe -- for your country. I would die for the United States, I guess. Of course I would, if it came to that. Someone said the idea is to make the other poor SOB give his life for his country, not give yours. Was it General Patton who said that?

Granddad's hero was Nathan Hale. He talked about him all the time. He told me Hale was an American patriot of the Revolutionary War -- hanged by the British as an American spy when he was only twenty-one. Hale was captured, but before the hanging, he made a speech that ended with 'I only regret that I have but one life to lose for my country.'

I'm not sure if the Academy is for me, but if I do stay it will be for Granddad's images, not my dad's.

Blake studied his roommates. They first met on their second day at the academy, when they were assigned to share a room.

Brandell had introduced himself, "Heidi, hire yew? Name's Brandell Sikes. Jawjuh. Call me "Reb." Where yew from?"

Blake didn't understand a word he said, but Stone did. He replied, "My name's Emerald Groler. Harlem. Most people call me "Stone" – get it? Emerald, Stone." He giggled like a kid but with the patois of a New York gangster.

Blake simply followed suit and answered: "Blake Lawrence III, Pittsburgh." But he sensed the contrast: a Negro from Harlem sharing a room with a rebel from Georgia and a blond-haired ex-sailor. Could be trouble.

Blake extended his hand to both but there was no warmth in the shakes, a sign of newness – already weary of the new system into which they'd been thrown like fish into a lily pond.

Six-fifteen a.m. Reveille. Bells broke the silence. The day began. But no one moved. For a few minutes, as if to resist the beginning of their venture, they delayed putting their feet on the floor. Finally bodies stirred. Then activity exploded: showers, teeth brushing, metal lockers clanging, desk drawers opening and shutting, and shoes being shined. Beds would be made after breakfast with powder blue bed spreads tucked stiff with the Naval Academy emblem in the center. Navy blue blankets folded at the foot of the mattress. Chairs screeching on hard decks, bright work shined until the brass sparkled like an evening star. Only one word was uttered by any of the three -- Stone said "shit" when he nicked himself shaving.

A knock on the door. It flew open. Three bodies jerked to attention and stood by their beds wearing only their Navy-issue skivvies.

"Rise and shine, plebes. Breakfast formation in ten. Move out, plebes!"

Bancroft Hall was a place with wide corridors and rooms filled with desks all pushed into the middle. Lockers were filled with rigidly folded uniforms.

The training had begun instantaneously -- like jumping into a swimming pool, with no turning back. Everything was new and fast and "on the double," even the meals. They were like jackrabbits -- up down, up down, lecture after lecture, days crammed full of activities.

"What's the schedule?" Stone asked.

"Same as yesterday," Blake responded in a bored voice. By now he had memorized a daily schedule that hadn't changed since his dad and granddad had been midshipmen: reveille 6:15, breakfast 6:50, classes 7:55 – 4:05, lunch 11:45 – 1:05, athletics 4:05 – 6:30, evening meal formation: 6:30, study: 8 – 10:15, taps 10:30. During plebe summer, study time was spliced between lectures about the history and heritage of the Navy and the Naval Academy.

"Not the schedule -- I mean what do we do today?" Stone persisted as he finished the final touch-up of his spit shine.

"Sorry. Thought you meant the times. We've got a bunch of military stuff. Shooting, sailing. Things like that."

They had been there for only a few days, but most of the time so far was spent standing in lines to receive new clothing and get their hair cut, military style. Blake's was already cut Navy-short, but after the Naval Academy barber was finished, there was barely a quarter-inch on top and none on the sides. His blond hair lay on the floor among the dark strands from the previous man in the chair.

Afterward they stenciled their name and laundry number on everything: their underwear, white works, even their Navy-issue jock straps.

The longest line had been at the tailor shop deep in the basement of Bancroft Hall. A skinny little man from Jacob Reeds of Philadelphia carefully measured everyone. One midshipman remarked that the tailor looked like he had been there since the founding of the school back in 1845. Their blue and white uniforms wouldn't be ready until just prior to fall when the brigade returned, mainly because the quality of the cloth and tailoring was among the best in the world. For most, their Navy uniforms would be the only "tailor-made" clothes they would ever wear.

As the midshipmen climbed on the small box to be measured, they were each asked the same question, "How do you dress?"

Only the men from wealthy families knew what the tailor meant, because they were the ones who bought tailored clothes. When it was explained that it had to do with the natural positioning of the male's private part, some answered "right," others "left." The remainder just shrugged their shoulders. For those in doubt the slightly built older man instructed, "Left side! Always say that you dress on the left side. I'll leave enough material in the crotch so your heavy artillery will hang comfortably in the left side of your trousers."

Even their vocabulary changed. Pants were now called "trousers," coats were "blouses." Bathrooms were "heads," walls became "bulkheads," and a ceiling was an "overhead." They also absorbed Navy talk and gentleman talk like osmosis -- without knowing it was happening.

Tom Blackstone, a junior year, second classman who herded their summer company through the lines and schedule, said there would be a lot of marching, sailing, rowing, and other physical stuff.

"This is the time to learn order, not after the "firsties" get back," Blackstone said.

Firsties. The nickname of senior year midshipmen word struck fear into even the most fearless.

For most, there had been little if any order to their lives. Most left that to their mothers.

"After breakfast, we go to a place called the 'Sail Loft.' You know -- tie knots, then to the obstacle course, and finally to the swimming pool."

"Oh, no -- swimming?"

"Why 'oh, no'?" Brandell asked Stone.

"Can't swim."

"Really? Whad chew expect? No swim'n? Wanna be a saila don't chew? Come hire to the Nava Academy? It's all about wata."

"Don't know. Guess I thought it was all about good food, girls, and lots of fun." A cynical smirk splashed across Stone's face.

"My god. Those a damn po reasons to be hea."

Blake caught the first sign of Brandell's dullness when his face and words showed that he thought Stone was serious.

For the next several weeks they marched everywhere in platoons of about thirty new plebes under the guidance of a second classman. Tom Blackstone let everyone know two things: he was from North Dakota and he wanted to be a Marine.

At the Sail Loft, the class met Shorty. "I'm a chief not an officer -- a chief boatswain's mate, but since you midshipmen outrank chiefs, you can call me 'Shorty.'"

He continued in his gravelly voice, "I'll teach you how to tie knots, but you'll learn a lot more than that from me. I love the Navy and when you get to the fleet, I want you to be good sailors, so we'll start right off with my philosophy. If you follow what I say, you can become good officers -- not pricks -- and you too can have a good life in the Navy. Doubt me, and you'll be miserable. Remember this: The good book says, 'So ye sow, so shall ye reap...' And that's the goddamn truth! Be a shipmate, not a shit mate! You understand? It means that the Navy is all about being a good player -- on a team. And that's the goddamn truth!"

Shorty proceeded to enlighten Blake and the rest of the class with what he called "marlinspike seamanship" -- the art of knotting and splicing various ropes and cordage. He held up a piece and explained, "Now you may think this is rope, and you could be right, but on the other hand you could be wrong. In the fleet everyone refers to it as 'line.' They call wire 'rope.' Got it? In the fleet this is line and this" he continued, pointing to a sample of three-inch round wire, and continued, "this is rope. Now, line is made by twisting strands made from yarn, which is twisted from fibers and slivers."

Shorty showed them how to seize the end of a line and coil, Flemish, or fake a length of line onto the deck for seaman-like storage. "This is the bitter end," he said as he held the end of line high over his head. "And this is the bight," making a bend in the line. "And this," he pointed to the straight length, "is the standing part. Now sometimes one line has to be joined with another or secured to an object like a stanchion or hawser or cleat." He explained the various knots, bends, and hitches and showed the difference between a granny knot and a square knot. He demonstrated a fisherman's bend, sheet-bend, bowline, clove-hitch, half-hitch, and rolling-hitch. Finally he made them practice several of the more practical knots and bends, always correcting them by gently showing them the proper method and adding, "And that's the goddamn truth!"

After marlinspike seamanship, which Shorty claimed was the rock upon which the Navy was built, they moved on to learn the rudiments of boats. For Blake, it was the whaleboat races that were the most fun. The lesson was teamwork again. The coxswain (one of the smaller mids) gave the orders: "Up oars, down oars, boat oars." A chief petty officer nicknamed "Doggy" explained the techniques of rowing, mixed with a few choice cuss words, as if indoctrination into the Navy was not complete unless new midshipmen could speak the language of the common sailor.

When they started pulling, each man was out of synchronization with the others, crashing the oars of the man behind or in front. But before the week was out the races became competitive. "Whose boat will be fastest?" Doggy shouted. "Pull. Pull together! It's like being in the fleet -- there it's teamwork that counts."

A week later it was on to the rifle range. Hot! Sweaty. Dressed like sailors in blue dungarees, leggings, and a caliber .30 M-1 rifle, the same one Blake trained with in boot camp. A Marine instructor told them, "Squeeze the trigger, and don't jerk it." Then the public address announcement came, "All ready on the left, all ready on the right, all ready on the firing line." Pause. Waiting. Nervous. Then it came: "Commence fire!" It was the first real experience of what they were at the Academy to do: learn to fight wars.

The sound of bullets cracked the silence of otherwise attentive, somewhat anxious midshipmen until the scream was heard, "Cease fire! Cease fire! Didn't we say never, never, point that GD weapon in any direction but downrange, mister?" Three Marines surrounded the pitiful mid, all screaming at once.

"Prone position. On your bellies, men -- keep that barrel pointed downrange. Spread those legs, tighten that position, now squeeze."

Blake's squad was standing behind the firing line waiting its turn when a squad from another company straggled by on the way to a break. "Pittsburgh, ain't this great?"

It was Erie, Blake's pal from sailor days. Since arrival they had been separated and too busy with the routine to visit each other.

"Stone, meet Larry Tallman. Erie – Emerald Groler."

The only two black midshipmen in their class nodded then bumped their hands in a strange ritual.

"How ya do'n buddy?" Erie asked Blake.

"OK. If you like sweat in your eyes and dirt in your face," Blake said as he leaned on his rifle.

"No, I mean we're *here*! We're midshipmen -- at the Academy!"

"Yeah, so?"

"Boy, would I like to see old Belly Checker's face right now." Erie loosened the rifle sling and slipped his M-1 over his shoulder.

"That SOB!" Blake said.

"What company are you in, Pittsburgh?"

"Ah, Larry, drop the Pittsburgh stuff. Call me Blake."

"Yeah, okay. What company? Gimmee your room number. I'll come over."

"Second company, first wing, second deck, room 1214."

The second classman who was herding them shouted, "Move out, Tallman. Who told you to sling arms?"

"See ya, Pittsburgh."

"Blake, Larry."

"Yeah, Blake, see ya." As he went off, Blake heard Erie explaining to his platoon leader that he had already gone through Navy boot camp and knew more about guns than the second classman would ever know.

*****

The class began its swimming training the next week. The instructor demonstrated the Australian crawl, the breast stroke, and the floating back stroke, then told the mids to jump in and try it. Most were swimmers of at least basic accomplishment. They splashed around and showed they could stay afloat, but Stone didn't move from the pool deck.

"Didn't I say get in the water, mister? Get in -- that's an order!" the instructor shouted.

"Ah, sir --"

"I said get in the water!"

Stone was right when he said he couldn't swim. He didn't rebel when the instructor insisted he jump in, but he looked scared. He jumped in, but didn't come up.

Blake shouted, "He can't swim!" then jumped in and swam Stone over to the side of the pool. The instructor and several others pulled him to the deck, where he lay coughing and spitting up water.

"You could have drowned! Why didn't you say you couldn't swim, mister?"

"You gave an order, sir"

"Order? Are you crazy, nigger?"

"Don't call me that!" Stone jumped up screaming. "Don't ever call me that!"

"What did you say, boy?"

With that, Stone shouted, "That either!" He charged. Swinging his skinny arm, he hit the instructor in the chest.

All sound in the pool area stopped; even those in the water stopped splashing. All eyes were upon Stone and the instructor he had just hit.

It reminded Blake of the time back in boot camp when Erie hit Chief Belly Checker. That was what started their problems -- and ended up, in a convoluted way, bringing the two to the Academy.

Another instructor backed Stone against the wall of the natatorium shouting, "You shit bird! You hit an instructor."

Stone shouted, "Let me go!" as he struggled to be free, but several others held him there until he calmed down. The class watched in silence as Stone was led away, still shouting, "I'm not anyone's boy."

CHAPTER 3

PLEBE SUMMER

Later that day, Blake and Brandell were sitting at their desks. It was evening and the shadows of the elms splashed across the green playing fields that bordered Bancroft. The last rays of light spanked the Severn, causing a sparkling sheen across the windless, flat water spoiled only by a few cat's-paws.

Brandell was spit shining his shoes.

Blake read *Reef Points*, the book of plebe knowledge. Looking up from the small pocket-sized reference, Blake said, "Stone's been gone a long time -- almost supper. Think they'll kick him out?"

"Back home wha ah come from, he'd be gone already. No doubt aboot it." Brandell held his shoe under the light. "I'll neva get these shoes to look like yo's. How yew do it?"

"Practice, my man. And good boot camp training."

It was not until well after supper that Stone returned.

"Where yew been?" Brandell asked.

"The commandant's office with Ensign Franklin. They're trying to decide if I'm stay'n or go'n. I don't care. But I won't forget about it, like some want."

"They're what?" Blake sensed his own anger erupting. "Deciding? Forget about it? Reb, isn't that crazy? The instructor called him a nigger. You heard him, didn't you?"

Brandell raised his hands to the sky as if to salute an invisible god.

"When are they going to decide? And who is 'they?'" Blake continued questioning Stone.

"He denied saying it," Stone responded. "He's an instructor. Regulations say you can't hit an officer. You do, you go home."

"The instructor denied it?" Blake asked.

Stone didn't answer. He just sat on the edge of his bunk and shook his head. Then he bent from the waist and covered his face and eyes with both hands.

"Ah did hea it. True, it did happen. But, that's not unusual talk -- it's just that, talk," Brandell said.

"The hell you say. It's not just talk!" Blake burst out, sounding very indignant. "Hell, I'm not putting up with it. I'll go see Ensign Franklin in the morning."

Blake didn't sleep well that night. His mind kept flirting with the fragments of Naval Academy history he had learned from his father and grandfather. He knew Stone wasn't the first Negro to be admitted as a midshipman. There was one in the Class of 1937 and another one before that in the Class of 1936, but they didn't graduate. He remembered his grandfather telling him that the first colored mid entered way back in the late 1800s, maybe 1870. But none graduated until Wesley Brown in the Class of 1949. None of them had an easy time of it but Stone's was a case of blatant stupidity. Everyone, that is everyone who didn't live in a cave, who had their eyes open to a changing America, knew that the one word that ignited rage in people of African descent was "nigger." Blake knew why he felt so strongly about that disparaging word. His own grandmother was an immigrant and although most people couldn't tell from his last name, Blake became just as incensed when he heard the taunting words, "Dumb Swede."

He remembered his basketball-playing buddy back in Great Lakes days. Stan Washington was smarter than anyone in Electronics "A" School and he passed the screening exam. However, somehow the paperwork for his application to the Naval Academy got lost. Stan was one of the most easy-going guys Blake ever knew, but everyone was mindful that one thing set him off -- the word "nigger." It was the same with Erie – *that* word set him on fire. Stan didn't get to the academy, Erie did, but only because of an obvious screw-up on the part of a chief.

Ensign Franklin, a member of the immediate graduating class, who stayed behind to train the incoming plebes, wasn't in his company office after breakfast. Blake was obliged to continue the day's routine, which took his company to the obstacle course. It was a series of running and strength tests intent on determining those who had endurance and fitness problems. If a midshipman didn't complete the course in the minimum time, he was required to undergo extra training. Stronger than his skinny build would imply, and fast as lightning, Stone excelled in the obstacle course. He had the best time in the entire class. When they returned from their morning of training, Ensign Franklin had already departed for lunch. Blake waited outside his office until afternoon formation, but still no company officer. One of the upper classmen winked and said, "Ensign Franklin has a new wife." Blake let the office know that he had information about the swimming incident and then went on to formation.

That morning the class assembled in Memorial Hall - - this time for a lecture about the Navy and the Naval Academy.

Blake remembered his grandfather's voice from the time he visited the room long ago. Now as he stood there, a chill crossed his shoulders. Humbled by the pictures and statues and battle flags that hung from the walls and ceiling, he asked himself, "How could anyone become like them?"

He listened intently to the instructor, a Marine colonel dressed smartly in his full dress white uniform with war decorations and sword. Blake assumed it was a costume purposely selected to impress the mids and add drama to the talk.

"The history of training midshipmen to become officers parallels the history of the naval service. You may be interested to know that a mutiny lead by a midshipmen was the reason for establishing this Naval Academy. You see, in 1842 a man by the name of Philip Spencer, son of then Secretary of War Caufield Spencer, led a mutiny to kill Commander MacKenzie, the captain of the Brig *Somers* and take over the ship. I'll get back to that, but first you should know about our naval service."

Clever guy, Blake thought. *Leaves us hanging on a mutiny -- wanting to know what happened while he feeds us the rest of his crap.*

The colonel paused and then continued, "To fight the British, our founding fathers built a fleet of ships and called it the 'Continental Navy.' For those of you who are interested, the Marine Corps was also founded by the Continental Congress at the same time, way back on November 10, 1775 -- we had two battalions serving then. They even fought for ol' John Paul Jones.

"Unfortunately, the Congress abolished the Navy soon after we won the revolution. They considered it an unnecessary expense. However, the world's largest oceans surround America, so merchantmen argued that they needed a Navy to protect them from pirates. Thinking better of their earlier decision, Congress passed, on March 27, 1794, an act to establish the United States Navy."

He paused for effect, and then began again. "Back to the midshipmen story. At that time mids were trained aboard ship. Like the British method: catch them young, about twelve years old, and send them to sea through their sixteenth year. But the French navy believed that land training was the better method -- which probably explains why the French kept getting their butts kicked by the likes of Lord Nelson. Ha, ha."

There was a sprinkling of snickers, mostly from the brownnosers in the class.

"In the beginning of our Navy, classroom work was conducted aboard naval ships by a handful of teachers," the colonel continued. "However, several training schools were eventually established on land as places where midshipmen could go to cram for the lieutenant's exam. One of the first midshipman schools was called the 'Philadelphia Naval Asylum.' It was founded in 1838.

"In 1839 the Navy ordered three steam-driven vessels; this made authorities aware of the need for officers who understood the principles of steamships. From that came a call for a school similar to West Point."

The colonel, obviously a Naval Academy graduate, stopped, cupped his hand over his mouth and said, "I should wash my mouth out with soap for uttering those foul words!" He smiled. "You know West Point, that school on the Hudson River which had been established in 1802. The school our Tar football team beats every fall. From those early days came the Navy motto you should always remember: A messmate before a shipmate, a shipmate before a stranger, a stranger before a dog, but a dog before a sojer. Ha, ha, ha.

"In April of 1842, William Chauvenet accepted an appointment to the Philadelphia Naval Asylum as professor of mathematics. Shortly thereafter he took over as headmaster. In 1843 he developed a plan to expand the curriculum to a two-year course of instruction and set about getting the Navy's approval.

"At first he was unsuccessful because there was resistance in Congress. However, on March 3, 1845, he had a stroke of good luck. George Bancroft was appointed Secretary of the Navy. Yes, the same Bancroft for which this giant barracks called 'Mother B' is named. Trading on their common academic experiences, Chauvenet, Yale Class of 1840, convinced Bancroft, Harvard 1817, that the two-year course of training was necessary. It took Bancroft only three months in office to acquire Fort Severn, an obsolete army post. On August 15, 1845, Bancroft appointed Commander Franklin Buchanan to be in charge and ordered co-founder Chauvenet and the other professors from the Naval Asylum to the new location."

Hope he doesn't expect us to remember all those dates.

"So there you are, gentlemen, that's how we ended up with a Naval Academy right here on the Severn River. Ever since, training has been about the same. Instead of going to sea then coming back to prepare for the lieutenant's exam, your training will consist of attending classes here during the four academic years. But every summer you will get practical training. Your program is very similar to the way it has always been done. When *you* are finished you will be appointed either ensigns or second lieutenants.

"Oh, about the midshipmen mutiny aboard the Brig *Somers*. Midshipman Spencer's mutineers failed to kill Captain MacKenzie. Instead the three were hanged. The scandal of it all became the main argument that convinced the Navy that it needed a permanent school to train midshipmen."

He finished his lecture with some bits and pieces of Naval Academy trivia, e.g., that the school adopted the word "plebe" from West Point. Which he supposed they had adopted from the Roman word plebeian meaning of the common people.

Blake scanned Memorial Hall once more. He again felt inspired by the history of the naval heroes whose stories were displayed along its walls. Blake knew that the words "Don't Give Up The Ship" on Oliver Hazard Perry's flag at the battle of Lake Erie were actually spoken by a Captain James Lawrence -- a man with Blake's last name. He didn't think he was a relation although maybe he was – perhaps way back in the family history? Captain Lawrence's words became the American Navy's battle cry. Perry's flag hung prominently near pictures and stories of George Dewey, Class of 1858, hero of the battle of Manila Bay and Chester Nimitz, Class of 1905, genius of World War II.

"Class dismissed."

Glad to be out of that tutorial history lesson, Blake and his fellow plebes were next off to the gymnasium. They were in the midst of learning the fundamentals of boxing from a pug-nosed instructor named Spike when a classmate wearing an armband that said "MOW" (messenger of the watch) came for Blake. "You are to come right away -- as you are, don't change uniform -- they said to double time -- to see the company officer."

"Midshipman Lawrence, Fourth Class, reporting as ordered, sir."

"At ease, Lawrence. Got your message. What is it you want to tell me?" Ensign Franklin asked.

Blake spread his legs to parade rest, one hand clasped behind his back, the other holding his white hat crushed against his leg. "Sir, my roommate is Midshipman Emerald Groler. He told me that he is being considered for discharge because he hit an instructor."

"Yes?"

"I heard the instructor call Stone... er, Midshipman Groler, the 'nigger' word, sir."

Franklin, who was tall (over six foot), came out of his chair and put his face near Blake's. He crossed his arms over his chest and asked, "So?"

Bristling at the officer's apparent effort to bully him, Blake tensed then raised his voice, "So, sir. Anyone would hit somebody who called them that word, sir."

"You think so, do you? What do you care?"

"He's my classmate, sir."

At that response Franklin seemed to relax. He returned to his desk, stoked his chin and said, "Good answer. You play basketball, mister?"

"Yes, sir."

"Coach know about you?"

"I think he does. My coach back at Great Lakes told us he did."

"Haven't seen you over on the basketball court."

"Been busy, sir."

"Get out there!"

"Aye, aye, sir." Blake snapped to attention, put on his hat, and did an about-face.

"OK, Lawrence. I'll pass your statement on to those who are investigating this mess with Groler. You can go back to your class. By the way, what is it?"

"Boxing, sir."

A sheepish grin appeared on Franklin's face, "Watch out for the old one-two."

That night while shining their shoes, the door to their room opened with a bang.

"Attention on deck!" The voice of authority shouted as the door slammed against the bulkhead.

Blake, Brandell, and Stone jumped to attention.

"Carry on, plebes."

"Erie, you SOB!" Blake said with a cry of relief. It was neither an officer nor even an upperclassman; it was Blake's buddy from his sailor days.

Erie raised two fingers on his right hand and gave the carry-on sign.

Blake introduced him. "Stone, you remember Larry Tallman. Brandell, Erie and I were at NAPS together. Don't mind him. He's just up to his old crap. Erie, these are my roommates."

Brandell nodded to his dark-skinned classmate.

"NAPS?" Brandell asked.

"Yeah, Naval Academy Prep School."

Erie took a seat on the radiator under the window. He asked, "You ready for some liberty? Heard the commandant's gonna change the rules and let us have a few hours out in town before the firsties return."

"You liberty hound," Blake said as he set his shoe aside. "I knew you'd be going over."

"Can't stay to shoot the shit too long. Big inspection tomorrow. Just long enough to set up a rendezvous. How about meeting me next to Tecumseh right after noon formation? We can see what's going on in Annapolis, or we could even go to Baltimore or Washington. You guys wanna come along?" Erie asked.

"Can't," Reb responded. "My fatha is coming. Got rooms at Ca'va Hall for the weekend."

Stone just shook his head, no.

"You the guy they're giv'n a hard time to about not swimming? Heard about it over in my company. Everybody's talking about it."

"It's not about not swimming," Blake corrected his buddy. "An instructor called him a name."

"Ah. Whatever." Erie backed toward the door. "Got to go. Nice meeting you guys. See ya in front of Tecumseh, Blake."

After Erie left, Blake said to Stone, "You should get out on liberty. Come along with us if you like. Can't stay in the room all weekend."

Stone's head still rested on his hands. "No. I got things to do. I'll be all right."

CHAPTER 4

LIBERTY

Blake and Erie made the rendezvous. Tecumseh, as the plebes had already learned, was the figurehead of an Indian warrior salvaged in 1865 from *USS Delaware* a 74-gun, line-of-battle sailing ship. The statue originally represented Chief Tamanend, the leader of the peaceful Delaware tribe. But midshipmen wanted it to represent a more warring character, so they changed the name to "Tecumseh" in honor of a chieftain who ravaged the American frontier in the War of 1812. From the beginning, most midshipmen went along with the belief that the stern-looking warrior possessed supernatural powers -- he was good medicine and became the "God of 2.5," the passing grade on a scale of 4.0. As they walked past the statue, Blake was reminded of photos he had seen of midshipmen throwing pennies as offerings for a passing grade. Little did he know that he would soon be flipping a few coins himself.

The two friends felt important as they strolled through the historic town, the capital of Maryland, in their new white work uniforms. No one else recognized their importance. Their baggy trousers and equally loose-fitting pullover jumpers worn with a black neckerchief tied under their chins marked them as freshmen at Annapolis. The Navy school and its students were invisible to the city's population except twice a year: the Army-Navy football game and graduation. The rest of the time the general public was unaware of the school unless something went wrong -- something that was newsworthy.

They marched in step as if they were in a parade, and their attitudes matched their strides. Changed from the happy-go-lucky sailors of less than a month ago, they felt confident and proud but strangely subdued. In other times they would already have been getting drunk in some slop-shoot bar on the sleazy side of town.

"Want a beer?" Erie asked.

"Yeah, but we're not supposed to. We get caught and we could get a Class A, even be booted. Ya know we're not allowed to drink within seven miles of the capitol building."

"We can take a cab out to Glenburnie or Arnold." Erie persisted. "They're outside the limit. I hear there's a couple of bars out there that serve mids."

"Ah... not sure we should," Blake said. "And we're not supposed to go outside the seven-mile circle either. Even if the bars would serve us, we'd be very visible. Too dangerous."

"Now or never, buddy. We better do it before the first class gets back."

They wandered the surrounding area of Crabtown's Capitol Circle along with hundreds of other plebes, just killing time. They walked the cobblestone streets peering into curio shops, hoping a cab might come by, but none did.

Finding a cab was a problem on a weekend when the state government was not in session. After a half-hour they headed toward the small harbor in the corner of town just off the Severn River. There they came upon a taxi discharging some civilians. Jumping in, Erie said to the driver, "Know any bars where we could get a beer?"

The driver, a scruffy-looking man by academy standards, replied, "A couple."

"Take us to the nearest one. We only got a couple of hours," Erie said.

"How much is it going to cost?" Blake asked.

Looking into his rear view mirror, the driver snarled. "Show me some money."

Erie pulled out a five-dollar bill.

"Not enough. Double it. Cost you ten bucks."

"Rip-off. I'm not paying that much!"

"Up to you," the cabby said. "Get out or stay. Your call."

Blake grabbed Erie's arm, which was raised to open the door and get out.

"Ah... make that for a round trip and you got a deal," Blake said.

"Twelve for a round trip and *you* got a deal," the driver said as he shrugged his shoulders. "Up to you."

"OK. Take us." Erie slid down in the back seat. "Go! Quick! Get down, Blake. They'll see you."

No more than fifteen minutes later, the two were in front of a dingy neighborhood bar just outside the seven-mile limit. "I'm not waiting. You ready -- call this number, ask for Jerome." The cabby handed Erie a card. "I'll be here in fifteen, twenty minutes."

The speed which Jerome put his taxi in gear and drove away made Blake suspect that he was either a sailor stationed across the river or Navy civilian moonlighting and didn't want to be caught delivering midshipmen to out-of-town bars.

It was a dark, sawdust-on-the-floor kind of place. Besides the bartender, there were only three other people in the room. Two of them, a middle-aged woman and man, sat snuggled in a booth in the corner. The other person was unshaven and dressed only in dirty pants and an undershirt. He sat at the bar sipping a beer and smoking cigarettes.

"What'll ya have?" the bartender asked.

"Two beers, no, make that four beers," Blake ordered.

"Two bucks," said the bartender.

"That's pretty steep," Erie said.

"Take it or leave it."

Blake and Erie each put up a dollar.

They took their seats in a booth away from the window. Their white uniforms made them look like two flakes of snow on a tar road.

"What's this place remind you of?" Erie asked.

"Good times past. Milwaukee, Newport."

The bartender, a bald-headed old man with a dirty apron wrapped around his waist, brought the beer. He put two bottles in front of each young man.

"How about that place in Florida, near Miami? After we played in the All-Navy tournament." Erie grinned and then took another sip of beer. "Remember those whores? They cheated Cadillac and me. You and Stan stopped a real good brawl. We'd a got the shit kicked out of us. Damn near had to fight our way out of that bar."

"Yeah." Blake smiled at the memory.

"How about that place we hung out at in Fall River?" Erie said shaking his head. "And some of those good look'n honeys -- they were something."

"You almost went to jail because of one of them," Blake said chugging his beer.

"I was sure scared," Erie said, and then he changed the subject. "You going out for the basketball team?"

"Well, my company officer, Ensign Franklin, mentioned it was starting soon. I don't think so. You?"

"Don't think so? Why not? Football will be enough for me. Academics'll be hard. Don't know if I can keep up."

"Two more beers," Blake called to the barkeep.

"Ok."

"Ah... Blake..." Erie stammered. "You better take it easy on the beer."

"Gonna get drunk."

"You better not." Erie sipped some beer. "You never could hold your drink. Remember that time back in boots? You drank too much and I had to fight you to get you to go back to the base. And then the other time -- it was too much booze that got you thrown in the brig."

The bartender delivered two more beers, interrupting Erie's thoughts.

"By the way, my name's Willy. You want anything else? Just ask. We got just about anything you middies would want. Even got a back room over there." He pointed a thumb over his shoulder and winked. "You like to play cards? Black Jack, Draw Poker?" Then he leaned down close and whispered, "There's a couple of girls live near by. I can get them quick. We got rooms upstairs."

Erie seemed interested, but Blake cut off the idea. "Thanks just the same."

"We're heading back after this beer," Erie told Willy. "Can you call this number and ask for Jerome?"

"You got it, middies," The bartender wiped the edge of the table clean with his rag and started to leave.

"Forget that "middie" shit," Erie said.

Blake thought, *Oh, oh here it comes. That abrupt change in personality that he had seen in his buddy before.*

Erie stood up and grabbed the bartender's arm. "Sounds like we're a bunch of kids. This middy will kick your ass."

"Easy. Didn't mean anything by it."

"Don't start any trouble, Erie," Blake said, pulling Erie's arm away. "Sit down!"

Erie sat back into the chair. They sat silently for a time sipping their beer. Then Erie groused, "Didn't you read *Reef Points*? It said "middie" is a term used by mothers, Hollywood, and for little old lady's blouses."

"Shit, Erie. The guy didn't mean anything."

It was as if they were each contemplating their new circumstances and reviewing their old friendship. They again fell into silence until Erie blurted, "Whataya think it will be like after the firsties get back?"

"Always the shame, a lot of childish nickel-and-dime shit." Blake's nose felt numb and his lips and tongue felt like a rag. "We hacked boots -- we should be able to hack plebe year. But I'm think'n of pulling out -- go'n back to the fleet."

"You thinking about quitting? Bullshit! Blake -- don't do it! Wait until after Christmas leave at least."

"Nah. Don't think it's for me. Besides my brig time will catch up with me -- I'm not cut out to be an officer."

"Blake, you're a puzzle. You're smart but you didn't want to come to the Academy. Now you're here and you want to quit? It's always been about your dad, hasn't it? It's not the brig time. No one cares about that. What's the deal with your dad, anyway, Blake? You're one of the Blake Lawrence family. You hate him or something?"

"I don't hate my family. And I don't hate my dad. Jush don't respect him. My granddad was honorable, a hero. My Uncle Charles died in the war, at Pearl Harbor. He was jush a second lieutenant. It's just I don't like what my dad did to mom and us kids, Charlie and me. Now he wants to make up, but five years ish a long time to make up. No one ever said, 'You look like your dad,' because he was never around. He never saw me play basketball -- never knew I made good grades. After a while you forget; well, you try to forget him. Most of the time he doesn't exist, but you know he does and one day he jush shows up. Shit."

"Yeah... well, your business."

"Yeah, my bushiness." The beer was affecting Blake's speech.

"Blake, you're always on the edge of eruption -- but you have talent. Your problem is you always keep it just below the surface. Since boot camp, you've always stood off, waiting for someone else to lead. Hey, everyone likes you and you are a de facto leader even if you don't step up and take charge. Look at me." Erie now seemed the more sober of the two. "Make me a promise."

"What?"

"Promise me you'll wait until after Christmas leave."

Instead of responding, Blake just chugged his beer. His eyes glazed from the alcohol.

"Come on, promise."

"Nah."

"That's why you're drink'n so hard. That's why you're not going out for basketball! It's your dad." Erie's face was red from his fury. "Knock it off!

Promise me you'll stay -- Come on, buddy -- just 'til Christmas -- come on, buddy. Promise!"

"Okay, I promise. Jush don't go pull'n your 'I was a shailor' shit on the firsties. I heard you at the rifle range giving that second clashman a load a crap. They'll jump on your butt and you'll be out on conduct."

"Fuck 'em." Erie's eyes were watering. "I can handle their bullshit."

"That's another thing. You better lay off cuss'n. Haven't heard many cuss words here. Not like back in sailor land. No more 'F' word." This time it was Blake who changed the topic. "What are your roommashes like?"

"A couple of kids right out of high school." Erie raised his hands. "They're boots -- don't know shit about the Navy. But they're okay. I'm helping them with all this military stuff. How about yours?"

"They're okay," Blake said. "They both want to play football."

"We get new roommates when the academic year starts. Maybe you and I'll be assigned the same company academic year. We could be roommates."

"Yeah. Wouldn't that be something?" Blake smiled before chugging some more beer. "The firsh guys to go all the way through boot camp and Annapolis in the shame company together. I'd stay if that happened. We could eat at the training table -- skip all the plebe bullshit."

"Talk about me cuss'n," Erie said. "You better clean up your language, too. Besides you're drunk. You still can't handle your liquor."

"I don't shay the big 'F' word. That's what I mean." Blake countered defensively.

Willy brought two more beers. "Your cabby should be here in about ten minutes."

"Better not drink that," Erie said. "You're already drunk."

"Am not," Blake laughed the words before taking another drink. "Only had two beers."

"Correction: I had two. You had five."

"Crap, we used to drink more than that in the fleet."

"Haven't had any for two months."

They got up when Jerome came in the door. Blake staggered into the cab and dozed off within minutes.

The next thing Blake heard was Erie saying, "Thanks, Jerome." He woke Blake with an elbow in the side and pushed him toward the main gate. "Better straighten up, buddy. Look alive going through the gate or you'll get fried. They catch you drunk, they'll Class A you."

"I'm okay now," Blake countered. "Wow! That beer really hit me. Out of practice."

"We better walk it off," Erie said.

Once through the gate, Erie guided Blake around the yard to sober him up before going to the Rotunda to sign in. Every time they saw an officer or upperclassman, Erie steered Blake in another direction. Before they separated, Blake said, "Hey, buddy. I'll try to be over to see you in a few days... at least before academic year begins."

Now sober, Blake slowly climbed the steps to his room, returning to a life he promised to maintain at least until Christmas. As he passed the MOD, he saw three mids wearing pillowcases over their heads and running toward the other wing.

"What's that all about?" He asked his on-watch classmate.

"What?"

"Those guys. Running. Why the masks?"

"Didn't see them. I was writing in the log."

"Kid stuff," Blake said to the MOD, who shrugged his shoulders. "You'd think they'd leave that back in high school."

Thinking little more about it, he opened the door to his room, went in, and began taking off his liberty uniform. Stone was lying on his bed, his face toward the wall.

"You awake, Stone?"

"Ahhh..."

"You okay?" Blake asked.

"Ahhh..."

Blake went over to his roommate and touched his shoulder. He asked again, "You okay?"

Stone rolled slightly toward him, and his face turned. Blake saw blood running from an ugly wound on his nose. His uniform was dirty, as if it had been dragged across the floor.

"What the hell? You look terrible. What happened?"

Stone didn't speak.

"Come on, Stone. Tell me. What happened?" Blake sat on the edge of Stone's bunk.

Silence.

"Stone, you got to tell me. How'd you get that cut on your nose?" He pulled Stone's shoulder to more fully see his face. It looked bruised but there were no other cuts or wounds.

"Some guys came in and took me."

"'Took you'? What's that mean?"

"They took me -- beat me up -- called me 'nigger,' they told me to resign -- get out. They don't want me here. I'm going. Don't need this bullshit."

"Who were they?"

CHAPTER 5

GO HOME, NIGGER

It was at breakfast formation the morning after their weekend liberty that Tom Blackstone, the second classman who bragged that he would one day be a Marine, took a look at Stone's face and said, "You fall down a ladder, mister?"

"Yes, sir!"

Stone had only a shiner under his right eye, but his left eye was completely closed. His cheeks were puffy with shadings of red, orange, and blue.

Blackstone moved closer. He lightly touched the wounded face; Stone winced. The second classman didn't ask how it happened. He just said, "You been to sick bay with that, boy?"

"Sir, no, sir. And I'm no one's boy!"

"Midshipman Lawrence! You Mr. Groler's room-mate?"

"Yes, sir."

"You know where sick bay is?"

"Sixth wing basement, sir?"

"Right -- take Mr. Groler there. Make sure a doctor sees him right away, then get right back to the chow hall."

"Aye, aye, sir."

As they waited for the doctor, Blake asked, "You have any idea who they were?"

"No, they sneaked up on me. Covered my head." Stone looked away as if he was hiding something.

"You sure?"

"I'm sure."

"Come on, Stone. This is bad stuff. You can tell me."

"I'm sure."

"Stone? Give the bastards up."

Stone turned and let his head sink to his chest as if he was meditating. Finally he said in a very low tone, "They all sounded alike. Rebel voices -- like Brandell."

"Like Reb?"

"Well, I'm sure he wasn't one of them, but they all talked like him, southern-like. I'm not saying he was one of them. Don't say anything, promise?"

"Okay, I promise. But didn't Brandell say he was staying with his parents at Carvel Hall? Where is he, anyway? Hasn't been in the room more than to sleep since after the weekend."

Their conversation was interrupted by the doctor's question, "What do we have here?"

"I was told to bring my roommate here, sir. It's his face and ribs, sir."

"Let me see," the doctor said. He gently touched Stone's face, then asked him to lift his t-shirt. "Hmm. Where does it hurt?".

"Everywhere, sir."

"You've been in a fight. Hope you got some of the other guy."

"Other guys, sir. He was jumped."

"Hmm. You can shove off, mister," he told Blake. "I want to take some X-rays. We'll get Mister --" He looked at Stone's stenciled name. "Groler back to his room."

Later that morning, after he came back from sick bay, Stone told Blake that the MOW had directed him to the company office where Ensign Franklin was waiting with the Naval Academy's public relations officer and a representative from the commandant's office. Apparently the doctor had told someone that a negro midshipman had been jumped, and a newspaper reporter in Annapolis had gotten hold of the story. Stone said the questions came at him fast. They wanted to know who did it -- what time, what did they do, and say. And why?

"I didn't have the answers to most of the questions except what they said. I told the public relations officer that they told me, 'Go home, nigger.'"

Stone's story hit the papers the next morning. The headlines showed it was of varying importance to area editors and publishers:

Third page of the local Annapolis newspaper:

Midshipman Beaten

Second page of the *Washington Post*:

Negro Midshipman Hazed

Front-page headline of the *Baltimore Sun*:

Negro Midshipman Called Name,
Told To Leave Naval Academy

The bell rang for noon meal formation. Stone went to the mirror to survey his face. "Swelling's going down, don't you think?"

Blake and Stone grabbed their blue-striped middy hats, checked their neckerchiefs and flew out the door. Blake asked, "You're not going to quit, are you? Just because of those guys? Not everyone is like them."

Brandell showed up in formation at the last minute, right before the march-off. He was in the squad just in front of Blake's.

"Right face!" the platoon leader ordered.

Now, Brandell stood shoulder to shoulder with Blake as they marched to the mess hall. Out of the corner of his mouth, Blake said, "Reb, where you been?"

"Wha you mean? Whea ah been?" Brandell whispered. "Busy. Football."

"You hear about Stone?"

"Somth'n."

"You know anything about it?"

"'Cos not."

They stood at rigid attention as the prayer was given over the public address system and the general announcements were made. Chairs screeched across the deck when they heard, "Brigade seats!"

After the meal Blake watched Brandell. He was shovelling down whatever food no one else wanted.

"Brandell, I need to talk to you."

"Wha aboot?"

"Stone."

"Don' know anyth'n aboot that," Brandell said as he continued to stuff his paunchy jowls.

*****

The next activity on their schedule was boxing class. Stone and Reb changed their uniforms in silence, and Blake sensed the stiffness and distance Reb gave his injured roommate. He thought about the possibility that Reb could be one of those who beat up Stone and insulted him. "You enjoy your family's visit last weekend, Reb?"

"They didn't come up."

"Didn't come up? Thought you were staying at Carvel Hall?"

Brandell didn't answer, he just finished tying his gym shoes, grabbed his "cover," slapped it on his head, and started to the formation. Blake stayed right on his heels. "You didn't answer me, Brandell. Where'd you stay last weekend, if your parents weren't here?'

"Got noth'n mo to say."

They fell in and marched toward Macdonough Hall. Again Brandell was next to Blake. He whispered, "There's a rumor that you were one of the guys who beat up Stone."

"Lie."

"Where were you Saturday night?"

"You the FBI?"

"Nope. But I may be your worst nightmare."

"Knock it off, you two. No talking in ranks!" Blackstone shouted. "Keep yapping and you'll be doing push-ups 'til midnight."

In the gym Blackstone ordered, "Fall out! Put on headgear and gloves."

Spike, the instructor who had over one hundred professional fights and had once been a champion spoke to them as they scrambled to get into their fighting gear, "Okay, listen up. Today it's time to practice what you've been taught. Keep your dukes up, defend yourselves at all times, but be aggressive in there. Show me some spunk."

"Okay, pair up," Spike continued. "With someone about your own size. I want to see how you defend and I want to see you throw a jab, a straight right, a hook, and the one-two."

"You and me, Brandell," Blake said.

"Suits me."

"I know you were one of the guys who beat up Stone," Blake said.

"You some nigg'a lov'a?" Brandell responded.

"No more, no less than I'm a rebel hater. I don't like cowards who need three guys to beat up on a skinny guy like Stone, and I don't like the word 'nigger.'"

Reb looked confident, bouncing around like a pro, throwing warm-up punches and juking. Blake remembered his fight at the smoker back in boot camp. He wanted to save enough energy for the third of the three one-minute rounds. He danced and jabbed Brandell for the first two rounds. He wasn't in shape and was an awkward, stumbly, roundhouse puncher with few boxing skills, but he landed a lot of punches. He hit Blake's arms blow after blow but seldom connected with anything of consequence.

Brandell was shorter by about five inches but was a hell of a lot bigger, and it was clear from the first bell he wanted to fight. He weighed about 220 pounds, mostly beer-fat.

In the second round, Reb rushed Blake, his arms whirling like windmills. It was all Blake could do to keep from getting hit. He danced and juked and tied Brandell up.

By the time the bell rang for the third round, the gym was buzzing. The guys in the platoon knew what was happening. It was more than a class boxing match and they began shouting for a knockout. They wanted action and blood.

Blake pushed Reb away from a clinch, then popped him with another jab. "Gonna give you a taste of your own medicine, Brandell. Don't you ever touch Stone again."

Sure enough, Brandell ran out of steam. He could hardly keep up his guard, and his legs were wobbly. Blake kept moving and jabbing and jabbing. Reb's nose began to bleed. One punch after another. Hit. Hit. Hit. Blake couldn't miss, but he couldn't knock him down, either. Blood was all over the canvas. Finally Spike jumped into the ring, looked at Brandell, and stopped the fight.

One day after the boxing match, Brandell got permission to move to a different plebe summer company. The matter of Stone hitting the swimming instructor faded away. Blake assumed it had something to do with the honor system. Either Stone had lied or the instructor had; the matter couldn't be resolved.

Blake remembered what Erie had said on their last liberty together: "The general public's unaware of the Navy school. It's as if it doesn't exist -- unless something goes wrong -- something that's newsworthy."

The beating and "Go home, nigger" incident probably saved Stone from being dropped during Plebe summer. Headlines such as "Negro student harassed at Academy" protected him from irrational adherence to school regulations that reflected the prejudices of the day.

Blake asked, "You're staying, aren't you? It was the same question Erie had posed to him. He felt uncomfortable asking Stone when he knew leaving after Christmas may be in his cards. He asked anyway: "You're not gonna quit?"

Stone replied, "My daddy served as a sailor during World War II, on a ship. He told me this would be tough. He also said if I decided to serve, I should be prepared to give my life for my country. I'm stay'n."

CHAPTER 6

THE FIRSTIES

Summer ended when the plebes moved into their academic-year rooms and waited for the return of the firsties. Blake spent the last hours before their arrival squaring away his locker, shining his shoes, and reviewing the contents of *Reef Points*. This pocket-sized reference issued to every plebe held as much folklore about the Navy and the Academy as could be packed between its covers. It included a section called "Plebe Knowledge," a dozen or so pages of trivia. During plebe summer, Tom Blackstone had made it clear that knowing -- even memorizing -- the contents of that book would lighten the load of plebe year.

Blake's grandfather had told him that plebe year was the worst of it. Most of the bilge-outs happened during that year, some because of the hazing, some because of the academics, some because of conduct, but most because of a combination of the three. He called it 'the inability to keep all the balls in the air.' Nevertheless, Granddad thought the lessons learned during that first year set the mold for a life at sea, where there was no sniveling and no excuses, just grinding it out to be ready for war, never knowing when or if you would be called.

The first working day after Labor Day marked the start of academic year. Except for the foreign language component, everyone took the same courses. The

no longer true

administration called it "lock-step" education. Classes began in elementary drafting, descriptive geometry, plane trigonometry, algebra, plane analytic geometry, and chemistry. There was also composition and literature, foreign language, and physical education; more than twenty-four to thirty units of total instruction -- about 135 hours of lectures, labs, and drills a semester. At most civilian universities, fifteen units was considered the maximum. The reading assignments alone could easily fill the two and a half hours allotted for evening study. However, on top of that came sports competition and preparations for meal questions. Of course there were also "come-arounds," the term used to describe time spent in an upperclassman's room undergoing "plebe indoctrination" or "hazing" -- depending on interpretation.

Blake's two new roommates seemed to be a stronger fit for the Academy than were Stone and Reb, both of whom ended up in other battalions.

Except for his fading sun-bleached hair, Pete Ettinger, a surfer from Santa Barbara, fit a Lincolnesque description. He was tall, broad-shouldered, barrel-chested, and often somber and quiet. The silent type, five minutes of conversation a day was his limit. After a year in the Air Force he was asked why he came to the Naval Academy. He made no bones about it: "To go back into the Air Force, become a pilot, and... the girls -- mids get lots of dates with pretty girls." His parents were both physicians and had hoped he would follow their path, but academics were not his strong suit. Pete wasted no time announcing that he would need help with his classes -- for him, anything over 2.5 would be gravy.

Sam Tallau, on the other hand, came bursting into the room like a grenade. Fast-talking and gregarious, he grabbed a desk and began doing things, rushing about stowing gear and cleaning. He was a wrestler type with short, bulky muscles and no neck -- just strong shoulders. He had straight black hair parted in the middle and a Romanesque nose. Because of his Napoleonic look, his plebe summer classmates dubbed him with the obvious, uncreative nickname "Napoleon." He said his parents came from an eastern European country near Russia, and they now lived in Philadelphia. In the first few days of living together, it was clear to Blake that Sam was the dynamic kind who would push the edge, knew all the angles -- a bit like Erie, who had ended up at the other end of Bancroft Hall from Blake. At the very first meal the upper class gave Sam several nicknames: "Shrimp," "Sand-Blower," and "Stump," all of which he hated.

When asked why he came to the Academy, Sam said, "Free. I didn't have the money to go to an Ivy League school, so here I am. I could have had a partial scholarship but my congressman offered me a primary appointment based on my high school grades and some tests. This is better than a full ride. Besides, a military life is a lot more exciting than civilian life. I watched my dad working a couple of jobs as a laborer, and I knew I don't want that."

In the mess hall, the three roommates sat at the same table with two other fourth classmen from their platoon. Hamm McClinton was barely seventeen and was instantaneously identified by everyone as a "grease (aptitude) bucket." He talked too much, showed no discretion, and puffed his accomplishments. He was careless and it showed. His shirt was seldom tucked into his trousers properly, and his belt buckle alignment was sloppy. The firsties immediately nicknamed him "Mr. Hambone."

Del Butler, nicknamed "Egg," occupying the seat closest to the second class end of the table, was quiet, studious, scientific, and brilliant. He always had the answers and never seemed to forget anything, yet he was already a member of the radiator squad: those who didn't play a sport and needed extra exercise.

"How's the cow, mister?"

"I'll find out, sir," came the response from all five plebes.

"Shove out! All of you."

Without moving his head, Blake discretely looked for the source of the order. Tucker Middleton wore the stripes of a platoon leader for the fall set of stripers. The winter set would take over after Christmas. Stripes were the symbols of rank bestowed on first classmen within the student shadow chain of command.

Middleton, who was the table captain, sat with two other firsties, squad leader Mark Greenfield and stripeless Dale Thompson. They sat at one end of the table. Two second classmen and three "youngsters" filled out the twelve. *"Green bench"*

It was Mark Greenfield who gave the order to shove out. Each of the plebes immediately executed this bit of minor hazing, which amounted to sitting without the benefit of a chair. Tolerated because it was a test of the strength of their legs, it also tested their will to take punishment.

"What's your name, *tool*? You, peeking out of your eye," Greenfield said.

No one responded.

"Oh, so all of you were peeking and none of you know it. Eyes in the boat, you bunch of trolls. Everyone come around tomorrow morning before breakfast and enlighten me. You also better know the headlines from the *Washington Post*, *Baltimore Sun*, and the *New York Times*."

"Aye, aye, sir!" came the chorus. They had already learned the five acceptable responses: "Yes, sir;" "No, sir;" "Aye, aye, sir;" "No excuse, sir;" and "I'll find out, sir."

The order to "come aboard" was usually given when the upperclassman who gave the order "shove out" saw that the plebes were beginning to waiver, their strength giving way to the possibility of falling to the floor. In this case the order never came. Blake could feel the muscles in the upper part of his legs tighten and begin to quiver. But he was determined not to be the first to give in. He was not. Hamm McClinton apparently had learned the key. "Request permission to come aboard, sir."

"What's your name, mister?"

"Midshipman McClinton Fourth Class, sir."

"Why do you want to come aboard, Mr. Hambone?"

"My legs are giving out, sir. I'm about to fall, sir." McClinton's voice wavered and sounded like he was in distress.

"Come aboard, all of you, you cry-baby, sniveling, pukes."

All the plebes pulled their chairs back to the table and sat, their aching muscles relieved.

"Sir, request permission to ask a question, sir." It was Hamm McClinton again.

"Permission granted, Mr. Hambone. What is it you want to know now, dufus?"

"Where can I find the headlines for the newspapers, sir?"

"Mr. Hambone, you negat. Is this the way it will be? You don't know shit and you want me to find out for you. This is going to be a long year, my man," Mark Greenfield said. "When you come around tomorrow morning I'll answer your question. Oh, and Mr. Hambone, you better be able to tell me about *The Message to Garcia*.

Blake peeked again and saw Tucker Middleton, the platoon leader, shake his head. "Mark, ol' buddy, this is too much. I'm already feeling very sad that I'm back from leave. I hate this frigging place and this guy is making our evening miserable with his stupid questions. We need quiet!"

"Second that," Dale Thompson said in a reserved tone.

Greenfield smiled at his classmates, but to the plebes he barked, "The whole bunch of you sick-looking pukes better bone up on eating square meals, better manners, and keeping your eyes in the boat!"

There was no doubt who was really in charge of the table after Dale Thompson spoke. Even the second classmen stopped talking; the rest of the meal was eaten in silence.

The fourth class remained at their seats until the upper class had all departed and the command, "fourth class, march out," was given.

"Hamm, you idiot," Blake said as they "chopped" back to their rooms. "You're going to get your ass chewed for asking dumb questions. You got to find out on your own. That's what *The Message to Garcia* is all about. We get the *Washington Post* and *New York Times* in our room and Del gets the *Baltimore Sun*. Come by before the morning come-around and bone up. You better tell Greenfield you already know the answer to your own question."

The next morning, all five were outside Greenfield's door at 6:24 and burst through his door at 6:25.

"Midshipman Lawrence, sir."

"Midshipman Butler, sir."

"Midshipman McClinton, sir."

"Midshipman Ettinger, sir."

"Midshipman Tallau, sir."

Greenfield looked like the grease bucket he was. He was still wearing only a t-shirt and trousers. His feet were bare. His side of the room looked like a pigpen. Shoes were sitting on the desk apparently waiting for a shine. He hadn't stored his luggage, his laundry was spread around, and he was still stowing his locker. Blake had learned from Sam, who learned it from a second class buddy that their illustrious squad leader, Greenfield, was a turn-back from the class that had just graduated. He had been hospitalized for a major sports injury and had to take a year of the same course work over. He was allowed to stay on because he was near the top of his class academically and was a jock who played varsity lacrosse.

On the other side of the room sat Dale Thompson. Sam, who seemed to already know everything about everybody, said Thompson would be the next set six-striper, the brigade captain. Already immaculately dressed, he sat reading his newspaper and didn't look up when the five plebes sounded off.

"Okay, you boobs. What were the headlines?" Greenfield asked. "Wait... mister. What is your name?"

"Midshipman Ettinger, sir."

"Why are you covered, dufus?"

Pete snatched his hat off his head. "Sorry, sir. Forgot. I was in the Air Force, sir."

"Okay, what were the headlines?"

"Sir, the *Washington... Baltimore Sun...*'"

"Wait a minute, you idiot. One at a time. Let's hear from Mister Butler."

"*Baltmore Sun* head line said, 'Vietminh Rebel Against South Vietnamese Government,' sir"

"Who gives a shit? Okay, now you, Mister Ettinger. What else?"

"Sir, *New York Times*: 'China Continues to Shell Quemoy and Matsu Islands. U.S. Navy Ships Convoy Supplies,' sir."

"Mister Tallau?"

"Sir, *Philadelphia Enquirer*: 'Democrats Expected to Win Big in Mid-Term Elections. Blame Eisenhower's Economy,' sir."

"You believe that bullshit, Stump?"

"I'll find out, sir."

"You'll find out? You some kind of a grease ball, Mister Tallau? No opinions of your own?"

"No, sir."

"Okay, Mr. Hambone. Tell me something I don't know."

"Sir, Pat Boone's song 'April Love' is at the top of the hit parade, sir."

"Hambone, you idiot, shit magnet! Who gives a shit about that? What paper had that as a headline?"

"Sir. Not a headline. Didn't think you knew that, sir."

"For christsake, Mr. Hambone -- you grease bucket. That song came out last year and everyone knows it. Oh, you found out where to get the headlines. Tell me about Garcia."

Most plebes already knew the meaning of *The Message to Garcia*. It was one of the first things every plebe had to read and understand.

Ham rattled off, "Sir, *The Message to Garcia* is an essay written by a man named Elbert Hubbard. In it he tells the tale of one Lieutenant Rowan, a West Pointer."

He pretended to spit and wipe his mouth for saying the words 'West Point,' then continued. "He was called into the office of the president of the United States and given the task to carry a message to Garcia Iniguez, a revolutionary general in Cuba's war against Spain, asking what aid the United States should send to help the Cuban revolt against Spain. Rowan didn't ask, who is Garcia? He didn't ask where is Garcia? Nor did he ask how do I get there? Rather, he answered the president with a simple, 'Yes, sir.' He then set out to ride and walk into the jungles to deliver the message."

"You surprise me, Hambone," Greenfield said. "Very good! For next come-around, memorize it."

Then he came close to Blake. "What's your name again, mister?"

"Sir, Midshipman Lawrence, sir."

"Lawrence, *Washington Post*. Go!"

"Aye, aye, sir. The headline of the *Washington Post* said, 'Jawaharlal Nehru First Prime Minister of India,' sir."

"Mister Lawrence. Tell us about yourself."

"Sir, I am Mister Blake Lawrence, Midshipman Fourth Class, sir."

"I *know* that," Greenfield sneered. "Aren't you a Navy junior... related to the famous Lawrence family of the Navy?"

"Sir, my grandfather and father served, sir."

"Your father. He is Captain Blake Lawrence the second. Is that not true?"

"Yes, sir."

"What'll we call you?"

Blake didn't answer.

"You're the third Lawrence. How about 'Trey?'"

Blake again didn't respond; but he hated the name, Trey.

"Your father. Wasn't he the prick who commanded a carrier last summer?"

"Yes, sir. He commanded a carrier, sir." Blake girded at the upperclassman's use of that word his father.

"Was it the carrier I made my first second class cruise aboard?"

"Sir, I'll find out, sir."

"You know about your father, don't you?"

"Sir, I'll find out, sir."

"He's a prick! You going to become a prick like him?"

Blake's jaw tightened. He felt his cheeks flush. He hadn't liked Greenfield from the start and now he liked him even less. But he was a firstie and Blake was confused about what he had to take from another mid. He felt like punching Greenfield on the spot. It was one thing for Blake to call his own father a prick, which Blake did from time to time, but not for someone else to use that term. He sucked a large breath of air and answered, "Sir, I'll find out, sir."

The bell rang. Thompson said quietly, "Better let them go, Mark. They'll be late to formation."

"Out! All of you. And you all better know *How's the Cow* when you get to the table."

Morning chow formation was like a zoo with all the animals loose. The upper class, after a night's rest, had recovered sufficiently from their summer vacation that they began to take back Bancroft Hall -- and all the plebes in it. During plebe summer, Blake and his classmates were used to one, maybe two, upperclassmen looking them over and chewing them out. Now every upperclassman in the platoon was on them. No sooner would one inspect them than another would come by to look them up and down, checking for loose strings or threads called "Irish pennants," their shirt and buckle alignment, examining their shoe shine by putting their own next to the plebes and generally harassing every plebe equally.

At their table the plebes stood at rigid attention, making chins, the art of tilting their heads forward to tuck their chin tight to their neck. They held their arms tight to their sides, hands back along the seams of their trousers. Immediately after the morning prayer, the brigade six-striper ordered, "Brigade seats."

Chairs scraped, conversation exploded, food was devoured. "Pass the eggs, Shrimp. Eyes in the boat, Trey. Pass the twins, McClinton. Why is the milk pitcher empty, Butler? How's the cow, McClinton?"

"Sir! She walks, she talks, she's full of chalk... the... the... lac... I'll find out, sir."

'McClinton, you bozo. Didn't I order you to know that for breakfast?" Greenfield's voice sounded like a battering ram.

"Mr. Lawrence."

"Yes, sir."

"Let's see if you did your homework. How's the cow?"

"Sir! She walks, she talks, she's full of chalk. The lacteal fluid extracted from the female of the bovine species is highly prolific to the fifth degree, sir!"

"Well, very good, Lawrence. Let's find out what else you know. What was the name of the first Commandant of Midshipmen?"

"Sir, I'll find out, sir."

"What time is it?"

"Sir, I'll find out, sir."

"Shit, don't you people know anything?"

"Recite the *Laws of the Navy*, Mr. Lawrence."

"Sir, I'll find out, sir."

Thompson said quietly, "Better let them finish eating, Mark. They've got classes."

"Eat, you bozos. You better know your *Reef Points* by noon meal. And come around tonight, Lawrence."

"Aye, aye, sir."

Blake was very well forewarned about come-arounds. His grandfather and father often laughed at the various games played during their time. "Swimming to Baltimore" was a plebe lying on his belly and pretending to swim. "Aircraft carrier qualifications" required a running dive and a slide on the belly. To "sweat a penny to a bulkhead," a plebe placed a coin on his forehead then against a wall; "greyhound races" was another idiotic running game dreamed up by bored upperclassmen to harass plebes.

After breakfast, while getting ready for class, Sam said, "Your dad's a captain? You never told us that."

"Well, it's no big deal."

Pete looked up from a book; he was trying to cram for a quiz at the last minute. "Bullshit, roomy. It is for us," he said.

"When we get back from class, you better fill us in, Blake. About this Navy family of yours."

After the quick stop in their rooms, the Plebes were off to class formations. Blake took classes with classmates from one other company as well as his own. Section leaders were appointed alphabetically. Everyone took a turn. Unlike others, who became excited and often nervous in their first leadership opportunity, Blake discharged this minor responsibility in a quiet, effortless manor. He had already had his chance when Lee Locke from the other company had the job. Blake liked Lee because he was the kind of guy who had smiling eyes and a mischievous Irish look to him. He was seldom in trouble because even the upper class saw his potential and liked him. Although a bit chubby, he excelled in his sport of 150-pound football. His classmates called him "Admiral" from the day he entered the Academy.

Section leaders functioned to march their classmates to and from the classroom. This meant crossing the yard on the several paths and roads from one building to another. It was a time to chat and exchange information about homework. But being a section leader also meant being vulnerable to getting a Form Two, the official paper that accompanied being placed on report. "Frapped" and "fried" were the other names for being caught breaking regulations. Of course, talking in ranks was forbidden, and not only the offender was fried, but the section leader also got it for not maintaining control of his section. Demerits came in units of five, which converted to either extra marching or loss of liberty. Plebes were permitted 350 demerits before facing expulsion.

Lee marched the section to the entrance of the academic buildings where the classrooms were located.

The courses had long ago been nicknamed by midshipmen. "Steam" was naval engineering; "juice," electrical engineering; "bull" was English, history, and government; "skinny" was physics and chemistry; and "dago," a foreign language. A section of midshipmen took their seats alphabetically and came to attention when the instructor entered.

By this time in Academy history, though civilians as well as military officers were teachers, their methodology was the same: "Carry on. Draw slips and man the boards." With that order, everyone went to the chalkboards. There they did the calculations of the problems written on slips of paper. The purpose was to demonstrate that the day's assigned homework had been completed and was understood. Several members of the section were then asked to explain their work. Terror struck those who had either not done their homework at all or didn't understand the material.

Del Butler came by his nickname "Egg" because he was brilliant, studious, and scientific. He avoided as much of the military "crap" as he could. He had a distinguished high school experience ending as valedictorian. Like many of their classmates, Del had been in the top ten percent of all the high school students in America who had graduated the year before. Now they were competing for "stars," the little emblem that signified they had a grade point average of 3.5 or higher. But for most of the plebe class the real target was 2.5, the passing number.

Blake's chalkboard was next to Del's, but peeking at his work would have been considered an honor violation. As soon as he was done, Blake stepped back and surveyed Del's work. "Oh, shit, wrong answers, wrong approach," Blake said to himself. He knew he hadn't studied the work because there was no time. He had just skimmed it and asked if anyone had the gouge – the expected questions and answers for the daily quiz.

Mr. Nichols, the instructor, came by as each student stepped back. "Lawrence, guess you've seen Mr. Butler's answers by now. Put in more time studying before tomorrow's quiz.'

"Aye, aye, sir," Blake responded. But he knew he wouldn't be able to because of all the stuff he had to learn for Greenfield. There just wasn't enough time to get it all done.

Blake's disdain for this unreasonable firstie began to grow. He felt like the bacon squeezed between two pieces of toast. What could he do to get out from under this prick?

*****

At noon meal that day, Greenfield asked Blake for the answers to more *Reef Points* questions. Some of the new questions were outside that reference such that when he arrived at his evening come-around, Blake owed the firstie more than twenty-five answers, almost none of which did he have time to find answers to.

"Where's the Mexican monument?" Greenfield barked.

"I'll find out, sir." Blake responded, not knowing the answer.

"How long have you been in the Navy?"

Blake cringed. He remembered the piece, but to answer with a partial or incorrect answer was worse than not knowing. "I'll find out, sir."

For the next several weeks, Blake made nightly come-arounds to Greenfield.

"Midshipman Lawrence, sir," Blake shouted as he slammed open the door, yanked off his hat, and stood at rigid attention in shower uniform alpha, which included a raincoat and rubber go-aheads. Under the slicker, Blake wore only undershorts and carried his small metal valuables box.

"Okay, Lawrence. Let me hear the first ten laws of the Navy!"

"Sir, *The Laws of the Navy*, by Admiral R. A. Hopwood, Royal Navy (Retired), sir…"

"In the shower, idiot."

Blake stepped into the shower.

"Turn on the water, cold, dumb john, and begin."

"Now these are the laws of the Navy,
                Unwritten and varied they be;"
"I can't hear you over the sound of the water, Lawrence. Louder. Start again."

"Aye, aye, sir," Blake shouted.

"Now these are the laws of the Navy,
                Unwritten and varied they be;
And he who is wise will observe them,
                Going down in his ship to the sea.

As naught may outrun the destroyer,
                Even so with the law and its grip;
For the strength of the ship is the service,
                And the strength of the service, the ship.

Take heed what ye say of your seniors,
                Be your words spoken softly or plain;
Lest a bird of the air tell the matter
                And so ye shall hear it again."

If you... "If you labor... from... morn until even.
And... And... sir, I'll find out, sir."

"I asked for ten, Mister Lawrence, not three. You planning to complete the course of instruction at the Academy?"

"Sir, I'll find out, sir," Blake shouted.

"Oh, you'll find out? You don't know if you'll complete the course and become an officer?"

"No, sir."

"You wishy-washy puke. Lawrence, what's the mission of this hellhole?"

"I'll find out, sir."

"Why am I not surprised you don't know? Well, I'll tell you. It's to prepare us, as mariners, to fight -- pure and simple. If you're not prepared to do that, get out. Shove off and come back tomorrow night -- dressed in shower uniform alpha, again. This time know all 27 verses! Maybe you'll grow some balls overnight."

Blake did an about-face and quickly marched into the corridor, leaving a trail of water. Squaring corners as he went, he ran back to his own room where he threw his wet things in the shower and grabbed his *Reef Points*. He scanned the words to the poem.

"If you labor from morn until even
    And meet with reproof for your toil;
'Tis well, that the gun may be humbled
    The compressor must check the recoil."

"Dummy," Blake said to himself. "I knew it all the time. But now he wants me to know all 27 verses?"

Pete Ettinger, who was studying math, looked up and frowned, but said nothing. Then, after a pause as if he was measuring his words, he asked, "How did your come-around with Greenfield go?"

"Shitty. I clutched... forgot the fourth *Law of the Navy*. I knew it but lost confidence and couldn't get it out. Now I've got to know them all and he has me coming around every night until I do."

"He has it in for you. I remember what he said about your dad."

At the beginning of plebe year, Blake had come clean with his roommates. They knew everything about the men of Blake's family who had served in the armed forces, and the several who had attended military schools including his father and grandfather. He even told them about his dad's break-up with his mother, that he lived with his new wife in D.C. and now was stationed at the Pentagon. They already knew about the strained father-son relationship.

"I almost hit the son-of-a-bitch. If he says it again, I'm decking him. I don't care. Then I'm quitting."

"Quit?"

"Yeah, I promised Erie I wouldn't until after Christmas leave, but I'm fed up."

"You hit him and you'll be kicked out," Pete warned.

"I have a better idea. Let's get him."

"What?"

"Wait until Sam gets back. He's down at Del's getting the poop about tomorrow's skinny quiz."

No sooner were Pete's words out of his mouth than Sam came plowing through the door like a locomotive.

"Got it," Sam barked. "Del thinks it'll cover only the first five chapters. He gave me the gouge as he sees it and you know Del... he's a cut... star-man potential."

"Blake's gonna quit," Pete told Sam.

"Like hell! What's this all about?" Sam leaned his short body against a locker.

"Greenfield is giving him grief."

"That's not the reason," Blake said. "You know why."

"Oh, poor baby. You don't like your daddy." Sam's voice had a whine to it. "Pete and I... just ordinary guys, just pick-your-nose kind of guys, not with the illustrious Navy background you come from -- we want it. And you don't? Bullshit, Blake! Don't let that prick Greenfield make you quit."

"I say, instead of hitting the prick, let's get him," Pete repeated his solution.

"Sam's eyes litup at the thought. "What do you have in mind, Pete?"

The three went into conference with Pete as the surprising leader. "It has to be simple but fool-proof," Pete said. "We do it in such a way that he doesn't know who did it."

"The old 'blanket-over-the-head' trick," Sam offered.

After throwing out several options, their conclusion was that they would carry out a plan to get even with Greenfield on a Saturday night, about midnight after he returned half-in-the-bag from one of his beer drinking parties in town.

CHAPTER 7

BILGE OUT

As the academic year progressed toward Thanksgiving followed the Army/Navy game, time passed more quickly than any period in the plebes' lives. Fall was all around them. Elm leaves across the yard blanketed the lawn with a quilt of reds, yellows, and deep browns. Things began to tumble into place. They got into the routine: up at dawn, meal formations, plebe knowledge, class formations, classes, study, quizzes, p-rades, and inspections. Firsties became bored with running them. Second classmen, testing their wings, wanted their right and proper due and tended to resent plebes who gave them less respect. They stayed at the hazing a bit longer. Youngsters, less than a year away from it themselves, quietly bided their time.

Life for Blake was a ride at the edge. Every week he raced for the grade postings. His name appeared regularly on the Bush, the weekly list of near-failures in academics, those between 2.5 and 2.8. The Tree, the list of those unsatisfactory, showed he was just below satisfactory in "skinny" at 2.4. If he didn't improve, he would bilge out by mid-term.

He knew his problem: too many things to do and too little time to do them. But mostly it was too much Greenfield who still had him coming around every night to recite the *Laws of the Navy* and answer many other questions. The urge to go back to the fleet resurrected itself. He began to hate this prick who wore his misplaced power over plebes as if he was a New York cabbie in rush hour.

During plebe summer he had made his battalion intramural basketball team and was invited by the coach to try out for the plebe team. Now, in addition to everything else, he attended practices every afternoon. Games with local small colleges would begin in a few weeks.

Erie had dropped basketball for football. He and Stone made the plebe team, Erie as a linebacker and Stone as a speedy pass receiver. Blake became one of the top plebe rebounders and knew that next year he had a chance to make the varsity, if he was around.

Blake's dilemma was that he had several options to overcome with regard to the Greenfield situation. He could go to his company officer, one very chubby Lieutenant John Jones, whom the brigade nicknamed TF^2 (Too Fat To Fly), but he ruled that out immediately. The world would fall on any plebe who did that. He could go to his midshipman platoon leader, Tucker Middleton. But Middleton tolerated Greenfield's table antics -- why would he interfere for one man? Then there was his own firstie, Dan Sloan. Long ago a system had been devised that assigned a firstie to every plebe. The idea was that the senior would teach his plebe the ropes, check his grades, and in general look out for any rocks or shoals that might get in the way of his surviving plebe year. But all Sloan wanted was to complete the course of instruction, get the academics behind him, and get out of what he called a "childish environment." His favorite acronym was IHTFP (I Hate This F---ing

Place). He often added with a chuckle, "And this place loves f---ing me."

Sloan played a lot of cribbage and seldom studied. "Twitch" (the commandant's nickname) was extraordinarily easy on the firsties. He gave them lots of liberty and Sloan took advantage of that by frequently slipping over the wall. He professed to anyone who would listen that he wanted to go into the Air Force, complete his obligated service, then get into banking or become a stock broker. Not dynamic, hidden from all forms of leadership, Sloan's daily routine included reading the *Wall Street Journal*, playing the guitar, and listening to Hank Williams records. Blake ruled out asking Sloan's help because he knew he had very little standing among his classmates.

All Blake wanted was time to do his lessons. Not a sniveler and whiner, he never mentioned his difficulties with Greenfield to Sloan or his company officer. He figured that if word got around that he complained, the other upper classmen would dump on him even more. He didn't want anyone to protect him, but he was pretty sure that most other plebes were not getting the same treatment. Blake's roommates thought Greenfield was a special asshole who had it in for Blake. Greenfield was the talk of Bancroft Hall. His reputation as a hard-ass was so well known that plebes from other battalions avoided his area. He harassed everyone who came within shouting distance. There were times when, in addition to Blake, six or seven other plebes were in Greenfield's room on come-around. The others were eventually released, but Blake stayed on.

Greenfield had Blake on a string, like a yo-yo. No sooner did he answer one question, the firstie would have him looking up another. Greenfield never challenged Blake to quit, but it was implied. Blake thought Greenfield would not be surprised if one day he got fed up and turned in his quit chit.

Greenfield first exhausted all the trivial information questions from *Reef Points* such as:

"The longitude of Annapolis is 76° 29' 08" West."

"The Chapel dome is 192 feet in height."

"Fidelity is up and *Obedience* is down on our bayonet belt buckles."

"The vulgar establishment of Annapolis is the approximate length of time between the transit of the full moon and the next high tide. It is four hours and forty-two minutes."

"The mooring lines of a ship are numbered from forward aft on the ship."

After memorizing *Reef Points* for Greenfield, the next set of questions bordered on hazing because they required heavy-duty research, such as, "What was the name of the first Japanese midshipman to enter the Academy?"

He was resentful, big time. Caught between failing an exam or complying, he had a strong desire to lash out at the firstie.

After a week of research Blake brought back: "Sir, Jiunzo Matsumura was the name of the first Japanese midshipman to enter the Academy in 1869, sir."

"Where is Archangel and who invaded it in 1919?"

"I'll find out, sir."

"Hit it, Trey. Give me twenty, then shove off."

"Aye, aye, sir." Blake hit the deck and pumped out twenty push-ups, then ran out of the room to do more research.

The next come-around he had the answer. "Sir, Archangel is in Russia, on the Northern Dvina River, 30 miles from the White Sea. Sir, Americans invaded Archangel with a force of about 10,000 in 1919. They suffered about 400 casualties, sir."

"What superintendent was the skipper of the *Monitor* in the battle with the *Merrimac*?"

After three days research: "Sir, Superintendent John L. Worden was the skipper of the *Monitor* in the battle with the Merrimac, sir."

"What was first class that was permitted to enter the Marine Corps?"

After a day's research and help from a Marine officer on the faculty: "Sir, 1881 was first class that permitted graduates to enter the Marine Corps, sir."

"Who was the first graduate to earn the Medal of Honor?"

After two day's research: "Sir, the first graduate to earn the Medal of Honor was Army Second Lieutenant Harry L. Hawthorne, Class of 1882, sir."

Each new question required Blake to go to the library at Mahan Hall and dig, with the aid of the reference librarian, through old documents and papers.

Often the answer to one question would lead to another -- and more research. "Midshipman Lawrence, who was Philo N. McGiffin and what is he famous for?"

This was an easy one. Everyone knew the legend. Philo N. McGiffin was one of the Naval Academy's most famous graduates. Blake gave the routine response, "Sir, Philo N. McGiffin, Class of 1882, is noted for his pranks while at the Academy. He rolled cannon balls down the dormitory steps and exploded six power charges as a midnight salute from the cannons flanking the Mexican Monument. As a passed midshipman, he was not given a commission in the U.S. Navy, so he joined the Chinese Navy, sir."

"What's a passed midshipman?"

"Sir, I'll find out, sir!"

Next evening Blake reported, "Sir, a passed mid-shipman is one who completes the course of instruction but doesn't get a commission, sir."

More research. Blake often wondered how Greenfield knew enough to ask the questions in the first place and how he knew that the answers Blake gave were correct. He thought of making up an answer to trick Greenfield, but decided against that on the hope that his misery would soon be over and a mistake at this point may only extend his time with his personal prick.

Letter writing was never Blake's strong suit. He wrote to his mother only three times during boot camp. He had written only twice since he had been at the Naval Academy. Of course she wrote every week, occasionally sent cookies and even a few dollars. One evening, the MOW came to the door and told him to get up to the Rotunda right away -- his mother was on the telephone.

"After a month without answering my letters, I decided to call and find out if there is anything wrong. I know you, Blake," she said with a fleck of sarcasm in her voice. "You always went silent when you had problems. What's going on?"

"I'm doing okay, Mom. Don't worry."

"You getting enough to eat? You need to eat good meals."

"I'm okay. They feed us well."

"How about rest?"

"It's okay. I get enough."

"How are your grades? I received a letter from the superintendent that said you have a grade below 2.5.

"I had a bad week. Failed a couple of quizzes. You getting stuff about me in the mail?"

"Oh, yes," she replied. "Your superintendent is very good about keeping parents informed. You were always such a good student -- all A's. What's happening? Why aren't you writing more often?"

"Nothing's wrong, Mom. I just get busy. You doing all right?" Blake tried to change the subject. "How's Charles?"

"We're okay. Charles is a junior and graduates from high school next year. Thinking about West Point."

"West Point? Why not Annapolis? He'd do better than me."

"But you haven't answered me, young man. What's wrong?"

"Nothing. Having a little hard time with the routine -- of getting everything done on time. Got a firstie on my ass."

He regretted the last statement as soon as he said it.

"Don't cuss. Hazing?"

"Aw, come on, Mom, that wasn't cussing. Well, I'm sorry. No, Mom, not hazing. It just takes time."

"What's his name? Does your father know?"

"Hell, no!"

"He can help, you know -- if he wanted to. He's close by."

Blake's dad had completed his command tour of his carrier and was now stationed in the Pentagon, only about an hour's drive away. His dad had tried several times to make contact, even dropped him a note, but Blake never answered.

"Mom, stay out of this. I don't need any help. And I sure don't want Dad to even know I'm having academic trouble. Damn it, Mom, forget I said anything."

"Don't swear at your mother." Her voice raised.

"I'm sorry. I'll write. Got to run, Mom. Thanks for calling. I love you."

"I love you too, son. Let me know if you need anything."

*****

The three roommates waited to enact their plan of revenge on Blake's mentor. Time was on the side of Pete, Sam, and Blake. Sooner or later Greenfield would come in from liberty, snookered, in the bag. And when he did they would carry out their plan.

Thanksgiving came and went. The football team had a chance to beat Army. If they did, plebes would rate carry-on, the relaxation of plebe rules, until after Christmas leave.

But Greenfield never let up. His questions to Blake were skewed toward the coming event, like, "In what year did the Academy adopt 'Navy Blue and Gold' as the alma mater song?"

After a day's research: "Sir, the Academy adopted 'Navy Blue and Gold' as the alma mater song in 1925, sir."

"Who kicked the field goal to tie Army and allow Navy to remain undefeated and become national football champions in 1926?"

After few hours of research: "Sir, Tom Hamilton, Class of 1927, kicked the field goal to tie Army and permitted Navy to remain undefeated and become national champions in football in 1926, sir."

"When was the first Navy football team formed and who started it?"

"I'll find out, sir."

"Give me twenty and shove off."

After several days of research, Blake responded during a come-around, "Sir, the first Navy football team was formed in 1882, by Cadet Vaulx Carter, Class of 1884, sir."

"When was the first Army-Navy football game and who won?"

"Sir, the first Army-Navy football game was played in 1890 and Navy won 24 to zero, sir."

Greenfield now only randomly asked for the *Laws of the Navy*. When Blake inevitably failed to recite them perfectly, the firstie would then ask Blake for their meaning, thus compounding the Blake's problem.

Blake continued to struggle with the feeling to lash out at Greenfield, but something inside him said, "Hold on. Don't do anything stupid."

It was two days before the game, after a pep rally in Tecumseh Court, that the three roommates saw their opportunity. Cheerleaders stood on the steps in front of Bancroft Hall inciting the young men to go to war and defeat their arch enemy -- West Point. They sang songs such as, "A Cheer for Navy," "The Goat is Old and Gnarly," "Up With the Navy," and "Anchors Aweigh". It was after the Brigade had sung the *"Navy Victory March"* that someone shouted, "On to Baltimore!"

The chant grew until a mob of midshipmen moved past Tecumseh toward the main gate, firsties and the cheerleaders in the front, then the mass of bodies marched past Tecumseh, now painted in bright reds, greens and yellow war paint. His face was striped to look war-like and ferocious. Through the yard, out the gate, past St. John's College, and through the town they went ostensibly to carry their fighting message all the way to the city of Baltimore, some 25 miles away.

What actually happened was that some firsties used the opportunity to slip away to a bar to down a few beers. The rest of the midshipmen pressed on until members of the faculty skirting the crowd in their cars turned the mass back toward the school.

Pete, Sam, and Blake figured that Greenfield would take advantage of the disorganization to go to his favorite watering hole and come back drunk. They took turns walking the corridor. To seem innocuous they pretended going to the head or to a classmate's room.

About midnight Sam came into their room. "He's on the deck. Drunk as a coot."

Their strategy was keyed to one word: "Surprise." The three peeked out their door. Greenfield was about 100 feet from his own room, talking to another firstie. They waited. No one else could know or be involved. They would act alone. Luck was with them: the MOD left his post to make his security rounds at the same time the other firstie turned and went into his room. Greenfield staggered toward his room humming "Navy Blue and Gold."

Pete, the tallest, went first. A pillowcase with holes for his eyes covered his head. Blake and Sam followed immediately behind, matching his steps right after left. Their heads were also covered with pillowcases. About ten feet away, Greenfield looked up and mumbled, "Who's that?"

But it was too late. The three jumped him. Before Greenfield knew what was happening, a Navy blanket was thrown over his head. Sam, the shortest but strongest of the three, held Greenfield's arms, and they picked him up. As if they were carrying a squealing pig to market, they ran with his slender body writhing and struggling, his voice muffled by a hand over his mouth.

Down the stairs, out the door, across the yard, and into the natatorium. They released the body, blanket, and all into the water and heard a splash.

"You bastards!" Greenfield shrieked.

Their mission complete, the three raced back to their rooms, never making a sound until they were in their beds. Adrenaline still revved their bodies. Snickers grew to laughter.

Blake felt redeemed. He had held his temper and didn't do what Greenfield wanted – quit or worse.

After a few minutes Blake said, "Hold it down. He'll come looking. Go to sleep, if you can."

CHAPTER 8

THE GAME

At breakfast the next morning, Blake, Sam, and Pete kept their eyes in the boat. Food was passed in silence, but they could hear the comments, whispers, guffaws, and giggles of the second and third classmen as well as their muffled remarks from nearby tables. Greenfield's chin was lower than usual. It almost rested on his plate. Apparently, he'd told a friend about what had happened -- and the word spread like a Montana forest fire.

After breakfast, while they were making last-minute preparations for class, Greenfield slammed his class ring against their door and stood straddling the entrance. "Okay, the word's out and I'm looking for the guys who did it. It would have been plebes, and my guess it's you three. Come around tonight after supper. All three of you."

*****

"Against the bulkhead, all of you!" he shouted.

"Aye, aye, sir," came the response in unison.

"Give me twenty!"

On their bellies they dived, shouting, "Beat Army, sir," after each push-up.

"Okay, I know you did it. Very clever! But I don't hold a grudge. Never hold a grudge. I just want you to tell me the story -- how did you do it? Was it planned or did you just get lucky? You could *never* do that to me if I was sober."

Silence.

"Well?"

"I'll find out, sir," in unison.

"Well, the way I see it, Lawrence, you're the ringleader and you other weasels went along. I'm going to have each of you for lunch and supper. But, Lawrence -- that's another story. Come around every night for the rest of the year."

"Aye, aye, sir."

******

In their rooms, they giggled. "The prick only thinks he knows," Sam said.

"F-you, Greenfield -- bring it on," Pete said. "We can hold out to the game. Then, when we win, we're home free."

"Ya, carry-on," Sam grinned.

But Blake thought about Greenfield's last words, "Lawrence -- that's another story. Come around every night for the rest of the year." *He couldn't mean it - or did he?*

******

On the train ride to Philadelphia, the plebes, color drained from their already-pale faces, looked too young and out of place in their blue service uniforms with white stiff collars. They acted like hunting dogs on a leash -- blustery and edgy. They picked at their box lunches; few could eat. Adrenaline fed their bodies as if they were playing the Army-Navy game. Songs, cheers, and boasts about the outcome went up and down the aisles. Everything rested on this game. At that moment it was the only thing that mattered at both schools. Records against each other in lesser sports such as lacrosse or basketball didn't count. Outcomes of other games like 150-pound football weren't relevant. For interschool rivalry, the only thing that mattered was winning this football game. The success of the entire year rested on the outcome.

For the first class, beating Army was a lifelong notch in their belt. Some classes never beat the opposing school. For the rest of their lives those graduates suffered a silent embarrassment when questioned: Never beat Army?

For the plebe class to win was most important because it meant carry-on until return from Christmas leave. For Sam and Pete it meant escape from the wrath of Greenfield for more than a month. For Blake it meant more of the same – Greenfield's bullshit -- the difference between passing and failure. Unless the firstie relented.

Knowing the possibility of carry-on, each plebe class struck an unwritten and unspoken contract with the first class. Work hard, scream like a banshee, win over Army, and we will let you alone for a month. Let us down and we will hold you responsible -- life will be hell until you go on Christmas leave, and then we will get you again when you return.

Blake once asked his grandfather why the Naval Academy, or any military school for that matter, played football at all. His answer: "Of course for the players it's about learning teamwork, but it's not really for the players, nor the sport. It's for the American public to know and take pride in these schools where the elite officers, needed to win their wars, are made. It's also about the notion that a team, like the Navy, can play bigger than its individual members. Just observing the play imparts a lasting memory, albeit often subliminal, on future naval officers. Of course, it doesn't hurt the morale of the school and the Navy at large if the team beats Army."

Off-loaded like a herd, midshipmen soon formed into company formations for the march-on. Much of the pageantry was the ceremony before the game and at half-time. There was no after-game show; the moment it was over, the stadium emptied and party-time sport began.

The march-on preceded the game. The home team, which alternated each year between the corps and the brigade, marched on first. In ranks by company and lined up on the field, the low pitch of male voices bellowed in unison. Cheers by the entire student body flooded the stadium. They then took their seats in the stands while the opponent student body marched to assigned field positions and performed their cheers. Before the National Anthem, all students -- blue and gold on one side -- gray and gold on the other, standing at their seats across the field from each other, competed to out-cheer the other. The Colors were paraded and a prominent voice exploded into the first notes of the "Star-Spangled Banner," silencing the hub-bub of onlookers, stirring their attention. The entire spectacle was worthy of a nation of patriots.

The game soon began with each team ferociously trying its best plays on the other. Back and forth they went until one or the other scored. Plebes of the scoring team, in their beautiful blue or gray uniforms, dove to the nearest open space and did push-ups to match their team's total points.

The first classmen of Army had thus far not beaten Navy in football at any time during their four years. All efforts by the Military Academy faculty were focused on not allowing their boys to graduate without a win. Colorful signs sprang from nowhere, each chastising the Naval Academy for producing a product that was more sissy-like than manly. The corps had successfully stolen the midshipman mascot, a grungy old goat named Bill. Near half-time with the Army team ahead, Bill the Goat appeared from under the stands. This caused a group of midshipmen to run around the stadium and wrestle for possession of the beast.

Of course, residents of Washington, D.C., Baltimore, and surrounding areas chose up sides. Many thousands of people attended the game. But the President of the United States, as commander-in-chief of the Armed Forces, remained neutral. At half time he was escorted to the center of the field by the color guard of the previous year's color company. There he was transferred to the protection of the color guard of the other school's previous year Color Company.

With the half-time pageantry over, the students began again the cheers and chants intended to arouse their respective teams to greater heights -- and victory.

Blake, Pete, and Sam's voices were hoarse from shouting continuously. Motivated by the need to avoid Greenfield's wrath, they gave the game great attention. By the fourth quarter it was not clear who would win. Although Navy had a remarkably talented quarterback, an All-American at that, the Army team was scratching for every advantage. Greenfield, sitting in a row behind them, occasionally remarked, "You three better pray we win. Or I'll have your asses as soon as the brigade gets back. You hear me? Cheer, Lawrence. Cheer, Ettinger, Cheer, Tallau!"

"Aye, aye, sir," came the unison response followed by, "And it's up with the Navy, boys. Down with the foe. Good ole Navy's out for a victory, She'll shoot her backs around the greylegs' line..."

"I said a cheer, not a song, you bozos!"

The three let out a yell and gave him:

"Na-vy! Na-vy! Navy!

N-N-N-N

A-A-A-A

V-V-V-V

Y-Y-Y-Y

Na-vy!

Fight! Team! Fight!"

The clock showed just a few minutes left in the game. Navy was losing by four points.

Blake said to himself, "Come on, baby, if I'm to pas my courses, I need the carry-on. Win, baby, win."

The quarterback, a slender, long-legged kid from Texas, rolled out to the right and threw a pass to a Navy end who dived to within twenty yards of the goal line.

Pete grabbed Blake's arm and said, "We can do it! I feel it. Oh, shit, don't let me down, Navy."

With less than a minute to play, the Texan rolled out again but this time he kept the ball and dodged though the black, gold, and gray uniforms, diving high in the air over an Army tackler to score the much-needed touchdown.

"We did it! WE WON!"

"Not so fast. They still have time and a time out," Blake reminded his roommates.

After a successful extra point, Navy, now leading by three, kicked off. With only seconds to play, Army needed a field goal to tie. It was up to the Navy defense. Greenfield shouted above the roar, "You better hope they hold, Lawrence!"

They threw again. Caught again.

Time out. Seconds.

The huddle. The snap. A 'Hail Mary' throw.

Navy held. The ball bounced on the hard turf rocking back and forth until a midshipman football player grabbed it, kissed its leather strings, and held it high over his head for the brigade to see.

The game clock ran out and the stadium exploded into cheers. Blake and his roommates jumped and hugged each other. Happiness was a cold day in Philadelphia as the brigade belted out the lyrics of Navy Blue and Gold.

> "Now college men from sea to sea
>   may sing of colors true,
> But who has better right than we
>   to hoist a symbol hue?
> For sailormen in battle fair
>   since fighting days of old,
> Have proved the sailors' right to wear
>   the Navy blue and gold."

Blake turned to look for Greenfield, but he was nowhere in sight. Liberty call. They were free until an hour before the train left to return them to Bancroft Hall. Blake told Sam that he would try to get to the party he was holding at his house in Philadelphia home. But first he had to spend some time with his mother and brother, whom he had told to stay at their seats, that he would find them.

By jumping from seat to seat around the slow moving mass of people, Blake bounded down toward ground level. As he reached the concrete path around the stadium, he ran into his pal Erie.

"Blake, what a game. You see them stop Army? And that run by the Texan? Man, what a game! Next year, I'll be playing. Where you off to? Let's find a beer."

"Can't, meeting my mom."

"Hey, Blake. You kept your promise. It's almost Christmas and you're still here."

"Well, I'm still undecided. My grades are lousy, but I think I can make it through the semester now that we've got carry-on."

"Greenfield still on your ass?"

"Not now, not until after Christmas leave."

*****

"You look so smart in your uniform," Blake's mother said when she saw him in his midshipman uniform for the first time. She looked relieved, like she had harbored doubts they would find each other in the crowd. Charlie, Blake's eighteen-year-old brother, seemed bored with the entire event.

His mother and brother still lived in Steel City because Pittsburgh was her hometown. Before their divorce, his parents had lived on Navy bases where he went to school with other kids called "Navy Juniors." At the time, Blake didn't know the real reason why his mother and father split up. One day life was good, and the next his father was gone and life was...

"Good game," Charlie commented after shaking Blake's extended hand. The two brothers were not huggers, never were. In their younger days they were more likely to punch each other in the arm as a sign of their unspoken affection. Charlie resembled Blake only in hair color, blonde. Otherwise, he was shorter and stockier with the shoulders of a football player.

"Too bad Army didn't win," Charlie said.

"You still thinking about going there?"

"Sure."

"Winning makes the season. I get carry-on until after Christmas leave." In Blake's mind, that was the most significant aspect of the trip to the City of Brotherly Love. "Where we off to, Mom? You hungry? Want to go back to your hotel first? I'm starved." He looked at his watch, already thinking about Sam's party.

"We could go to supper, if you like. There's a nice restaurant in our hotel, isn't there, Charlie?"

"Uh huh."

They took a cab. Dodging through the dark, snowy streets, Blake saw midshipmen and cadets with beautiful girls on their arms beginning their night of revelry. He had no girlfriend. For him, plebe year had so far smothered all thoughts of romance. He did remember his days as a sailor when he dated one girl after another, never finding one that tickled his go-steady-maybe-marry button. He looked forward to Sam's party.

His mother insisted they wait in the lobby while she made a short trip to her room to freshen up. It was while she was gone that Blake's father strolled in the door with his wife on his arm. He was in his blue service uniform, and the four stripes on his sleeves seemed to grab the attention of nearly everyone nearby. Charlie couldn't take his eyes off them even though he too had seen them many times.

"Blake! Charlie! What good fortune. What are you two doing here?"

"Waiting for Mom. She's staying here." Blake's voice carried the strain of their relationship. It stemmed from the image of his father, whom he viewed as a "prick" -- a ruthless egoist who would sacrifice all for the sake of his career. He knew why he felt that way. It was because when his father left five years before, for what his mother called a "flag wife."

"You remember Rose-Ann, don't you?" His father introduced the woman who Blake thought stole his father from the family. Besides her curves and cleavage. her hair was her dominant feature. It was reddish blonde, cut in the current Hollywood style. Her clothes matched her coiffeur, right out of *Vogue* magazine. She hung on her husband's arm like the wrapper on a loaf of fresh bread.

"Evening, ma'am." Blake's words sounded like they were right out of *Gone With The Wind.*

"Captain Lawrence said we might see you." Rose-Ann purred. "Nice to know you, Blake -- the Third, isn't it? And Charlie --"

"Yes, ma'am," Blake responded politely, submerging his feelings about her use of his father's rank as if to remind him of their superior status. It was then he noticed her thin lips, the small creases near her eyes, and the lines at the corners of her mouth all covered by heavy makeup.

"It was a good game, wasn't it, Blake?" His father said.

"Good outcome, sir."

The tension between the two caused the words to sound awkward and stilted.

"You received my letter and invitation, I assume."

"Yes, thank you, sir. But mother was coming." Blake had indeed received a note asking him to join his father for supper after the game, but, impolite as it was, didn't answer it.

The atmosphere became even more chilly when Blake's mother walked out of the elevator. In contrast to Rose-Ann, she was still in her comfortable football outfit of a plaid skirt and a turtleneck sweater. For Blake, she looked like a mother should, a little plump, a little rosy, and very nice. Blake saw her hesitate, then stride boldly into the awkwardness of the moment. But she didn't speak, just stood at the side of her sons.

"Mary." Blake's dad acknowledged her presence. "Ah -- we have to be going. Charlie, I'm in Washington again. At the Pentagon. Maybe you can get down to see us soon."

"I'll try, Dad. Maybe after mid-term exams. I, I'm a junior this year and -- playing on my high school football team."

"Good for you. Keep me posted on how your team does. You playing for the plebe basketball team, Blake?"

"Yes, sir."

"Well, we're on the way --" his father said one more time, then taking Rose-Ann by the arm, departed toward the cocktail lounge.

"I'm starved, Mom," Blake said looking at his watch.

"What are we waiting for?" The three took seats in the crowded room that was still buzzing with the exuberance of Army-Navy football. Waiters. Drinks. Menus. Blake looked at his watch.

"You keep looking at the time. You have some place to go?" his mother asked.

Blake tucked his chin as if it was nothing. Then as an afterthought, "My roommate is from Philadelphia. You know I told you about Sam. Sam Tallau. The wrestler. Anyway he invited me to his place... later. Ah... I have plenty of time."

"Hum," she said. "Well, I'm very tired from the trip and the game. We do have to drive back first thing in the morning. What time is your train leaving?"

"About midnight."

"Don't you be late and don't get into trouble."

"I won't."

Their small talk was of home and humorous stories about the two ornery brothers. Halfway through their meal Blake looked up and said one word, "Greenfield."

"Who?" Charlie asked.

"That's him. The guy I told you about, Mom. Been running me."

"Seems to be a nice-looking boy."

"He's not. Not to me."

His mother began giving him the third degree. "Do the authorities know about him? Should I write a letter? Will you pass your courses? Should your father know?"

"I'm out of the woods, Mom. I have carry-on. I'll be okay."

"Well," she said, "at least you'll be home soon -- for Christmas. Some good home cooking will put some meat back on your bones. You look so thin."

"I'll come home for a few days. But I've got to get back and study. I'm really behind."

The meal ended when Blake's mother decided she and Charlie would go to their room and get some early rest. Blake knew it was her way of letting him go off to his party. Before catching a cab to Sam's place, Blake decided to stop in the hotel restroom. As he approached the door, Greenfield came out and caught Blake by the arm. "Don't think this is over just because we won the game, Mister Lawrence. Come around tomorrow night after evening meal... Know the *Laws of the Navy*, all of them! Or I'm gonna have your ass."

CHAPTER 9

VIVA AND THE CHALLENGE

Streetlights glowing over snow-covered roads. Children sledding across open lots. Icicles hanging from bare tree limbs. The cabby carefully maneuvered through the slippery streets, stopping in front of a red brick house with brown stone steps set on a boulevard full of identical homes.

For Blake, Philadelphia didn't look too much different than Pittsburgh, lots of older houses with small porches and too few windows.

It wasn't the high end of town, but from the sound of the music, laughter, and voices it was the high end of fun. Blake knocked. A tall, vivacious-looking girl wearing a tight sweater opened the door. She said, "You must be Blake. Sam and Pete are waiting for you -- in the kitchen.

"They call me Viva -- Viva Voce. My real name is Kathy Velenochi -- I'm from the neighborhood. Everyone calls me Viva -- I guess it's because I sing."

"Hi, Viva. I'd like to listen to a song."

"Congratulations on winning the big game. It's cold out, don't just stand there."

She shook his hand and ushered him in with a sweep of her arm, away and up like a stage actor might in a Shakespearean play. Her dark brown eyes, almost black, seemed to grow into large ovals. She had the kind of face and eyes that became animated when she talked; they moved like movie star's in front of a camera.

Blake waited, still sizing her up. He realized she was almost as tall as he was; in Blake's world, those kind of girls were rare. When she turned to lead the way he watched this leggy woman and saw that her black hair was pulled straight back over the top of her head. It hung down to the center of her back and bobbed side to side in rhythm with her skirt.

"Well, come on in. Make yourself at home. Sam's in the kitchen."

He instantaneously felt something that he had never felt before. *Viva looks good! Wonder if she's taken?*

She led him to the kitchen where Sam and Pete were standing by a table with several other classmates from their company. Blake smelled highly seasoned food.

"Hey, Blake. We thought you wouldn't make it. Party's just getting good. Here, have a beer." Sam thrust a cold bottle into his hand. "You met Viva already. She's a neighbor. Went to high school together. Get some food and meet some of the other people."

Blake's eyes followed Viva as she disappeared in the direction of the living room.

"My, she looks good!" Blake said.

Sam elbowed Blake. "Careful. In case you didn't notice, Pete has his eyes on her too. She's his date for tonight. You both need to be careful; she's a bit different -- may be too much for either of you."

"Why?" Blake asked.

"I grew up with her in this neighborhood. Went to school with her. Comes from a poor family. She has a one-track mind: gonna make it, no matter what. Noth'ns gonna get in the way of that girl -- never has -- not since grade school."

Pete, who was a few inches taller than Blake, elbowed him and winked, "Lay off, roomy. I saw her first and I like spunky girls. But for the more important stuff, wasn't that a great game? Blake, we won! Think of it: carry-on until after Christmas!"

"Not me. Guess who I ran into at my mom's hotel?"

"Not Greenfield?" Sam asked.

"Yep. He was in the same restaurant where we were eating. I thought I avoided him, but as I was leaving we ran into each other coming out of the head."

"You talk?" Pete asked.

"He did; told me to come around tomorrow night."

"That's bullshit -- chicken shit! He can't do that!" Pete exclaimed, slamming his beer bottle on the table.

"You going?" asked Sam.

"Sure. Got to. Who knows? When we get back, he may make you two come around also."

"Well, he better not. My firstie won't let him get away with that," Pete said.

"That bastard," Sam said. "He is, without a doubt, the biggest prick in his class, no question. Enough about Greenfield. Follow me, and don't fall in love with the first girl you meet -- besides Viva. Have some of this good food." Sam took Blake's almost-empty bottle and replaced it with another, then pointed to the dining room table, completely full of plates and dishes heaped with strange-looking fare. "My mother and sister made it. Just like the old country."

"I'm not very hungry. Already had supper with Mom and Charlie."

"Well, come and meet everyone. Mom, this is Blake Lawrence, my roommate. Everyone, everyone, this is Blake, my roommate."

Blake paid his respects to Mrs. Tallau. "Thanks for having us tonight, ma'am. The food looks real good."

"Oh, you must be the boy Sam talks so much about. The basketball player." Sam's mother was short; her head barely came even with Blake's chest. She was very plump, but her face and eyes had the same expression as Viva's, open and radiant in her welcome. *It must be something in the wate*r.

Sam disappeared into a living room full of young men and women. Some were standing; others sat on the couch and chairs drinking beer and having intense conversations. Blake watched as some danced in a section of the room where the carpet had been pulled back to reveal a wooden floor.

"You must be a friend of Sam's -- from Annapolis." A hand touched his arm from the side.

Blake responded, "How did you guess? I bet it's the uniform." He turned to face a girl who smelled of cheap perfume, like a street hooker. Shorter and much younger than Viva, she had fiery red hair and wore an outlandishly tight sweater over breasts that didn't fit her body.

"Oh, sorry about that remark -- forget that," Blake apologized. "I've been known to have a trace of sarcasm in my blood."

"My name is Flame. Well, my real name is Crimson Mallon, but they call me Flame."

"Don't tell me. Yunz're from the neighborhood."

"Sure, most of us are. We grew up with Sam. You're from Pittsburgh, aren't you?"

"How did you know that?"

"You said, 'yunz.' Everyone from Pittsburgh says that -- it's your trademark."

"Hmm. I've been trying to stop saying it."

A body whirled past Blake in the crowd and replaced his empty bottle with one that was full. Without thinking he took a sip and kept on talking. "Does everyone have a nickname like you and Viva?"

"Oh, you met her. Not everyone in the neighborhood... but most. Somebody says the word... just once, and everybody picks it up, and we have it for the rest of our lives."

"Sounds like a good place, this neighborhood. By the way, if you don't mind my asking. How old are you?"

"Almost sixteen." Flame smiled as if the year made a difference. "This neighborhood is a good place. All the boys go in the service. Sam's the first to try to become an officer. He's so smart, and an organizer. He's the only one who got to college -- so far. But I'm going to go when I finish high school. I don't live here any more. We moved to the Main Line last year, but they still invite me. You the first from your hometown?"

"Not sure about that, but I'm not the first in my family. By the way, how old is Viva?"

"Oh, she's old -- eighteen. She started at Juilliard this fall."

"Juilliard? Hmm." Blake let on that he knew what that was.

"Only the most talented get to go to that school. She's giving a recital next month," Flame offered. "I bet you like her, don't you?"

"I only met her. But I'd like to know her."

"Wanna dance?" Flame asked, her body already swaying to the music.

Blake looked at her for a moment then looked around the room. He wondered what his classmates might think about him dancing with a kid. But they were all engaged in romancing and dancing themselves. "I, I, okay. Why not?"

Flame knew something about dancing because as soon as they arrived at the tiny carpet-less area, she began moving her hips. Blake first learned to dance with the "Wisconsin Honeys" when he went on liberty with Erie at the Eagles Club in Milwaukee during his sailor days. Having learned a more sedate style at the Naval Academy prep school and a few tea dances since, he now merely shuffled his feet and stayed in one place. When someone changed the record from Elvis Presley to an old Sinatra standard, Flame came in close, rubbing her body tight against his, reminding him of dances at the Eagles.

They swayed slowly to the beat of Frank's voice.

Her face nestled into his chest and one of her hands reached up and began rubbing the back of his neck. Flame whispered, "You want to go neck for a while?"

"What? What did you say?" The music and chatter in the room was so loud he wasn't sure what he had just heard. He wasn't expecting that kind of forwardness.

"We can go upstairs." Her voice was low and throaty. "And you can kiss me."

Blake stopped dancing. "Flame, you are something. How about some food instead?"

He looked around as he walked toward the table. There were now more people in the small house. Bodies were everywhere. Laughter. Giggles. Music. Loud talk. The room was whirling, the beer made his nose numb. He looked for Viva, but she was lost somewhere in the mass. He saw that Flame was already dancing with Hamm McClinton and would probably, before the night was over, find someone to neck with. Blake only hoped it didn't go any farther than that. *Jail bait.*

"Hey, Blake." It was Sam. "There you are. Saw you dancing with Flame. She had her body all over you." Sam pushed another beer into Blake's hand. "Having a good time?"

"Yeah. Too much. Get'n a bit tipsy from the beer. Where's Viva?"

"Don't know. Think she's with Pete. Look upstairs. A bunch went up to the bedroom."

Blake made a sandwich of a sausage on a bun and weaved his way toward the stairs. He stopped on the steps half-way up and looked down on the party below.

The house smelled of body odors and years of good cooking. It was a good smell, the smell of street Americans who enjoyed their lives.

Maybe they were the root of the nation he was just beginning to think about. At first he didn't want to come to Annapolis. Then as he told Erie, he wasn't sure about staying. But now that his remaining a midshipman was hanging in the balance, pass or fail the first semester, his desire to stay deepened. He realized it was strange to have such lofty thoughts in the midst of a party -- maybe it was the beer.

But he couldn't get Greenfield off his mind. Even though his class had carry-on, he had to go around to tomorrow night, and it was against the rules to have to do so. But it was one of Greenfield's more difficult questions that began Blake's search for a greater meaning to his question of whether or not he should become a naval officer. It happened at supper two weeks before the Army-Navy game.

"Lawrence, what did George Washington say on June 29, 1788?"

"Sir, I'll find out, sir."

The Naval Academy librarian told Blake that the first president said a lot of things and Blake would need to know the place and circumstances of the obscure quote.

Blake searched the archives for two days until he found a quotation attributed to George Washington on the date Greenfield mentioned:

> "No one can rejoice more than I do at every step the people of this great country take to preserve the Union, establish good order and government, and to render the nation happy at home and respectable abroad. No country upon earth ever had it more in its power to attain these blessings than United America. Wondrously strange then, and much to be regretted indeed would it be, were we to neglect the means, and depart from the road providence has appointed us, so plainly; I cannot believe it will ever come to pass. The Great Governor of the Universe has led us too long and too far on the road to happiness and glory to forsake us in the midst of it. By folly and improper conduct, proceeding from a variety of causes, we may now and then get bewildered; but I hope and trust there is good sense and virtue enough left to recover and the right path before we shall be lost entirely."

Blake wondered again where and why Greenfield even had enough information to ask the question, but he did and it was Blake's duty to find the answer. Greenfield was a strange man. Even though he was a hard-ass, his questions seemed to have a deeper purpose.

He never seemed to study, but Blake heard that he got very good grades. He did read a lot. Was that the source of his inquiries?

As he stood in a slightly-inebriated state at Sam's party, Blake wanted to be a part of the future with the chance to be involved in the historical things to come. These were solemn thoughts that would most likely be laughed at if he were to tell them to his classmates. But he knew the Navy was always a part of the things that really mattered to the country. Maybe a decisive battle, or only an incident that changed the world. It was at that instant that he made up his mind.

Dammit! That bastard Greenfield! He's not going to break me! Nor is he going to be the cause of my bilging out.

Blake turned and continued his quest to find Viva. At the top of the stairs he found classmates talking to other neighborhood girls. A few of his classmates had brought their own girlfriends. Crammed into several bedrooms, some were talking, some listening to music, and some were necking with girls they had met at the party.

Blake looked in every room.

"Seen Pete?" he asked.

About to return to the dancing, he heard, "If you're looking for Pete and his girl, thought I saw them out on the balcony."

Even though they had barely spoken, Blake couldn't get Viva out of his mind and wanted to barge in on the two, but he thought better of it. *My roomy saw her first. Drop it.*

As he started back down the stairs, he saw Pete sitting on the floor talking to a different girl.

What the hell? Where's Viva?

He looked at his watch. It was twenty-two thirty. Time to get back to the train. He was returning to the kitchen when he heard the voice. To Blake it seemed to be opera. Viva was standing in the corner of the living room next to a piano. A crowd surrounded her. Blake stayed off to the side. He marveled at her voice. He had no training and no real appreciation of the talent required to perform, but to him she sounded professional. When she began singing Christmas songs, everyone joined in. The crowd took on the feeling of merriment that her emotional singing conveyed.

Before the next song began, Sam shouted, "Okay plebes. Travel time. One more dance and we leave. Got to be back to the station by twenty-three thirty. I'm calling cabs!"

Viva stopped singing and the guys grabbed their girls for one last dance. Blake bolted in front of another Mid and quickly asked Viva if she would dance.

"Of course," she said.

He took her in his arms. He had never before danced with anyone who just melted with his body to the rhythm of the music. She was a dancer as well as a singer.

"We didn't get to talk."

Viva smiled with her eyes. "Didn't think you were interested."

"I thought you were Pete's girl."

"I'm not anyone's girl."

"There's not much time left. Will you come to a dance in Annapolis? Sing me a song?"

"Will you be there?"

"Why wouldn't I?"

"Sam says you're getting a lot of heat from a senior and you might quit."

"Well, the heat part is true."

"Don't let him make you quit. Everyone thinks you have a future in the Navy."

"Yeah, who?"

"All your classmates."

"Well..."

"Fight back. At least don't quit. Pittsburghers are not quitters, are they?"

"Cabs are here! Who wants a ride?" Sam shouted.

Blake squeezed her and said in her ear, "Have to go but I don't want to."

"You'll be late."

"Not sure I care."

"Don't they call that AWOL?"

"You know too much." He tried to kiss her but she turned her head and he settled for a light peck on the cheek. Then he spun her and they ended the dance.

Viva joined Mrs. Tallau who was standing by the door saying good-bye to Sam's friends.

"That invitation to a dance. Is it still on the table?"

"That's an invitation. I'll write – no, I'll call."

"I want to come," she said. "But only if you are there."

Blake touched her hand and said, "I'll work on it." Then he was out the door and running to catch the cab.

*****

The day had been exhausting. Most mids slept during the return train ride, but Blake couldn't. His mind was on a delicious girl named Viva. He felt like a high school kid going to his first dance, giddy and excited. He thought of her coming down to Annapolis. She would be in her formal and he in his full dress uniform.

They would dance to big band music and later he would take her back to the drag house and get more than a kiss on the cheek. But now he had the challenge to make the fantasy come true. But Greenfield stood in his way.

Getting back on a Sunday morning gave the brigade time to catch up on any missed sleep and neglected studies during the pep rally week before the big game. Blake, Pete and Sam slept in but made it to the chow hall in time for lunch. Greenfield was absent. The three surmised he stayed in Philadelphia for the weekend, which meant he didn't have to be back until supper.

"Maybe he'll come back feeling so good he'll forget the come-around."

"Don't bet on it," Blake said.

It was wishful thinking on their part because, for whatever reason, Greenfield was meaner than a snake at the evening meal. "I expect all three of you to be in my room right after evening meal."

Pete, Sam, and Blake reported as ordered. Greenfield toyed with them, "So, we won the game and you three think you're getting a free ride? Well, it's not that easy. There's no carry-on for you three as far as I'm concerned."

Fortunately, Dale Thompson, Greenfield's room-mate, interceded. He reminded Greenfield of the bargain between the first class and plebes and suggested that the three be back immediately after returning from Christmas leave. Greenfield agreed and dismissed everyone. But as Blake was leaving, he said, "I want you one more time, Lawrence. Be here at 2200."

Back in their room the three agreed that Thompson had proved again that he was six-striper material.

"Ya, he stepped in just in time and had saved us a serious problem," Sam said.

"It's almost as if he's above the rest – quiet, ethical – older than his age," Pete said.

Although they did not know exactly what they would have done, they did know they would not have put up with coming around when the rest of the plebe class had carry-on.

*****

Blake stood at ease outside Greenfield's door. Every other plebe in Bancroft Hall was walking around enjoying his first free time since plebe summer. He felt embarrassed that he had been singled out to make what he supposed would be one more come-around. He expected this to be his last come-around for the ensuing month. He questioned why he accepted it at all. Although he didn't fear Greenfield, he did lose sleep and lots of study time over the man. He did everything he was told despite wondering whether all Academy grads became pricks who thought they knew more than the system and lost the big picture of what the place was to accomplish. Why was Greenfield giving him this big dose of shit? If it wasn't the last come around, Blake had to decide what he would do. It had turned into a personal thing between him and Greenfield. Why was he here at all? He could have quit already. Lots of his classmates already had. Why hadn't he just turned in his suit and left, gone back to the enlisted navy, which he really enjoyed. Something was driving him, and it wasn't Viva's challenge, although he would like to date her -- in uniform. No, it was the possibilities, the things he didn't understand about being a grad. Back in boot camp he had told Erie that he didn't want to come here, but something told him to go along -- see what happened. Now, under the surface, he really did want it; he didn't want to fail. It was probably the family thing, his obligation.

The hell with heritage. Now it's for me. I want it but not to become a prick. There has to be more to being a grad than that. I don't know what it is -- but I knew I have to find it for myself. To hell with my prick father. This is not about him. I'll do this... for me, for the possiblities.

The clock struck 2200. He burst into Greenfield's room. "Midshipman Lawrence reporting as ordered, sir."

"Against the wall, Lawrence," Greenfield snapped.

Dale Thompson was absent. Blake assumed he was somewhere in Bancroft Hall working on one of the many committees he served on or... getting ready to take over as winter set six-striper. For that he had to move to a special room near the commandant's office. What ever he was doing, he wasn't around to save Blake from Greenfield's bizarre behavior. Greenfield could only keep Blake for ten minutes, until taps. Blake figured whatever he was up to, he had to get to it very fast, before Thompson returned. For a minute or so, Greenfield remained silent, shuffling around the room as if he were contemplating. Finally he said quietly, "Saw your father in Philadelphia. The prick remembered me from last summer's cruise."

Blake felt his face flush in anger. *This is the second time he's called my dad that name. I'm gonna deck him. Should I? If I do, my grades won't matter; I'll be dismissed.*

"Trey," Greenfield sneered as if mocking the Lawrence family. "You are without a doubt the most sniveling, whining puke I have ever met. You couldn't pull your weight in a whaleboat of Goucher girls! You passive bastard, you don't have the backbone of a garter snake. You don't know if you want to be here, but you keep soaking up Uncle Sam's money. Why don't you take your ambivalence and go home, you whining piece of shit; I know your problem. You forgot the First Law of the Navy: To seek the best. You're unworthy of this place because it's the unworthy who see the best and don't even try. All right, Mister Lawrence, here's how it'll be. You recite the *Laws of the Navy* without a mistake and you are free of me forever. But if you make one mistake, I get your ass and you come around continuously until I graduate or you quit. Bet your ass? Fair enough?"

"Sir, request permission to speak?"

"Go ahead, pussy. You got the guts to take the bet?"

"Sir, not a fair bet."

"Not a fair bet? To get me off your butt?"

"Sir, there are twenty-seven laws of the Navy, and the probability of me screwing up are very high. Besides, an upper classman can't hit a plebe without his permission. Against regulations, sir."

"Well, since when did you become an expert on the regulations? You taking the bet, or not -- you chicken?"

"Not taking the bet, sir."

"You're not? You are the pussy I thought you were. Like father, like son. Okay, give me the *Laws of the Navy*, mister."

Blake began. He knew the front end of the twenty-seven four-stanza rhymes cold but he still had not mastered the last four or five. His only hope would be that Dale Thompson would come back before the come-around ended. He slowed his delivery, but Greenfield was too smart. "Speed them up, Lawrence the third.

Don't try to pull a fast one on me. I want them all before taps. You have four more minutes."

Finally Blake came to the end without an error. It was the morals portion at the end that always got him.

> "As the wave rises clear at the hawse pipe,
>   Washes aft and is lost in the wake:
> So shall thou drop astern all unheeded
>   Such time as these laws ye forsake;
> Take heed in your manner of speaking
>   That the language ye use may...

"That the language ye use may."

"That the language ye use may -- I'll find out, sir."

"Too bad, Lawrence. You were so close. Assume the position."

"Sir, I didn't give permission."

"Assume the position, pussy."

Blake hesitated. His first thought was not to assume the position at all, just walk out. But then he decided his course of action. He would do it -- he would carry out the order, but if Greenfield hit him it would be all over. He wasn't going to quit. He cared about what happened to him, but he would get satisfaction, one way or another.

I'm not an animal for a firstie to toy with. I'm tired of being pushed around.

Blake grabbed the edge of the nearest desk and bent over, exposing his rear end. Greenfield picked up the largest book in the room, an atlas. He paused for a few seconds to get the right angle for delivery, then swung full strength and hit Blake across his buttocks. At that moment, two things happened that Greenfield didn't expect. The door opened and Dale Thompson came in, and Blake stood up and faced the two first classmen.

"Mr. Thompson, did you see Mr. Greenfield hit me?"

"Ah, yeah, I guess so."

"Then, you are my witness. I'm calling you out, Mister Greenfield."

"Calling me out?"

"Yes, sir, and I want it in the gym with boxing gloves tomorrow night after supper. My roommates will act as my seconds, sir."

CHAPTER 10

THE DUEL

A feeling of colonial days spread across the Academy at Christmas time. Garlands of wreaths and bows hung on the gates. Music rang from the chapel. Billowing red ribbons hung across the green limbs. Midshipmen made their way through fresh snow wearing heavy overcoats, gold buttons reflecting the colored lights. Candles flickered in the windows of Captains Row as the glee club strolled the yard.

Sam sat by the radio. It was dialed in to the *Perry Como Show*. The singing barber from Canonsburg, Pennsylvania, sang, *I'll Be Home For Christmas*. Snow sprinkled the windowsills of Bancroft Hall. Few could study for counting the days until the start of Christmas leave.

"You called Greenfield out? What the hell does that mean?" Pete asked.

"It means I want to fight him," Blake responded.

"Fight? Fight a firstie? You nuts?" Sam exclaimed.

"But – duels – er -- fights are against the regs," Pete said blowing a smoke ring after a hardy puff of his Camel cigarette.

Blake stood with his feet apart, hands on hips. He had a determined look on his face. "This is not a duel -- at least not with swords or a gun like in the old days. It's just a chance to punch him in the mouth -- in the gym, with boxing gloves. And I want you guys to be my seconds."

"Seconds?" Pete said as he smashed the butt of his cigarette into the ashtray.

"Yeah, you go to Greenfield's room and make the arrangements. I'm sure it will be Dale Thompson. Tomorrow evening after supper, in the gym, as many rounds as is agreed to. You'll need a referee and a timekeeper. It isn't like it hasn't been done before," Blake said.

"Plebes have fought a firstie before?" Pete questioned.

"Well, I don't know what class they were. My granddad told me way that back in the beginning of the Academy, mids fought duels all the time. About Granddad's time, a mid named Meriwether fought a guy named Branch for twenty-three rounds. Granddad said one of them died afterward; he thought it was Branch, and there was a big investigation. And there was Dan Gallery, class of '21, who accused a guy named Daniels in the class of '22 of being a draft dodger for resigning. They fought over that one."

"Why do you want to fight Greenfield? We already threw him in the pool."

"Lots of reasons. That was a prank. This is for real. First of all, he hit me without my permission; second, he made me come around when we had carry-on; and three, he called my dad a prick."

"Hell, I've heard you call your dad a prick," Sam said.

"He is a prick. And I can call my dad anything I want, but no one else better do it. Not within earshot of me!" Blake sounded angry. "I'm tired of his shit."

"You're serious about this?" Pete asked.

"Damn right I am."

"Well, Greenfield does deserve a licking," Pete said. Then as an after-thought he asked, "Do you think you can win?"

"Hell, I don't know," Blake threw his hands up. "I just want the chance to poke him in the nose. Now, you guys with me on this or not?"

"We were with you when we threw him in the pool," Sam answered. "Why not?"

"Okay, but this has to be done on the QT. No one can know about it. The problem is, Dale Thompson is going to be the next set six-striper. He may not go along. You guys need to go to him and get his agreement for tomorrow evening: After supper, in the gym, no one else there except the participants, the timer, and the referee. The fewer the better and everybody sworn to secrecy."

"How many rounds?" Pete asked.

"As many as the seconds agree to," Blake answered.

Pete and Sam left the room and returned in less than a half-hour. They told Blake that, to their surprise, Dale Thompson agreed, but only because Greenfield insisted. But Blake knew there was another reason. Thompson was the only witness to Greenfield hitting without permission. He probably thought he had to go along with the fight. If he didn't, and Blake reported the matter to the authorities, he might lose his stripes. Thompson also agreed it had to be done in secret -- that it would be done in an honorable way. He would referee and Pete would be timekeeper. No one else was to be involved or know about it.

*****

Supper the next evening was a quiet affair. The plebes at surrounding tables, usually braced up and answering questions, were at ease and chatting among themselves. Pete, Sam, and Blake sat in silence. Greenfield and Thompson sat just as quietly at the end of the table. No one ate very much -- they picked at their food, and as soon as the meal was over, Blake and his roommates went directly to the gym where Blake changed into sweat clothes and put on his gloves. Greenfield and Thompson showed up a few minutes later.

While Greenfield changed into his fight clothes, Thompson discussed the situation with the plebes. "This can't go on very long -- don't want to get caught. Would you be satisfied with a five-round bout, Mr. Lawrence?"

Blake looked at Pete and Sam, raised his gloves and beat one into the other. "All I want is a chance to hit him. I don't care how many rounds. Up to him."

"Okay, five rounds it is. We stop and get out of here after the last round. No one speaks of it again. Agreed?"

"Agreed," Blake said.

The two climbed into the ring. Greenfield was six inches shorter but more fit than Blake thought. He wore boxing shorts and a T-shirt tucked over a flat belly. His biceps were long and sinewy. Blake could see that his legs were strong from running the lacrosse fields for the varsity team. Pete rang the bell and said, "The first one-minute round begins."

Blake glared at Greenfield, but the firstie just smiled and said, "We'll see if you're like your pussy dad."

Blake charged Greenfield and swung a haymaker hook intended to end things early. Greenfield, who obviously knew what he was doing, slid under the punch and began jabbing under Blake's guard, slamming well-aimed fists into his stomach. Blake became so furious that he charged again in retaliation, this time tackling the firstie to the floor where they lay for a moment wrestling, legs and arms flailing at each other.

After they were untangled, Greenfield said, "So, you want to play that way? Well, protect yourself, plebe!"

Blake had little experience in the ring -- a few short lessons during plebe summer and his two previous fights, one in boot camp and one against his old roommate Brandell. Those had been against slugs -- two guys big and out of shape with fewer skills than he. This was the first time he was in against a good fighter. For Blake, Greenfield was the door he had to go through. Maybe he could have laid back and accepted everything Greenfield had to offer without issuing this challenge, but it had to be settled. Passing or failing his academics no longer mattered. This had to be done. For him it was a matter of honor. All he wanted was one good punch into Greenfield's face, but he felt like a gooney bird trying to land on Midway Island -- he kept swinging, stumbling, and missing. The sound of arm slapping and grunts echoed through the otherwise empty gym. Greenfield, as it turned out, was like a rabbit, fox, and reptile all rolled into one. To Blake he looked like the latter -- a snake as he crouched and slithered round and round the ring, striking then dodging. His quickness kept Blake off balance while the smaller man slashed in and out, often swinging as if to cut Blake's face with his glove laces.

At the end of the second round, Blake knew he was up against a skilled, fit athlete. Greenfield wasn't a varsity lacrosse player for nothing. He was a mean, rough fighter who asked no quarter and gave none. The third and fourth rounds were more of the same; Blake could only land an occasional glancing blow as Greenfield kept punishing him and talking to him as he did so.

"You're a pussy, Lawrence. Come on, see if you can hit me."

Even though his arms felt like he was carrying an anchor, Blake struggled to keep his guard up. He brushed off most of his opponent's punches -- but many got through.

Greenfield hit him in the face and Blake's head jerked back. Blake swung hard but only found air. Blake's glove finally raked Greenfield's cheek. For his trouble Greenfield hit Blake in the eye and it immediately swelled — he could barely see through it.

Blake's face felt like it did when he had the mumps. With one of his eyes was almost closed, he could only plod after a moving shadow. He had to find a way to get to Greenfield. He began to match the firstie jab for jab. This was the last round, and it couldn't end without his landing a serious blow. He became like a robot lumbering after Greenfield. He swung wildly, determined to catch him with a roundhouse, but hitting only air.

"Oh!"

"Oof!"

"You bastard," Blake mouthed.

"Ha, ha." The firstie just laughed as he stayed out of range except to stab Blake occasionally in the eye but mostly square in the face.

"Oof!"

"Ah."

Blood from Blake's nose spashed across the mat on which they were fighting. The referee called a halt, took a rag, and wiped Blake's nose.

As he chased the smaller man, Blake remembered that his earlier charge had at least gotten him within hitting range. Blake faked a step to the right and as his opponent moved toward the corner, he ran hard into him and tied him up. The referee said, "Break." As they pulled apart, Blake swung a left hook followed by a right cross and Greenfield went down.

Although he jumped immediately to his feet, the damage had been done. The bell rang. Blake was satisfied. He might look like hell, but his honor had been avenged. The fight over, Blake started for the ropes. Greenfield grabbed Thompson and shouted, "One more round!"

Sam jumped into the ring and said, "It's over, sir." And Dale Thompson agreed.

As they were changing back to their blue service uniforms, Greenfield came to Blake. Dale Thompson stood next to him. Pete and Sam stood close by, as if ready to fight.

"Okay, Blake. You did well. You showed you have some fight in you -- I'd like to have had another round to get even, but -- it's over."

To Blake's surprise, Greenfield took off his gloves and held out his hand.

Upper classmen never shook hands with a plebe; it would mean a spoon, the equalization of their relationship, a sign of friendship. Blake thought for a moment, then slipped off his gloves and shook Greenfield's hand. He thought it was the gesture of sportsmanship and only meant that the fight was over. Never thinking he would get the response he received, with a twinkle in his eye and an impish grin he asked, "This mean I'm spooned?"

"Call me Mark, Blake. If you need a place to hang out, come on in. Okay with you, Dale?" It was a noble gesture from a man known as the biggest prick in the brigade.

Thompson was caught off guard. He thought for a second, then said, "Okay, call me Dale, Blake." They also shook hands.

"And Blake, ah -- I'd like you to come around to my room -- when it's convenient -- just for a talk. You don't have to do it, up to you."

The five men then evaporated into the night.

*****

In their room, Pete slapped his hands together, "Man, you are a lucky shit."

"Lucky? That was a clean punch. I got him good!" Blake said defensively.

"That's not what he means," Sam said. "He means, *you* got spooned by the meanest prick in the brigade!"

"Yeah," echoed Pete. "That's what I meant. You lucky turd."

"You going around to Greenfield?"

"Sure, he asked me. I'll go." Blake said. "Don't know what it's all about though. But it's the least I can do after he spooned me."

CHAPTER 11

DARK AGES

Beginning the day after the fight, Blake's life as a midshipman changed. Neither he nor his roommates ever mentioned what happened that night in the boxing ring, but word got out somehow. Everyone knew something happened between him and Greenfield. Although most mids didn't know exactly why, their respect for Blake took off like a Bancroft Hall rumor. He was tagged as a man of superior character. His grades took an up-turn and he became the person in his company the other plebes deferred to in class matters. One even suggested he run for class president.

Stranger things had happened. Most often the one elected was a mid who had been president of his high school class and still had political leanings. Blake never thought of running for office. In high school his athletics kept him too busy for extracurricular matters. But when Sam urged him to try, Blake said, "Okay, but only if you organize the campaign. Just don't do anything until I have a chance to get my grades up. Hell, the election isn't for several months. We'll start next fall, after we get back from youngster cruise."

"Like hell we will," Sam stated. "Candidates or their reps have to go room-to-room asking for each classmate's vote. Outside of their company, no one really knows their classmates. Your early notoriety puts you in position for the 'halo effect.' It'll bring stripes and a reputation; we have to work on that now!"

Sam's energy level was always on max, but he seemed to keep a little extra available for the things that really challenged him. Even for a plebe, whose schedule always over-spilled a reasonable day, Sam's was like a flood. He already worked for *The LOG* and *Splinter* staff and several other extracurricular activities available at the Academy. Nevertheless, the challenge of running a campaign moved him to accelerate his normally-explosive thought processes. "You want me to run the campaign, you got to let me do it my way. Here's what we do. We'll do a preemptory strike. Right after Christmas leave we'll go door to door. Raise your level of awareness within the class. Let everyone know you'll be a candidate next fall. Put the other chumps who want to run on the defensive. Maybe run off some of those who might otherwise have run."

*****

For Blake, Christmas leave amounted to three days at home and two weeks of cramming in the silence of his Bancroft Hall room. He wrote his mother about his problem and she agreed that a short visit was enough -- just so she knew he was all right. After he got back to the hall he called her often so she wouldn't worry. She encouraged him to keep focused on his studies.

Dark Ages began when everyone returned from Christmas leave and lasted until spring leave in early March. It was the dull period when the days were short and nights were long, when snow blanketed the yard. Because everyone felt glum plebe year, the rite of passage to become an Annapolis officer continued but without enthusiasm.

One way to liven an otherwise boring existence was to toy with the plebes. But for Blake the days of hazing came to an end. As soon as the upper class learned he was running for class president, they left him alone.

Sam was an organizer. He got the plebes of the company involved, then the battalion, and from that base came posters, hand-outs, and personal, door-to-door campaigning by others on Blake's behalf. His name zinged through the hall as if he had invented a new weapon or made a scientific breakthrough. All of this took place during the time he was bringing his grades into the rarefied atmosphere of 3.0's and higher. Once he got Greenfield off his back and caught up during the Christmas holidays, it seemed that the course work fell into place. He cruised through algebra, trig, and chemistry. He began to have time to think. He hadn't gone back to Greenfield's room as the upperclassman had asked. So, finally, well after he had his midshipman life reasonably under control, he decided the time was right.

Blake wasn't certain how to enter the room. Should he just walk in as if Greenfield was a friend, or should he sound-off like it was a regular come-around? He decided to be on the safe side. "Midshipman Lawrence, Fourth Class, sir."

"Carry on, Blake. You don't have to sound-off in our room any more. Relax. Glad you're here. Sit. How you doing?"

"Good. More time to study, now that..."

"Now that I'm off your ass." Greenfield smiled.

He seemed like a regular guy, but Blake was still uncomfortable with the situation. He sat tall in his chair, somewhere between a full brace and at ease.

"You can hang here any time you want. No one will bother you."

"Thanks."

"You gett'n all this shit?"

"What stuff?"

"The plebe crap."

"I suppose. Don't understand the sense of it... but..." Blake said.

"You know my reputation?"

Brigade's biggest prick.

Greenfield answered the question himself, "Brigade's biggest prick, right?"

Blake judiciously remained silent, still wondering what the line of questioning was all about.

"You won't believe this, but you never seemed like the other plebes I had around. They came and went, one day, maybe two. Some quit under the pressure, some just rode it out until I gave up on them, but no one fights an upper classman like you did. You kept coming for a half year. You seemed to have another layer more than the others. I first thought you lacked fiber. But you never showed emotion -- no cracks in the armor. Like a robot, you just did whatever you were told, even when it began to affect your grades. In other words, you just took it and never showed any grit. I never had doubts about you, but I could never get a gauge on your relief valve. Anyway, someone helped me make my decision, so I decided to help you. I'm not out of the Academy yet, obviously. But I think about what being a grad means, even more than my roomy, who is the new six-striper. The difference between us is that he does it and I just think about it. I think about the top drawer officers, in any walk of life, particularly military officers. What makes them the way they are? One of the things I think makes them different is they must sometimes stick their asses out. Sometimes things go over the edge and officers must take a stand or... get out, maybe both. What do you think, Blake?"

"About what?"

"About what I've been talking about. What's the essence of becoming an Annapolis officer? Come on. This isn't easy for me to be talking to you like this." Greenfield seemed embarrassed.

"Well – I -- I think everybody is different. Sticking out our backside isn't something I think about. I believe the circumstances dictate what to do."

"Like calling me out for saying your dad's a prick?"

"Yeah. Like calling my dad a prick. And hitting me without permission. And running the shit out of me for no apparent reason."

"Good. Well you took the bait and risked a whole lot. I admire you for it. Not sure if I would have done it exactly the same way, but it worked for you."

Blake had the urge to smile, but didn't.

"I'm gonna make a prediction. You will do well in the Navy."

"Thanks." Blake smiled at the compliment.

"I hear you're running for your class presidency."

"Thinking about it."

"Do it. And – ah – Blake, let's talk again."

"Right," Blake said as he got up and left Greenfield's room, feeling better about both Greenfield and himself.

*****

Blake did have one other thing on his mind besides his studies. One night during the darkest of the Dark Ages, in the dreary Annapolis February, he called Philadelphia and asked to speak to Viva. He was told he'd find her at the Julliard School in New York.

Blake dialed the number. "May I speak to Viva -- I mean Kathy Velenochi, please?"

"Wait. She's at the other end of the hall. I'll get her," the voice said.

"Hello. This is Kathy."

"Viva, this is Blake Lawrence. How are you?"

"Who?"

"Blake Lawrence. Don't you remember -- from Sam's party after the Army-Navy game?"

"Oh, Sam and Pete's roommate at Annapolis."

"Yeah. Can't talk long. Got to get back to study hall. Can you get away and come down for a Tea Fight?" he asked.

"Fight?"

"Tea Dance. It's what we call a dance."

"How did you get my number?"

"I'm a Russian spy in midshipman clothing -- will you come?"

"Ah, Blake, how nice of you to ask. But, Pete already asked -- through Sam."

"Did you say you would?"

"Not yet. But," she said sarcastically, "they somehow got me on the Naval Academy's list of approved and suitable girls you plebes can dance with."

"You coming down?"

"I'm thinking about it."

"Okay, it's up to you. Let me know your plans."

"But, ah, Blake, I think I'm committed to go with Pete. He's your roommate, isn't he?"

"Yeah, Sam and Pete, and my good friends at that. I'll see you. Save me a dance."

"Bye, Blake."

*****

For a Tea Fight, girls were invited to come to Annapolis on a Saturday afternoon. It was a chance to meet midshipmen, maybe a future husband. The mids who were not bashful took to the floor immediately; those who didn't lined the walls of Carvel Hall. Blake was among the latter. But he had his eyes on Viva. In her chiffon, ankle-length afternoon gown with a corsage pinned to her shoulder, she looked every bit the budding diva. She and Pete seemed to be enjoying themselves, but he wanted to get just one dance with her. At a break, the two came to join Sam and Blake. Sam was standing with his girl, another Philadelphia beauty named Julie. Hamm McClinton, one of the youngest members of Blake's class and by far one of the better students, was dancing with Flame, who was wearing a yellow angora sweater. The fuzz was all over Hamm's blues.

She must have lied about her age because the girls are supposed to be at least seventeen. I hope Hamm knows what he's was doing, dragging a high school girl.

In their dress blues and white gloves, the brigade was at its romantic best. Girls from all over the country liked to be invited to drag (be a midshipman date) at the Academy, even when they knew that they had to pay for their own transportation and lodging. But this was not a brigade ball. It was only a "tea fight," and afterwards the mids went back to Bancroft and the girls went home. Most of the girls at tea fights were locals, daughters of Navy officers or students at nearby colleges. Some of those from out of town booked in at a local hotel, but most stayed at one of the many nearby drag houses in town. These were private homes, often owned by widows of Naval officers, who took the girls in and chaperoned them during their weekend stay in Crabtown.

"May I have a dance? You don't mind, do you, Pete?"

"Blake, you snake. Don't try anything; she's mine!"

"Just one dance, wifie. Never fear."

On the floor, Viva's face was almost even with his own. "You're a tall girl," he said. "And much prettier than I remembered."

"Why, thank you, kind sir."

"How's school going?" he asked. "What do they teach you at Julliard?"

"Well, a lot of stuff. Mostly music composition, the masters, and in my case, voice training."

"You sounded very accomplished at Sam's party."

"Thank you again, sir. But I have a lot to learn. I give my first recital in February."

"Where?"

"In New York. At the school."

"Too bad. Wish I could be there," Blake said.

"How are you doing in this school?" Viva asked. "Sam tells me you're going to run for class president."

"That's not a lock. I have a lot of stuff to do before that happens, like get my grades up."

"By the way, why did you call Pete "wifie?" Viva asked.

"Probably sounds dumb, but since we can't marry while we're here, we jokingly call our roommates our wives."

"Oh." Viva's brow wrinkled.

The music stopped for a moment and began again with a Glenn Miller standard. Pete tapped Blake on the shoulder. "Cut in?"

"Ah, Pete. I just had one dance."

"That's all you get, my man. Take off." Pete pushed Blake playfully.

"Bye, Viva. I enjoyed the dance."

"I did too, Blake."

He walked back to join the other bachelors. He waited a few minutes to watch the strikingly beautiful Viva swing in the arms of his roommate. When the music changed to fast dance songs, he left to return to his room and his studies.

*****

During a visit to Greenfield's room, he learned about service selection, the process whereby firsties crossed the bridge into active service. Not everyone could go to a ship, become a pilot, or Marine. There were quotas for each. Although, through summer cruises and other practical experiences they should have easily made up their minds, it seemed that everyone had procrastinated in their decisions. At the last minute they ran around talking to their friends, learning about the possible choices. Greenfield was considering the Air Force.

The visits to Greenfield became one of the most stimulating things Blake did during his plebe year. Without as many come-arounds to other upperclassmen, Blake spent a great deal of time in discussions about things he never would have talked about with anyone else. Greenfield, it turned out, fit into the intellectual category of midshipmen. He didn't have to study as hard as his classmates, so he filled his time reading books.

His father practiced medicine in the small town of Tulare, California, and his mother taught school. Greenfield graduated at the top of his high school class, fully intending to follow his father into medicine by attending Berkeley. Somewhere along the way, he became infatuated with the military and decided to go to one of the three major war-fighting academies. There was an appointment opening at Annapolis, and he took it.

For the rest of the year, Greenfield and Blake talked about world affairs and military history. They entered into grand debates about the meaning of civilization, nationalism, collectivism, Marxism, democracy, federalism, air power, power projection, and on and on. Blake even researched questions voluntarily just to get the upper hand over his new friend.

Blake knew he wanted to serve on ships. But even as an enlisted man, he had not gone to sea. Observing the confusion of service selection, he wasn't as certain as before. He realized his choice would become more complicated. During the rest of his Naval Academy training he might find another part of the armed forces that interested him just as much as ships.

Greenfield challenged him to keep an open mind because there were many new and innovative changes to warfare on the drawing boards. He thought the near future would be a good time to become a part of technologies that would change the way wars would be fought and the Air Force would be the place of greatest change. His heroes were Billy Mitchell, Curtis Le May, and Jimmy Dolittle. He called them "Bombs," "Brains," and "Balls."

They argued about the standards for a graduate. Should plebe year be more difficult or not? Greenfield told him, "In my opinion, the only standard for graduates is living up to those heroes who have come before."

"Search for your own heroes," he added.

CHAPTER 12

IT'S OVER

If plebe year came in like a dynamite explosion, it went out like a basketball dropped on a court -- bop, bop, bop -- and then it was over.

Blake's summer cruise as a youngster would be aboard a ship in the Atlantic, maybe crossing into the Mediterranean Sea or possibly going to Northern Europe. For the first time since he arrived, he could actually smell the sea; it beckoned him and he couldn't wait to get started. But he had to wait. There was a plebe basketball schedule to finish, the remainder of plebe year to weather, then final exams.

As the year came to a close, self-interest took hold. Class standing required attention to course work. Plebes still got a few come-arounds, but the duration in an upper-class room was reduced to slamming against a wall, reporting, giving the answer, and getting out. All the fun had already been sucked out of the process. Upper classmen didn't have the time nor the inclination to keep indoctrination at the high level it had been during the fall and winter. By the time the final spring set of stripers took charge, plebe year was essentially complete. They still had to march in the center of the corridors, know headlines and sports scores, but the days of hard questioning were over.

The Farewell Ball was the first ball the plebes could drag. Pete, who would survive first-year academics by a very thin margin, again asked Viva but she had already left the country for what she called a "European voice experience." It bothered Blake that he wouldn't see her, but not Pete, who turned around and invited another of his many girlfriends. Blake ended up dragging a blind date, the sister of one of his company mates and got "bricked" (the mocking of a mid who dated a girl who was less than very attractive).

The first class had their final P-rade and the second class had their ring dance. Graduation hats flew into the air, and plebe year was a thing of the past. It would always remain in their minds, an accomplishment to refer to for the rest of their lives.

For Blake, it marked a life change. He had begun first year at the academy in an ambivalent mood. In fact he was certain he would not stay. Erie pushed him into trying it for the first half, but it was Greenfield who became the catalyst for his change. He thought of the year as a growth period in which he was challenged every step of the way. Would the remaining three years be equally demanding? *Well, bring them on – I can handle anything after my plebe year.*

Blake made it a point to greet Greenfield in his new second lieutenant's Air Force uniform and be one of the first to give him a salute, which earned him a silver dollar. They shook hands and agreed to stay in touch. Greenfield then quickly became a fading image as he went off with his parents and friends. He went into the Air Force, where it was unlikely Blake would ever see him again.

The rest of the brigade seemed to disappear like a flash flood in a desert as soon as the sun burned through.

The new first class went off to the summer cruise with the new youngsters. The second class began their indoctrination into amphibious warfare, naval aviation, and submarines. Everyone would get several weeks of summer leave before the academic year began again.

Blake, with every one of his classmates, ran to Herndon Monument, where they climbed the slimy sides to place a cap on top -- they were now youngsters. For Blake, wearing one diagonal stripe on his shoulder boards felt good. He surmised that it would be the biggest promotion he would experience in his life. Hazing was gone forever, unless they trained for the Marine Corps at Parris Island or in Coronado for the UDT/SEALs. Now all they had to do was to obey orders and live up to the things they learned plebe year (if in fact they had learned anything) for the rest of their lives.

The lists assigning midshipmen to ships were posted on a bulletin board near the mate's desk on each deck of Bancroft Hall. Blake first scanned the list for the name and location of his ship. He would be on a 692 class destroyer. He then scanned the list for other classmates' names. Stone would go to a cruiser whose homeport was Norfolk, Virginia, a town not known for its racial tolerance. Pete would be on a destroyer. Sam and Erie's summer cruise would be aboard a battleship. Missing from the list was the name Brandell Sykes. When the final plebe year grades came out about a week after the final exams, Blake noted that the racist had failed three courses. Blake had moved up from the bottom third, where he was after mid-terms, to the upper third of the class. Although he had lost track of Brandell after they joined their academic companies, he now knew that the bigot had bilged out. Blake always thought Brandell was dumb as a stump anyway and would not be a serious loss to the Navy. As it turned out, more than 25 percent of the plebe class who entered the previous summer had already left for one reason or another. Some just quit on their own to go to civilian colleges; others couldn't take the hazing. But most couldn't hack the difficult examinations in math and science required to become an engineer.

Massive four-by-four-by-three wooden Cruise boxes were issued to them to store their belongings until the next academic year. Sea bags became stuffed with uniforms needed aboard ship: dungarees, blue service, white service, and khakis -- rain gear, boon dockers, and very little money. They were off to the briny deep, which was only a vague notion for most of them. Finally the word came down, "Mount out at 0600. Tomorrow morning you're going to sea!"

CHAPTER 13

AT SEA

Smells. Freshness of the sea, ocean spray, and salt. They filled Blake's nostrils stronger than the smell of a first cup of coffee in the morning. He scanned the heavens. Clouds folded one over the other, flying across an otherwise passive sky. Out of nowhere the ships had appeared in Chesapeake Bay in the deeper water just outside the Severn River. Except for an occasional ripple, the water in the school's small boat harbor looked flat. The only waves were those from a passing barge and a captain's gig making the inboard side of the wooden dock.

Blake felt like the cartoon character Kilroy of World War II fame -- his fingers grasping the top edge of a wall, the tip of his nose just above it. He felt like he was just beginning to swim his way from his shallow understanding of the Navy toward the next layer of awareness: what was the world really about? He knew about the Cold War, he knew the Korean War had left that peninsula in turmoil, and he also knew there was conflict in Vietnam. But he had no real understanding of a naval officer's place in all that except it seemed there was strife everywhere in the world, and American ships were somewhere nearby.

His grandmother Hildur, a Swedish woman his grandfather met and married while an attaché in Europe after World War I, often criticized her husband and the naval service. Blake once heard her say, "With your constant show of force and power, you Navy men miss opportunities to make the world a better place. After you fight a war, you should strive to be sure that it leads to a more peaceful planet." Blake called her his farmor, the Swedish name for father's mother. A statuesque woman, she stood almost six feet tall with high cheekbones and a lower lip that she extended when she lectured her husband. "Remember," she would say in her Swedish-accented English, "To be noble is not a character trait limited to those of high birth as the Europeans might wish, or English knights in silver armor with a halo over their heads. American naval officers should show moral character of an admirably high quality." To granddad's greater irritation, she would go on with her high-sounding and preachy lectures to Blake, encouraging him to search in life for his better angels. "Nobleness reaches beyond everyday decisions for a facet of your character that transcends material and monetary rewards. You should search for the greater truths."

In those days, Blake thought her words were just the ramblings of an old woman that got on the nerves of his grandfather. Hell, at the time, he even thought her a bit weird and didn't understand most of what she said, especially on days when her accent was heavy or she spoke in Swedish. None of the parents or grandparents of any of his buddies ever talked like that, but she was not ordinary. Now her words were taking on far greater meaning for him in his search for the truth.

Ships painted haze gray stood tall at their anchorages. For Blake they were a portrait of majesty, his Rembrandts. Their stacks showed wisps of white smoke

and their halyards were filled with colorful flags
swaying with the wind.

Destroyers, the workhorses of the blue-water Navy,
had a sleek look beginning with a high stem sloping
toward a stern that sat only a few feet above the water.
The black water line that followed the shape of the deck
kissed brine as it slapped against the hull.

It was not Blake's first time aboard a ship. Actually,
his earliest memory was when he was about four years
old the time he visited his grandfather's ship. It was in
port, and he held the captain's hand tightly as they
strolled from the quarterdeck to the pilothouse and from
the bow to the stern. It was a long walk for him, scuffing
his shoes, tripping over hatches, but listening intently to
the strange words like "fo'c'sle" and "transoms" and
"bulkheads." That day was a vague memory, but he
knew it had happened.

Blake and his classmates boarded the motor launches
that took them to their assigned ships lying at anchor in
the deeper water of the Chesapeake Bay. Some would be
his shipmates for the cruise, giving him a chance to
know them better.

Blake climbed the ladder with his sea bag over his
shoulder. He paused to see how the ship was made up.
Was it like Chief Shorty had told them in seamanship
class over in Macdonough Hall?

*There's the anchor chain tending into the current.
The Ensign is flying from the stern, a Jack in the stem.
The ladder leading to the quarterdeck shows clean white
canvas. Life rings are hanging nearby on the lifelines.
All just as Shorty said it should be.*

He thought a moment about what he was to do on
boarding. He rehearsed in his mind the routine, then he
proceeded. He shifted his sea bag to his left shoulder

and saluted the American flag flying from the stern, then saluted the officer of the deck. "Request permission to come aboard, sir."

"Permission granted," came the forceful reply from a very young-looking ensign as he returned the salute.

"Midshipman Lawrence, reporting for duty, sir."

"Okay, Lawrence, hand your papers to the mate and stand over there out of the way until we get everyone aboard" The OOD pointed to an open space near the five-inch gun.

The line of new youngsters and first classmen flowed across the gangway. They formed in a group all standing at parade rest waiting to be taken to their places in the ship.

"My name is Ensign Rhode. Our ship's name is *U.S.S. Ingraham* DD 694. She's the third ship to be named after Captain Duncan Ingraham. She's squared away and we're proud of her so don't screw up; leave her better than you find her. Okay, you will live in your division's compartment. Here is a list that shows where you will be assigned." He held the paper in the air. "Your guide will show you where to go and which rack and locker will be yours. After you unpack and make your bunk, hurry to the chow hall. You still have time to catch noon meal. Cookie knows you're coming. He has rations set aside for you. Don't linger. The mess hall has to be cleaned for evening meal. We get underway right after lunch. Underway time is 1330. We join up with the squadron at 1430, then sail south to meet the rest of the training task force tomorrow.

"One more thing. A division petty officer will show you to your sea detail station after lunch. Look lively and do what you're told. Look squared away. We have the smartest ship in the squadron -- keep it that way."

Blake's was assigned to the First Division. Their bunks lined both sides of a passageway in the forward part of the ship that led into a space called the bos'n locker. "Take that rack -- the upper. And that locker." A seaman named McMichaels pointed to a shiny silver-colored box about two feet high and a foot wide that was sitting on a stack of about three others. They extended to the overhead.

"I won't be able to get all my stuff in that," Blake said.

"What you can't get in there stays in your sea bag. We stow them forward in the locker," McMichaels responded. "By the way, my nickname is Curly."

"Wonder why," Blake laughed.

McMichaels, who stood almost as tall as Blake, had no hair. "The doc had me shave it all off because of a fungus. I like it better this way. I never get put on report for needing a haircut."

The shrill sound of a bos'n's pipe pierced the stale passageway air. "Now hear this, you haze gray and underway sailors, the uniform for getting underway is dress whites."

The loudspeaker was bolted to the bulkhead right next to the pillow end of Blake's top bunk. A main heating line was at the other end where his feet would rest. Blake's choice was simple: Find someone to trade or get accustomed to the noise for the entire cruise.

He rummaged through his hanging gear bag, pulled out his dress whites, and was about to put them on, wrinkles and all, when a firstie came by and said, "Youngsters will wear working whites with a neckerchief."

After lunch, the bos'n's pipe again blew a song he didn't recognize followed by the words, "All hands set the sea and anchor detail."

Blake went to the fo'c'sle where a thick-jawed, stocky petty officer named Willowby asked his name and said, "All right, Lawrence, for the first phase of your training you will be in the First Division. You'll be on the foc's'le for anchor detail. Man the hose to wash the anchor chain and anchor as they come aboard. After the anchor is aboard, stand at parade rest over there with the division, at quarters for leaving port."

"I'm in my whites."

"I'm in whites, too. Don't get dirty, mister."

A sailor wearing a sound-powered telephone headset shouted, "Stand by to heave in the anchor to short stay." A few seconds later the same sailor said, "Heave in to short stay."

Petty Officer First Class Willowby, his white hat almost on his nose, ordered, "Heave in to short stay!"

As the cat marched the anchor chain up and around and dropped it into the anchor locker, Blake dutifully sprayed the mud from the chain as it came aboard.

"Heave it right on in!" came the order.

The ship moved slowly astern and Blake stood at attention alongside the sailors of the First Division. Willowby, who had the swagger of a confident, fearless man, took a position in front of the division. Blake surveyed his new shipmates. He'd already had a cursory introduction to Curly McMichaels. Buck Barber and Pumpkin Head Jones were young also; each was no more than eighteen years old, but all were solidly built. From the back, Willowby was of medium size, but he had no neck. His head seemed to grow out of powerful shoulders, from which hung equally mighty arms with biceps as big as pineapples.

"Shift colors!" came the order from the bridge.

Blake watched a petty officer lower the Jack. He looked up in time to see the ensign raising smartly to the top of the main mast over this ship of war.

Blake was finally underway aboard an American ship. He felt a chill across his shoulders.

I'm where I wanted to be from the day I enlisted. For the first time I feel like I'm in the real Navy.

The Naval Academy, with all its Bancroft Hall mysteries, slid away and faded with the sunset as the bow swung and the ship began its turn to face the channel. As she slowly gained headway to follow the long line of buoys, the bos'n's pipe again pierced the silence. "Aboard *Ingraham*! Attention to starboard! Hand salute."

The first division faced together to starboard and Willowby saluted as the ship passed an American flag flying from a flagpole on the shore adjacent to the ship's passage. Blake felt the same shiver again and stood tall with pride.

"Two."

Willowby's hand came smartly down.

"Carry on."

As she passed buoy number one, *Ingraham* gained speed; her bow dipped into the sea, sending spray across the deck.

"Now secure the sea and anchor detail."

The order came over the 1 MC (public address system) from the bridge and Willowby growled, "Fall out."

The fo'c'sle crew of the first division made a dash for the nearest hatch, but Blake waited and walked forward to the stem of the ship.

"You can go below, Lawrence," Willowby reminded him.

"I know, sir, but I'd like to stay on deck for a few moments."

"First place, you don't have to say 'sir' to me. And second, this area gets dangerous when green water starts coming aboard. Don't stay up too long, mister." Willowby's tone sounded a bit motherly, but Blake knew this bull of a man would not be a first class petty officer if he had been too soft.

The wind and spray cut across Blake's face, watering his eyes and leaving his cheeks tingling from the bite of salt water. The horizon disappeared, reappearing as the bow rose and fell. He sucked air into his lungs and felt his heart expand from the excitement of the moment, an exuberance he had never known before. He went to the very stem of the ship, where the lifelines come together. He put one hand on each line and then leaned into the wind. Looking down he could see the bow diving into the waves deeper and deeper as the ship gained speed. More and more spray and green water came into his face, but he didn't care. It was like finally climbing a mountain, his Everest. He was at sea in the mystery of the ocean. His mother wouldn't understand, but his grandfather would. So would his dad.

Over the 1 MC came a voice, "Now, the midshipman standing on the fo'c'sle! Clear that area, immediately!"

Blake looked around to see if there was another mid with him, then turned and carefully walked aft, embarrassed by the PA system announcement that had just singled him out.

The PA then blared: "All midshipmen muster on the fantail. That is, all midshipmen muster on the fantail -- immediately." Blake continued aft and joined the others in a formation facing a hastily placed lectern.

No sooner were they in place then a voice announced, "Attention on deck for the captain."

He wore three gold stripes on the shoulder boards of his white uniform and seemed relaxed and at ease, showing the confidence of a man who knew he was in charge. Not too tall but muscular with pitch-black hair, he gave the impression that he might once have been a swift, hard-running football halfback. "Stand at ease, men. I'm Commander Gui Andriso. Welcome aboard *Ingraham*. The crew and I are pleased to have you for this short training cruise. *Ingraham* has a glorious past and an incredible future. It is named after Captain Duncan Ingraham, a noble naval officer who, in 1853, while in command of the sloop-of-war St. Louis in the Mediterranean, he interfered with the detention by the Austrian consul at Smyrna, Turkey of a man by the name of Martin Koszta, a Hungarian who had declared in New York his intention of becoming an American citizen. Koszta had earlier been seized and confined in the Austrian ship Hussar. For his conduct in this matter Ingraham was voted thanks and a medal by Congress. It took great courage for Captain Ingraham to stand his ground alone so far from America.

"*Ingraham* has four battle stars from World War II and one from the Korean War. She earned the Navy Unit Citation at Okinawa. During that invasion she shot down four Japanese kamikaze planes. Another crashed into the ship, leaving her with 51 casualties. This ship is a fighter. She didn't sink and was eventually repaired so we can again take her into harm's way if it comes to that.

"This is an eight-week cruise and you will spend about three weeks each in engineering, gunnery, and operations.

"I am not a Naval Academy graduate. My training came from the Merchant Marine Academy at Kings Point, New York, but I like the program Annapolis has laid out. Hopefully, by the time you complete this cruise, you will be comfortable and know a great deal more about ships and the Navy than when you began.

"The task force is sailing southeasterly. We will clear the Chesapeake by tomorrow morning. We will then refuel immediately. Then the task force, under the command of Rear Admiral Spencer, will follow a track for the Mediterranean. During our trip we will conduct every kind of training possible including engineering drills, gunnery shoots, and seamanship evolutions. You will stand one and three watches -- that is four hours on and eight off. First classmen will stand officer watches, OD, and engineer of the watch. Third classmen will stand enlisted watches. During your eight hours off watch you should not only perform the duties of your division but also take notes about what you learn. The sea is an unforgiving environment, so be careful. Your safety is paramount. Remember the first law of the sailor: One hand for yourself and one hand for the ship. You are of no value to the Navy or me if you get hurt. I spend most of my time on the bridge, but I want you to know I am interested in your training and am available to talk at all times. If you have any personal problems, don't hesitate to come to me or the exec. I expect my crew to do the same. I love the Navy and enjoy talking navy and seamanship any time -- seek me out. Let's get to know each other. Oh, and I will enjoy reading your notebooks at the end of the cruise."

The captain was gone as quickly as he came, heading at a fast pace back toward the pilothouse. Blake's first impression was that he was certainly different from what he expected. His preconceived notion that sea captains were petty martinets had already vanished. This man, who spoke with a decided New York accent, was articulate and clearly sure of himself but not overbearing. His confidence showed that he was secure in his position in the Navy.

*****

The next morning, Blake was aroused by a hand on his shoulder. "You have the morning watch, Mr. Lawrence." As the body disappeared into the dark compartment, Blake looked at his watch. It was 0330. He had fifteen minutes to get on deck and relieve the messenger on the bridge.

He climbed down from the top rack and quickly dressed in his dungarees. Except for a red passageway light, the ship was totally dark. In the nearby head he washed the sleep out of his eyes and scrubbed his teeth. He checked his appearance in a mirror and dashed up the starboard ladder, arriving at the door to the pilothouse with about five minutes to spare. He took out his handkerchief and rubbed the polished toes of his shoes.

Blake entered for his first underway watch. He stood off to one side, marveling at the process he was witnessing. The ship was rolling much more now than when he went to bed. In the dark, bodies moved back and forth and in and out of the pilothouse. His eyes slowly became accustomed to the change from light to the pitch-blackness of the moonless night. He finally said, "Midshipman Lawrence reporting for watch sir."

"Flashing light message, sir," a sailor wearing the insignia of a quartermaster said to the Officer of the Deck. "Turn 30, sir. Standby, execute."

"Right standard rudder," the OOD ordered. "Come to new heading of 170."

The bos'ns mate of the watch grabbed Blake by the arm. "Don't bother the OD. We're joining up with the task force. Relieve the man on the starboard lookout."

Blake took the binoculars and put on the sound-powered headset. The sailor he relieved disappeared quickly down the ladder, heading toward his bunk for a few hours sleep before the upcoming replenishment.

The outlines of other destroyers surrounded *Ingraham*. As his eyes became more accustomed, Blake could make out a line of ships to starboard. Ahead he saw the stern of another; looking aft, he could see the stem of yet another. He wondered if this wasn't the same formation his grandfather, and father's ships used as they sailed into battle during their two world wars. For that matter he could imagine the British in the Napoleonic wars sailing into danger in two columns, ready to maneuver to unmask their guns.

"Use those binoculars, Midshipman Lawrence," the bos'n mate of the watch growled. "They don't do us any good hanging around your neck. We're looking for the tanker and the task force. The tanker is supposed to join us at the rendezvous." The bos'n mate's tone was sharp and certainly different than the sound of classroom professors at the Academy. It reminded him more of Greenfield's tone before they became friends.

"Aye, aye," Blake responded. He put the glasses to his eyes and scanned the dark horizon of the Atlantic Ocean.

The weather had changed during the night. High waves slapped the side of the ship. Green water foamed over the bows of the adjacent ships. He heard the OD say that they were at the edge of a tropical storm.

Light peaked through at the edges of the eastern horizon dead ahead. Blake strained to sight something through the gray light. He scanned from ten degrees on the port bow to abaft the starboard beam 30 degrees, just as he had been taught in boot camp. All he saw were ugly-looking clouds against a gray sky. On his fifth such scan he thought he saw a speck dead ahead. He came back to it a moment later.

What now? Do I sing out or call the bos'n mate over?

"I have something, sir," Blake heard over his sound-powered headset. It was the port lookout. "Can't make it out. Has a tall stack – no, two tall stacks. It looks like a single ship, hull down crossing from starboard to port, sir."

Damn, I saw that. Beat me to the report.

"What about you, Lawrence? You got it?" The junior officer of the deck asked.

Morning, a fine glow of light grew from the east. Blake took his glasses off long enough to respond to the question. "Yes, sir. I have it. Sorry for the late report, sir. Hey, what are you doing here, Mr. Blackstone?"

"I'm here for the same reason you are, Blake. Training," Blake's plebe summer squad leader said.

"Thought you were gonna be a Marine?"

"I am. Got to learn how the Squid Navy works first. I'll tell you this: I'm impressed with this Captain

Andriso. He already has us standing OD watches and eating in the officers' wardroom. Okay, back to work. Keep your eyes open."

"Aye, aye, sir," Blake said.

He immediately scanned forward where the speck he had seen earlier had now grown to the full silhouette of a Navy tanker. But behind it he saw a new sighting. Several specks were growing on that horizon.

"Sails ho!" he reported. "Multiple ships on the horizon bearing 010, right behind the tanker, sir."

"That'll be the task force. Let's get ready to replenish. Bos'n, pass the word," Captain Andriso ordered.

The bos'n's pipe shrilled its song. "Now hear this! Set the replenishment detail. All hands set the replenishment detail."

Bodies began to move quickly. Men ran onto the foc's'le, dragging line and attaching rigging to bulkheads.

"Okay, Lawrence. I've got it. I'm the replenishment lookout. Go to your station."

Blake ran down the ladder and onto the deck as his ship came into a position behind the tanker. The bow of *Ingraham* dipped and rose in stormy waves. Green water and spray came across the deck. The men on deck were already soaked in salt water.

"Don a lifejacket, Lawrence!" Willowby ordered.

As he was tying the last strings of his lifejacket, the ship made its final approach. It came alongside the tanker, slowed to match the tanker's speed, then nestled into a position with not more than sixty feet separating the two. Across the water Blake could see sailors waiting on the tanker. A police whistle sounded. Blake saw Willowby twirling a line. He shouted, "Stand by for my bolo!" It was a long thin line with a heavy hard ball on the end. Willowby twirled and twirled it over his head, then let the ball on a string fly across to the tanker where it landed amid sailors who grabbed it and began the process of rigging hose lines between the two ships.

"You men, grab that line and run with it!"

The deck was slippery from wave after wave of salt water flooding across. Like in a tug-of-war, Blake, McMichaels, and Jones pulled a two-inch line that dragged the end of the oil line across to be implanted into a receptacle to receive the flow of black oil.

As they were holding the line so a petty officer could secure the nozzle, a giant wave swept across the bow, drenching the crew and knocking Buck Barber off a line he was tending near the stem of the ship. The water rode the slightly built seaman down the deck toward the edge where the lifelines had been removed. Without a doubt, Barber was going over the side.

Willowby shouted, "Grab that man!"

Blake instinctively reached out and grabbed Barber's arm with one hand. He held the two-inch line with the other. But the combined weight of Barber and the water caused Blake to begin sliding toward the edge himself. McMichaels and Jones tried to control the sagging two-inch, but they also began to slip. To the deck they all went, grasping for a purchase, a cleat, a rail, anything.

Blake held Barber and McMichaels while Jones held the two-inch. Blake struggled to pull the sailor back aboard. Barber's body hung partially over the edge, his face white with fear. Another wave would sweep them both over the side and into the sea.

CHAPTER 14

THE CROSSING

Blake kept his eyes on Barber's frightened face. His fingers ached from the slippery salt water and the weight. He felt his grip slip, at first no more than a half inch. He squeezed harder, and shouted, "I got ya." But then his hand slipped again. This time to Barber's wrist. He shouted again, "I'm losing him!" In his peripheral vision he could see *Ingraham's* bow as it rode a wave high into the air. He knew that in a moment the bow of the ship would crash downward into a trough and the next wave would bring another mass of green water rushing across the deck.

Bos'n Willowby, who was standing below the line handlers, dove forward from under the oil transfer line. Extending his powerful hands and arms, he grabbed the edge of Barber's life jacket. With one great lift he threw Barber back aboard. Blake, still holding onto Barber with one hand and the two-inch line with the other, crawled away from the deck edge.

Willowby screamed, "Get up! Get on your feet! Both of you! Barber! Grab that line and hang on!"

From the bridge Captain Andriso shouted through a megaphone, "Shall I break away, Bos'n?"

"No, sir. We're okay, sir. Keep fueling."

Just then the mountain of water crashed over the deck, but now the seamen held on and continued the refueling. The smell of black oil filled Blake's nostrils. For him it was a new smell, but he knew he had to get used to if sailoring was to be his calling. Steam-powered vessels drank the fluid like humans take air. Soaked and hungry, Willowby's boys clung to their line, obeying as he gave orders: "Lay back on it, men!"

"Slack off, boys."

"Hold it."

"That's well."

On one occasion the two ships came together, their sides threatening to touch. The line slacked, causing the oil hose to pinch. Then the ships veered wide in compensation. Blake was amazed at Willowby's strength when he jumped from his perch to help with the line. It was as if a gorrilla or a giant bear took hold, the line came in and went out so easily.

Willowby seemed to have little respect for those driving the ship. Shaking his fist, he shouted up to the bridge, "A baby could steer better than this. You're driving like a New Yorker!"

Blake looked up and saw that midshipman Tom Blackstone had the "conn" and was giving orders to the helm. Captain Andriso stood calmly behind, training him.

With the fueling complete, and all lines aboard and stowed, the high line detail was set. A sailor from the *William M. Wood*, DD-715, had come back late from liberty in Annapolis. So as not to miss movement, he climbed aboard *Ingraham* and asked to be returned to his ship.

Willowby had Blake and the others rig an aluminum chair to be hauled back and forth between *Ingraham* and *Wood*. With Tom Blackstone still conning, *Ingraham* pulled away from the oil tanker and maneuvered astern of the destroyer.

Signal flags ran up and down the halyards, flashing lights barked messages. *Ingraham* maneuvered alongside Wood and soon lines were across between the two. The ships rose and fell in the heavy seas no more than 40 feet apart. The AWOL sailor came forward, and under the instruction of Willowby, donned a life jacket, was seated, and strapped into the chair.

"Lay back on it, men!" Willowby ordered.

The men on the high line lifted the chair high off the deck, and it slowly began its travels across the water boiling between the ships.

Willowby shouted, "Keep her taut, men! We don't want a Wee Willie Wood sailor to get his ass wet now, do we, boys?"

As the basket crept over the side, swaying in its trolley, the sailor unwisely responded, "Fuck the *Ingraham*! Get me to a good ship."

Willowby smiled and said quietly, almost in a whisper, "Hold her taut, boys. When I give the word, everyone take one step forward. Let the bastard get his ass wet."

"Hold her, hold her. Wait. Not yet." When the basket was exactly half-way between the two ships, Willowby spoke in quiet tones, "All right, men. One step forward, two."

The line sagged and the man in the chair dropped instantaneously. His feet were still well clear of the water but spray began hitting him in the face. There was a fearful, wild look in the sailor's eyes. He held to the chair with one white-knuckled hand. He checked his life jacket with the other.

"One step forward, two," Willowby said.

The line sagged again and this time the man's feet touched the water, soaking his legs.

"You *Ingraham* bastards!" he shouted as green water hit him hard in the face, drenching his uniform and the bag he was carrying.

"Lay back on her, men!" Willowby shouted. A tongue-in-cheek smile crept across his sea-weathered face. "Didn't I tell you not to get that Wee Willy wet? Lay back on her!" The line sprung taut again and the basket chair was quickly hauled aboard.

A chief aboard the *Wood* shook his fist and shouted across, "Willowby, you SOB. You did that on purpose. I'll see you in port and kick your ass."

"That'll be the day, Chief Jones. That'll be the day that any Wee Willy could kick an *Ingraham* man's ass. All right, men, let's let our midshipman ship driver get out of here. Get that line back aboard."

*****

At breakfast on the mess decks, several midshipmen and sailors came by to congratulate Blake on saving Barber from going overboard. As Willowby himself explained it, "Blake here is a goddamn hero."

"You were the one who pulled us all aboard, Petty Officer Willowby," Blake countered. "You must be the strongest man in the fleet!"

"That I am, Mr. Lawrence, and Chief Jones from the Wee Willy Wood better not mess with me."

The watch messenger came down the nearest ladder and approached Blake. "The executive officer wants you and petty officer Willowby on the bridge right away."

"What's this all about?" Blake said as he followed Willowby and the messenger of the watch.

Captain Andriso was in his chair examining some papers when Blake and Willowby entered the pilot house.

"XO, sir. Midshipman Lawrence and I are here as ordered," Willowby said to the executive officer, the number two man on the ship.

"Good, I'll tell the captain."

The XO and Captain Andriso conferred for a few minutes before the two approached, then the captain ordered, "Bos'n mate of the watch, sound attention on the PA."

The bos'n piped his tune followed by, "Attention all hands."

Captain Andriso took the microphone and held it to his mouth. "This is the captain speaking. This morning we almost lost a man over the side. I've told you before the sea is unforgiving and we must constantly be vigilant of safety. Fortunately the man was saved from possibly drowning by the quick thinking of a midshipman third class and one of our top bos'n mates. Ordinarily I would wait until we were in port to do this, but I want to emphasize to you the importance of safety. I am hereby commending Midshipman Blake Lawrence and Bos'n's Mate First Class Willowby for their brave and alert actions. Congratulations, men. That is all. Carry on throughout the ship."

Captain Andriso handed Blake and Willowby a piece of paper and said, "Petty Officer Willowby, I heard that exchange between you and the chief on *William Wood*. I don't want any brawls on the beach."

"Oh, no, sir."

*****

The transit of the Atlantic Ocean in July turned out to be uneventful but hot. The hurricane season was still more than a month away, so the seas were flat and the sun bright. Temperatures in the living compartments were often in the 90's and even 100's.

Blake worked for Petty Officer Willowby in his off-watch hours, chipping and painting and cleaning heads. He worked in dungarees alongside Barber, McMichaels, and Jones.

Blake's general quarters station was on a three-inch battery where he was given the responsibility of first loader. These were the guns designed to replace the 40-mm's used against the Kamikaze raids at the later stages of World War Two. His job was to take the rounds of three-inch shells that were passed to him from the deck and insert them into the breech. All this happened as the gun trainer rotated the turret to keep the barrels pointed toward the target, which in wartime would be a fast-flying airplane. Now, in practice, they were challenged to point and fire at a sleeve towed on a long line behind a passing airplane. As midshipmen became proficient at one station, the officers rotated them to other positions to learn the techniques of war-fighting. The training included demonstrations of every weapon. An anti-submarine depth charge exploded so close that it erupted in a mass of water, which slammed into the hulls of every ship within miles. Five-inch guns were fired at distant surface targets. Even the sixteen-inch guns of the battleships were fired to show the force available to an afloat commander. A carrier returning from deployment passed nearby and its aircraft flew demonstration bombing missions to show them the power of naval aviation.

*****

In the evenings, with the temperature in their compartments unbearable, Blake and his new shipmates Barber, McMichaels, and Jones dressed only in their undershorts and often carried their mattresses topside to sleep under the stars.

"Spread them out along the deck but not too close to the edge," Barber joked. "Don't want to lose one of you middies." By now the First Division had accepted the midshipmen as part of the crew. They worked, ate, slept, and stood watches together.

They lay now on their backs looking up at the diamond-sky staring at the brightly lit southern stars.

"Barber," Blake said.

"Yah.'

"Where you from?"

"Iowa."

"Iowa? You a farmer?" Blake asked.

"Yah."

"No shit? How in the hell did a farmer from Iowa get in the Navy?"

"Dad."

"What's that mean?"

"My dad was a sailor during the war."

"How come they call you 'Buck?'"

"I broke horses."

"Broke horses in Iowa?"

"We got horses in Iowa!" Barber said defensively.

"How about you, Jones?"

"Look! A shooting star," McMichaels pointed.

"There's another," Jones said. "That's three in a row! What did you ask, Blake?"

"Where you from?"

"All over. We lived in a trailer. My dad worked in the oil fields wherever he could get on. When I get out I'm going back to Texas where I lived the most, I guess. Only got 243 days before I get out."

"No shit? You know exactly how many days you have left in the Navy?" Blake asked.

McMichaels growled, "Why don't you guys shut up? I'm trying to sleep. Got the mid watch. Everyone counts the days, Blake. We're short timers, not like you lifers."

"Where you from, McMichaels?"

"Ask me tomorrow. G'nite."

*****

They entered the Mediterranean in the late afternoon, passing through the Strait of Gibraltar. Blake could see the huge rock that dominated the scene. It was one of the world's most important sea-lanes -- a narrow body of water that connected the Mediterranean Sea to the Atlantic Ocean. During one of the rotations of the watch, he took a moment to go into the navigator's chart room. The chief quartermaster, who looked like Captain Ahab and sounded like a professor, pointed to the place on the chart. "You middies show interest -- we're glad to teach," he said. "The strait separates southernmost Spain from the northern coast of Africa. Cape Trafalgar in Spain and Cape Spartel in Tangier mark its western limits. Its eastern boundaries are Gibraltar and Point Almina in North Africa."

The chief ran his fingers across the chart. "The waters of the Mediterranean are circular, like this." He drew a big circle. "It flows east on the surface from the Atlantic through the strait -- an undercurrent carries it west back into the Atlantic. Gibraltar is an island with several huge rocks they call the Pillars of Hercules. The island's not very big -- no more than three miles and the Rock of Gibraltar occupies most of it."

"How do you know all that?" Blake asked in amazement.

"Want to know Gibraltar's history?"

"Don't have much time. Got to go aft and relieve the after lookout."

"Won't take much time." The chief quartermaster handed Blake a book called *Sailing Directions* and pointed to a library on the shelf above the chart table. "Take a gander."

Blake leafed to the part about Gibraltar. He didn't want to be late relieving his watch, so he simply scanned the material. He marveled as he read about the place that had played such a major part of naval history. It seemed to have been owned, at one time or another, by everyone who lived nearby. But in 1704 a British naval force captured it and used it to keep enemy ships from entering or leaving the Mediterranean Sea. During World War II the Allies launched an attack from Gibraltar against the German and Italian forces in North Africa.

"Thanks, chief. I'll be back. Got to run," Blake said as he returned the book to its place on the shelf.

"Glad to have you. Help yourself to the books anytime."

*****

The task force separated, and the ships sailed independently for the southern ports of Spain and France. *Ingraham* would go to Cannes. Blake made his way back to the quartermaster's shack near the pilot house where he read about the town:

Cannes, a luxurious resort city on the French Riviera in southeastern France, lies on the Gulf of Napoule, an arm of the Mediterranean Sea. Its best-known boulevard is the Promenade de la Croisette, which runs along the shore and has elegant hotels and casinos. The first settlement at what is now Cannes was a fortress built about 700's B.C. on Mont Chevalier by an ancient Italian people called Ligurians.

Blake read further:

Cannes is also known for the beautiful women who come to bask in the sun, often without cover above the waist.

He ran down to the compartment where the first division was getting dressed to enter port.

"Barber."

"Yeah."

"You know what?" Blake teased.

"What?" Barber said in a bored tone.

"The women here don't cover their tits!" Blake exclaimed.

"Getoutahere. How do you know that?"

"Read it in a book. Up in the quartermaster's shack, on the bridge."

Barber grinned. "No shit? I'm go'n over as soon as I get my liberty card from Willowby."

McMichaels' eyes were cast downward. He looked dejected. "I forgot to tell you guys, but we may never get ashore in Cannes. The forward head didn't pass captain's inspection -- Willowby's pissed."

"He wouldn't hold our liberty, would he?" Blake asked naively.

"You don't know Willowby," McMichaels said. "He can be a real prick. He won't give us our liberty cards until he re-inspects and finds that head spotless."

CHAPTER 15

THE MED

The ship anchored in sight of Cannes, France. Waves rolled from the sea, breaking in lines that splashed gently over long sandy beaches filled with women sun bathing and men playing in the surf.

To the naked eye, the people on the beaches were just specs but as soon as the sea detail was dismissed, *Ingrahman's* bridge was flooded with sailors and midshipmen waiting their turn to use the ship's "Big Eyes," the powerful lenses usually used for navigation and reading distant ship-to-ship messages at sea. Others passed binoculars back and forth. The entire ship's company had heard of Blake's discovery.

"Look at that one," came a shout from one of the men on the glass. "Man, her tits are like two mountains."

A midshipman shouted, "Oh, look at those!"

"Hey, I'm go'n ashore -- meet one of those honeys!" Jones said.

They were in a hurry. Shower. Shine shoes. Change into dress whites. Carefully tie their neckerchiefs. Roll the rim of their white hats. All in order to pass quarterdeck inspection and get ashore in this town famous for its beautiful, bare-breasted women.

"Where you going, McMichaels?"

"Ah – nowhere – ah – boats," the young sailor stammered.

It was Willowby. He was already in his dress whites. "I haven't inspected that head yet."

"Ah, come on, Willowby. You're not going to hold up our liberty, are you?" Blake asked.

"If that head doesn't pass my inspection, I am," said the burly petty officer.

Jones elbowed McMichaels. "You clean it?"

"Well..."

"Let's go, McMichaels. We'll take a look."

Blake and the three seamen followed Willowby forward into the first division crew's head. On entry Willowby bellowed, "This is a shithouse!"

"Hell, that's because we used it to get ready for liberty, Boats," Jones said, trying to make a logical excuse for his shipmate.

"The showers are dirty, the pisser is stained, and the sinks look like the bottom of a shit house! You should have come and got me before you guys messed it up. That is... if it was ever squared away. You know how the shit flows: it goes down hill and stops with me. McMichaels. None of you ain't get'n your liberty cards until this place meets my inspection, and you're now mess'n with *my* liberty -- I'm ready to go over. I'll be on the mess decks. Come and get me when it's ready and don't take too long, cause I'm going over soon. If you don't have it ready by the time I'm ready, I'm taking your liberty cards with me."

Willowby left.

Blake, Jones, and Barber looked at McMichaels. "You didn't tell us Willowby hadn't inspected this place."

McMichaels looked at his toes. "I didn't think..."

"You didn't think?" Blake said. "Think in one hand and piss in the other -- see which one fills up the quickest. You didn't think? Now we all have to change clothes and help you..."

"You don't have to do that. Go on ashore. I'll catch up later," McMichaels mumbled.

"Yeah, you will. You'll never get this place clean by yourself, not before Willowby goes over. Besides he's holding all our liberty cards. Let's get to work."

The four raced back to the compartment and stripped out of their liberty whites. Back in the head, dressed only in their skivvy shorts, they blocked off the entrance and went to work. Blake scrubbed the showers. Jones did the urinals. Barber washed and shined the sinks. McMichaels got the overhead and then as the rest finished, scrubbed and squeegeed the deck.

As they worked, other crew members came to the door. They wanted to use the head but were told to go aft. A few said they would wait until it was opened again. Before long there were seven men waiting in line. One said, "Hurry up, you guys. You're screwing with our liberty. We want to go ashore."

"Okay, we're done," Blake said. "McMichaels, you stand by here while we get Willowby. On risk of losing your life, don't let anyone in until after he inspects."

Blake ran to the mess hall and found Willowby drinking coffee with one of the cooks.

"Ready, is it? We'll see."

Willowby was met by a line of crew members wanting in the head that had now grown to more than ten. "Hey, Boats, he won't let us in."

McMichaels stood, blocking the entrance in his underwear and holding a swab handle at the ready, threatening to clobber anyone who tried to get in.

"Hold your water!" Willowby said. "This won't take long." His inspection was tougher than the captain's. He looked into every corner. He rubbed his hand over every horizontal surface and checked every mirror for smudges.

"Miracle. McMichaels, you did this all by yourself?"

McMichaels gave him a sheepish grin.

"Okay, I know what really happened. I'm buy'n all of you a beer at the first slop shoot we find ashore. Meet you on the quarterdeck in five minutes. I'll have your liberty cards. Don't be late -- or no liberty"

*****

They scrambled into their whites and the four raced to the quarterdeck. Willowby was waiting, and as he handed them each a card, he reminded them that they had Cinderella Liberty. "Don't miss the ship," he warned. "You have only until midnight."

"Only midnight? That's bullshit, Boats," Barber growled.

"Captain's orders. Seems there's been an upgrade in our DEFCON -- another goddamn Cold War crisis. Wants us to stay close to the ship -- may have to get underway. Besides, the weather's turning bad."

Everyone knew what the Cold War was -- the intense rivalry that developed after World War II between groups of Communist and non-Communist nations. The struggle was called the Cold War because it did not actually lead to fighting, or "hot" war, on a wide scale.

Characterized by mutual distrust, suspicion, and misunderstandings, these conditions increased the likelihood of the next mass war, one that could destroy humanity.

343

Blake surmised that all parties saw every international incident as part of the Cold War, and this, whatever it was, was one of those.

He and his buddies saluted the quarter-deck, then the flag, and climbed down the ladder to the liberty boat, one of *Ingraham's* motor whaleboats. It was early afternoon in the Gulf of Napoule, ordinarily noted for its mild, dry climate. The sun was still shining, but clouds were gathering in the east. The boat rode in broad swells upon which a brisk wind whipped frothy waves that splashed over the gunwale. They made a bumpy landing at the same pier where boats from other ships came and went, dropping off sailors.

A broad tree-lined boulevard with quaint shops led through the town that sat nestled at the foot of mountains. A castle called the Chateau des Abbes de Lerins sat on Mont Chevalier, overlooking the gulf. The Promenade de la Croisette ran along the shore. Blake could see elegant hotels and casinos.

"Let's go down the boulevard. Look for some of those braless broads with the big tits," Jones said.

"Hey, don't you guys want a beer? I'm still buying," Willowby said.

"Okay, but not long. Girls before beer, Boats."

"No! Beer before girls," Willowby argued.

"No! Tits before beer," Jones countered.

They went into a small bar where Willowby ordered the drinks in English. "Everybody speaks money talk, right, Frenchy?" He paid for them in dollars. His change was in French currency.

"Let me see that," Blake asked. He examined the paper and coins. This was his first time in a foreign country. "How do you know you didn't get cheated?"

"Got to know the exchange rate," Willowby explained. "But, not to worry. Sailors won't come in if the bar cheated. Word gets around. Cheat'ns bad for business."

The four talked for about an hour as they drank Willowby's beer -- and a few others, which they all chipped in to buy. A few girls came in and sat at a corner table. McMicheals and Willowby found them interesting, but the rest wanted to check out the beach and boardwalk. When they left, Willowby was talking in broken French to a cheaply dressed girl.

Along the boulevard they swaggered into shops and stopped in each hotel and casino as if they owned the places. They saw several French girls sunbathing without their bras. They walked into sand up to their ankles to say hello and gawk at their bare breasts.

"Mamsielle," Blake mispronounced one of the words he remembered from his French class. It seemed to make the girls smile at the obviously-drunken Americans. But when he added, "Say vois play? Vooly voo? Coo shay a vec ma se swa," all hell broke loose.

"Would I sleep with you?" one of the girls said angrily in English, swinging to slap his face.

Blake ducked just in time.

"What did you say?" Jones asked Blake.

"I think I asked how the hotels were."

"Getoutahere. You must have said something else."

"That one's smiling."

"The others are not. They're getting the cops. Run!"

Their feet grew heavy as their shoes filled with sand. As they were running, a female voice rang out. It had throaty characteristics that Blake had heard before. "Blake, is that you?"

He stopped and scanned the faces of the many people enjoying the beach.

"Blake. Over here!"

He knew the voice. *A woman's voice, but who -- and from where?*

"Blake. Here."

What female would know me in Cannes? Thousands of miles from home.

He remembered her eyes. They were deep and dark. Her hair was pulled from her ears and bundled at the nape of her neck. Unlike the others, she wore a bra. But her bathing suit was no more than a bit of cloth.

"Viva? Is that you? Can't be. Viva? What are you doing here?"

Blake left his buddies and ran across the white sand to where she stood. He remembered her from the time he met her at Sam's party in Philadelphia and the tea dance during the Dark Ages. He liked her, but she was Pete's drag. He liked the fact that Viva's hair was still long. He guessed that if that bun at the nape of her neck was released, the length would still hang to the middle of her back, maybe even longer. He also liked her skin, unusually translucent for a person of Italian heritage. Maybe her folks came from the northern part of that country. He liked her full-breasted body, slim and tall. Her dark hair and eyes gave her the look of the diva she said she wanted to be. He also liked her husky voice, it seemed to add to her new elegance.

The other three raced across the sand to join him. "Who's this, Blake?"

"This is Kathy Velenochi. A friend from Philadelphia. Viva, this is Barber..." They shook hands. "Jones -- and McMichaels -- I work with these guys in the first division aboard my ship."

"Delighted to meet you." Viva sounded and looked more sophisticated. She pushed her sunglasses to the top of her head. Her eyes smiled as boldly as her lips. Blake liked that, too.

"Thought you said her name was Kathy?" Jones questioned.

"I did, but everyone calls her Viva -- Viva Voce. She's an opera singer."

"Oh." Jones seemed satisfied with the answer. Then he added, "You got any girlfriends?"

"Afraid not," Viva said, shrugging her shoulders. "I'm here with one of my instructors and a few artists. Sorry -- all males. Blake, can you come and meet my friends?"

He looked at his sailor buddies. The questioning expression on his face must have spoken the words he wished he could say, but wouldn't.

"It's okay, Blake. Go ahead. Go with her. Who would have believed you'd meet a friend over here? Have fun. You look good with her -- a blond-haired mid with a dark haired-beauty."

"Where are you guys off to? I'll meet you someplace – later," Blake said.

"We don't know. We'll probably find Willowby," Barber said. "Don't forget be on the pier no later than midnight. Miss the boat you'll be known as the AWOL Boat School Boy. See ya, Blake."

Viva introduced him to her friends, an artist, a musician, a professor. Their voices sounded as if they were bored with the world. They mixed their languages, speaking words alternately in French, Italian, German, and English. Blake figured it was to impress him, a military man who they surmised was much less cosmopolitan than they -- and they were right. She told him the artist was studying the history of modern painting. The musician concentrated on woodwinds, and her professor sang tenor with an Italian opera company. After the introductions they chatted for a few minutes about art and artists before they excused themselves. She seemed to want to be alone with Blake as much a he wanted her company. Blake cautioned her friends that the wind was picking up and the weather was expected to take a turn before morning. She took a moment to wrap a light cloth skirt around her waist and slip into high-heeled, open-toed sandals. They began walking.

"You're --"

"You --"

They laughed at their simultaneous effort to start the conversation. She was different than when he first met her at Sam's party after the Army-Navy game. He guessed her first year at Julliard had already begun smoothing of any rough spots from the streets of her Philadelphia neighborhood.

"You go first."

"No, you," She said. "You were going to ask?"

"What are you doing here?"

"Oh, I'm just over on a holiday from Italy. I'm studying there just for the summer -- no time off for singers or, it would seem, for budding naval officers. What about your ship? Is it a fun summer for you?"

"Actually, this is my first time at sea and I think it's wonderful. I work with the guys you met. And they're great. One's from Iowa, another from the South. One is from Pennsylvania. What do you want to do?"

"Just walk and talk. Where is Pete?" She asked.

Blake wanted to make something up that discredited him, but thought better of it. "On one of the ships, but in another port. Does he know you're here?"

"Don't think so. We don't write anymore."

Blake's mind spun a new web. Pete was his class-mate and, although he roomed with him, he didn't know everything that was going on in his personal life. This was a new revelation, one to his liking.

"How did your election turn out?"

"What election?"

"President of the class."

"Oh. I'm not running until the fall. How did you know that?"

"Sam told us. You're famous in our old neighbor-hood.

"Actually, I win, I'll give the credit to Sam. He's organizing the campaign."

"Just like him. In high school he organized every-thing."

By now the wind came in strong gusts. To keep her dress from blowing, they stopped at a coffee shop for espresso. Their conversation was so easy that time passed like a jet at altitude. Seemingly interested in his every word, she leaned forward, exposing the tops of her breasts. She crossed her long slender legs. His heart pounded. For Blake even her body language was sensual. She reached across and touched his hand. He had to take a deep breath.

"This is great fun, Blake. I'm so glad we met again. Did they say you must be back by midnight? Do you really have to? Things here really only get started here about that time. It is almost midnight, you know."

Blake jerked his hand away and looked at his watch. "Oh, my gosh. Viva, I have to go. Will you be here tomorrow? I think I can get liberty. Where are you staying?"

She walked him to the door of the coffee shop. "I'm at the Hotel de Cannes. You can't forget it. Just ask anyone."

"Got to go or I'll miss the liberty boat. If I'm AWOL from my ship, I won't be around to see you tomorrow. I'm glad we found each other, Viva." He bent to kiss her goodbye. This time she didn't pull away for a light peck on the cheek as she had at the party. Instead she pulled his face to hers and kissed him on the lips, passionately.

"I'll be back." His heart pounded. "I'm glad you found me, Viva."

"I'm glad too," Her smiling eyes were almost even with his. "If I'm not in the hotel, I'll be on the beach."

He began to run. Over his shoulder he shouted, "How far am I away from the pier?"

"Only about a mile. Come back tomorrow!" she said.

"If I don't miss the boat!"

CHAPTER 16

STORMS AND SUBS

Like Cinderella, he ran. He tried to put Viva out of his mind but couldn't. Instead of leaving a slipper behind, he had left a beautiful woman he already cared about. His wristwatch showed that the time was past midnight. Panic gripped his heart. Missing ship was next to murder in the eyes of the Navy -- and Blake was just getting started in his naval officer life. He ran past couples meandering along holding hands. As he raced, pretty girls waved and shouted "come hither" in French. Grimy little men made dirty hand signs that offered sex in dark alleys.

Rain sprinkled, clouds burst, then water beat angrily against the boulevard's many awnings and windows. In the distance, through the vague visibility, he could see the outline of destroyers still at anchor. However, people were moving around as if they were ready to get underway. Dull lights showed across a dingy pier. As he got closer he saw a crowd of sailors milling around.

Still have a chance to make it.

When he saw a group of midshipmen, he stopped running and slowed to a quick walk. He looked for his First Division shipmates. Many of the sailors and mids he passed were milling about the pier, drunk. Some carried bottles of cognac, others had French beer, but none seemed concerned that the clock showed they were past liberty. He did hear many express their irritation at having to be back so early. Some were angry because the boats were slow in returning them to their ships.

Looking at the state of the sea, Blake could understand why the ship's C.O.'s shortened liberty: the fleet was in for a bad storm. There was no moon, but he could see clouds low and blossoming. The rain came like a waterfall, blown in sheets by gale-force winds. Swells broke heavy against the pier. Salt spray flew high into the air from arching waves. Liberty boats pounded hard into the wooden pier structures. A boat officer directing the pick-up of a group of sailors shouted, "Get aboard quickly! As soon as your boat makes the dock. Every one put on lifejackets! Immediately!"

Blake spotted his First Division buddies. Tired from the late hour and the watch routines their bodies had become accustomed to, they lay sprawled under the metal roof of an abandoned tackle shop. Their uniforms showed the stains of booze and bars. Jones and Barber were sleepy drunk, but McMichaels and Willowby were in a state of falling down, slobbering drunk. They sat on a wood piling leaning against each other and singing songs of the sea. Willowby drooled as he bellowed old ditties that Blake supposed had been passed along to him long ago by as a boy in New England. McMichaels only added a bit of drunken harmony.

> "Whiskey is the life of man.
> Whiskey Johnny.
> Whiskey is the life of man.
> And it's Whiskey for me, Johnny-O."

"Shing it, Boats," McMichaels encouraged.

For Blake, Willowby was an enigma. He had a memory for sea chanteys and the details of sailor life, but after almost twenty years in the Navy, he was still only a first class boatswains mate. He should have been a chief by now. Something got in his way. Blake wondered if it was the booze.

McMichaels and Willowby sang the four lines of the whiskey chantey several more times, then switched to another which Willowby called "Stormalong." His sea chanteys were less about the words than about rhythm. He kept the tempo by slapping his hand against his right leg as if he were keeping beat for imaginary sailors heaving on an imaginary rope. McMichaels' part was to add emphasis to the word "Stormalong."

Willowby sang: "Stormalong, Stormalong my boys, Stormalong,"

"Shtormalong," McMichaels said, beating his leg to the same emphatic rythm.

"Yankee Johnny, would you Stormalong."

"Stormalong."

"Brave bad Johnny, would you Sormalong."

"Shormalong."

"Ah, shut up. Can't sleep with you two clowns bellowing," Barber shouted over the ballad-singing sailors.

"Well, shcrew you," Willowby said, his chin on his chest. He went on singing the long chanty.

"Yankee John, Stormalong. Brave bad Johnny Stormalong."

"Yankee John, Stormalong. Oh, brave bad Johnny, would you Stormalong."

Willowby stopped singing when he recognized Blake. "Sho, you did make it. Heard about your girlfriend with the big tits. You get any, Mr. Lawrence?"

"Come on, Boats. Get off that stuff."

Blake took a seat next to Willowby, out of the rain. "You think we'll get back tonight, Boats?"

"You darn toot'n, mishter midshipman. Shkipper'll want to get out of the way of this shtorm. He'll need us to up anchor as soon as we're aboard. You can bet on that."

A shore patrolman, now finished with his work in the city, helped out on the pier by acting as a boat officer. He shouted, "Any *Ingraham* sailors? Your boat is making the pier. Hurry up! Get aboard quickly -- we have a *Wood* boat right behind it."

As the *Ingraham* sailors made their way through the crowd, the Chief from the *William M. Wood* stepped in front of Willowby. "Been looking all ova town fo you, Boats."

Willowby smiled, showing his missing teeth. "To kish my assh, Chief Jones?"

"To kick yo ass!" the Chief said. "Fo dipping my man in the wata dur'n the high-line transfa."

"Well, 'Wee Willy'! Kick away," Willowby's down-Mainer voice challenged. His eyes pinched like those of a cat ready to strike, then widened into a ferocious, wild glare. He rolled back his sleeves; his tattoos ranged from his fingers to his upper arms.

With that, Chief Jones pushed Willowby in the chest with both hands. For a moment the bos'n mate lost his balance and rocked back on his heels. Then he lunged forward, drawing back his muscled arm to make the first punch. Blake had an instantaneous vision of the pier becoming a mass of bloody bodies. Without thinking, he jumped between the two. He grabbed the arm in mid-flight almost losing his balance from the force of the swing. "Boats! Stop! You're drunk!" he shouted.

"Remember what the captain said. No brawls. You'll be busted."

"I've been busted before. Don't worry me none!" Willowby said.

The thought again flashed through Blake's mind that drunkenness and fighting were why Willowby remained only first class. After all, Blake mused, it had been his own inability to handle alcohol that had caused his brig time before the Academy. After that he swore never again.

Now maybe I can make a difference for Willowby.

"Chief! Stand away," Blake shouted above the storm. "We're not looking for a fight."

"Well, mista. We expect an apology or yo gett'n one."

"We'll not be apologizing," Willowby said, drawing back his arm again, his jaw set tight, his eyes glowing like a panther at the ready.

"Oh, yes we will. Chief, it was an accident. But we're sorry. No brawls, okay?"

Chief Jones showed a grin of large white teeth that gleamed in contrast to his dark skin. "Okay, ah... accepted. No brawls, but that asshole betta look out."

"Let's get aboard, Boats," Blake said, pushing the staggering bos'n toward the pier.

Willowby lowered his head until his chin rested on his chest. He cast his eyes toward Blake. They had a wild glare -- that first moment of hate.

Blake knew he had made an enemy. He was an outsider and only a midshipman, not yet an officer.

Had I overstepped?

If he had, it was for the right reason.

The trip to *Ingraham* challenged the coxswain's skills. Angling across the swells, the bow of the boat rowed up and down into the waves, soaking the sailors and midshipmen, at times almost swamping the craft.

Looking back toward Cannes, Blake had two images. The first was that of beautiful Viva standing on that sandy white beach. The other was of an eternal sailor standing on the dock, in the rain, waiting to get back to his ship and the sea. He would never forget either vision.

At the ladder leading up to the quarterdeck, the boat rose and fell against the rolling ship, green water and foam flying into the air. Despite their state of inebriation, they scrambled off and climbed the ladder to safety.

Almost instantaneous with their arrival on the quarterdeck came the order from the bridge, "Now go to your stations, all the sea and anchor detail."

Blake, still wet from the treacherous ride back from Cannes, joined the foc's'le detail. The wind whistled and rain cut their faces as they waited for the orders to heave in the anchor.

Talk about practical training. This is sailoring at its best and worst.

Willowby shouted above the roar of the storm. "You shouldn't have got into that back there -- none of your bushiness." He sounded hurt and a bit more sober.

"Probably not. But there would have been a big fight. We all could have been court-martialed. You could have been busted."

"Not your worry."

"I thought it best. Do you always drink like that?"

"None of your business. You're no longer in this division. Get off my deck!" the bos'n mate said angrily.

"Why, because I called you a drunk and wouldn't let you brawl on the dock?"

Willowby didn't answer the question. "You're now in the sonar gang. Report to Ensign Rhode, the sonar officer."

Power rests with the powerful, and Willowby doesn't want me anymore. Okay. Screw up, move on, and learn. If I'm going to lead enlisted, and there are a lot of them -- they run the Navy -- I better learn to understand them. They have feelings and pride just like me. Was I wrong?

Underway. Green water. Crashing like a bomb exploding over the foc's'le. With practically no visibility, the fleet moved on a course mysterious to all except those who understood hurricanes. By the time he found Ensign Rhode, it was very late. Blake had the morning watch in the forward sonar room, so he crawled into his bunk and tried to sleep. Waves pounded the ship. She shivered and shook like a dog soaked with water. She rolled then rose and fell. Bulkheads creaked. The stench of black oil mixed with salt air.

"Hit it, Mr. Lawrence. Time to get up." The face was unfamiliar, one of the sonar gang.

He looked at his watch. 3:30 a.m.

Shit, only an hour of sleep.

He made a quick trip to the toilet then made his way forward. To keep from losing his balance as the ship rolled, he held onto bunk stanchions and pipes. In the dark he found the hatch that led to a ladder that took him down three decks, deep into the stem of the ship into the sonar operation room. A third class petty officer stood beside another petty officer who was sitting in front of the sonar control. Another sailor stood up when Blake entered.

"You Midshipman Lawrence?" the third class petty officer asked.

"Yes, sir."

"Take a seat... over there." He pointed to a chair, "What'd you do to piss off Willowby?"

Blake didn't respond. He just shook his head.

Down deep in the bow of the ship, the noise of the stem plowing into the ocean and slamming into waves was more pronounced, the rolling quicker.

"Petty Officer Cunningham is relieving on the stack. You'll learn from him." Blake watched and listened as the watch exchanged information, then the two off-going petty officers climbed up the ladder and disappeared.

Blake and Cunningham were now alone but no words were spoken. The on-watch petty officer-in-charge began manipulating dials on the front of the box they called the "stack." Each time he turned the dial, a pinging sound seemed to emanate from the ship. Loud at first, it grew weaker with time. Thus far Blake had not experienced sea sickness -- but he knew he was not immune. "Everyone can become ill from motion sickness," his grandfather had told him. In fact he had said, "Everyone sooner or later does, in one form or another. Some just experience a tiredness while others vomit uncontrollably, sometimes without relief until the motion that caused it subsides. Some are even discharged from the Navy when it is diagnosed as chronic."

The storm had worsened. Blake could tell because the rolling and pounding was much more intense now than when they got underway. Still the other man kept silent, his face buried in his work on the stack. Blake offered, "My name's Blake. What's yours?"

No answer. He kept turning the dial.

Finally Blake asked, "You okay? You're not sick, are you?"

With that, Petty Officer Cunningham reached down, pulled the trashcan between his feet and put his head down. The vomit exploded like a ripe orange thrown against a bulkhead. Over and over and over, in convulsions he wretched. Most of it hit the bucket, but some splattered over the edge onto the deck, even onto Blake.

"You okay?" Blake asked.

"What's it look like?" The greenish-colored face turned toward him. Blake saw dribbles of yellow and orange fluid on his chin.

"You want me to take the watch?"

"Yeah," Cunningham said.

Blake switched seats with Cunningham. He pushed the trash can, now partially full of puke, toward the sailor's chair.

"What is it we're trying to do?" Blake asked.

"Catch submarines, idiot!" Then he bent down and puked again.

"Yeah, but how? I don't know this stuff."

"Hit that button." He pointed, then vomited again. When he came up for air, Cunningham added, "Then turn that dial five degrees and listen."

Blake quickly put on the earmuff headset. He hit the button and heard the explosion of sound, turned the dial five degrees and listened. His eyes followed the representation of the burst of sound as it expanded toward infinity from the center of the circular television-like screen. Blake had no training in the technology, but the concept seemed simple enough. Broadcast noise through water and listen for it to hit something.

Over and over he smacked the button and turned the dial. Boring. His mind drifted. For a moment he could see Viva in Cannes.

She would know why he hadn't returned when she no longer saw the ships at anchor.

The smell of vomit quickly brought his mind back to the present. Blake's stomach rumbled. Cunningham vomited again. The smell deepened. Blake's stomach weakened.

I'm not going to get sick.

But the smell of Cunningham's puke permeated the small room. The rolling ship, the pounding up and down, the vibration, the smell, the smell. Blake couldn't hold it. He retched into the same trash can. Up it came. The espresso, the asparagus sandwich he had when he was with Viva, yesterday's lunch and supper, everything. But once it was over, it was over. His seasickness subsided almost immediately and he went back to his ping-train-listen routine.

"Got something," Blake said.

"Oh, no," Cunningham responded between vomits.

"It's like a bleeping sound every time the noise spoke goes over the same bearing. I don't know what it is."

"Here. Let me listen." Cunningham said, still looking pale. "Same bearing. Hit it again."

Cunningham listened.

"Again," the sonarman said.

Cunningham leaned forward and touched a button on the bulkhead and shouted into a microphone. "Bridge, CIC, this is sonar. Sonar contact bearing 030 true, range 3000 yards, classify submarine."

Cunningham seemed to come alive. He wiped the drool from his mouth with his handkerchief and took over from Blake on the stack. Into the microphone he said, "Bearing 035, drifting right, belay that... steady bearing. Range 2500. Closing."

"Confidence?" CIC asked.

"High. A no-shitter. This is a 'sewer pipe.' Speed slow. Bearing steady. I'm going passive."

"No! Don't!" came the order from CIC. "We don't want it to know we got it."

"Torpedo doors opening. Christ, it's gett'n ready to shoot!" Cunningham said, now looking pale for a different reason. His voice raised an octave. "She could shoot a torpedo!"

Cunningham sat up straight, concentrating. He hit the sound button, took off the headset, and turned on the speaker that broadcast the sonar sounds into the compartment. Blake could hear the ping bouncing off something solid. It sounded like a hammer hitting a steel drum.

So that's what a submarine sounds like.

"Evaluation, sonar?" Bridge asked.

"Evaluation, sonar? Captain wants to know what we have here?" Bridge again.

"A frigging submarine! I said it before! It's ready to shoot a goddamn torpedo!"

Ingraham picked up a bit of speed. The pounding increased, less rolling. Blake heard the orders over the speaker. "General Quarters, General Quarters. All hands man your battle stations. Make anti-submarine weapons ready."

Blake glanced at his watch. It was about five o'clock in the morning. He could imagine the sleepy faces of the crew bounding out of bed, running to their battle stations in the dark, donning lifejackets, and breaking out ammunition. His first division buddies would be taking green water showers rinsed with drenching rain.

The door to Sonar control opened and a chief sonar tech entered. Ensign Rhode, a boyishly looking young officer, followed the chief.

"What you got, Cunningham?" the Ensign asked.

"I think I heard the winding sound of a Russian screw – just like in sonar school."

"Let me hear," the chief said.

"Skipper won't let me go passive."

"Bridge, sonar. Request permission to go passive. We think this is a Russian but need to verify," Ensign Rhode said.

"Captain says go passive, but not long."

The chief put on the headset. His face showed the strain of trying to discern sounds in a normally noisy sea.

"I agree. Check me, Mr. Rhode." The chief handed the earmuffs to Rhode. He listened.

"Agree."

"Bridge, sonar. Sonar classifies it as Russian. Depth 500 feet, but she is going deeper. Range closed to 2000 yards. Recommend changing course -- attacking the sub."

"Sonar, bridge, send her an 'uncle joe' signal on Gertrude (underwater communications). Ask I.D. -- nationality."

The chief keyed the Gertrude with the appropriate letters.

"No response, sir!' Ensign Rhode shouted. "Recommend changing course -- attack the sub."

Blake asked, "Isn't that risky? We could start a war!"

"You think we should wait until we have a torpedo in us?"

*****

During the long delay after the sonar chief sent their signal to the submarine over Gertrude, *Ingraham* had remained ready. Captain Andriso would have launched his anti-submarine weapons; Blake was sure it was the kind of officer he was, straight up, no fear. *Don't any sonofabitch threaten my ship!*

Seconds became minutes; *Ingraham's* crew were prepared to release ASROCK, torpedoes, hedgehogs, and depth charges – the proverbial kitchen sink.

Tension. Blake could sense from the chief's body language that the Cold War could become hot. This wasn't John Wayne play-acting in some "B" movie. This was not midshipman training. This was Captain Gui Andriso prepared to attack, and it was better than training -- it was the real thing. The state of the world was in the hands of a few sonar techs on a submarine and captain of the destroyer U.S.S. *Ingraham.*

But Captain Andriso did not attack.

"Got a signal, sir."

"Quick check the code book," said Ensign Rhode. "Did it give a proper response to Uncle Joe?"

"Confirmed, sir. It's a damn Brit, sir."

Ensign Rhode called the bridge over the microphone: "Classify English sub, captain. Sorry."

Had it been a Russian submarine and no positive response, Navy ships were under rules of engagement to protect themselves. Through the clear thinking of Captain Gui Andriso, the incident turned into a false alarm.

CHAPTER 17

LEAVE AND LOVE

The remainder of Blake's youngster cruise was much like the beginning -- a transit across the Atlantic, lots of watch standing, plus divisional work. During this phase he was transferred to the engineering department where he spent his time in the engine rooms. He worked with the sailors who maintained the boilers, steam turbines, and other machinery. They often referred to themselves as "snipes" or the "black gang."

By the time *Ingraham* made its anchorage in Chesapeake Bay at the mouth of the Severn River, he had been exposed to every part of the practical side of shipboard duty. Commander Gui Andriso was true to his word. He reviewed every youngster's workbook. The captain was the kind of man who worked long hours, often into the wee hours of morning, far longer hours than his crew. Blake's book came back with red pencil marks throughout, showing where his system diagrams were incorrect and suggesting he spend more time during the next academic year on engineering subjects. Captain Gui Andriso wrote:

"A Naval Academy student should do better than this. Work harder!"

Despite the stinging remark, Blake had learned a lot about engineering. At first the odor of fuel oil and grease had bothered him. It permeated his clothing and he couldn't seem to get away from the engine room even when he was topside. After a while he got used to it. The petty officers seemed to be miracle workers, keeping the engineering plant sparkling clean, ship-shape and, most importantly, operating efficiently. Often they didn't have the right parts, so they just made them. His job, besides listening and learning practical engineering, was to brew the coffee, which had to be done just right. Snipes prided themselves as having the best coffee on the ship. Just so many scoops of coffee -- add water from the evaporators, then let it perk to a dark, black color. Finally, let the chief of the watch give it the taste test. Then and only then could it be pronounced engineer's coffee. As far as machinery was concerned, the chiefs all had the same philosophy. Machinery was like the human body. To really know what was going on inside, it had to be seen, touched, and listened to. Gauges told only part of the story. The real diagnostics had to do with feeling for vibrations and touching for temperature changes. Enginemen often set their coffee cups on equipment, then watched and listened. It wasn't voodoo, and it wasn't taught at the Academy, but as Shorty used to say, it was the goddamn truth.

Blake had made his rounds of the ship the day before. He said good-bye to the black gang, then the First Division bos'n boys as well as the sonarman and radarmen with whom he had stood watch and worked.

Finally he went to Willowby, whom he found in the bos'n's locker making up a new line for underway replenishments. His good-bye would be quick. The motor whaleboats were already alongside to take the midshipmen ashore.

"Boats, we're go'n ashore now. Want to thank you for a good cruise."

"Well, if it ain't *Mister Midshipman* Lawrence." He shook his head in an understanding way. "Maybe this has been a good first step to make you a decent officer. You might guess I don't like most officers. They act like asses and don't know much. But you might turn out okay."

Uncharacteristically, he reached his tattooed arm across the pile of line he was working on and shook Blake's hand. "Ahh... I want to thank you also. Want you to know you probably saved me from losing my crow back there in Cannes. Might make chief yet." He dropped his eyes as if he were embarrassed at saying the words, but in a very gruff voice added, "Good luck to you. I'm expecting you to work hard to become a sailor's officer."

*****

It was not until the small boats rounded into the Severn River and they could see the chapel dome that the third classmen could officially declare themselves youngsters. Mother B, sitting stately on the peninsula, was a commanding sight. This time it looked more like a home than the prison of plebe year.

Midshipmen who had to stay back to take exams again or attend sub-squad (special swimming lessons) were generally unhurried; however, most raced to begin their leave as soon as they arrived at the dock. They ran with their gear to their rooms in Mother B. Laundry went in one direction. Cleaning in another. Cruise boxes were re-stowed with things not needed on summer leave. Suitcases came out of storage and were filled with gifts bought in Europe.

Like Blake, Pete and Sam were in too much of a hurry for any extended small talk. Blake did mention to Pete that he'd seen Viva in Cannes.

"So?"

"So. She still your girl?"

"Met another girl. English. London. She's coming over his summer," Pete said as he slid the girl's picture in front of Viva's in the photo frame centered on his desk.

"What about Viva?"

"What about her?" Pete looked surprised.

"Nothing. See ya in September," Blake said. His heart took a jolt at the news that Pete had lost interest in Viva. His mind was already weaving a plot to find her, explain what happened at sea in the Mediterranean, and resurrect their relationship, as shaky as it was. "Sam, "I might come over to Philadelphia to visit -- before going back. Okay?"

"Okay. Give me a call." Sam winked. He knew what Blake had in mind.

Airline reservations were confirmed, cabs were called, and within a few hours Bancroft Hall was again empty of all except the lowly plebes in their summer training.

Blake took the bus to Pittsburgh and arrived that evening to a welcome home sign his mother and brother had made.

Charlie Lawrence, named after their mother's Uncle Charles Nichols, had grown at least an inch since Blake last saw him. Charlie wanted to know about the Academy. Blake told him plebe year was rough, but if the rest was anything like youngster cruise, it would be a great experience. Charlie said he leaned toward going to West Point, where his uncle graduated and was commissioned.

Blake's mother was still going with a man named Jack, but Blake could never remember his last name. The romance was now about three years old -- an on-again, off-again thing. Jack owned a tax accounting business and often hung around Blake's mother's house with little to do between May 15 and December 31. The relationship must have heated up since Blake last saw her because his mother had changed the way she acted and dressed. She seemed more cheery and no longer wore her housecoat all day. Blake didn't dislike Jack; however, he was a stranger, an outsider, and more important, not his dad, whom no one could replace. For those reasons, Blake thought it was doubtful he and Jack would ever be close. But Jack did seem to make his mother happy -- and that was important. When Jack was at the house, Blake tried to be elsewhere.

His only other leave since joining the Navy more than two years before had been boring. Blake's high school pals hung out at the same places. Now, during his summer leave, it was still that way -- only more so. The writer Thomas Wolfe once said, "You can't go home again," and as far as Blake was concerned, he was right. His pals Henry Anderson, Tom Wojciechowski, and skinny Billy Frasier still lived at home. They went to the Saturday night dance at Sullys, just like they did during high school. Henry still had a severe case of acne and Walter Szabo was still in the Army.

For Blake, still struggling to mature as a naval person, hanging out on a corner was far from his ideal of becoming a noble person.

After two weeks at home, Blake told his mom he was pulling out. He had called Sam Tallau and learned that Viva was in town.

"Philadelphia?"

"Yeah, Mom. Sam says I can stay with him for a few days."

"What's Sam like?"

"Well, he's a very good student and a hell of an organizer. He's organizing my election campaign for class president. He's from an eastern European family -- nice folks. Met his mother at that party after the Army-Navy game. Don't know about his dad. Sam's short, like a stump -- big muscles, a wrestler. You'd like him, but he takes some getting used to because he's so dynamic. He can't stand to be idle and comes off a bit pushy. The firsties called him 'Napoleon.' He liked that. They also nicknamed him 'Shrimp.' He hates that."

"And this girl?"

"Her name is Viva."

"Viva? That's an unusual name for a girl." She frowned.

"Nice girl, Mom. Her real name is Kathy -- Kathy Velenochi. She's a singer. Get it? Viva Voce. She studies at Juilliard!"

"A singer? Viva? Hmm. Sounds Italian to me."

"So? Just a date, Mom."

*****

Blake said his good-byes, different now than the time he went off to boot camp. Then it was all new. Now he was a seasoned young man, having been through the Navy's toughest sorting out processes and having been away from his mother's home for more than two years. He would miss his mom and brother, but now there were new challenges.

He arrived in Philadelphia after a hot bus ride across the Pennsylvania Turnpike in August. Sam was waiting for him at the station. Sporting a colorful short-sleeve shirt that showed off his rippling wrestler muscles, Sam threw Blake's luggage in a Chevy convertible. As he gunned away from the curb, Sam offhandedly said, "She's gone. I checked with her mother today -- she left already -- had to get back to New York."

"Sam! Why didn't you tell me when I called?"

"Didn't know. I thought you wanted to surprise her so I didn't inquire until this morning. Didn't want to give you away."

"You got her number?"

"No."

"What good are you?" Blake jabbed his roommate in the shoulder. "Know where she is? She's still at Juilliard, isn't she?"

"Yeah, but she's not living there this summer," Sam said impishly. "But her mother did tell me Viva stays at a YWCA in Manhattan."

"How put-out would your mother be if I only stayed the night? I'll take a bus to New York tomorrow."

"She'll hate it. She cooked you some great old-country food."

To the contrary, Mrs. Tallau didn't blink an eye that Blake was just staying overnight. In fact, her eyes twinkled, "How romantic! Just like my Homasu when he won me back in Estonia. He walk two days from the front to be with me. You like Viva? She nice girl. Very talent."

Blake left late the next morning. Sam took him to the bus station. "See you back in school. Sure you don't want me to drive you to New York?"

"I'd rather do this, thanks. See ya back at the Academy. Next week."

*****

He stayed in the YMCA and walked to the Juilliard School. Although he wore a sport shirt over a pair of khaki uniform trousers, he still looked military. Juilliard was in an old building that looked like it had been built about the turn of the century. Inside he asked for Viva only to find that she was auditioning for a part with a small production company off Broadway.

He bolted to the street looking for a cab. After a twenty-minute edgy wait, he finally waved one to the curb, gave the driver instructions and watched New York pass by. At the theatre he slid into a back-row seat of the empty theatre. On stage several dancers finished practicing a routine. Viva stood off to the side. A moment later she was called to center stage.

"Okay, Miss Velenochi. Give us your good stuff. From the top, please."

Viva wore her black hair combed in a long pony tail that fell to her waist, the way Blake remembered her when they first met. She staged a pose as if she were a girl of the street and began. The song was a popular ballad and when she was finished she left the stage.

Blake marveled at how she had grown since he first met her after the Army-Navy game. She was poised and professional, and her voice made him shiver in its beauty.

"Thank you, Kathy. We'll call," The casting director said through a false smile.

She came up the aisle toward Blake. Her head was high but her face showed disappointment. He waited until she was adjacent to his row of seats. He clapped his hands. "That was very good!" he said loudly.

Viva, surprised and obviously upset, didn't even acknowledge who he was. "It was terrible. I won't get a call-back." Her head shook back and forth in anger, hair swinging like a pendulum. Then she recognized him. "Blake! What on earth are you doing here?"

"I'm here to see you. How about lunch?"

"Oh, I'm starving. Come." Her smile lit up like the sun in the morning. She reached out, pulled him from his seat, and led him to a small deli next door where they ordered foot-long submarine sandwiches.

They sat on the street, drinking soda and watching the passers-by, chatting as they ate. It was as if they had never left Cannes.

"Why didn't you call?" she asked.

"I wanted to surprise you."

"And did! Did you come all the way from Pitts-burgh?"

"No, I stopped at Sam's place for a day."

"How's Sam?"

"Good. Can't wait to get back to school."

"That would be Sam. High energy. Wants to organize the world. What about Pete? What's he up to?"

"Don't know. He went home to Santa Barbara on leave."

"How was the rest of your cruise? Obviously you made it back to your ship on time. But you never came back."

"The cruise went well. Sorry about the storm. And your work in Italy?"

"Could have been better. Damn Italians. So snooty... and brazen. Men can't keep their hands off women."

"You're Italian."

"I'm an American -- from Italian parents."

"How's your training going? Thought you didn't start back to school until later."

"We don't. I wanted a part in *that* musical. Under *that* director."

"I thought you wanted to become an opera singer."

"I may not be good enough. I also like light opera and musicals."

"What's Juilliard like?" Blake asked.

"Well --" she paused to swallow the last of her sandwich. "Just as Annapolis is the leading school for naval officers, Juilliard is the leading school for the performing arts." She added, "That is, in America. Many of the stars of music, dance, and drama prepared here -- lots of movie stars."

Blake studied her. She was dressed like he expected they dressed in the artsy world of New York. Tight pants cut off at the thigh, low-cut top, soft shoes.

Must be the uniform for fitting into the culture.

"How'd you get here?" he asked.

"Where?"

"Juilliard."

"Oh, passed the audition. They liked me."

"Audition?"

"Sure. We had to have good grades in high school -- pass tests and all that. Just as you do, but talent is everything here. They don't like you, you don't get in."

"They allow you to perform while you're going to school?"

"Of course. You go to sea on cruises for practical training. We perform."

They finished their sandwiches and the conversation waned. Blake could see that Viva's mind was in other places.

"What are you doing tonight? How about dinner?"

"Oh, Blake. I do want to, but I've got to practice. And food? I only eat one meal a day. I'm going back and try out again for that show tomorrow. This time, I'll go for a different part -- a back-up or anything, a dancer. I dance well, you know. I want it."

"How about after you practice?"

"Hmm."

"Viva?"

"Maybe."

"Viva?"

"Tempting. Oh, all right," she smiled, then added, "How about the concert in Central Park? Seven o'clock. Meet me at the Y. We'll walk."

She stood. For a moment Blake thought that she was inviting a kiss. But she turned away and waved as she headed toward her school.

*****

At seven o'clock, he was at the front desk of the YWCA asking for Viva. A woman in her forties smiled and paged the second floor. After a few minutes, Viva came down the stairs wearing slacks and a sweater. Glasses gave her the look of a student instead of the sultry singer she was trying to portray at the afternoon try-out.

Her hair was now pulled straight back into a bun at the base of her neck instead of the more casual way she wore it the first time he saw her at Sam's house. Her dark eyes smiled when she said, "Right on time. Come along. It's not far."

"Never saw you in glasses before."

"I only wear them off stage, so to speak. I'm a bit near-sighted."

He shrugged his shoulders, "They do give you a different look."

"Like me still?"

"Of course."

They entered the park on the south side and went directly to seats facing the orchestra. Music already filled the air. The place was full of casually dressed people, mostly older. They found two seats near the front and slid across the aisle, stepping carefully around other people. They sat between two women. The one on Blake's left was dressed in slacks just like Viva but the lady on Viva's right wore a beautiful evening dress. Her small purse lay next to her leg.

The music was a selection of Cole Porter melodies -- springy tunes from light operas. By now the stars were full against a darkening night. The audience sat in semi-darkness, a breeze brought coolness. A spotlight focused on a vocalist as she strolled on stage. Everyone stood to clap. The lady next to Viva stood, as did many others. She held a paper toward the meager light to read it. "Can you help me? What time does it say?"

Viva said, "Seven p.m."

"Thank you, dear. Too late. I can't get there in time." She placed the paper back in her purse and sat down to listen to the music.

Blake noticed that Viva kept eyeing the lady's purse. She would turn sideways slightly and tilt her head as if she was studying something. Finally, she took off her glasses, squinted, then put them back on for a better look.

A few moments later everyone stood again to applaud, and while the lady was standing, Blake saw Viva slip her hand into the purse, pull out the paper, and slip it under her sweater. Then she reached for Blake's hand. "Let's go," she said. The vocalist began to sing, and before the audience was completely seated, Blake and Viva excused themselves. Viva crossed the park with Blake in racing to keep up.

"What's up?" Blake asked. He didn't want to directly ask about the theft.

"Hurry! Call a cab. How quickly can you get into your uniform?"

"Why?"

"Don't ask. Just take me to the Y and come right back in your uniform."

"Does this have something to do with what you took from that lady's purse? That's larceny. We could go to jail, you know."

"It's not like I stole money, silly. Just a paper -- an invitation -- an invitation to a cocktail reception that started less than a half hour ago. Besides, everyone has a little larceny in them."

"Not me."

"Oh. Poo. Mister perfect. In this business, you have to want it. If you want it, you go for it, one way or another. And I want it!"

This is a side of Viva I've never seen before.

"She obviously wasn't going -- the lady in the park, I mean. She said it was too late for her to get there, but not us. That's why we have to hurry. Everyone will be there, and I want to meet him."

"Meet who?"

"Fosse. Mr. Bob Fosse."

"Who's he?"

"Blake. Don't you know anything about the theater? He's only the biggest director and choreographer ever. You need broadening. You have no understanding of the arts and literature."

She's right. I have not been exposed to the arts – engineering and military took all my time. Nevertheless her insult hurt. This is a different woman than I thought I knew. She's a schemer and what else? I guess I'll go along, but how far?

He hailed a cab, dropped her at the YWCA, then held the cab in front of his own Y. He changed into his khaki uniform in less than five minutes, knotting his tie on the way. He found Viva waiting on the curb looking her vivacious self in a short evening dress that accentuated her height. In her high heels, her long legs looked even better than any movie star's. She wore a shawl across her shoulders. But she was obviously anxious and asked Blake, "What took you so long?"

She directed the driver, "Take us to Radio City,"

"You know you're making me a party to this lar-ceny," Blake said.

"You want out? I'll go alone."

"No. But --"

She waved the invitation at the doorman as they passed into a room with high ceilings, a glass roof, and curved arches at every entrance. Blake's out-of-place uniform caused many people in the room to do a double-take. These were the show business elite. Their hair was styled, their clothes perfect. They hugged each other on greeting, a very foreign thing to Blake. The talk was loud and animated above music coming from a band in the corner.

"Be a darling. Get me a drink of something, anything -- to carry. Maybe white wine, or a martini." Like a well-behaved pet dog, he crossed the room to the bar and asked for a martini and a glass of white wine.

Viva was chatting with two couples.

"Thank you, darling," She said in a falsetto voice he had never heard before. She took a sip from the martini. "Good -- very dry." Then she looked around and said, "Where is he now?" she asked of the couples, all of whom seemed to be following the movements of a tall, balding man on the other side of the room.

Viva took Blake by the arm, directing him through the crowd until she stood just outside a ring of beautiful women surrounding the man. They listened for a few minutes as he discussed his new musical and expounded on several of his past hits. With Blake on her arm, Viva kept pushing ever so slowly into the ring until she was right in front of the man.

"Is that a Navy uniform I see? I was a sailor once."

"Yes, sir. I'm a midshipman at the Naval Academy," Blake responded.

"Well I had the time of my life when I was in the service. Memories. I was in Europe during the war. Helped produce some shows for the boys. Never went to sea. You been to sea yet?"

"Yes, sir, just got back from an eight-week cruise in the Med."

"Hear that, girls? He sir'd me. That's the Navy. I loved it!" Fosse said. He started to turn away, but Viva said. "Mr. Fosse, he's my friend, but I'm the one who wants a part in your musical."

Fosse was tall but not as tall as Viva. His eyes started at the top and ran down to her toes before settling on her breast line. He finally raised his eyes and said, "What's your name and what do you do?"

"Viva -- Viva Voce -- and I -- I'm at Juilliard. I mostly sing but I can also dance. I'll do anything for you."

"You will, will you?" He smiled. "Viva Voce – catchy -- an interesting stage name. Show up tomorrow. I'll take a look. Good talking to you, midshipman. Looks like you've got good taste in women." He shook Blake's hand then continued to discuss his work with the growing crowd.

On their way home, Viva told him, "Someday I want to see my name in the headlines and on a theatre marquee."

"Viva, you are a whiz at getting your way. There's no doubt in my mind it'll happen for you."

She leaned over and kissed him on the mouth, "I'm not totally work, darling."

They "necked" in the back seat until the cab came to a screeching halt in front of the YMCA. Viva jumped out and said, "I must get to bed, Blake. Good night. See you tomorrow?"

He could still taste her lips as he mumbled the words, "I'll be there."

*****

The next day, Blake went with her to the rehearsal hall. They sat in a middle row, well behind the directors. Viva sat on the end seat. She waited patiently to speak to Fosse. At the right moment, she bounded down the aisle and introduced herself. Blake could see her hand point in his direction. Fosse turned to look and waved to Blake. Viva removed her dress to reveal tights, put on a pair of dance shoes, and took her place on the stage to begin her audition. Her long legs spun and kicked and swung. Her body flowed in rhythm to the music. Blake had always sensed her gracefulness, but now he saw how beautiful she was as she demonstrated her elegance and style.

As he watched, he remembered the kisses from the night before, and his heart took several tumbles.

This girl is so desirable, but is she for me? She'll take some getting used to, with her attitudes about. getting ahead at any cost and about larceny, even if minor.

*****

Drawn like a moth to a flame, the rest of Blake's leave was spent sitting, watching, walking, and talking with Viva as she made her way through the maze of New York theatre life.

When she got her call-back and the part they splurged on a dinner at Sardi's, a restaurant where famous people came and went.

By the time he left, their romance had grown to the point where they touched often, kissed passionately -- but on the run, after lunch, before her rehearsals, and just before she entered the no-man's land of the YWCA. The night before he was to return to the Academy, they had dinner at a street café not unlike those at Cannes.

His hand drifted across the table and touched hers. By now he was sure he was in love – and for him it was the first time. They smiled across the candles set in the middle of the table.

"You'll write?"

"Of course. You'll come down?" he asked.

"If I can get away."

"It's not far," he insisted.

"I have to pay?" she questioned. "I don't have much money. They hardly give me enough to pay my tuition."

"We'll work it out," he said.

They walked hand in hand along the streets back to her dorm. Blake took her in his arms. She squeezed him and ran her hand along the back of his neck. They kissed. Hard. Hungry. Long. Finally they broke apart.

"I can sneak into the Y," he suggested.

She smiled, "Silly boy. I'm up too early tomorrow. Rehearsal."

"Me too." He kissed her one more time. "I'll call you from Annapolis."

"Do." Her eyes smiled a lingering, hungry look. Blake's heart beat hard. Midshipman Lawrence was caught in the magnet of love.

CHAPTER 18

YOUNGSTER YEAR

The bus ride, boring, tiring, and sad. Blake's thoughts were only about Viva, Viva, Viva. He felt empty. He could still smell her perfume, feel her lips on his, her tall, slender body, the touch of her fingers at the back of his neck, on his cheek. Without effort, without consciously knowing, like a good vitamin or a bad virus, he didn't know which, she had crept into his body.

She's in my head more and more -- like a flood or a train wreck. You don't see it coming and can't stop it even if you wanted to.

The Greyhound headed south across the bridges into the farmlands of New Jersey and Pennsylvania, stopping at several towns along the way. Blake transferred in Baltimore and arrived at the main gate mid-afternoon. By the time he found his new room, dragged his cruise box near the door, and stowed his summer uniforms, it was evening meal. The brigade wasn't required to be back until noon the next day. Some upperclassmen arrived early as Blake did, but he knew most would make it a last-minute thing. The mess hall was only partially filled. The early birds were separated at one end of the mess hall from the new plebe class, still moving to their new companies and exempt from hazing. After supper he sat alone in a silent Mother B. Tomorrow the building would roar with activity. He took out paper and pen and put a picture of Viva on his desk. Not one for long letters, his one pager to his mother reviewed his trip to Philadelphia, then New York, and described his visit with Viva. He told her he was back at the Academy and would try to write more often. His next letter was to Viva. His mind swirled. He always struggled with words; numbers and machinery were more to his liking. What was happening? His pen wouldn't move. To write a love letter was more difficult than a Greenfield come-around.

"Dear Kathy..." He stopped and started again.

"My dearest..." He wrote.

"Darling Viva..." Started another.

He crumpled his first few tries and dropped them in the waste basket. His attempt at a love letter was either too solemn or too syrupy. Poetry was not his thing either, but he tried:

Love is like a rose
A petal that grows

He tried again, then said, "The hell with it." He put on his B-robe and walked to the pay phones. The desk lady at the YWCA said she would page Kathy Velenochi. After a few minutes she came back on the line and said that Kathy was not in her room. "Do you want to leave a message?" Blake told her, "Only that... ah... leave my name, Blake Lawrence... and... ah... just say I called."

Back in his room he scanned the fall midshipman activity calendar. He picked a weekend when there was a football game and a dance.

The thought of Viva coming for a weekend motivated him -- the words began to flow. It was as short as the one to his mother, but at least it was a letter. He told Viva that he had a great time in New York and hoped her stage and schoolwork were going well. Then he invited her to come down for the weekend he had selected. He explained that there would be a lot going on and to bring clothes for the afternoon as well as an evening dance. "I will understand if you can't make it. Love, Blake."

A day later, everyone returned and academic year began. Mother B returned to life. Another class of plebes joined the brigade. The upper class, including a few youngsters, began the process of introducing them to the core values of naval service: obedience, honor, grit -- then reinforcing those values through daily practice, not merely by words.

*****

During plebe year the three roommates hardly had a chance to get to know each other. Of course they shared the same space, saw each other between classes and come-arounds, but except for the party at Sam's, they had spent little time really talking. Now they had time. With no come-arounds to distract them they talked while facing each other across desks pulled together in the center of the room. Pete Ettinger, the surfer from Santa Barbara, was usually the first to break the silence of study hour. Of the three, his concentration was the least sustainable. He fell into what was known as the "bucket" (low grades) category. He finished plebe year with a 2.503, as close as one could get without flunking out of the academy, but for him, anything over 2.5 was gravy. Pete came back from his vacation with long hair frosted at its edges and yellow as the California sun. He would have to have his hair barbered before the first formation or be "fried" with a "Form Two" worth ten demerits and two hours of marching punishment.

Their conversations were seldom lengthy and seldom controversial. As in the wardroom of a ship, the topics of religion, politics, and women were taboo. Well -- not women, because Pete always talked girls. A typical topic was the rule, indelibly inked in their minds since Plebe year: never "bilge a classmate," that is, never be a witness to a violation. Another topic was about "snaking" another midshipman's girl. Although frowned upon, it was particularly taboo to steal a roommate's girl. Blake felt obliged to tell Pete about his interest in Viva.

Blake waited a few days before he broached the subject. He wanted to tell Pete in front of Sam because Sam was in on it. "Fighter, I went to see Viva during leave, in New York."

To Blake's pleasant surprise, Pete simply shrugged his shoulders and said, "That's okay. Viva and I never were right for each other. I don't know shit about art, and she didn't understand engineer talk. Besides I can't have a girlfriend who lives that near. Distractions. Came close to bilging out last year -- this year's got to be a different story." He took out a photo of a girl and began the process of putting it into the frame on his desk. "I found a new girl in Santa Barbara – Nancy. She's a student at UCLA. I'm going to buck up my grades, you watch." He now had three pictures in the frame, stacked one in front of the other. He slid Nancy's in front of Barbara, the English girl. Viva was now on the bottom.

"How do you keep track?" Blake asked.

"Not easy."

"Thought you were going out for tennis?"

"I am. I'm good enough to make varsity, I think."

"Napoleon," Blake asked as he flipped the pages of a new textbook. "What about you? You going out for wrestling again?"

Sam had a brain like a Swiss watch and had already settled into a regimen of study which, as he said, was intended to make him first in the class academically.

"Yeah, I'll wrestle and I'm gonna kick Army ass! I'm also on the chess team. But first things first. I'm gonna get you elected class president."

"How you gonna have time to do all that and work on *The Log*?" Pete asked.

"I'll get it done. But you guys have to swear to secrecy. They're gonna let me concentrate on doing my irreverent cartoons. You know, capture the dominant characteristics of the many wonderful targets here in Bancroft Hall... like company and battalion officers. Old "Twitch," the commandant, won't be exempt. Some dull upperclass'll get it too, those who've never had a creative moment in their lives. That's why I hate this lockstep academic shit. No majors and no minors. Everyone taking the same engineering courses. Hell, most of our classmates are just happy for 2.5, right, Pete?" He waved his hands in exasperation. "It's the sup's continued struggle for dominance over our military minds. No creativity!"

"Yeah, talk about no creativity, how about engineer-ing materials and calculus? Differential equations?" Pete said as he scratched his head. "None of that soft shit. Get it right or bilge out. There's not enough time, particularly when infantry drills and physical training are thrown on top. *I HATE THIS FRIGGING PLACE!*"

"You hate it? Hell, you've only been here a year. Wait 'til next semester," Blake reminded them. "Physics, mechanics, naval machinery European history, foreign policy plus a language. I guess I'm stuck with French. What about you, Sam?"

"They're gonna let me switch to Russian."

"Russian?"

"Yeah, it's closer to my Eastern European roots than German. I already know a lot of Russian, but not fluently." Sam didn't look up from the book he was reading. But he added, "You guys hear about Hamm?"

"What about him? Nothing would surprise me, that immature asshole grease bucket," Pete murmured while flipping the pages of his book.

"He came to Philadelphia during summer leave. Spent some time with none other than the famous Miss Flame."

"Yeah," Blake shook his head from side to side. "I heard Hambone bragging at breakfast formation. Puffing his accomplishments with that jail bait."

"That klutz," Pete added. "I bet he's gonna ride the radiator again this year."

"Shit, no one wants him on a team. In P.E. he's always the last to be picked."

"Hey, he's on the sailing team!" Blake said.

Everyone laughed.

"How'd he get in this place?" Sam asked.

"Smart," Blake said.

"You mean book smart," Sam remarked. "He has no common sense."

"You see Lee Locke?" Pete asked.

"What about Lee?" Blake perked up, wrinkling his brow. Lee was Blake's competitor for highest grease (aptitude for the service) grade in the class.

"I saw him," Sam responded. "He came back even chubbier than last year. Says he gonna make the 150-pound football team."

"Yeah. The admiral will have to lose fifteen pounds," Pete said.

"If he says he will -- he will," Blake said in clipped tones.

Sam looked up and smiled as if he understood the respect Blake had for Lee, but also the competition that had already begun for stripes, even in youngster year.

"Blake, you going out for basketball again?" Sam asked.

"Yeah, I showed up for practice with the other four starters from the plebe team. Guess what? Coach said everyone who tried out would get a fair look. But he made it clear that there were only three spots open on the varsity. His work outs are hard. He believes in pain."

"He's a relic of another era," Sam said. "But he wins games. We beat Army last year."

"Fundamentals, fundamentals, fundamentals." Blake shook his head. "Quote the coach: 'To prepare for basketball properly, imagine a game having five quarters instead of four. Those who win, can play tired -- at least the style Navy plays -- fast break and defend like a tiger protecting her cubs.

"If I make it, it'll be because I work harder. I'm gonna be first to practice after classes and last to leave -- run extra laps. Coach likes players who show grit and determination -- so I'm gonna give it to him. I have a chance to be the third man to make the team. Even if I do, I'll ride the bench. If I get a chance to play, it'll be as a substitute in some easy game, like against Cornell or Yale -- never against Princeton. And never, never against Army."

*****

IHTFP was embedded in the thinking of some midshipmen, particularly those who didn't participate beyond the basics. But most mids took pride in involving themselves in various extracurricular activities. They knew, as difficult as it was, the school provided excellent training for its purpose, which was preparing them for war from the sea. Nevertheless, pessimism prevailed. Everything became a target of morbid, irreverent humor. None of it serious, it was just the thing to do. No longer required to march in the center of the corridors and square corners or any of the other things plebes do that make them the center of unwanted attention, youngster year became the time of playfulness. Invisible, the third classmen went to class, hid in their rooms studying, and read. Their spare time was taken up with card playing and thinking up ways to be mischievous. Everyone became the target of their creative, impertinent, cheeky humor.

When the new first class took over, they exercised their "rates" (privileges) as if they were the profits for surviving the previous three years of their isolated, demanding life. The commandant, known to all mids as Twitch, went along. He permitted the firsties to expand their rewards to a corridor here, a chair there, where only first class were permitted to walk or sit. They even received extra liberty hours. In addition, there were the old privileges with names such as Lovers' Lane, Smoke Park, First Class Bench, First Class Ladders.

The second class had similar but fewer rates.

Youngsters, now feeling their oats, were often the targets of violations. Being ratey, as a mid who exceeded his class rates was called, often got not only a bark from the firsties, but could find his "grease" (aptitude for the service) grade dropping if it became chronic. On the other hand, the fun was doing it and not getting caught. Of course, woe unto the plebe who usurped a third class privilege such as using Youngster Cutoff.

Not long after the academic year was well underway, the three roommates sat in their room just before evening meal formation cramming for an exam the next day.

Blake put down his book and began the process of tying his tie; the knot had to have a precise dimple and be snugged close-up just right into the stiffly starched collar. As he looked in the mirror, he off-handedly said, "I got a letter from Viva today. She's coming for a weekend."

Sam said, "I heard. Flame's coming too."

"How'd you know?" Blake asked.

"Oh, you know Hambone. He has to tell all. Says he's pumping Flame."

"He's nuts," Blake said. "Everyone knows she's jail bait. Is she sixteen yet?"

"Jail bait," Pete nodded his head in agreement.

"That's what I told him," Sam said.

After marching into the mess hall and being dismissed, they gathered around their table.

The order came from the six striper, "Brigade seats."

Midshipmen, who all marched to the mess hall at once, expected to be served within five minutes of arrival. On this evening the food servers were late distributing the evening meal. Soon after the command "seats" was given, the mids began stomping their feet and rattling spoons against empty glasses.

Three hundred servers stood around waiting to deliver, but the food for the 3,500 midshipmen was not ready.

The brigade commander, a midshipman of fine reputation, tried to calm the situation by announcing, "Be patient. Food should be here very soon."

But the minutes passed and the noise grew louder until there was a frenzy. Plebes were ordered to stand on the center of their tables and "hook them up" which meant to shout "Food! Food! Food!" Some played the drums by beating a metal serving spoon against a pan. Soon after the meal was delivered, to the delight of the youngsters who were always at the center of mischief anyway, Sam shouted, "Food fight!"

It was too late for the stewards to turn back, for they had been under heavy pressure to deliver to the hungry young men. Everyone seemed to sense the avalanche coming. Soon the flood of food thrown from table to table grew until every mid at every table joined in. Laughter filled the air along with lettuce, tomatoes, slices of bread, meatballs, and even spaghetti. Working white uniforms were soon stained red and green.

Back in their room the three couldn't stop laughing. Not since they had thrown Greenfield into the Natatorium had they had so much fun.

But a ring-knock on their door quickly brought a sobering silence. It was a firstie named Gladmore, a two-striper who wanted everyone to know it. The three roommates stood for the senior, but not at attention, sort of at a relaxed parade rest.

"Which one of you guys started that food fight?"

No one said anything; their faces remained expressionless.

"Well?"

"Well, what? Mr. Gladmore?" Pete asked.

"Well, did you start the food fight?"

Silence. Their faces continued expressionless. It was a question not to be asked.

Sam's face reddened. "Are you trying to trap us into an honor violation?"

"Well if it happens again, I'll have to put you on report."

Sam said sarcastically, "That's fair."

As soon as Gladmore left, the messenger of the watch knocked on the door.

"Mr. Lawrence, you have a phone call."

Thinking it was a call from Viva, Blake raced through the corridors. He picked up the phone and said, "Hello?"

"Blake, is that you?"

"Yes. Who's calling?" It was a male voice. His heart settled back to normal.

"Your old squad leader... Mark Greenfield."

"Where are you? What are you doing?" Blake was caught off guard because he figured he'd never again hear from the guy who had made his life so miserable for about three months but then strangely became his friend.

"I'm at the Air Force's fighter school. Moody, Georgia."

"You are! How do you like it?"

"I soloed today."

"Congratulations! What's next?" Blake wondered if this was the purpose of the call, to tell him that he had soloed.

"Advanced, then F-100's"

"Sounds great," Blake said.

"What are you guys up to? Brigade back?" Greenfield asked.

"Yep, we're back. Same old stuff."

"You and your roommates tearing up the place?"

"Whataya mean?"

"Well, after the pranks and stuff you played as plebes, I figured you'd really get with it as youngsters."

"Actually we had our first food fight tonight."

As if he hadn't heard Blake's food fight remark, Greenfield said, "I'm getting married."

"No kidding? Congratulations! You never told me about a girl."

"Met her this summer -- a southern girl."

"Congratulations -- again."

"I'll send you an invitation."

"Yeah. I'd like that," Blake responded, "and, I, ah, appreciate the call."

"Give my best to the old company. Mention me to Lieutenant Dean."

"I -- okay. I'll do that, but I don't come in contact with him very much."

"See ya at 15,000 feet, Blake. Go aviation."

"Yeah. Maybe. Bye. And congratulations again."

Back in his room, Blake told Greenfield's story. The other two weren't interested in the report of marriage, but the fact that he had soloed caught their attention.

"He say what kind of aircraft he'd be flying?" Pete asked.

"Fighters."

"Hey, he'd be perfect for that," Pete said. "Always thought he had a fighter pilot mentality. I remember them from my enlisted days: cocky, big attitude. I'm gonna be one!"

Sam added, "He could go up against the Russians very soon in this Cold War shit."

"Greenfield mentioned our Natatorium prank and wondered if we had been up to anything else. I told him nothing so far except the food fight."

"That Gladmore's an asshole! He tried to trap us into an honor violation. Asking who started the food fight. That SOB needs a Greenfield."

"Well, I have an idea," said Sam. "Remember the story of Philo N. McGiffin?"

"Yeah, sure." Blake said.

"Well, let's do a Philo McGiffin!"

"Like what?" Blake asked.

"Remember, he rolled some cannon balls down the dormitory steps?"

"Yeah?" Pete said.

"Well, where does Mr. Horseshit Gladmore live?" Sam asked.

"Got it. First deck, two decks below us, and right at the foot of the ladder," Pete said as he rubbed his hands together. "Great idea. But where do we get cannon balls?"

Sam frowned. "Didn't think of that. Forget it. Bad idea."

"No. Good idea," Blake said. "What about bowling balls?"

"What about a trash can full of water?" Pete said.

The planning phase of "Operation Bowling Ball down the ladder of the third wing of Mother B" went into effect.

"This has to be foolproof," Blake said. "With Viva coming down for the weekend -- I can't risk a Class A."

"Well, Mr. Class President-to-be, who do you think you are? The Lone Ranger? None of us want that," Sam said. "But this should be simple. We get one of those big laundry carts and fill it with about six bowling balls, two. Take the moke (nickname for civilian cleaning personnel) elevator from the basement to the deck below ours and stow them in back of the moke's closet. Then when we do it we go there quickly and let them all go at once. He'll hear them coming and have a baby. He opens his door and the trashcan of water floods him. We run up one deck and into our room."

"What about the mate of the deck?" Pete asked.

"That's a problem," Sam agreed. "We'll just have to chance it -- hope they won't recognize us."

"Why don't we wear stocking caps? Cut holes for eyes and pull them over our faces," Blake said.

"Good idea!"

Three evenings in a row, after sport practice they each blatantly walked out of the bowling alley with two balls and took them in a laundry cart to the closet nearest the ladder above Gladmore's room. They also filled a trash can with water and asked the mokes of the deck not to betray them. Having watched boys' pranks for years, they agreed. Despite being called moke, which was short for jamocha mocha, a coffee and an irreverent racial nickname referring to their skin color, they were loyal to midshipmen when asked.

The roommates set an alarm clock. They got up in silence and looked out their door. When the mate of the deck was making his rounds at the other end of the corridor, they ducked down the ladder and went into the moke's closet. There they waited until fifteen minutes to the hour, the time when the watch was changing. Dressed in dark pants and shirt with their stocking caps pulled over their faces, they looked like John Wayne in a World War II movie. They rolled the trash can into position, tilted just right resting on Gladmore's door. Then they crept up a deck and along the dark corridor.

Hugging the bulkhead, fingers of each hand in a bowling ball, they silently walked single file until they were opposite the ladder. Running as fast as they could, they paused at the top of the ladder and let them go. They waited long enough to hear the bop, bop, bopping of the balls and the bang they made slamming into Gladmore's door. As soon as they heard Gladmore's voice, they took off running back to their own deck.

Behind them they could hear the pandemonium of screams and cursing as the water swashed into Gladmore's room.

Class loyalty is a strange thing. Even the biggest asshole is to be defended if the class believes he has been wronged. The search by Gladmore's classmates began. In this case, the firsties weren't sure if the stunt was just a spurious Philo N. McGiffin replication or if it was aimed at Gladmore. Nevertheless they came out in hordes to solve the mystery. Because Gladmore was a hard case, most firsties thought it was plebes out for revenge. Others thought it was Gladmore's platoon, who were ready to mutiny anyway because of the zealous way he inspected. Apparently the MOD's didn't know or wouldn't tell whom they saw running in the middle of the night, so it was a general mystery, and the three culprits felt secure.

Gladmore never came around to confront them. Instead the next night their own company commander held an all hands meeting. In the passageway outside the company office, with Lieutenant Dean present, he said, "Anyone who knows anything about the bowling ball prank should come forward. This is serious."

The three played it dumb, just the same as they did when they dumped Greenfield in the natatorium. While standing among the other midshipmen they mumbled such things as "bowling balls?"

"Down a ladder? Sounds like fun."

"Wish we'd thought of it. Where'd they get them?"

Lieutenant Dean stepped forward. "The bowling balls and water caused a lot of damage, and the commandant called the naval investigative service; they're checking the fingerprints. The entire executive department is involved in this investigation."

In their room Blake asked, "Fingerprints? He's pulling our leg, right?"

CHAPTER 19

PRANKS AND DRAGS

For the next several weeks, the Academy buzzed with the thought that the ghost of Philo N. McGiffin, a member of the Class of 1882, had struck. Philo was not the only memorable graduate of that class. There was also Second Lieutenant Harry L. Hawthorne, U.S. Army, who was the first Naval Academy graduate to earn the Medal of Honor. But McGiffin was the most colorful. Plebes were required to recite his story. As a student he was full of devilment. Discipline bored him. Rolling cannon balls down the stairs was just one of his pranks but the one which landed him in the brig on the old *Santee*. He was colorful not only because of his exploits while a midshipman but because, when declined a commission in the U.S. Navy, he took China's offer to join their Navy. His classmates were not even lieutenants when he was promoted to commander and was wounded fighting a battle against a Japanese naval force in which he, as the naval advisor, took command of a Chinese battleship after the cowardly captain ran from the bridge.

Apparently the bowling balls and trash can full of water that Pete, Sam, and Blake used for their reenactment did even more damage than McGiffin's cannon balls. The executive department, which was Captain Robert O'Brian's Bancroft Hall staff, held meetings to prevent an outbreak of similar pranks. Company officers conducted discussions about being serious in the business of building naval officers. The fall set stripers were required to use their chain of command to reinforce the danger of rolling bowling balls down ladders.

The more the school focused on the prank, the more the brigade got into the humor of it all. Sam, whose identity as the artist for *The Log* remained an editorial secret, unleashed at least a dozen different cartoon entries. Blake and Pete gave him the ideas and he sketched them. Several showed caricatures of officers wearing Dick Tracy style hats sneaking around the corridors trying to catch midshipmen bowling. One showed the commandant (better known as "Twitch") standing in front of his battalion officers shouting, "I want those bowlers!" Others showed the superintendent chewing out the commandant for not finding the source of bowling balls. Twitch gave the search his best effort, but the culprits were never discovered. Rumor had it that he secretly took it in stride, believing it funny, and that he joked with some of his officers that it was just kids letting off steam.

What did get out among his classmates was the name Blake Lawrence III. Sam, political strategist for Blake's campaign for president of the class, leaked just enough that his candidate's name was connected to the supposedly secret Greenfield fight as well as the Philo N. McGiffin prank. When asked why they voted for Blake, classmates would say because his name was on their minds at the time.

Sam got the classmates of their company and battalion involved. He designed the posters and handouts, then organized the door-to-door hand shaking by Blake and others on his behalf. Came the day for the election, Blake and another mid with top-of-the-class grades were locked in a dead heat. But Sam, without Blake's knowledge, had the last word. Just before the votes were to be collected, he put out the word that the other guy was a chess-playing yacht sailor while Blake had been the star of last year's plebe basketball team. In the world of all things superior and inferior, chess and yachts were near the bottom of the macho list and although brains were important, macho played a bigger part in who would become president of the class.

"Blake won! Class president!" Sam exclaimed. "Our strategy turned it. Actually he won by a lot. We just finished counting the votes. He'll be here in a few minutes. Get ready."

Sam's audience was Pete and the entire group of classmates who worked on the campaign. They had all squeezed into Blake's room to surprise him.

'Shhh. He's coming," Sam said from his position at the door where he was peeking through a crack.

The door opened and everyone shouted, "Congratulations! Into the natatorium!"

Pete, Sam, and a couple of others grabbed Blake and rushed him back out the door. With all the other classmates following, they carried his squirming body down the steps and out the door of the third wing, shouting, "Dunk the pres! Dunk the pres!"

Blake figured it was inevitable, so he only pretended mildly to seek freedom. Past upper classmen and "jimmy legs" (civilian security), they took him to the edge of the pool where they swung him back and forth, and on the count of three let him fly.

They stood along the edge singing, "For he's a jolly good fellow, for he's a jolly good fellow, for he's a jolly good fellow, as nobody can deny."

As he splashed about in the water, Blake thought how quickly his life had changed. As class president, he was now brought into the higher echelons of academy life. Things would never be the same.

*****

Blake met Viva at the bus station. She looked sensational, dressed for the football game in a plaid skirt and bright yellow sweater that nearly matched her short blonde hair. He decided not to comment on the color change. He just assumed she wore it like that for a part in a musical or play. He took her luggage and led her toward the drag house where he had made reservations three weeks before. Drag houses, a carry-over from when midshipmen were paid only $3.00 a month, continued to be a blessing for their dates because they were less expensive than hotels.

Mrs. Plumbly, a matronly Navy widow, came well recommended for two reasons. She was popular with the drags because she seemed to understand and sympathize with them. She kept an assortment of solutions to recurring weekend problems, like missing buttons. But the primary reason her place was so well liked by midshipmen was because she had a basement room full of couches and chairs where she permitted the lights to be turned low after the proms.

After introducing Viva to Mrs. Plumbly, Blake waited in the living room of the colonial-style brick home while Viva stowed her luggage in her assigned room. She came down the stairs with Mrs. Plumbly, who already knew that Viva was a student at Juilliard, a singer and dancer who had set her sights on an entertainment career.

"She doesn't know anything about the academy, Mr. Lawrence. You must show her around before the game."

It took them only about ten minutes to walk to the Maryland Avenue gate, where Blake began pointing out the various training buildings on the campus. There was the museum, and the academic halls Mahan, Maury, Griffin, and Sampson, all named after naval heros. "They're where we study engineering."

He also pointed out the administration building where the superintendent flew his flag. As they passed the chapel he told her it was where John Paul Jones was buried.

"I thought he died in France."

"How did you know that?" Blake asked.

"Don't remember. Maybe high school history," she said. "No. It was in a play I saw."

"You're right. But he has been here in a crypt since 1913."

"I know. Don't tell me. He said -- What's your famous Navy slogan? Wait, don't tell me, I remember." She lowered her voice and said, "'I have not yet begun to fight!'"

"You know more about him than I do," Blake said.

"I know he was a murderer."

"Was not! You don't know that," Blake said.

"Well, Congress wouldn't promote him to rear admiral but the Russians did and he ended up in Paris, where he died."

They continued their stroll through the yard. She seemed sincere in her interest about the place. Blake noticed that she seemed to have a bent for history.

"When was the academy founded?" Viva asked.

"1845."

"Old... Very old place," She said. "But not as old as West Point."

"Ugh! Wash your mouth. That's a dirty word."

"Oh, pooh. I know West Point too, and what a history it has! Probably shouldn't tell you this, but I went to a dance there -- last month. Dreary place on the Hudson River, not as far from New York as this is."

She's not my girl. Why should I feel this way? Jealous of a Woo Poo.

He pretended not to hear that she had dated a cadet, so he just babbled on, telling her extraneous information about the place. "Midshipmen were trained on ships before the academy was founded. This place used to be an Army post -- old Fort Severn."

"How do you know so much about the place?" She asked.

"Good plebe year. Upper class make you learn it."

"Plebe year sounds just like the entertainment business. It's so hard to break in, most quit. Only a few make it. I'm going to get a contract soon."

"Contract?"

"Yes, for a show or even a movie. I want to be a star someday."

"I've no doubt you will. You're certainly pretty enough."

"Well, thank you, sir." They walked shoulder to shoulder, Viva on his left so that his right hand was free to salute. She reached to take Blake's left hand. As she tried to slip it into his, he made a fist.

"No hand holding," he scolded.

"You're kidding! No hand holding? That's silly."

"I can be fried."

"Fried?"

"Put on report, demerits?"

"For holding hands? I knew the military was rigid, but holding hands?"

"Crazy," he smiled and joked. "You know we're gentlemen by act of Congress, and it's against regulations for a *gentleman* to show affection in public."

"Are you all crazy? You are! And I obviously have a lot to learn about the military. What happens after you graduate?" she asked.

"We're commissioned as ensigns in the Navy or second lieutenants in the Army, Marine Corps, or Air Force."

"How do you get in?"

"By nomination."

"That's another thing similar to Juilliard. I had to be nominated to go there."

"What kind of nomination?" Blake asked.

"High school teachers. Juilliard has to believe we have talent."

As they approached Bancroft Hall, he saluted a passing officer, then led Viva near the statue of Tecumseh. From there he pointed out Mother B as well as MacDonough, Luce, Dahlgren, and Ward Halls. "Much of our practical ship and war training like seamanship and gunnery are taught there."

"Your buildings -- they all look alike," Viva said. "Same architect?"

Blake shrugged his shoulders. "Don't know. Never thought about it. An architect named Earnest Flagg did Mother B."

"I wonder what the architects were trying to portray. Whatever it was, they had no sense of art. For me the buildings have the drab hide of a battleship with long, square, sharp edges. The lines remind me of a fortress; the only thing missing are the guns. But where's the soul? It might reflect a weakness in your education; lots of engineering, but no sense of art or literature."

"I've got to go to noon meal formation. We get inspected," he said, passing off on her disparaging remarks about the buildings and their training.

Nobody said she couldn't have her own opinion.

"Wait here near the Indian and watch. I'll find you."

"Oh, look," Viva said. "There's Flame. I'll wait with her."

"Yeah, guess you didn't know. She's dating Hamm McClinton."

"She's too young to be dating here," Viva commented.

He took off in a run toward the ranks of midshipmen waiting to be inspected.

*****

When Blake returned, Viva and Flame were standing together. Although they were in the same company, Hamm McClinton had somehow arrived first. Flame had her head resting against Hamm's chest, her hands were wrapped in his. The messenger of the watch (MOW), a plebe, came double-timing toward them. Hamm stepped away from Flame, but it was too late. The MOW stopped in front of him and said, "Sir, the officer of the watch sent me to get your name and company number. He said to tell you that you are on report for conduct unbecoming a midshipman and public show of affection, sir."

Blake and Viva separated themselves from the embarrassing activity of a MOW taking a name, so the

OOW could dispense a Form 2, the record of the offense.

Everyone stood for the National Anthem and stayed on their feet for the entry of the team.

A huge roar went up from the midshipmen as their team ran onto the field. Signs came out of nowhere that said "Philo McGiffin has returned!" and "Who threw the bowling balls?"

McGiffin even became the hero of the team. Their chants while doing warm-up exercises before each game included the chant: "One, two, three, four, who are we fighting for? Philo! Philo! Philo!"

The brigade came up with two new cheers: "Balls, balls, who's got balls? Balls, balls, who's got balls? Balls, balls, we got balls!" And "Bowling balls, bowling balls, Navy! Bowling balls, bowling balls, Navy! Roll it over 'em, Navy! Roll it over 'em, Navy!"

Viva had to shout above the noise, "What's that all about? Who's Philo McGiffin?"

"Oh, some old grad. Did some colorful things about seventy years ago. Some mids rolled bowling balls down a ladder inside Bancroft Hall, just as Philo did when he was a mid. The brigade is having some fun with it."

"Why do some midshipmen have more stripes on their arms than others?"

As if he hadn't heard the question, Blake said, "Well, strange that you ask. Midshipmen have always been pranksters."

"You mean like the Philo thing?"

"Yeah, I guess," he shouted above the screaming and cheers of a spirited brigade. "My granddad told me the early boys here were very undisciplined, so the Navy created a way for the mids to govern themselves. Now there's a shadow command organization from a one-stripe midshipman ensign up to a six-stripe brigade captain."

"Why don't you have more than one stripe?"

"Different stripes. Mine's one diagonal, next year two diagonals, then as a first classman they'll be horizontal. Only firsties can be stripers."

"Is that a goat?" she shouted.

"Bill the Goat. Our mascot."

"He's beautiful."

"They groom him for the games -- a fresh bath and brushing. Stinks otherwise. A goat's been around almost from the beginning of Navy football, which began way back in 1882."

Kickoff. The game began. The opposing teams ran at each other and collided mid-field. Viva had a more-than-passing interest in the game. The opposing school, University of Pennsylvania, was located in Philadelphia.

"I'll bet you Navy wins!" Blake shouted.

"No bet! Penn plays lousy football," Viva said.

And they did. Navy scored almost at will. By the half the score was 26-0 and nearing the end of the game, Navy had racked up 34 points. "Viva! Blake said. "Look, they're putting Erie in the game."

"Erie?"

"Yeah. My buddy. His real name is Larry Tallman. We went through boot camp together -- and a lot of other stuff."

Erie played linebacker and although he was tall and slender, it seemed to Blake that he hit as hard as anyone on the varsity. Navy held and Penn kicked. "There goes Stone." Blake shouted. "They put him in, too."

"Stone? He and Erie are negros?"

"Yeah, so? Stone was my plebe summer roommate. Real name is Emerald Groler. Look he's going out for a pass. Ah, he missed it – bad pass! But Stone is fast. Did you see him run?"

The whistle blew and the game was over. Score 34-7. Penn's only score came at the expense of the Navy substitutes.

Afterwards, Blake took Viva to The Hitching Post, a small restaurant not far from the Maryland State House. When they finished he told her, "The dance starts at 1930, er -- 7:30 so we haven't got much time. I'll leave you at the drag house and be back after I change."

*****

"You look beautiful!" Blake said as he watched Viva descend the steps from the second floor of Mrs. Plumbly's house. She was wearing a below the knee blue pastel formal that left the tops of her breasts exposed.

"You do, too! What is that uniform?"

"Our full dress. It's turned chilly -- may snow. Better take a wrap with you."

"And white gloves, no less. Let me count your buttons... hmm. Eighteen. It's a bit like the West Point uniform."

"But better."

*****

They went through a receiving line that included the commandant and his wife and several of the senior officers of the academic departments and their ladies. Blake and Viva then made their way to the dance floor where they moved to the slow music of a full orchestra playing music from the big band era. The song was

Claude Thornhill's "Snow Fall." Viva's perfume rose like an evening mist over a warm river. It seeped into Blake's nostrils like an intoxicating potion. He held her tight. She rested her head on his shoulder, a hand on the back of his neck. Their bodies swayed to the pleasant sounds. Inside he felt the same as he felt after he left her in New York, heart pounding, nervous like a puppy. She was fun and loving. She seemed to concentrate on him and only him. She aroused him. When the beat changed to a more vibrant rhythm, Viva left Blake shuffling his feet in one place as she spun around, demonstrating her considerable dancing skills. The center of the floor became hers and everyone stopped to watch. She liked the attention. She had an audience.

When it was over, the band took a break. He pointed her in the direction of the punch bowl and looked around for familiar faces. Erie and his girl stood nearby. "Saw you play today, Erie. Looked good."

"My first game. I wouldn't have got in except they were so bad. You remember Patty, don't you?"

Blake did remember Patty. She was Erie's longtime girl friend from his hometown whom Blake had met on a weekend in Chicago when the two young men were sailors.

"Of course. Long time since I met you, Patty. Back when we were at Great Lakes, wasn't it? Larry Tallman, this is Viva -- Kathy Velenochi. She's from Philadelphia."

"So we finally meet. Weren't you in Cannes last summer?" Erie asked.

"Yes, how did you know?"

"Blake talks about you all the time."

*****

They climbed the stairs to the gallery of Dahlgren Hall. It overlooked the large room that served as a ballroom and indoor basketball court. Below was a sea of couples dancing, dressed alike, pastels and blue uniforms. Blake explained, "I play basketball on a portable court right down there." As they listened she leaned her head against his shoulder and remarked, "I hope this isn't showing too much public affection, but this is kind of romantic."

"It's getting close to the time we can leave. Let's go down and stand by the door. I only have a half hour after the dance to be back in Bancroft Hall."

"Only a half hour? That's another silly rule."

*****

Because the air had turned brisk, they half-walked and half ran from Dahlgren Hall to Mrs. Plumbly's. By the time they arrived, others who were regulars at the dances were already there. The lights were very low. Blake and Viva stumbled their way over bodies occupying every chair and couch. She whispered, "Blake, this is silly." They found an unoccupied chair in the dark basement. He sat first and pulled her on to his lap. "This is silly --" she said again. He kissed her. "Blake --" They kissed again, passionately. Silence.

His heart felt like a piston throbbing in ecstasy. He wanted to stay, but he heard the other mids leaving. "I have to go."

"Don't go," she said.

"I have to. But, I'll be back out after church. We're required to attend chapel. Would you like to come?"

"Not tomorrow. Can't you stay?"

"Nope. Bye."

"Can't you come back? I heard that some guys sneak out over the wall."

"Maybe. Don't wait up."

They kissed and he ran all the way back to Bancroft Hall. As he was passing the chapel he spotted Hamm McClinton and Flame behind a bush necking.

"Hambone. You better hurry. You'll be late for sign in."

"Coming."

As part of what was called the "flying squadron," the two ran and, on arrival, found a long sign-in line. The cold snap had caught most without coats. Midshipmen stomped the ground to keep warm. Hamm McClinton whispered, "Blake, we're going back out. Want to come?"

"Going back out? Over the wall?"

"Shhh. Not so loud. Going over the wall. Later, about one o'clock. Want us to come get you?"

Although not everyone did it, everyone knew what "going over the wall" meant. Midshipmen were required to be in their rooms from taps to reveille, no liberty. A brick wall surrounded the landward side of the Academy, which provided enough resistance for most midshipmen. But for some, the wall served as a challenge. Defeat it and you were among the silent heroes who took liberty when they damn well wanted, not when the superintendent permitted. The penalty for getting caught was a class A offense worth many hours of restriction and marching under arms.

Blake weighed the relative benefits of going over the wall with Hambone. If he did he could be with Viva.

CHAPTER 20

HALF WAY

Blake lay awake. It was a silly thing to do – go over the wall. But then he could be with Viva. Should he or shouldn't he? He looked at the clock. It was after midnight. Where was Hamm?

Blake closed his eyes.

He woke to one of those special Annapolis mornings that seldom happen in the mild Maryland climate. An early blanket of fresh white snow covered the windowsill. The yard looked like a Christmas carol. Dark-colored tree limbs contrasted with the wind-blown powder that covered bare branches. The sky was perfectly blue except for high streaks of stratus clouds. The room was chilly, so he stood by the radiator and pulled his bathrobe under his chin. He watched the early church boys, the ones who went out to the town to services. They wore their heavy overcoats, the ones with their gold buttons from chin to knee. Their high collars were turned up, partially covering white scarves that matched the color of the snow.

Breakfast formations were straggle affairs: form up and march without regard to platoon order. When Blake and his two roommates took their seats, they sensed a difference. Ordinarily, the brigade came and went to a Sunday morning breakfast in subdued silence. But this morning the mess hall was like a chicken coop when a fox is nearby.

"What's going on?" Pete asked a classmate at a nearby table.

"There's a girl in the mess hall," came the response.

"No shit? Where!" Sam asked.

"Right over there -- with the sailing team." He pointed at a table nearest the galley, where eleven members of the sailing team surrounded a midshipman with hair tucked into a bun. Hamm McClinton sat opposite her. He had a silly grin on his face as if he enjoyed the notoriety.

Blake saw it as an act of stupidity; he could tell from the hair color that it was Flame. Apparently they had changed their plans and didn't go out, because here she was in the mess hall surrounded by men. Her body language showed that she was enjoying it.

Sam jumped to his feet and ran to the table. "Flame! What in the hell are you doing here?"

"Why, Sammy. There you are. Isn't this fun?"

"Hambone! How did she get in here?" Sam asked.

"Through a window," she responded innocently.

"Hamm, are you nuts?" Sam cautioned. "You better get her out of here."

But it was too late. The midshipman officer of the watch, a four-striper (lieutenant commander) arrived. He had been at the main table and just followed the trail of whispers about a girl in Bancroft Hall. He asked, "How did she get in here? Who's she with?"

"Ah, she's with me," Hamm said. "We're leaving. I'll get her out." The other members of the sailing team quickly faded out of the mess hall, leaving only Hamm and Flame.

"What's your name?"

"Hamm McClinton."

"The two of you better follow me to the main office."

*****

Chapel services were a non-denominational event for all Christian midshipmen, but they were mandatory except for those who had special permission to go out in town to a service.

After chapel, Blake returned to the drag house where he found Viva and several other girls curled up on a couch still in their pajamas, listening to Mrs. Plumbly's stories about Navy life as the wife of a naval officer. The drags seemed to find her story humorous because they held their sides laughing. Blake, who didn't find them interesting at all, had a hard time getting Viva to come outside for a private conversation. When he finally got her to stop giggling, he said, "Hamm McClinton and Flame are in trouble. What time does your bus leave? I have to get back to Bancroft Hall. They have Hamm in the commandant's office. Gonna hang him. Flame's there also, but they have to let her go. Can you come with me and make sure she gets home okay?"

"What did they do?"

"He got her into Bancroft Hall last night. He might have got away with that, but he took her into the mess hall for breakfast this morning. Guess he thought he'd show her off or something. Dumb. Immature. For a guy who is the top of the class academically, he isn't very smart. Anyway, he's not going to see daylight for a couple of months -- they'll Class A him."

"Class A?"

"Heavy-duty punishment. They used to put mids in the brig for a Class A. But now they just restrict them to Mother B -- lots of marching and no liberty."

Viva seemed unconcerned about Flame. "I'll come over with you, but Flame can take care of herself. She got down here on her own -- she can get back the same way. I won't take long."

Blake scratched his head. *There she goes again. She can be loving one minute and show total lack of concern the next. A little like her getting ahead at any cost. Skirt the unpleasant.*

Sunday mornings are normally quiet in Bancroft Hall. Midshipmen come and go to church services in a reverent manner. Even the main office is a passive place. But on this Sunday, the commandant, a battalion officer, and Blake's company officer huddled around a table where fifteen-year-old Crimson Mallon (alias Flame) and Hamm McClinton sat. In addition, the six-striper and several other midshipmen officers surrounded the group.

Flame no longer wore her borrowed midshipman uniform. Instead she was dressed in the short evening gown of purple and greens she wore the evening before at the hop. Hamm sat at attention, looking very much like a plebe instead of a youngster. Blake and Viva stood off to one side. Flame, totally oblivious to the seriousness of it all, seemed to think it was just a prank. "Don't all the girls get to stay overnight in Bancroft Hall?"

The commandant, Captain Robert O'Brian, the same gray-haired man who had given Blake's class the oath of office before plebe summer began, hovered across from Hamm. Captain "Bobby" or "Twitch," as the midshipmen called him behind his back, was the kind of officer who saw his charges as nice kids who sometimes did dumb things. The "Twitch" part of his nickname came from the way he moved his chin up and down, apparently because of the discomfort caused by the stiffly starched collars when he wore a blue service uniform. As the equivalent of a college dean of men, Captain O'Brian actually was immensely popular among the mids. His Irish good humor permitted the brigade to take a growing number of privileges that at other times were considered taboo. Earlier classes pronounced the. place "loose" compared to the way it was when they were midshipmen. But having a girl in Bancroft Hall even exceeded Bobby Twitch's boundary of playfulness.

"I want this woman out of the hall immediately!" He shouted.

"Sir, there's a young woman here who says she knows Flame... er Miss Mallon," the six-striper said.

"Who? Where is this person?" Twitch asked.

Blake stepped forward. "She's my date, sir. But she's from Crimson's neighborhood in Philadelphia."

"Oh... it's you, Lawrence. Well, introduce me."

"Captain O'Brian, I'd like you to meet Miss Kathy Velenochi."

"Captain," Viva said.

"You know this girl?" The commandant asked, pointing to Crimson.

"Yes, Flame... er Crimson Mallon. We grew up in the same town. I can get her on a bus. She'll be all right."

"Miss Velenochi, may I speak to you privately?"

"Of course, sir," Viva said respectfully.

She followed the commandant into his office where they talked for a few minutes. Captain O'Brian then asked Flame to go into the room with Viva. When the two girls came out, Viva went to the commandant and whispered into his ear.

"Well, thank heavens for that..." the commandant shook his head. "Thank you, Miss Velenochi. I would be obliged if you would see that she gets safely home. Oh, Lawrence. Talked to your father the other day. Fine man. Was a plebe when I was a firstie."

In the passageway outside the office, Blake, Viva, and Flame could hear the commandant when he said, "Fifteen years old?"

They walked toward the giant rotunda doors out of earshot of the unpleasantness going on behind them. Viva asked, "Flame, where are your things?"

"At Carvell Hall. Why?"

"The commandant asked me to escort you home."

"Escort me home? Why? You're still with Blake, aren't you?"

"I don't have to do as he asked, but Flame, you're only fifteen, and he now feels responsible for your safety. Otherwise he would have to assign an officer to get you home."

"What will they do to Hamm?" Flame asked meekly, finally grasping the seriousness of the situation.

"I don't think they'll kick him out," Blake said. "They could, but my guess is he'll be restricted until after Christmas. I want to get back to find out what's going on. It's best if you take the bus with Viva, back to Philadelphia."

"Why do you have to get involved?" Viva asked Blake.

"Because he's a classmate."

They made their way to pick up Flame's suitcase, then to the drag house where Viva said goodbye to Mrs. Plumbly, then hurried to catch the bus.

"You don't have to come with me. I can get home myself," Flame told Viva.

"Might as well. Blake's turned party poop on me."

While Flame was buying her ticket, Blake took Viva outside. They stood against the wall of the bus station, shivering even though they wore heavy clothes. They clutched each other as much to keep warm as anything else. Through the fog of his breath he said, "I'm sorry, but the weekend's almost over anyway. We could have had lunch and seen more of the school, but I'd have to be back by six for evening meal formation anyway. Will you come again?"

She kissed him. "Of course, if my schedule permits and it's not this cold. Did I tell you I'm in a new show? I'm an understudy again, but I get to sing this time."

"No! That's wonderful. Why didn't you tell me earlier?"

"I was having too good a time."

"Well, break a leg!"

"Thanks, darling."

"I really had a good time," he said.

"I did too, Blake. When I come again I think I'll stay at a hotel. We'll have more privacy." She kissed him again, this time with great passion.

CHAPTER 21

AMPHIBIOUS TRAINING

Youngster year came to an end. The class had put another year behind them. But now, in the minds of many, the countdown to graduation had begun even though they were only half-way there. Looking back, Blake could identify three significant things that happened during the year. He was elected president of his class and he had achieved his first stars for high grades in academics. The third thing was the best. He had a girlfriend, albeit they never had another date after Hamm McClinton got Class A demerits for the fateful "girl-in-the-hall" escapade. Based on his showing in a few games, there was one other thing. He had a chance to make the varsity basketball team again next year.

On the other side of his tally was the low light of the year. Navy had lost again to Army in both football and basketball.

Viva was supposed to come back for spring dance but she suddenly became popular on Broadway and her schedule as a performer kept her in New York. They talked occasionally and he wrote, but the school year ended without a chance to see her again.

Hamm McClinton survived the year but due to his Black 'N' (Class A offense), he spent several months on confinement to Mother B. In fact he stood last in conduct and his accumulated demerits knocked him off the Star Man list. There was also a rumor going around that Flame was pregnant.

Blake received one more phone call and a couple of short letters from Greenfield. He had completed flight training and been assigned to a fighter squadron in Europe. He and his new bride, as part of their honeymoon, would take a ship across the Atlantic. Greenfield expected that would be the last time he would see the ocean except from 15,000 feet. He ended his last letter with, "Blake, I really love what I'm doing. Flying jets is exciting but very demanding. It's not drone-work like much of my 'Four Years by the Bay.' When I'm not flying, I actually have time to think. Keep struggling for the meaning of it all. What makes an academy officer different, if we are?"

Shortly after the firsties became ensigns, Blake and the rest of the new second class boarded several large troop ships anchored in the Chesapeake, which then made their way to Norfolk, Virginia, the home of the Atlantic training command. Soon after arriving at the naval base the lectures began, some by naval officers and a few by Marines.

This period of training, which continued their practical growth, was for the entire second class from Annapolis as well as some cadets from West Point, taught conduct of military operations by naval, air, and land forces for the purpose of seizing a beach or coastal area was complex. Blake looked forward to it because his grandfather had told him about its success during World War II.

The class knew it was in for a hot summer. They were billeted in quonset huts on Virginia Beach. The huts were surrounded by sand and had no ventilation except four small windows on the sides and small end doors, all of which were kept closed much of the time to discourage mosquitoes and flies.

In the evening after their first day of lectures, the cadets and midshipmen made their way across the hot sands to their liberty. They found the gedunk stand, a wall-less quonset hut that held a number of long tables. The beer stand offered green bottles of Regent beer, which tasted much like the color of the bottle. Throughout their time together, the students of the two academies exchanged curiosities about the others' school. Why do you say this? Why do you do that? Blake mentioned to a cadet named Frank Nichols that his brother was considering attending at West Point and that he was named, on their mother's side, after an uncle Charles Nichols, who had graduated in the early 30's. Blake offered, "Wouldn't it be something if we were related?" But Frank said, "It's doubtful. Don't think anyone else from our family ever got above private first class, but we had lots of those. They were all warriors and the reason I'm in the Army." As the two drank the green beer and talked, they came to realize how similar the two schools were. Each had a plebe summer, each had a rough plebe year followed by immersion into the practical side of their services. Both had an honor system based roughly on the same elements of ethics: they would not lie, steal, or cheat, nor tolerate those who do.

Neither Blake nor Frank could handle their alcohol very well, and before the night was over, ended up staggering back to barracks arm in arm singing songs and talking too loudly for those who had already gone to bed.

*****

The next day they were back in their seats and the training began. "Thank you, gentlemen. Let's get started. I'm Lieutenant Commander Daggett R. Sherman, and this will be your introduction to amphibious operations which are considered the most complex form of warfare." To the discriminating eyes of cadets and midshipmen, Sherman looked squared away. His foggy voice emphasized, "An amphibious operation is the art of landing troops over a beach to take property during war. The ancient Greeks and Romans carried out early forms of these seaborne landings. As early as 1066, the Normans undertook a successful amphibious landing when they invaded England."

The beer from the night before rested heavily and soon Blake, along with most of the students who had consumed the green stuff, dozed off.

"The Normans were aided in their successful landing by a chance happening. While Harold, then King of England, was waiting for the Normans to arrive, he received."

"Zzzzzz."

"Known as the historic Battle of Hastings, it established the Norman rule of England. That amphibious landing went well..."

"Zzzzz..."

"Harold was defeated and slain. William marched on to London and was crowned king of England on Christmas Day, 1066..."

"Zzzzz..."

"But not all amphibious landings go well," Lieutenant Commander Sherman continued. "The battle for Gallipoli..."

"Zzzzz..."

By this time most of the class was snoring quite loudly but nothing disturbed Sherman's march through time.

"The Gallipoli landing was ..."

"Zzzz..."

"The Allied forces -- especially the ANZACS -- suffered severe casualties during the landings. Allied naval attacks in the area had alerted the Turks, who had strengthened their military defenses on the peninsula..."

Blake woke up in time to see Sherman point to a map of the Gallipoli area.

"The ANZACS were never able to penetrate very far inland and they suffered heavy losses and they were ordered to withdraw from the Gallipoli Peninsula. The campaign was a failure. A total of 5,833 Australian soldiers were killed in action during that campaign. Almost 2000 more soldiers died of wounds, bringing Australian battle losses to 7,818. A total of 19,441 Australian soldiers were wounded. A total of 2,721 New Zealanders were killed and 4,752 were wounded."

Blake looked around and discovered the entire class awake and listening closely to Sherman. The count of dead and wounded brought them back to the lecture that was all at once turning out to be damn interesting.

"The lesson of this story is to learn from our mistakes -- and the U.S. Navy did just that. We perfected this method of warfare by learning from the disastrous British operation in Gallipoli as well as others.

"Amphibious operations played a major role in World War II. In the Pacific, a common objective of our amphibious operations was to seize islands on which to build advance air and naval bases for operations against Japan. Early in the war, the Japanese carried out amphibious assaults on the Philippines, Malaya, and the East Indies. American forces counterattacked with amphibious landings. Beginning at Guadalcanal in the Solomon Islands, they worked their way toward Japan by landing on numerous Pacific islands. Allied troops also made amphibious invasions of North Africa and Italy. The Allied landing at Normandy in northern France on June 6, 1944, was the largest amphibious invasion in history. During the Korean War, U.S. Marines made a difficult but highly successful landing at the Korean port of Inchon on the Yellow Sea."

*****

The class returned the next day for more lectures. The buzz among the midshipmen was that although there were spots of interesting stuff, most of what they had heard so far was boring. If the rest of their training was similar, it would be a long, hot summer. The next instructor, a ramrod straight Marine captain dressed in sharply pressed fatigues stood with his pointer before a visual prop and droned like he was reading from a technical manual.

"I am Captain Steven McQuaid, United States Marine Corps." He clicked his heels and saluted.

He went on, oblivious to the snickers from some of the mids.

"This lecture will be about the steps in amphibious operations. But first let us review what we learned from Gallipoli. We learned to provide clear command channels..."

Midshipmen began snoring in their seats again. "Zzzzz..."

"We learned never to attack prematurely with insufficient forces, and finally we learned to have our supplies and equipment stowed aboard ship in the order they will be used ashore.

"Gentlemen, that completes my lecture." He clicked his heels and saluted.

A roar of approval went up from the audience, not because it was good -- but because it was over.

*****

The next day the captain in charge of their training stood behind the lectern. He wore the wings of an aviator and looked younger than the Marine Corps captain who preceded him. He wore a tailored uniform that perfectly fit his tall, slender body. "Gentlemen. Get in your seats. Thank you. Now settle down. After this talk you can get on to liberty call. I am Captain Frank Jellico, Class of 1939, USNA, and my topic is one of my heroes. His name is Richmond Kelly Turner. Admiral Turner was born in Portland, Oregon, and graduated from the U.S. Naval Academy in 1908."

The mid next to Blake said, "Here we go again. Time to get some more sleep."

But Blake's thoughts immediately jumped to his grandfather. *Turner entered just as my granddad, who was in the Class of '04, was graduating – wonder if they knew each other?*

Captain Jellico went on, "Admiral Turner learned to fly in 1927 but wanted command of a ship, so he left aviation and eventually, despite his inexperience in the relatively new field of amphibious warfare, became the leading American naval amphibious commander in the Pacific Ocean during World War II.

"In December 1941, as a rear admiral, he became assistant chief of staff to the commander-in-chief of the U.S. Fleet. He then went to the Pacific in July 1942 to direct amphibious operations in the Solomon Islands campaign. While in that command, he worked out highly efficient and successful techniques of ship-to-shore movement. Turner served as amphibious commander in most of the naval actions in the central and southern Pacific, including Guadalcanal, New Georgia, the Gilbert, Marshall, and Mariana Islands, Iwo Jima, and Okinawa."

Unlike the marine captain who clung to the lectern and his pointer as if they were chains, Captain Jellico now moved to the center of the stage. "What I want you to remember about Admiral Turner is what I call the characteristic of 'winning at war.' He had it and you'll need it if you stay in the military. You see, Admiral Turner was a mark one, mod zero *prick*."

Those in the audience who were dozing immediately awoke. Everyone sat up straight. Midshipmen and cadets nudged each other. The cadet next to Blake snickered and snorted as he asked, "Did he say prick?"

It wasn't that they didn't know the word. They just never expected to hear a senior naval officer say it in public and certainly never to disparage a four-star World War II naval hero.

"There is, as you know, more than one kind of prick," Captain Jellico continued. "I don't mean the kind who are vengeful and vindictive -- always ready to hang an imperfect world. And I don't want you to have the impression that I am disrespectful of Admiral Turner. He was the best kind of prick -- the kind who wins battles and wars. I'll pull no punches about Admiral Turner but intend no disrespect. I believe he would endorse that he was the 'pull no punches' kind of man needed to run amphibious operations. Why? Because of the complexity of this business! They called him "Terrible Turner," and he was as greatly admired and loved as he was hated by a few others. They say he was the kind of man who could see the trees and at the same time comprehend the entire forest. He had all the characteristics of a leader: courage, drive to win, knowledge, integrity, and generosity of spirit. True, he was hard and he did lack patience, but only with those who lacked capacity in the rough, tough, complex amphibious game played out in the Pacific. The Army had their Patton and we had Turner. And thank God for it!"

"During your training at Annapolis and West Point you may have time to reflect on your personal heroes -- those whom you might wish to pattern your life after. You could do no better that to become like this man -- Richmond Kelly Turner. At this time you may not like those who you think are of the prick variety, but someday you may not find that so."

He paused then went on. "Let me tell you about 'Terrible Turner of Tarawa.'

By now the students were on the edge of their seats. They wanted to know more about the kind of prick who won wars.

"At the time the Japanese Imperial Army's book on Americans was, and I quote, 'The character of the American is simple and lacking in tenacity and battle leadership. If they have a setback, they have a tendency to abandon one plan for another.' But they didn't know Admiral Richmond Kelly Turner. He had recently had his flagship shot out from under him in defense of the Guadalcanal Marines during the disastrous American defeat of Savo Island. In his noble way he said, 'Whatever responsibility for the defeat is mine, I accept.' Admiral Turner went on to say, 'We got up off the deck and gave the Japs one hell of a beating.'

"Instead of firing Turner, Admiral Nimitz promoted him and put him in charge of American naval forces when they invaded Tarawa in the Gilberts in November 1943. Tarawa is only about as big as Central Park in New York City, but the attackers met heavy fire from Japanese troops in concrete bunkers. After four days of savage fighting they inched forward and captured the tiny island. About 4,500 Japanese soldiers died defending the island. Only 17 remained alive. The number of American naval officers killed in action was 62; Marine officers 58; Marine enlisted 922; and Navy enlisted 684. Total American casualties, wounded and dead were more than 3,000. Ours is a grim business.

"The Allies improved their amphibious operations because of lessons they learned at Tarawa. As a result, fewer men died in later landings, and Terrible Turner of Tarawa went on to command landing after landing. He was poised to make the invasion of Japan at Kyushu when the atomic bombs were dropped ending the war.

"Now take your liberty and be back here tomorrow, ready to go to sea and actually put into practice what we have learned here in the classroom by making a real landing. Be ready!"

CHAPTER 22

THE LANDING

"All right, listen up! Remember this," the chief bos'n mate shouted. "When you're climbing down the cargo nets, keep your hands on the vertical ropes. The horizontal rungs are for your feet! Step carefully into the LCTs and LCVPs. Hunker down and be ready to charge when the doors open. And, remember that the good ladies of Norfolk will be waiting at the cotillion tonight as the reward for a good amphibious landing."

They were dressed in their green fatigues. Each wore a combat helmet and, slung over their shoulders, a rifle without ammunition. After three days aboard the cargo ships, they were in position and ready to execute H-Hour of D-Day. Blake could see boats cruising in circular patterns waiting to make the side of the ship and load these new soldiers for their baptism into cross-beach landings. LCTs (landing craft tanks), which were nicknamed "large vomiting tanks," came alongside. The mids and cadets scampered down the cargo nets to the waiting craft. As soon as one boat was loaded, another came alongside.

LCMs (landing craft mediums) and LCUs (landing craft utilities) would bring the larger equipment after the troops aboard LCTs secured the beach. Round and round they circled in the heavy seas until all the troops were loaded. Finally the LCTs lined up parallel to the beach and upon signal began their approach.

"Keep your heads down!" It was Marine Captain McQuaid, standing beside the boat cox'n. Assigned as a safety observer he wore marine fatigues and a combat helmet. Instead of a weapon. he carried a bullhorn.

Blake was a squad leader for about thirty other midshipmen and despite the warning to keep his head down, he peeked and saw line after line of landing craft heading for the beaches off Little Creek, Virginia.

I bet this is what it was sort of like D-day at Nor-mandy: excited and nervous. What will happen when the ramp falls forward and we all rush ashore?

He remembered his grandfather telling him about the hundreds of soldiers who died at Normandy when they stepped off into deep water with heavy loads on their backs. They drowned without firing a shot at their enemy.

"I said, keep your head down, Mr. Lawrence. This is no game."

With a thud, the boat rammed into the sand. They pushed forward. Shouting "Arrrgh!" like lions needing a good meal, they jumped into the water and waded until they could race onto the sand. Blake led the charge across open space cluttered with old rusty tanks and other obstacles. Diving behind whatever would provide cover, they pretended to fight an invisible enemy.

"Bang, bang, bang!" they shouted. Like playing soldier when they were kids, the new students of amphibious warfare crawled along, popping up from time to time and pretending to fire their rifles and throw grenades. In the distance they heard recorded sounds of bombs and cannons going off.

The objective for Blake's squad was a small hut from which gunsmoke blossomed into the hot air. Captain McQuaid again shouted, "Keep your heads down! Those could be live rounds!"

Using a crablike creep, one elbow after another reaching out, pushing the rifle ahead, the squad slithered slowly toward the box-shaped building. Sand blew into their eyes. Sweat drained from under helmets, down their faces and across sunburned noses. They reached a point about twenty feet from the target.

This is just training. The sooner it's over, the sooner I can get these guys their liberty.

He rose up, shouting, "Follow me!" He ran toward the hut and threw a practice grenade, but the puffs of smoke from the small building continued as the rest of his squad came after him. He heard Captain McQuaid shout, "You're all dead! That was stupid, Mr. Lawrence! I told you how to take that place. Your John Wayne impersonation got every single one of your men killed!" McQuaid stood nose to nose with Blake. His facial coloring matched the red on the tips of his ears. Worse than plebe year, the humiliation hurt. In front of his classmates, this salty Marine said, "Stand at attention and tall! Carry yourself like the officer you want to become! You are stupid, an idiot, and a numbskull."

"Okay... you, mister... yes, you! What's your name?"

"Jackson, sir."

"Okay. Lawrence, you're fired. Midshipman Jackson, you're the squad leader now. Back to the LCT and we start over. This time, do what I tell you."

For another hour they raced from the beached landing craft and drilled in the techniques of attacking a building. Finally, tired, sweaty, and hungry, they boarded busses that returned them to their quonset huts and preparations for the Cotillion organized by the society ladies of greater Norfolk.

Blake's thoughts were not about girls. He thought about his screwup and Captain Steven McQuaid, United States Marine Corps. He knew McQuaid was right, but still the public embarrassment ground deep. He wondered if his classmates would remember the tongue-lashing or his leadership mistake. The amphibious phase was over and he was to be the senior midshipman of his class for the aviation training. Would they willingly follow him like they followed their classmate Lee Locke? Blake's new duties would begin the day after they went aboard the U.S.S. *Valley Forge* CVS-45 in Norfolk. In the meantime, Blake had various administrative matters such as rosters and watch bills to attend to. He would have preferred to stay and work; nevertheless, he was obligated to put in an appearance at the Cotillion.

In their dress whites with the high collars and gold buttons, the cadets and midshipmen strode into the hall looking very much as if they came right out *of Gone With the Wind*. Norfolk's best stood waiting. They looked as if they were from a century earlier, a time when there were magnolias, mansions, masters, and mistresses. Some of his 20-year-old classmates had leering eyes; others seemed above it all. So it was with the girls: coquette-like smiles, but bored body language.

The midshipmen and cadets went through the receiving line and were introduced by senior naval officers and their wives to the mayor and his wife, as well as the members of high society who had organized the ball.

"Midshipman Lawrence, sir," Blake said to the first person in line, one of the lesser lights of the ball, who repeated his name to the next in line and so on as he moved toward the senior end and eventually the already dancing classmates and ladies.

The orchestra played southern music, songs such as "My Old Kentucky Home" and "Old Folks at Home" by Stephen Foster. Blake remembered learning about the man when he was in high school, before the Navy. Foster was one of America's best-loved songwriters. He wished Viva was with him now.

He joined Lee Locke and his new cadet friend Frank Nichols, who were trying to decide which of the many girls they would ask to dance. Stone, Blake's plebe summer roommate, joined them and commented, "Not many Negro girls – in fact I don't see one. And I know better than ask a white girl to dance, there'd be a lynching right here in old Virginy."

"I'm not seeing anything too sweet myself," Blake commiserated.

Their conversation flitted from talk about the girls to the amphibious operation and back to girls when an officer came and asked, "Which one of you is Midshipman Lawrence? I was told he was in this group."

Thinking about his episode with Captain McQuaid, Blake said, "Afraid I am, sir. What did I do now?"

"Oh, you haven't done anything wrong, Mr. Lawrence. But I would like to talk to you -- in private."

The two walked to a side door and into a small unoccupied room. As soon as the door was shut the officer, a commander wearing pilot's wings and a chest full of decorations, said, "I'm new on the faculty at the Academy. A new assistant to the new commandant."

"New commandant? I guess I'm the proverbial 10 percent who didn't get the word, sir. I didn't know that Captain O'Brian was leaving." Actually, this was a bit of a fib because everyone was aware that there was bad blood between O'Brian and the superintendent. The sup thought Twitch was too soft.

"The reason I'm here is to tell you that your father is relieving Captain O'Brian and wants to know if you wish to come back for the ceremony."

"Commandant of midshipmen? My father?" Blake's forehead wrinkled into a frown, and his mind leapt to his last meeting with his dad more than two years before. Except for a few telephone calls from him, which Blake never took, their lives never mixed. His dad was serving in the Pentagon, and he was a student.

"Ah, before you answer, you should know that your dad knows you are a second class striper and slated to lead your class for the aviation phase. He said he would understand if you put duty first."

*****

The next morning at 0630 an official Navy car was waiting in front of Blake's quonset hut to take him to Annapolis and his father's change of command ceremony. Blake knew things like this happened in the Navy, but never before to him. Without being told, the driver laid Blake's hanging bag with his full dress whites into the trunk of the customized Ford.

Blake had considered not going to Annapolis for the ceremony. If he didn't go, it would be a way to get even with his dad for his hurt. The Navy had removed most of his good excuses. He was told someone else could temporarily handle his duties for the aviation phase. No one else knew about the arrangements for a military car and airplane to get him there, but it would get around the Academy sooner or later. The school was like a small town where rumors spread faster than a California wildfire. He struggled with his conscience. Blake worried about the perception of nepotism. He worried about what his classmates might think of their class president, who took advantage of his father's rank and new job to fly around the country in a government plane. But he knew to ignore his father's ceremony would not be the right thing. It would mean disrespect, not just to his father, but to the Lawrence name. He didn't need to like his father, but he did have to attend. This way he could get to the ceremony and back to his duties the same day.

Before 10:00 that morning he was sitting in a line of chairs in Tecumseh Court adjacent to the superintendent of the Naval Academy, Vice Admiral Delargy Williamson. The gray-haired sup dressed in impeccably tailored dress whites, acknowledged the new commandant's son's presence with a sharp return of Blake's salute. However, the sup spent most of the pre-ceremony moving among the civilian guests, shaking hands and chatting with the ranking civilians and officers who obviously came from nearby Annapolis and the Washington, D.C. area.

His father had earlier come to greet him. "Thanks for coming," Captain Blake Lawrence II said to Midshipman Blake Lawrence III, "I heard you want to get back to your duties right away. Don't you want to come to our reception after the ceremony?" The question sounded like an order.

"Thank you, sir. But as I understand it, the plane is waiting, and I do have work to do. We get underway aboard *Valley Forge* tomorrow."

"Well -- chip off the old block. Your grandfather would be proud. Give Captain Smith, the CO, my regards. We flew together in VA 124. I've got to take my place. If you change your mind, Rose-Ann and I would like to see you." Then, as if an afterthought, "You know your brother entered West Point this summer. I watched him get sworn in."

"Yes, sir. Mom told me, but I couldn't get away."

A change of command at the Naval Academy has all the pomp and ceremony that can be brought to bear for such occasions. Often the outgoing chief of naval operations and even the chairman of the joint chiefs of. staff used the place for the occasion of their final service appearance. The band played "Ruffles and Flourishes," the colors were paraded, and a chaplain spoke the appropriate words. The superintendent decorated the outgoing commandant and spoke glowingly about his naval service.

In this instance, Captain Robert "Twitch" took the opportunity to retire from the Navy. His body language told the story. Shoulders slightly rolled forward, head and eyes pitched downward, he gave his speech in a monotone delivery. His talk reviewed his service since graduation, which sounded to Blake like a very distinguished, flag-officer. But Blake also knew that the naval service was as political as any other occupation, and one miss-step as captain sent otherwise superb men to the bone-yard of civilian life. Captain O'Brian had begun to look like a very old man.

Finally, the commandant turned to Blake's father and said, "I am ready to be relieved, sir."

Captain Lawrence stood, saluted, and said, "I relieve you, sir."

With those few words the Academy had a new commandant of midshipmen.

Rows of medals splashed across the left breast of a ramrod-straight body. At six feet, almost as tall as Blake, the new commandant presented an authoritative figure. Compared to Twitch's paunchy frame, Captain Lawrence's slender body structure gave the notion that he could still wear his midshipman uniforms. Before he spoke he removed his cap theatrically displaying hair cut shorter than a midshipman's crew cut.

Every officer who assumes command thinks deeply about this first opportunity to speak. Most forego any lengthy address because it is the outgoing officer's day in the sun. Blake had never heard his father speak in public. The new commandant thanked Captain O'Brian for an excellent turnover and bade him smooth sailing, fair winds, and following seas. He recognized the ranking guests and placed both hands on the lectern. He gazed back and forth across the many people seated in rows of folding chairs and began an unusually short speech. "The Naval Academy is the womb and bud of life for our modern Navy. From this place come the men who shape the preparation for future wars as well as those who will fight them. It has never been a place for mollycoddled whiners and snivelers, and it will not be under my watch. I am grateful for the opportunity and hereby accept the responsibility to take my place among the long chain of men who have maintained the high standards of rigor and discipline needed to fight our country's wars."

Blake was stung by the biting message. He saw a smile on the face of Superintendent Williamson but also noted the frown that grew across the forehead of "Twitch," who must have felt deeply the slicing words.

Trouble. I know my dad's reputation. The academy is in for a hard right turn.

He waited long enough to shake his father's hand; to do otherwise would have been disrespectful. He paid his respects to Rose-Ann and took time to say good-bye to Captain O'Brian, whom he didn't know except through Sam's cartoons after the bowling ball caper and Hamm's stupid mess hall escapade with Flame. He thought the man deserved better than his father's words. Apparently, what made his relief so imminent was his token punishment of midshipman involved in an incident that happened at the graduation parade. midshipmen are what they are, sometimes irreverent school boys. The last company in the last parade of the year marched off the field barefoot, leaving their shoes lined up on the field. Most didn't even notice, but once it was discovered by the audience there were a lot of laughs, but just as many people took it as a terrible sign of disrespect to the academy and its governance. The superintendent, who would have liked to jail the entire graduating class but couldn't, blamed the commandant. His days were numbered after that.

Captain O'Brian did call in the midshipman company commander and his company officer. When asked why they did it, the answer given by the midshipmen of the offending company was, "Just because – a prank."

When word got out to the fleet, most senior officers around the globe took the story in stride. Outwardly they laughed it off as a prank, but behind the scenes several powerful admirals lambasted the administration for being lax: giving the first class too many privileges like weekend liberty and permission to ride in cars. The solution would be a new commandant, one who was known to wield a mean hammer.

CHAPTER 23

AVIATION

On arrival back in Norfolk that afternoon, Blake immediately joined his classmates. They were living in an enlisted barracks on the base, waiting to move aboard the carrier in the morning. They wanted to know about his father, the new commandant. Blake shook his head and repeated what he had said to himself, "Trouble. The academy is in for a hard right turn. My bet is that the first class will lose some of their rates and you know what that means. The shit will flow downhill. Stand by for some mean firsties. I wouldn't want to be a plebe this year."

They went aboard the *Valley Forge*, a carrier that had seen hard fleet duty during the Korean War. Now it was used as the flagship for advanced anti-submarine warfare. They were herded into the hangar deck, a large space below the flight deck extending the length of the ship. There they milled about for a half-hour, waiting for their indoctrination to the ship. From a makeshift podium, an officer whose name Blake didn't remember, finally greeted them, "Welcome aboard Happy Valley," as we lovingly call her. Gentlemen, you are aboard a very proud ship with a very proud crew. She was built in 1944 with money raised by the citizens of Philadelphia in a special World War II war bond drive. She was fitted out as CV-45 and sent to the Western Pacific, arriving there in 1948. After a short visit to her homeport of San Diego in 1950, she deployed again to the Far East. This time she was first on the scene when the North Koreans streamed across the 38th parallel into South Korea. Happy Valley launched the first carrier air strike of that conflict. Waves of "Spads" -- Douglas AD Skyraiders and Vought F4U Corsairs -- struck North Korean forces while our F9F-2 Panthers flew top cover. In late 1952 she was redesignated CVA-45 and continued her work supporting our Marine and Army forces fighting over bitterly contested battle lines. During that war, Happy Valley air groups delivered over 3,700 tons of bombs. When it was over she was transferred to the Atlantic fleet here in Norfolk and again redesignated. This time to CVS-45 and outfitted as an antisubmarine warfare support carrier. We now are heavily engaged with special Task Group Alpha, concentrating on developing and perfecting new devices and tactics for countering enemy submarines in the age of nuclear propulsion and deep-diving submersibles. Any questions?"

Silence.

"All right, enjoy your stay aboard *Valley Forge*. You'll now be taken to your living quarters and begin your training."

*****

The midshipmen were given bunks among the more than 3,000 regular crew. The tour of the ship took Blake and his classmates from stem to stern of the giant ship. Over 800 feet long and displacing 36,000 tons, *Valley Forge* was to *Ingraham* as the Empire State building is to a waterfront cottage. The anchors themselves were as large as a gun turret aboard *Ingraham*; the entire destroyer could be put into the carrier's engineering rooms.

To Blake, flight ops seemed like a busy corner in Pittsburgh without a policeman in charge. Young looking sailors in yellow, green, and brown shirts scurried about pulling chocks, carrying hold-down chains, and climbing in and out of the planes to repair broken electronics or weapons systems. But there really was someone in charge. The head of the air department, known as the "air boss," was to coordinate and monitor the cycle as well as manage the hundreds of crew who made the whole intricate operation of the flight deck and hangar work. In small groups, the class crowded into a small glassed-in room at the rear of the bridge called "Pri Fly" and watched as the launch and recovery was ordered. Planes catapulted off the bow of the carrier on a precise schedule, flew their hops, then returned to find a place in the landing oval and hook a wire erected across the deck to catch their tail hook. That cycle of about an hour and a half was then complete, but another overlapped it and was already in the air.

Blake was well aware that the Navy had converted to jet aircraft in the operational fleet. Carriers now had canted landing decks. This meant that, in addition to the normal straight deck, an additional slice stuck out to the port side of the straight deck like one leg of the letter Y. The pilot of a jet lined up his landing with the angle instead of the straight deck. If he didn't catch the wire, he could pour on the power and take off again instead of crashing into the barrier.

An aircraft carrier, like a city, but floating in the ocean, houses so many people that the midshipmen were lost in the hustle of activities. Blake's duties as senior midshipman were to coordinate their training and get them from one place to another, on time.

The carrier phase amounted to a practical indoctrination into naval aviation, which had grown from its beginnings in 1910, only seven years after the Wright brothers made their first flight, to become a major element of modern naval warfare.

Now roughly thirty years after the first carrier, the *Ranger*, midshipmen were able to gain the "Cat and Trap" experience of being catapulted off a carrier and catching a landing wire. Of course the *Happy Valley* came along before jet aircraft and was a straight-deck carrier.

"You ready?" asked the lieutenant in the forward cockpit, a pilot trained in older World War II and Korean War propeller-driven planes.

"Yes, sir." Blake, still strapping on his flight helmet, sat rigid, his body tensed with adrenaline.

As soon as the pilot's hand made a quick salute, Blake was hit in the back with the force of a rocket. His head jerked backward as the force of gravity, never previously experienced, as if someone had dropped a blind -- a cloud covered his eyes. Seconds later the grayness disappeared as if the plane jumped airborne, climbing and turning into blue sky pockmarked with white puffs of clouds.

Blake had been briefed that it would slap him in the back and he might lose consciousness momentarily due to the G forces, but that had all been understatement. In a way Blake liked it. Oddly, it gave him a feeling of power. He had done something all midshipmen would be trained in but street Americans could only imagine. Planes take off from land all the time, but to do it from a landing field as short as a carrier was the real marvel of naval aviation. A carrier rolled and tossed, bucked and bent like all ships during bad weather, but even then the Navy could launch a strike made up of fighters, attack bombers, and support aircraft.

The AD Skyraider, called affectionately "Spad," was an old propeller bomber used in World War II and the Korean War. Pilots loved the Spad because it had a big engine and was very safe to fly. Spad drivers liked to say it was the last real airplane. The electronic version carried two pilots side-by-side. Blake and his classmates took turns during what the Navy called a "fam flight" or familiarization.

"Look down to your left," the pilot said. "Looks like a matchbox already, doesn't she?"

They flew around for about an hour, all the time listening to the pilot explain the various instruments. They did a few basic maneuvers, then turned into the landing pattern. Blake watched as they turned downwind, flew up the starboard side of the carrier, then rolled into the break to come around into the groove. The pilot slowed the Spad and Blake heard him go through the checklist, the last of which was, "Gear down and locked. Hook down."

He then turned steeply and dove to trail the carrier. With the ship now dead ahead, the picture Blake saw through the cockpit window was a deck bouncing up and down in the water like a cork. The airplane dropped quickly until it was on a line flying right up the center of the carrier. The landing signal officer held a large colorful paddle in each hand and held them up if the plane was too high and down if the plane was too low. The directions helped the pilot fly the proper slope into the floating runway.

Blake's pilot slowed the plane even more until it seemed to be wobbling just on the edge of flight. Just as they were approaching touchdown they heard the LSO's voice scream, "Wave off! Wave off!"

"Roger," Blake's pilot calmly said as he rammed the throttle forward, gathering immediate speed.

Next the Tower called, "Spad, er... Call sign Cabby Two on final... wave off and anchor starboard 500. We have an emergency. Cold Cat... Starboard."

"Roger. Waving off. Anchor starboard 500. Cold Cat Emergency." Over the intercom he explained to Blake, "It'll be nip and tuck to save the pilot."

Blake had been told that a "cold shot" happened when the old hydraulic catapults sometimes lost power as a plane was in the middle of launch. When that happened the plane dribbled off the bow of the carrier only to fall upside down as the ship ran over the plane. Most often it was just luck if the pilot lived.

Blake's Spad flew an oval pattern above the downed plane upside down in the water floating alone the starboard side of the carrier. A destroyer, from its plane guard position directly astern, raced in its direction. As it came close, the ship lowered a boat from its port side. He saw a man, presumed the pilot, standing on the wing of the plane. Just as the plane sank out of sight he jumped into the water and swim away. The destroyer stopped nearby, launched its boat and the pilot was saved.

"Spad in starboard anchor, pilot picked up. Come aboard now." The order came from Pri Fly.

"Roger, making approach." Blake's pilot again turned downwind and followed the landing pattern. As he made his final, he kept rocking the throttle back and forth to keep the right airspeed. At just the right moment, on a signal from the LSO, he closed the throttle, and the plane's wheels touched the deck. The tailhook caught the first of four wires – a perfect landing. Blake felt the jerk of his body, not unlike the slam when he was catapulted off. Had the pilot missed the last of the three wires, the plane would have to fly into a barrier named "Tilly," which was a big crane used to move planes around the deck. Their pilot pulled back the throttle to idle as the reverse retracting machine loosened the wire and dropped from the hook. A sailor wearing a green shirt waited nearby to do the dangerous work of unhooking in case the machines didn't work.

They then taxied to a parking place. Blake climbed down. On deck, he looked around to see if any of his classmates had noticed that he had survived his first trap. He felt relieved that the pilot who took the cold shot was picked up. But also felt puffed that he had endured the macho activity of Navy flying. He had always thought he would serve in ships but now -- maybe it would be flying.

The pilot asked, "How'd you like it?"

"Great! Great fun! I liked it a lot."

"Well, maybe we'll see you at 15,000 feet, but it'll be jets all the way from now on. At least you can say you flew in a real airplane. Spads forever!"

"Maybe. We learn how to fly later this summer -- back at the Academy -- the old N3Ns we keep back there. I'll see how that goes."

CHAPTER 24

FLYING

In the beginning Viva wrote every week, sometimes twice. But lately it was as if she were too busy. She did tell him she was having one of the most interesting times of her life, singing and acting in short ensemble pieces with people from other nations. When he learned she would be away for the summer, this time in England and France, and would not return until her new school year at Juilliard, he lost interest in his summer leave.

Blake thought of going to Europe during his leave to find her, but he just didn't have the money. Instead he decided to spend the time at home -- maybe finding a summer job.

In the meantime, until they were released for a few weeks sandwiched between learning to fly and second-class year, Blake's class bounced from amphibious training to carrier training. But before they could get out of Annapolis, it was their turn to learn the aerodynamic magic of the airfoil. When they weren't in class, they took turns helping to put the old bi-wing single engine N3N seaplanes in the water at the naval air station across the Severn River at Greenbury Point. As it turned out, flying the N3N was the most fun of the summer. The planes had two seats, the pilot-instructor in the forward seat and the student in the back. After an appropriate length of engine warm-up time, the pilot let

Blake taxi into the Severn River and head into the wind. The instructor took over for takeoff, increased power, and the plane picked up speed until the pontoon was "on the step," ready to break the suction of the water and take off. At just the right moment, he pulled back on the stick and the plane lifted off the water and began to fly.

The first several hops were familiarization. Blake's instructor, Navy Lieutenant Spellman, talked to him through a tube that ran from the forward cockpit aft. He generally showed how fast or slow the plane would fly, how to use the instruments, and did a few slow dives and turns, then explained the rudiments of a landing. "To land the seaplane, slow it to about sixty knots, then carefully touch the pontoon to the water. Once down, taxi carefully using the propeller wash and the rudder. Simple." Spellman said.

Blake's instructor, a seasoned jet pilot who was a company officer during the academic year, confessed to Blake that he found flying the old N3N quite amusing, compared to a night landing aboard a carrier. On the other hand, he thought the plane was just the right tool to teach beginning flight because it was so simple and flew so easily. "It's practically impossible to have an air accident in a plane that has a top speed of about eighty knots."

"You ready to take her up, Mr. Lawrence?" Lieutenant Spellman asked before climbing into the seats.

"Yes, sir. Ready as I'll every be."

"Okay, climb aboard and give the signal to cast us off. You can taxi us to the takeoff lane. Let me know when we're lined up and ready to go."

In his leather helmet and goggles, Blake secretly thought about what it must have been like in the days of Lucky Lindbergh crossing the Atlantic fame or the Red

Baron Manfred von Richthofen, the famous German World War I fighter pilot ace. He had seen pictures of the two with their scarves waving in the wind as they flew in open-cockpit planes similar to the N3N.

"We're in the lane, sir," Blake shouted above the prop noise.

"We really ready to go?"

Blake gave a "thumbs up" sign.

"Go when you're ready, mister," Spellman said through the voice tube.

"You're on the step."

"Got it, sir," Blake responded as he pulled back on the stick.

The fragile old plane came off the water.

It's flying. I'm flying. Wow!

"Okay, good so far, Mr. Lawrence. Take her up to 1,000 feet and head for the bridge."

Thumbs-up.

The bridge across the Chesapeake lay to his left, so he slowly turned and began his climb. The altimeter showed about 950 feet when the engine stopped and Blake felt the plane lurch strongly to port. The nose then raised abruptly, then dropped off as the plane went into a spin.

Blake's adrenaline shot over the top. He slammed his foot into the rudder pedal to right the plane and restarted the engine, which came to life quickly. He pulled back on the stick and came out of the emergency.

"Not bad, Mr. Lawrence. Now take us in for a touch-and-go landing."

After several touch and go's, Spellman ordered Blake to again take her to an altitude of 1,000 feet. "You can fly us home."

It's got to be joke. But what if it's not?

Blake inquired, "You want me to land the plane, sir?" No response. It was as if Captain Miller hadn't heard.

Coming in toward the landing, Blake's hands began to sweat. He dropped the speed to forty and after touching down, pulled the throttle back to provide enough speed to taxi. He arrived at the ramp feeling like a hero.

"Okay, I have it, Mr. Lawrence." And Blake felt the plane turn no longer under his control.

At the debriefing, Spellman praised Blake's coolness. "You made a good emergency landing. If this were flight training, I'd let you solo -- today."

Blake felt like he could actually do something. *I know if I wanted, I could become a pilot, like my dad -- if I want.*

On return to Bancroft, Blake found a note in his mailbox from his father. "Come by the quarters before you go on leave. Rose-Ann and I would like to see you."

Blake called, "Rose-Ann, dad invited me over to your quarters but I have to beg off." He lied, "Mom is expecting me tonight and I just have time to catch the bus to Pittsburgh."

"Of course, Blake. Your dad will understand. There's plenty of time to get together during academic year. Do have a good summer leave. I'll tell your father you called."

Her voice sounded nice, but she knows – and he will too.

With two cruises under his belt, Blake felt he had a much better understanding of the Navy. He was ready to get on with the next two years and graduation, but life had all at once become more complicated, with his father driving the good ship Mother B.

CHAPTER 25

ANOTHER GIRL

For Blake, the city of Pittsburgh, with its rivers, mountains, tunnels, inclines, and the red glow of ashes at night, never changed. He loved the people who made the city what it was. From differing ethnic and religious backgrounds, they were the friendliest he ever met. Hard working and fun loving, they seemed to take America for what it was, an opportunity. And they were grateful.

Shortly after returning to Steel City on summer leave, watching television on a scorching August afternoon, he told his mother he felt restless. "I wish I had something to do. It really gets boring just hanging around the house."

"You could visit your brother at West Point."

"Nah, he's a new cadet -- in beast barracks. He won't have time to see me. Besides I'll see him on our exchange weekend this winter."

"You could go back to Annapolis and spend time with your father, the new commandant." Her voice spit of sarcasm. "Did I tell you I received an official letter from him as if I were just another parent?"

"Getoutahere, Mom. I'm staying away from that scene."

"Thought you were going to see that girl in New York again?" Blake's mother asked.

"Would, but she's in Europe -- London -- this summer. I can't afford that."

"France and Italy last summer, now London. What kind of work does she do?" Jack asked.

"Actor."

"Hmm," his mother tilted her head as she made the sound. It was her not-sure-I-approve sound. He had heard it his entire life. The words that usually accompanied the head tilt were, "Are you doing the right thing?" It often rang in his ears when he was ready to embark on some escapade with Erie or his roommates. It seldom stopped him but it made him pause and think.

"Maybe I can get a job, make a little money -- anything to keep busy," he said.

"Ask Jack; he has several offices around town." Blake's mother offered. Jack, who had been her boyfriend for about three years, was sitting quietly next to his mother. Her proposal was as if he was in another town. He never took his eyes off the *Perry Como Show*.

She added, as if he were in another room, or town, "This is his off season, but he may need someone."

Earlier that evening Jack had come over for his weekly visit for one of her dinners. The man was obviously good for her. She seemed much happier than those days before Blake left for the Navy, days spent in a sour mood never changing from her tent-like housecoat.

"Jack," Blake said, "you have any part-time work?"

"Hmm," Jack said, never changing his gaze at the television. "Matter of fact, I do need somebody in the downtown office."

"I can only work for about three weeks, then I'm back to school."

"When do you want to start?" Jack's voice sounded distant. He was still engrossed in the show.

Blake swung his feet from the arm of the chair to the floor. "I'm ready right now. I don't know anything about accounting and taxes, but I can file or run errands."

"Okay." Jack finally looked at him. "Beverly Brown, my new permanent hire, is still getting her feet on the ground. You might like Beverly. Your age. Already graduated from -- la di da -- Vassar College."

"You mean that *liberal* all-girl school in Poughkeepsie, New York," his mother interjected sarcastically, playfully bumping Jack's shoulder with hers. "I have a degree from there, remember? A Vassar-trained girl – she can't be all bad."

"Why is Beverly Brown in Pittsburgh?" Blake asked.

"Pittsburgh is *not* the end of the world," she snapped.

"I didn't mean that. But there is more work in New York."

"Grew up here -- Fox Chapel," Jack said.

"A Pittsburgh girl. I'll reserve judgment about her then," Blake joked. "By the way, Miss or Mrs?"

The next day Blake showed up wearing a tie and slacks to begin a few weeks of work for Jack, a man from whom he had remained at a distance, but who had now became more interesting. His downtown office was on the twenty-third floor of the Grant Building, the tallest in Pittsburgh. Jack's personal office filled the entire corner of the floor with a view of the confluence of the three rivers: Monongahela, Allegheny and Ohio. It turned out that Jack was an attorney who specialized in tax matters, and by the look of his office, his business obviously made money. Blake soon learned that Jack had some very rich clients. Jack Hollingsworth was different in his office than at home with Blake's mother, where he wore open-collared shirts and drank a few Iron City pilsners. In the office he wore expensive suits and measured his schedule in minutes, bouncing from one project to another. Medium height, with straight black hair and a small mustache, Jack reminded Blake of the manly, handsome actors Earl Flynn or Clark Gable.

Jack introduced the two new employees to each other right away. He was right about Beverly. Blake did find her attractive. As he went about his work he watched her and was unable to resist comparing her to Viva. Beverly was the kind of girl who stood out in a crowd for her slender and aristocratic appearance, Viva for her flamboyance. Beverly wore earrings and tasteful, conservative, modern clothes, usually a suit with a blouse underneath. Her eyes were large and round, her dark hair was cut short. Even though she was a civilian, Beverly had the military look: squared away. Viva, well, her look changed with the situation. Her hair changed color with the character she was playing in the show. Viva was of the Broadway set and becoming more so every time Blake saw her. Despite Beverly's business-like look, her body language was very feminine, more so even than Viva's, who often acted like a tomboy.

Later that first week, Jack called them both to his office. "Beverly knows a lot about finance, taxes, and accounting. We have a client down in Sewickley Heights that needs help with his tax planning. He's an old Navy hand so I'd like you to go along, Blake. It'll smooth thin gs for us. You'll have to wear a jacket."

Beverly drove. At the point where the three rivers joined, she crossed over to the north side. Paralleling that river, she made her way in silence past Belleview, Avalon, and Ben Avon toward one of the richest towns in American history, Sewickley Heights, the place where iron and steel tycoons of yesteryear and today made their homes in big, isolated, tree-surrounded mansions.

Blake tried to pierce the quiet by offering small talk, but she seemed to be pouting about something. Finally she said, "Sorry, Blake. It's not your fault. I just hate this sort of thing. It's about women. I can do this by myself, but the reason you're along is these jerks don't like to deal with women. Ordinarily Jack takes these calls or comes along with me. You're the appeaser today."

"Well, I certainly don't know anything about what you do. I'll just keep my mouth shut."

"Oh no, you won't. You watch and see. You'll become the center of conversation. Just wait. I'll be lucky to get the old man's attention."

Big, brick, and bold was the way Blake described the house. They entered and followed a butler into a large living room that came straight out of the eighteenth century: dark drapes, overstuffed leather furniture, chandeliers, and doilies on every horizontal surface. It reminded Blake of several of the rooms in Edinburgh Castle.

"Have a seat; the gentleman will be here directly," the butler said.

Admiral Spaulding dragged one foot behind his stoop-shouldered, slender frame as if he had recently suffered a stroke. "So you're Lawrence. Jack said you were coming along with this young lady. Knew your grandfather. Class of '04, wasn't he? Commanded the old *Mississippi* -- I'm Class of '14 -- was his first lieutenant. Wonderful man. And your father? I know he had a son -- Class of '38, true? Where is he now?"

"At the Academy. He's the commandant, sir."

"Commandant, good. A demanding assignment. Good. Well, you must be the third Lawrence to attend. You like it?"

"Yes, sir."

"Well, tell me about what you youngsters do there nowadays. In my day, plebe year was rough."

For the next hour Blake and the admiral chatted, Blake reviewing the curriculum and training, while Spaulding explained what he did in the war, Beverly sat demurely waiting her turn. Finally he got around to the reason they were there. He had inherited the house and sizable other assets when his mother passed away the previous year. He had explained it all to Jack. Beverly was sent to finalize Jack's remedy to the admiral's tax problems. She showed Admiral Spaulding a few papers, explained them, and then had him sign. It took all of fifteen minutes.

On the way back to the office, she seemed more willing to talk. "Didn't know you were a midshipman. All I knew was that you were in the Navy."

"Sorry, I thought you knew."

"When do you graduate? She said without looking at him.

It was as if he now had some standing beyond being Jack's helper.

She's not bad looking – wonder if she'll go out? Viva's away doing her thing.

So he asked her, "You like to stop for a drink?"

There was a momentary pause before she said, "Sure. Where?"

They stopped at the Brass Rail, a bar on Diamond Street within walking distance of the Grant Building. Afterwards she drove him home, stopping long enough for him to change clothes and for her to meet his Vassar alumni mother.

For the next two weeks, Blake and Beverly worked closely together and went dancing every night. At the William Penn Hotel, they listened to Bill Haley and the Comets play "Rock Around the Clock."

By the time Blake left to return to school they both agreed they needed a break -- they were worn out. He liked Beverly — found her lively and fun -- but that was all. His feelings were still focused on Viva.

He did think about inviting her for a weekend during football season.

CHAPTER 26

SECOND CLASS YEAR AND WEST POINT

Blake settled in to second-class year which, by now he had to a routine: study hard during the week -- Sunday through Thursday, poker most Friday nights and drag Saturday.

By naval regulations, gambling was forbidden, but his first poker game included Pete, Erie, and Stone who were in because they had a football practice early the next day. Lee was dragging, and Sam was off to one of his mysterious trips to DC where everyone suspected he had a secret flame.

"Read 'em and weep, boys," Erie said after Pete cut the cards. Erie dealt them across a blanket-covered desk.

"Blake, old buddy, you ready for this year?" Erie asked as he continued to deal.

"Never! Already on the bush in fluid mechanics and juice." Blake said, holding his cards close protect against roaming eyes.

"You pass the quiz today?" Stone asked.

"Probably not. Amperes, volts, and resistance? Help!"

"Yeah, you need the gouge. With a 3.6 average last year!" Pete said. "I'm the one who needs help. My grades are always hanging on finger nails."

"My problem is spherical trig," Stone said then added, "Who dealt this mess? I'll take three."

"Wait 'til you get to thermodynamics next semester," Pete said. "No one gets it. If electricity doesn't get you, thermo will."

"Is there a fruit course at this place?" Erie asked using the word "fruit" to refer to the academic courses midshipmen considered easy.

"Who's this new girl you're dragging, Blake? Saw her picture on your desk."

"Beverly Brown. Met her in Pittsburgh last summer."

"You and Viva finished?" Pete asked.

"No way! I'm seeing her on my exchange weekend at the Point."

"You hear about the new commandant, er -- your dad?" Erie, who knew about their stormy relationship, grinned at Blake. "He's really turning up the heat on the firsties. They're pissed at him for taking away their weekends."

"They can't ride in cars either," Blake said.

"Yeah, Sam's cartoon got him – oops. I didn't say that," Pete said, then wiped his mouth with his cards.

"So Sam's the cartoonist!" Stone said.

"You are hereby sworn to secrecy, Erie, Stone. Say it!" Blake pointed. "Come on, say it."

"Okay. I swear." Stone crossed his heart.

Erie nodded.

"How you gonna handle this, Blake? Your dad bein' commandant and all?" Stone asked while realigning his hand with the three cards he drew. "Shit! I'm folding." He dropped his cards in the center of the table.

"I'm trying to stay out of it -- lie low. A few firsties have already started pinging on me. Heard one of them call him a prick the other day."

"He have a nickname yet?"

"Not that I know of," Blake said.

"Heard Sam call him 'Super-P.'" Pete said without taking his eyes off his cards. "I reminded him that the last guy to call him a prick was Greenfield. Remember when we dunked him in the natatorium? By the way, whataya hear from the old prick, Blake?"

"Nothing lately. You know he got married. Flying jets in Germany."

"Hear you lost Hambone," Stone said.

"Yep. Surprised us all." Blake stopped and shook his head. "When he knocked up Flame, he resigned and married her. He's at Penn this semester."

"I always thought he was a jerk," Stone said.

"A smart jerk," Pete said as he lit a cigarette. "He was at the top of the class academically."

"The Academy rubbed off on him. He did the right thing," Blake said. "Quit to marry her."

"Maybe too noble," Pete commented. "Shame of it is, it won't last. She's too young."

"So's he."

"How many we lost so far?" Erie asked.

"I heard about 200," Stone said. "Fewer than 800 left."

"We'll lose a lot more this year -- academics," Blake said.

"I hate stud. Blake, you always play the same damn game," Erie said. "When you going up to Woopoo?"

Blake threw down his cards. "Quit whining, Erie. King bets. I'm scheduled with the first group -- next week. How about you?"

"None of the football team goes until the Dark Ages. After the big game."

"How's the team look this year?" Blake asked.

"Not bad. How about the basketball team?" Erie asked.

"Better, I think," Blake said.

*****

The bus ride to West Point took about six hours. The basketball team got to go early in the year because their season started later than football. Blake felt excited about the trip because he hadn't seen Viva or his brother since before the last spring leave.

Viva was booked into the Thayer Hotel where he would meet her as soon as he could get away from his duties.

The weather was still beautiful in Annapolis the morning they left, but at West Point it was already dark, damp, and dreary. On arrival, Blake's class was met by a group of Cadet Cows (second classmen) who paired off with the visitors and welcomed them as their weekend roommates. Because Blake made friends with Frank Nichols during amphibious training, the two arranged to host each other during their exchange visits.

Frank was dressed in matching light gray blouse and trousers and wore a cadet cap with a shiny West Point emblem above the bill. The blouse had a black stripe around the high collar and down the center. A similar black stripe ran down the outside of each trouser leg. Frank looked like pictures Blake had seen of Douglas MacArthur and Dwight D. Eisenhower when they were cadets. The school had served the nation since 1802 and Blake guessed the uniform hadn't changed since the beginning.

President Eisenhower and five-star General MacArthur were constant newspaper headliners and among Greenfield's favorite come-around topics. MacArthur had graduated in 1903 with one of the highest academic records in the school's history. Eisenhower followed in the class of '15. He too was an excellent cadet, a star football player, but became a remarkable leader in the complex international environment of World War II and after.

"Here, let me help you with your bags, Blake. Follow me, I'm in F-2 Company -- in the North area barracks"

Blake picked up his bag, slung it over his shoulder, and followed Frank into an area that looked like a medieval fortress. Two giant Army barracks, each with four floors of rooms, were built like parapets with high towers on their roofs. A large open area as big as a football field separated each barracks. The academic buildings surrounding the barracks had a similar look, that of ruggedness, built to last forever.

How different this place is compared to our school. Annapolis is open and airy like the sea. This place is gloomy and depressing like a battlefield. Maybe it's on purpose, preparing each for their future environment and the kind of wars we will fight.

Once in his room, Frank showed Blake his bunk for the weekend and explained the routine. "So that you're not surprised, first call for reveille is at 6:00 a.m. Taps sounds at 11:30 p.m."

"Very much the same as ours," Blake said.

He took a seat and looked around at the room. Stark, rudimentary, bare floors, a room simply laid out with desks, book shelves, reading lamps, an iron bed, a steam-heat radiator, uniforms hung neatly in closets, and lockers full of sharply folded clothing. Frill-less, like the general architecture of the Point, it was made to convey a theme of sacrifice.

"You're scheduled right now for a briefing about the Point. We could skip it, if you like. I warn you it will be boring."

"I don't mind," Blake said. "Actually, I want to know more about the place. My uncle graduated from here and my brother Charlie is here -- he's a plebe. Run across him yet?"

"Yes, I have," Frank said. "And. this is as good a time as any to tell you. Once the weekend gets rolling, we probably won't have much time to talk. Your brother is up on an honor charge."

Blake blanched at the news. *Not Charlie! Hell, he's like me -- wouldn't ever... must be a mistake.*

"Honor?" Blake said.

"Yeah, I'm not supposed to tell you about it. But since we know each other -- I'm on the honor committee, so I can't talk about the details. No one can. You'll have to get that from your brother, but he may not want to talk about it. He's 'in room' waiting the results. We meet next week."

"When can I see him?"

"After chow. First the briefing, if you still want. As I said, it's optional."

"Might as well," Blake responded, but his thoughts returned to his brother.

Honor violation? What could he have done? He's never been deceitful and he knows better, especially growing up in our family.

The exchange midshipmen were sitting on folding chairs in an otherwise empty room. A firstie, gold hash marks from his elbow to his shoulder introduced himself as the first captain. He stood on a platform in front of them. "Welcome to the Point, gentlemen. Our school opened officially under Colonel Sylvanus Thayer. Under him the Academy became a pioneer in civil engineering..."

Blake's thoughts strayed to his brother. *Charlie had always been a good kid. He wanted a military career. Long before I enlisted, Charlie had set his sights on one of the academies. West Point was his first choice -- because of our uncle. To be kicked out plebe year? For an honor violation? That would be devastating. What could he have done?*

"Cadets are members of the Regular Army," The first captain continued. "The student body is called the Corps of Cadets. The corps is broken down into regiments, battalions, and companies. The Academy's honor code is a cherished possession of cadets and graduates. Administered by the cadets themselves, the code states simply that a cadet will not lie, cheat, or steal, or tolerate those who do. The code requires complete integrity in word and deed. It is strictly enforced, and any intentional violation is a cause for dismissal.

Lie, cheat, or steal, or tolerate those who do. Pretty simplistic, but a hell of a sight more severe than the rest of America. On the other hand it's not unlike our own. I wonder if I could sneak out of this boring stuff. I could read about it in about fifteen minutes on my own. Maybe I can find Charlie before supper. I wish I had asked which company he's in.

"The cadets receive training in military skills in courses taken during the academic year, and in summer training sessions held at nearby Camp Buckner and at selected military posts around the world. Training includes instruction in Army weapons and field maneuvers. A cadet also spends time as a platoon leader with a real combat unit. Students develop physical fitness skills through varsity or intramural sports and physical education courses. Any questions?"

Silence.

"Dismissed."

*****

Blake fell in beside Frank and marched with company F-2 to the Washington Hall, where he took his place at the mess tables. Just like at Annapolis, the mess hall had hundreds of tables where plebes stood among the upper class shouting responses to questions. The exception was the high balcony where the cadet staff officers ate. From that perch the senior cadet called, "Battalions attention! Attention to Orders. By order of the commandant, there will be a review at 1200 hours tomorrow. Battalions, seats!"

Chairs scraped hard floors, the noise returned to its normal full level. "Frank, I forgot to ask. What company is my brother in?"

"C-1, but I got the word to him to come around right after supper. He has about ten minutes before study hall begins. But I can't be there."

*****

"Cadet Lawrence reporting as ordered, sir," Blake's brother took off his Tarbucket, the kind with the chinstrap and high furry plum. His blond hair was cut short - - military style. He was thinner than when Blake last saw him, but then Beast Barracks does that to young men who come wearing baby fat. Otherwise Charlie looked fit. His posture was exactly like every other cadet: tall, straight, his uniform squared away. He wore parade dress grays with two white belts crossed through a brass plate centered on his chest.

"Hey, Charlie. Relax." Blake got up and shook his brother's hand. "Good to see you. How ya do'n?"

Charlie's eyes found the floor and his shoulders slumped. "Not so good. I might be found!" he blurted it out immediately as if he had been waiting to tell someone, anyone, who might help him. "Honor violation."

"Found?"

"Kicked. Booted out."

"Really? How did it happen? Sit down." Blake feigned ignorance. He didn't want to give his friend Frank away. "Tell me about it."

Charlie took a seat across from Blake, but he sat at erect attention as if he was on come-around. As he spoke his eyes blurred as if on the verge of tears. "I was at the library and came back late. The librarian let me work right up to closing so I thought it was okay to be late. The cadet on duty at the company asked if I was authorized and like a stupid dummy I said, 'All right.' As soon as I got to my room I realized what I had done: I lied. I thought it would have been no more than a few demerits and a walking tour in the area. I immediately went back and corrected it. But it was too late. The honor committee meets next week to hear my case." He began to cry then choked it back and quickly wiped his nose. "I'm thinking about resigning."

Blake came out of his chair. He grabbed his brother by the shoulders. "Like hell you will! Sit up! Tall! You think they want to throw you out? They don't! Not really. The Academy wants everyone to make it, if they can. How's everything else going?"

"What do you mean?"

"What do your classmates think of you? How are your grades? Have you had any other problems? It could make a difference. They sometimes overlook a marginal violation for a plebe who's doing well."

"Well, I think they like me. And I haven't had a lot of problems with classmates. Grades are okay, not starring -- about a 2.95 over all."

"Do Mom and Dad know?"

"No! And I don't want them to know," Charlie stated. "Mom will know soon enough when I show up at her door."

"You know I won't tell them if you don't want me to. These things are handled totally by the cadets. But you can bet that the sup up here, if he learns about it, will get the word to Dad. The bosses sometimes don't know until it's over; it's too late then."

"What should I do, Blake?"

"Let me think." Blake took his seat. His hand scrubbed his chin, and after a few moments of silence, he stroked his forehead and said, "They have to give you a hearing. It's the way the honor committee works. They call you in and hear your side of the story. Look. Here's what I would do. First, I'd call Dad and let him know. They don't like whimpers and whiners, so at the meeting act like a man, stand up tall, and state your case. Be noble enough to acknowledge wrongdoing -- that it was an impulse -- a wrong impulse and that you're sorry. That it won't happen ever again. That you learn from your mistakes. Just tell it and shut up. Don't snivel. Don't plead. People do get a second chance. When it happens, no one knows about it. Life goes on. If they give you a second chance, you may never talk about it."

Charlie, still sitting tall as he was told to do by his brother, stood and broke out into a smile. "You always knew what to do, Blake." He stepped to his brother and reached to hug him. Though the two had never been huggers, and Blake's first instinct was to avoid an embrace, he knew his brother was lost in the emotion of his terrible plight. Blake took his Charlie's hand and squeezed it, then pulled him to his chest and squeezed.

"No matter how this turns out," Blake said. "I know what kind of a man you are. Straight arrow all the way. Take off, plebe! And keep your chin up!"

*****

That night Blake tossed and turned. The unfamiliar bed caused some of his restlessness, but most was brought on by his thoughts about Charlie. He didn't feel competent to counsel him and worried that what he said was the best advice for his situation.

Reveille didn't surprise Blake, but the morning formation did. Into the brisk weather the cadets raced to line up for a muster before breakfast and their first classes. Blake stood shivering in the cold.

This weather has to be the greatest price they pay for duty, honor, and country.

After the Saturday morning classes, held in much the same style as those at the Naval Academy, Frank, with Blake in tow, ran back to his room to change for the parade. "Sorry, Blake, but you guys don't do it like we do. Can't march with me, but you can see it from the reviewing stand."

"Can I bring my drag to the parade?"

"Sure. Didn't know you were dragging. Is she here?"

"At the Thayer."

"I'll see you after the parade," Frank said.

*****

Blake made his way to the Thayer Hotel where he told Viva to wait until he could get away from his exchange duties. Looking very much like an Ivy League student, she sat in the coffee shop wearing a pleated skirt and a sweater.

"Viva." He wanted to take her in his arms and kiss her. Instead he took both her hands in his and said, "Let's look at you. Gorgeous. Ready to go?"

"Go where?"

"To see a parade, West Point style."

"So what's so great about seeing a parade? We have them in New York all the time."

"This is not like Macy's on New Year's or Thanksgiving. These are cadets doing their drill. It's beautiful, like you."

"Blake, since when did you become so complimentary?"

"I don't know, I just feel good today. Come on, we'll be late."

"I must be back in time to change for the ball," Viva said.

"No problem. We'll even have time for dinner."

The two took their places on the fringes of the Plain, the large grass-covered field overlooking the Hudson River; the cadets lined like corn-rows in their company formations.

"Pass in Review!" The first captain ordered.

When each platoon paraded past the reviewing stand, their straight lines and white gloves came into perfect synchronization as if they were one person.

She touched his sleeve and he hoped that it was a sign of her warmth toward him. While he couldn't take her hand, he did brush her shoulder with his.

Following the parade, Blake changed into dress uniform, then returned to take Viva to dinner at the Thayer. In her ball gown, she looked like the movie star she wanted to become. Blake knew she had her sights on a career as a professional entertainer, but he hoped to change her mind.

The dance, held in the Washington Hall was the same place the cadets took their meals. A band played at one end, the other end held refreshments. On entering, they met and shook hands with the superintendent, commandant, and faculty members in the receiving line. They chatted with Frank Nichols and his "drag," then danced to the music of a local New York band. On one break, while standing near the punch bowl a cadet first classman came near and said, "Hi, Viva. Good to see you again."

"Hi, Mark. Nice to see you, too."

As soon as the cadet disappeared into the crowd, Blake said, "How about a walk?"

"Sure, I like walks -- with you."

They meandered along the pathways that paralleled the river, enjoying the late fall evening that had turned surprisingly pleasant.

"Who was that guy?"

"What guy?"

"The firstie who said hello back there." Blake's eyes remained straight ahead.

"Oh, just a friend of a friend. I told you I've dated here before."

He turned and took her in his arms. "You know what this place is?"

Viva looked around. "Sure. It's called Temptation Walk and you've maneuvered me under the Kissing Rock."

"You've been here before."

"Well..." She smiled impishly. "In the words of George Washington, I cannot tell a lie."

"Want to try on my cap?" he asked.

Very willingly she did, and Blake took her in his arms. "Ah, I was hoping --" They kissed passionately. "Viva, you must know I like you very much."

"Oh, Blake. I like you very much too."

They kissed again but she pulled away. "But, Blake, don't -- I'm not ready for a serious relationship. Let's just have fun together. I look forward to our dates, but let's leave it that way. At least for the time being."

Blake shook his head in agreement, but inside he felt the day crumble back to its beginning.

However, she has left a smidgeon of hope.

He took her arm and guided her back to the dance where they swayed to romantic music. Afterward he escorted her back to the Thayer Hotel where they kissed and hugged until it was time for him to return.

"Write me," he said.

"Of course."

CHAPTER 27

LOSING THE BEST

Blake put Viva on a bus for her return to New York, Juilliard, and Broadway. They hugged good-bye, but it was not the same. He spent the entire long ride back to Annapolis thinking about Viva and what she had said after the dance, when she rebuffed him. *She must have sensed I was on the verge of "pinning" her with my class crest, the act of pre-engagement. In the back of my mind my next step would have been to invite her to the Spring Dance where I had intended to propose. If she accepted I would invite her to the Ring Dance during June Week. Then present her with a miniature of my own class ring as an engagement ring.*

On the outside, he maintained a carefree show, but inside he felt like a worm had crawled in and was eating his gut, his soul, and his heart. She hadn't out and out dumped him, but he did expect to receive a "Dear John" letter any day.

Sam caught him in a sour mood one afternoon and reminded him of his plebe-year warning about Viva. "She's fickle. I told you and Pete that when you two met her at my house. She knows where she's going and she hasn't changed. Come on, Blake. Quit mooning over her and get on with your life."

Blake took Sam's advice. He focused on school and making the basketball team. Coach made it clear that the new class had several All-American high school stars and that the roster for the coming season was open. No one had a firm position; everyone had to show him during practice that they deserved to make the team. Blake's mind was on his brother. He had been back a week and heard nothing.

As class president, he devoted time to almost all of the class committees. He was on the ring committee, the ring dance committee, and was the presiding member of the class brigade executive committee, which was a part of the honor committee. In a moment of weakness he even volunteered to be an occasional writer for the *Splinter*, the bi-weekly brother of *The Log*. It was in this "little magazine" that Sam published his irreverent cartoons. Blake agreed to be a writer only if it was anonymous -- it wouldn't be proper for the class president to be caught writing impudent stories for the column titled "Salty Sam."

The article he wrote told the story of four drunken midshipman who fell asleep in the back seat of a lady's car. They were given a place to stay overnight to sober up at a United States Senator's house. Blake signed off on the anonymous story with, "Sorry, Super-P. Your crusade to square away the First Class isn't working."

The Super-P salutation referred to his dad's new nickname. Blake reluctantly let Sam include it to his puckish article when the cartoonist said, "It'll add spice to the piece and complement the cartoon character wearing a cap with scrambled eggs and a big 'SP' on his chest."

Of course, Blake had to be in the presence of his father from time to time. The two exchanged pleasantries and his dad always asked how he was doing, but

Blake realized the awkwardness of their positions and kept his distance.

On the day after his article came out in *Splinter*, Blake received a call to come to the main office; the commandant wanted to see him. His first thought was his dad had read the piece and somehow connected the disparaging reference to Super P to him. On the other hand, maybe he would be asked if he knew who the drunken mids were in Salty Sam's article. Of course he knew that they were four football players including his buddy Erie. He also knew he would never give up Erie. Besides, without Erie the team wouldn't come close to beating Army this year. Navy's quarterback was lousy and they needed Erie on defense.

"Midshipman Lawrence reporting as ordered, sir." Blake stood at attention with his hat in his right hand.

"Carry on, Blake. Have a seat, son. How are you?" His dad got up and came from behind his desk. The four stripes on his blue service uniform were in stark contrast to the two slender ones running diagonally up Blake's left arm. "Actually, I know you're doing well. I keep track of your grades and other statistics that cross my desk. I'm so damn busy. I should see you more often."

Blake was still standing.

"Sit down."

"Aye, aye, sir."

"Drop it, Trey. Once that door closes, we're father and son. Well, anyway... have you got the sad news?"

"What news?"

"Charlie. He's been found... er, dropped from West Point." Captain Lawrence's jaw tightened. "Got a call from the commandant last night. Seems an honor violation. General Martin said Charlie handled it very nobly. Too bad. Charlie would have made a fine officer."

Emotion swelled in Blake. His eyes teared. He stood up and looked away. He took out his handkerchief and quickly blew his nose. "Permission to leave, sir. I have classes."

"Ah, Trey -- come on." He advanced toward Blake as if to take him in his arms. But Blake stepped back. "I know how you must feel," his dad said. "Didn't you know anything about this?"

"You don't know how I feel!" Blake screamed as he walked to the door. He let it all out. "You don't know how good he is -- you were never around. West Point is chicken shit to not give him a second chance. It was my fault. I went off to join the Navy. I didn't give Charlie enough of my time. There was a time when I would like to have had hugs from you, but it's too late. I don't need them now."

Captain Lawrence reached again to touch his son.

"Dad, I know Charlie. What happened was unintentional. Kids do dumb things, sometimes out of fear. But Charlie is not an honor case. Deceit is not in him. They should have counseled him and let him stay. I know him well enough that he *will* make a great officer, if he wants to -- maybe through officer candidate school. Maybe better than me."

"I know, son."

"You knew about it." Blake's voice rose. "They would have told you... and you didn't do anything. You could have."

"There was nothing you, I, or anyone could do." Blake's dad's brow wrinkled and he shook his head from side to side. Tears welled up in his eyes. "Few people pay such a high price to learn the value of honor. My sons now know."

*****

Back in his room, Blake went to his bed and lay with his face in his pillow.

"What the hell?" said Sam when he came charging in. "Blake in bed? Never saw that before. Did hell freeze over?"

Blake rolled over then sat up. "Charlie got kicked from the Point. Honor."

"No shit! You said he might have a chance to stay. They're a bunch of bastards."

"It's the difference between their code and our concept. It's too damn rigid."

A knock on the door brought the messenger of the Watch. "Mister Lawrence, sir. You have a phone call."

Blake got up and checked his dress in the mirror, then hurried to the phones in the rotunda. Thinking it might be his brother, he was already rehearsing what he would say, what words of encouragement he would give.

"Hello."

"Is this Midshipman Lawrence?" It was the voice of a southern female.

"Yes, ma'am."

"This is Mrs. Laura Greenfield." She paused for a moment. "I'm calling to tell you that my husband, Mark Greenfield, was killed last week in an aircraft accident." She paused again. "We are burying him at the Naval Academy next week. He would have wanted me to let you know. He spoke of you from time to time, very highly."

ANNAPOLIS 289

Blake didn't know what to say. He said nothing. But he felt doubly terrible.

First Charlie, and now Mark?

"Would you tell the others in his old company?"

"Yes, ma'am. I'm sorry, ma'am. My condolences, ma'am. Mark was a good man." He wanted to know more of the details, but it was inappropriate to ask. "When will the service be held?"

"Next Wednesday." She sniffled. "We weren't married long." She started to explain then, stopped. "Thank you Mr. Lawrence. Good-bye."

"Good-bye, ma'am."

That night his sleep was again fitful, in fact he hardly slept at all.

In class the next day his mind wandered.

What the hell else can go wrong? First Viva dumps me and Charlie gets kicked out, and now Greenfield is dead. What a hell of a week! What next?

*****

It was snowing lightly on the day of the funeral. Flecks of white covered the tops of the grave markers in perfect lines across the hillside cemetery overlooking Dorsey Creek. The chaplain said his words. Riflemen aimed their guns into the air and fired three volleys: a bugler began to play *Taps*. In his mind, Blake heard the words:

"Day is done
Gone the sun
From the lakes
From the hills
From the sky.

All is well,
Safely rest.
God is nigh.

Fading light
Dims the sight
And a star
Gems the sky,
Gleaming bright
From afar,
Drawing nigh,
Falls the night."

A lump came to Blake's throat. Tears formed in his eyes. He knew the story behind the music -- the haunting melody. He memorized the story of how "Taps," used at military funerals, was born, for one of his many come-a-rounds to Greenfield.

To himself he recited the story: *It all began in 1862 during the Civil War, when a Captain Ellicombe heard the moans of a soldier who lay severely wounded on the field. Not knowing if it was a Union or Confederate soldier, the captain risked his life to bring the stricken man back for medical attention. When Ellicombe lit a lantern and peered closely at the face; he suddenly caught his breath. It was his son. The following morning, heartbroken, the father asked permission of his superiors to give a full military burial despite his enemy status. The request was denied. But, out of respect for the father, they did give him one musician. Ellicombe chose a bugler and asked him to play a series of musical notes he had found on a piece of paper in the pocket of his son's uniform.*

Blake now said the rest of the words to himself as he listened to the notes being played in honor of Greenfield.

"Thanks and praise,
For our days,
Neath the sun,
Neath the stars,
Neath the sky,
As we go,
This we know,
God is nigh."

An officer walked solemnly to the very young woman sitting on a folding chair opposite the casket. He handed her a folded American flag and mumbled a few words. She took it to her breast and dropped her head to her lap in sadness and reverence.

Blake waited until all the family had approached her and made their remarks. He placed a midshipman anchor on Mark's casket, then introduced himself to the widow. Blake knew she was about his age, but up close, behind her veil, he could see that the lines of sadness and tear streaks made her look older. The frail-looking girl raised her eyes and gave a half smile when he said, "I'm Blake Lawrence. I want you to know that no one, so far, has had the same influence on me as your husband did. Please accept my condolences. He was a hell of a man. If there is anything I can do, just call."

"Thank you, Blake."

He introduced himself to Mark's parents, then walked slowly back toward Mother B. He kicked at the snow that covered Chauvenet Walk. He looked to the sky with tears still in his eyes. He then diverted his stroll toward the chapel by way of Chapel Walk. He went through the huge open bronze doors and glanced at the motto inscribed in Latin that Mark had made him memorize plebe year. "Not for self, but for country." He took off his cap, then knelt. He attended church every Sunday; it was required, but he didn't always feel spiritual. Today he did. He looked at the stained glass window portraying Sir Galahad, the symbol of the highest, most noble motive of military service. Light shone through it onto a simplistic altar that represented the sacrifices of sailors. He prayed quietly for the souls of the dead .

That evening, on arrival at basketball practice, the midshipman manager called him over and said, "Blake, coach asked me to tell you that he wanted to see you in his office before practice today."

He said to himself, "Everything else has gone wrong. I guess I'll be cut."

*****

Sam and Pete kept their distance. They knew about Blake's relationship to Greenfield, strange as it was. He was a prick firstie who leaned heavily on a plebe, then spooned him and they became close friends. Mark's death and burial had had a great effect on Blake. The company officer had called him in to revealed the cause of Greenfield's death. Apparently he was shot down during a routine flight when he inadvertently crossed a boundary into Soviet territory. Cold War stuff. Sam and Pete also knew that Blake's brother got kicked out of the Point and that Blake and his father had crossed swords again. Everything added to Blake's irritableness. Though his two roommates didn't know about the dashing of his romance with Viva, they knew something was up when he invited Beverly to the spring dance. On top of all that, Blake got into only two games during the season. The basketball team lost to Army again -- for the third year. When the coach called Blake in to his office, it was to warn him that because of the talent on the plebe team, Blake would probably be cut before his senior year.

The spring dance and spring leave came and went. He wrote occasionally to Viva, but there were few responses. Then one day the letter came.

Dear Blake:

Don't be mad at me. Please. I know I haven't been responding to your letters, but it isn't because I don't like you. We had fun at West Point. I like being with you -- don't stop inviting me. I know I hurt you when we were on Temptation, after we kissed. At the time, I couldn't tell you the reason I discouraged you but now I can. You see, I was on the verge of an opportunity to be in a Hollywood movie. It wasn't final, and I didn't want to jinx the deal; I'm very superstitious, as you know. Anyway, I've finished my work here at Juilliard, and I'm going to Hollywood. I signed a movie contract! I hope to see you again, someday. Please keep writing.

Love,
Viva

PS: I'll send you my address in Los Angeles as soon as I know it.

She didn't dump me! She still cares!
His mind read things that were not there.

Maybe she will come to the Ring Dance. He ran to the phones and made the call. "May I speak to Viva, please?"

The woman who answered at Juilliard said, "Sorry, she is no longer a student here."

He tried her home. Viva's mother told him that she had already gone west and gave him a number in Los Angeles.

A male voice answered. Blake asked, "Is Kathy Velenochi there? May I speak to her?"

"Sure. Wait."

"Yes, this is Kathy."

"Kathy. I got your letter. How are you?"

"Blake. How did you find me?" Her voice sounded strained.

"Through your mother. What's it like in Hollywood?"

"Actually, Blake I don't have time to talk. I'm in rehearsal."

"That's okay -- I won't talk long. I just called to invite you to the Ring Dance. Can you come? It's in June."

"Oh, Blake. How nice of you to ask, but sorry, I'm tied up out here. I have a small part in another movie. Contract stuff."

"Well, I'm glad for you. Your career seems to be taking off. I'll miss you. Contact me when you're back east. Break a leg."

"Thanks. I *will* call. Good-bye, Blake."

"Good-bye."

Before the sound of plastic on plastic, both voices had a touch of sadness. Blake felt like crap. Like a puppy dog on a leash, he'd bolted right back into the Viva fire and gotten burned again. Sam had accused him of being one of those love-starved mids who jumped for the first girl who looked his way -- it went right to their pecker. There was a doubt in Blake's mind whether he really felt love -- or lust.

*****

Beverly agreed to come over from Pittsburgh. He met her at the Greyhound bus station and took her to her lodgings next door at Carvel Hall, one of the oldest hotels in the city of Annapolis. Because of work, Beverly arrived only the afternoon before the big dance. After supper he left her at the hotel to dress and returned wearing white gloves and his dress white uniform. She looked stunning, dark hair against her snow-white ball gown.

In Dahlgren Hall they stood in a line of second classmen soon to be firsties. As they came ever closer to the binnacle, Beverly removed Blake's ring from a ribbon she wore around her neck. Second classmen could not officially wear their rings until after the Ring Dance. Their class crest would be worn closest to the heart until after graduation, when, for the rest of their lives, the Academy crest would be worn closest.

As they waited, Beverly saw the midshipman imme- diately in front holding a ring. It was smaller than the one she held but looked exactly the same. "Is that a class ring? Why is it so small?"

"We're engaged to be married," the young woman said.

Blake's classmate joked, "It's a miniature of her future husband's class ring."

"Oh," said Beverly. She glanced at Blake. The corners of her lips turned down momentarily. "How nice."

According to the christening tradition, Beverly dipped the ring into the binnacle containing the waters of the seven seas. Then they walked into the giant replica where she placed the ring on the ring finger of the Blake's left hand, sealing the bond between the class and the naval service.

Blake was briefly reminded of Viva and his vain attempt to become engaged. It was not the same with Beverly. There was a lot of difference between the two. Viva wanted to become a movie star or at least be a professional entertainer, and Beverly had her sights on a career in business. Both were beautiful, both stylish in different ways: Beverly a bit more chic, Viva more flamboyant, but both knew where they were headed. But Blake knew he loved Viva.

CHAPTER 28

BACK TO THE SEA

Blake stood on the bridge of the battleship, *USS New Jersey*, BB-62. Once again he was at sea, a place that at one time was strange; now he felt very comfortable. He liked the excitement of it, the way it made him feel important as one always does who is in charge of something large or small. He liked the openness of it -- the unobstructed view that a clear horizon gave, no high-rise buildings, no bridges, no clutter of cars and wandering people. He liked the cleanness of it, the air, the sky, the smell of sea spray and rolling waves. He liked the comfortable simplicity of its hierarchical life. Everyone knew who was boss. He liked the feeling of trust, honesty, and strength working with friendly men all trained the same way. He also liked the inherent danger sea-going evolutions brought and storms that could break men and ships.

His job as a simple watch stander wasn't very important, but it felt so. As assistant to the assistant officer of the deck, he was to take bearings on all ships moving nearby as well as report stadimeter ranges, a tool to measure distances. The admiral and captain on board *New Jersey* wanted to ensure that the screening destroyers were in precise station. They got nervous when any ship's bow pointed in their direction. Important or not, the watch got him out of the bunkroom he shared with a dozen other new first class midshipmen on the third deck of this giant vessel.

Through the glassed-in open bridge, he could see the enormous flared foc's'l with its sun-bleached wooden deck, polished bright work, and powerful 16-inch guns. The bow dug lazily into the ocean swells, rising slowly bringing a burst of sparkling ocean spray.

Blake wondered if ships didn't have souls, a product of their activities during their lives. Ingraham's would be that of a "fighter," which came from having recovered from almost sinking after being a target of a Japanese kamikaze. New Jersey's soul would be that of "steadfastness," having always been there in every war with her big guns blazing away in support of the fleet and troops ashore.

"Mr. Lawrence!" Blake turned away from his thoughts to the voice of an advancing Commander Bruce Fellows, faculty officer and midshipman coordinator for the cruise. He served as the link between the training organization and the ship. As the ranking firstie, with the title of midshipman navigator, Blake worked for Commander Fellows. "Thought you were to have the training schedule to me by noon today?"

"Blew it, commander, sorry. But I can have it to you right after this watch. There are a few holes I have to fill."

"The reason I'm on your ass is that the XO is on mine. He's itchy about the big shoot tomorrow -- mount captains and all that."

"No sweat sir. Give me about a half hour after I'm relieved."

"One more thing -- the in-port watch schedule. I'll also need that before we get in to Barcelona next week."

"Got that too, commander."

Commander Fellows retreated from the bridge, where he knew no one was to be on administrative business. The sanctity of the pilot house and open bridge on a battleship was for war fighting and control of ships only. Blake liked Commander Fellows, a tall, gangly man who wore his unwrinkled uniforms as if he never sat down. Blake suspected he seldom did; highly conscientious, he was constantly on the go. Although he was clearly hyper about his responsibilities, he treated Blake almost as an equal, leading Blake to take liberties he wouldn't ordinarily take with someone so senior. Blake thought most of Commander Fellows' problems were that he was an aviator who taught meteorology. He had never been aboard a ship other than a carrier since midshipman days, and he spoke like a man not used to giving orders.

From Blake's short but recent experience on both, battleships were the antithesis of carriers. Spit, polish, and smartness were *New Jersey's* hallmarks while the carrier *Valley Forge*, if it was typical, was quite a bit less surface and more get-on-with-it in style. Neither was wrong and both were war-fighting ready but one was a bit more intimidating than the other.

Blake went back to standing his watch. On the horizon, surrounding the battleship, were a dozen destroyers. Having spent his third class cruise aboard a "tin can," Blake had grown to agree with the reputation that destroyers were the greyhounds of the Fleet. Rear Admiral Alexander, the commander of the training cruise, used them like one might use an errand boy.

"Signal *Decatur* to go alongside *Putnam* and fetch us two midshipmen to join me for dinner tonight," he ordered.

No sooner did the flashing light and flag signal go out than a belch of smoke from her pipes was seen from *Decatur* as her stern squatted deep into the ocean, churning a boil of water. Racing for the other ship, she glided alongside, made the transfer, and soon came alongside the battleship with the four firsties, two from *Decatur* and two from *Putnam* to join the admiral in his private mess.

The summer cruise was about first classmen in their last practical shipboard training and youngsters in their first. Thus the upper class were to observe firsthand by living and eating with officers at the same time they gained leadership experience putting the third class through their paces.

Blake found the officers' mess aboard *New Jersey* a place of congeniality where gentlemen took respite from keeping the ship. Men dressed in immaculate serving uniforms with wine-colored vests and white trousers moved silently from table to table. More than three times the size of a destroyer's, the battleship's wardroom was a place where rank mattered. Seniors occupied chairs at one end, juniors at the other, and with each promotion, the order changed jealously. Blake had eaten at an early sitting prior to taking the noon-to-four watch. But tonight he would dine in the admiral's private mess with four *New Jersey* firsties and the four transferred by high line from the destroyers.

Once he was relieved of his bridge duties, he hurried to his small office where he kept the schedule matrix that showed which midshipmen were assigned to their new divisions and battle stations. After tomorrow's battle exercises and just prior to entry into their various Mediterranean liberty ports, everyone would rotate. After changing a few entries and filling in the final data, he scooped up the paper and delivered it to Commander Fellows' stateroom. Blake then raced to the admiral's mess where he joined seven other firsties waiting to be invited into the flag mess. The speed with which he had to bounce around to get everything completed reminded him of plebe year come-around to Greenfield.

On entry to the mess, to his surprise he found his old buddy Erie.

"How'd you get aboard?" Blake asked.

"From *Decatur*. High-line. It sucks."

"What port you going to?"

"Barcelona," Erie answered.

A steward motioned them to come in and take their seats. "Me, too. Let's take the tour to Madrid," Blake said just before he took his place at the chair next to the admiral.

Erie winked and said, "Sounds good."

Rear Admiral Alexander was, according to the buzz in the wardroom, a "comer" in the Navy. According to Blake's grandfather, there were admirals and there were Admirals. There were those who were just functionaries, promoted to serve a few years to fill a specific staff or management need for a specific assignment. And there were those who were promoted because they were destined to run the Navy. Alexander, so it was said, was destined to be a fleet commander or even chief of naval operations. Blake wanted to satisfy his curiosity. What set this man apart? What set the really good ones apart from the rest?

The midshipmen stood at relaxed attention carefully placed between staff officers of various ranks. Because he was the senior midshipman, Blake sat across from the Admiral's chief of staff, a gray-haired captain with a chiseled jaw and tired eyes.

"Attention on deck," a voice said.

Tall, youthful, and perfectly groomed, Admiral Alexander reminded Blake of a six-striper at the Academy and guessed the admiral had been one during his days there.

"Take your seats, gentlemen." He leaned over and whispered something into the chief of staff's ear. They both laughed. His eyes next scanned the table. In a voice that exuded confidence, "Now," he said, "let's see. You're Lawrence. I know your father." He nodded. "And down the table -- please introduce yourselves. Start there." He pointed to Erie. "Tell us your family, your ship, and what you have done on the cruise."

Each of the midshipmen in turn gave a treatise about who they were and their training thus far. When they were through, the admiral was silent as he picked at his food. He seemed to be contemplating his next words.

"Gentlemen, we've been at sea for over three weeks now, training in weapons systems and various naval maneuvers. Beginning tomorrow I want you midshipmen to demonstration your prowess. I sent out a message to that effect. I've told the ships captains' that I want only midshipmen at the controls -- maneuvering the ships, shooting the guns, operating the engineering plants, etc. How else can we know if you've really learned anything?"

"What do you think about that, Mr. Lawrence?"

"Well, sir. As long as the chief is behind me when we shoot the sixteen-inch gun I'm assigned to, I'm all for it."

"Don't you feel confident as turret captain?"

"To a certain extent, I do, sir. But, still, I haven't even seen it fire. That will bring the confidence."

"Exactly. It's about feeling the 'sailorly existence.' Being ready for combat. You'll all feel it after tomorrow." Then he added, "Mr. Lawrence, I've decided to make you part of my staff -- midshipman liaison. Of course, this would be in addition to your other duties."

Blake thought about all the other things he was responsible for, particularly those already late for Commander Fellows, but he knew it was an honor to be on the admiral's staff. *I'll get it all done.*

Near the conclusion of the meal, during desert and conversation, the admiral turned to Blake. "Of course, the name Lawrence is famous. In our Navy there is your grandfather and now your father. Commandant is a special job. But have you heard the name T. E. Lawrence?"

"I think I've heard it but don't know anything about the person, sir."

"Well, he's one of my personal heroes -- I've put in some time studying the man. Born in 1888, died in 1935, he was a British soldier and writer."

The admiral sat back and scanned the table.

"Maybe some of you have heard of him as the world famous Lawrence of Arabia. He was one of the most adventurous and noble personalities of World War I. We are entering the Mediterranean where Lawrence worked much of his life in a foreign culture. But also there are men -- and women, I suppose, who chose to serve without notoriety. Call it a lesson from an older sailor. We all need heroes; maybe you will become one of ours."

With that he excused himself.

The others stood then dispersed back to their duties.

Erie grabbed Blake's arm. "You're going to be a busy mid."

Blake shrugged his shoulders, "No sweat, I think. See you on the pier in Barcelona."

At 0630 the next morning, the training fleet went to general quarters and the admiral ordered the practice battle to begin. Everyone donned helmets and life jackets. They were to stay at their battle stations day and night, just like in wartime. Midshipmen received last-minute instructions about their duties, but nothing happened. Two days later the fleet passed by Gibraltar.

Suddenly and without warning a ship reported incoming bogies. Planes dropped out of the sky in realistic patterns, racing by the ships simulating strafing, torpedo runs, and dropping bombs. The ships simulated return fire, but it was too late; the surprise air attack caught most of them off guard. Without anyone knowing except the admiral's staff, an aircraft carrier returning to the States was diverted to attack the fleet.

As part of the training, ships were ordered to track and simulate attacks on several submarines previously ordered into the area. Destroyers darted back and forth slicing through green water, sonars blasting away, simulating weapons drops in defense of the convoy. Finally the ships were ordered to conduct live fire. Blake, in his position as turret captain for *New Jersey's* forward 16-inch battery, ordered rounds to be brought to the loading trays. Their target would be a sled being pulled on a very long wire behind an ocean-going fleet tug that had been diverted from another part of the Med.

"Locked on and tracking," came the report from the radars. To prepare everyone for the terrible noise, Blake gave a ten-second stand-by before he said, "Shoot!"

No sooner did Blake squeeze the trigger and unloose the first round -- a blast so strong that the ship actually moved sideways -- than he heard, "Cease fire! Cease fire! Secure from general quarters!"

Not knowing why the exercise was curtailed prematurely, everyone on the *New Jersey* took off their sound-powered telephones, stowed their gear, and retreated to their living spaces to clean up after three days in the exercise.

Blake left the forward battery and made his way to the flag bridge to find out what was going on.

Huddled around a chart table, the admiral and his chief of staff conferred with the staff meteorologist and Commander Fellows. Because of his faculty status in the subject of meteorology, he had been called in for consultation.

Blake stood to one side and listened.

"It's one of those flukes, sir. The Med gets them. They just jump up out of nowhere," the meteorologist stated.

The chief of staff shook his head in agreement. "True. I've heard about them."

Blake knew about them from a course he had taken at the Academy. Called typhoons, cyclones, and tornadoes, in various locations of the world they were all the same -- hurricane-force winds of 75 miles an hour or more with its accompanying rain, fog, and high seas, bringing enormous damage to ships at sea. Usually, through a series of weather reports from stations around the world, the tracks of these storms are plotted and carefully avoided.

"How bad can it be?" the Admiral asked.

"Bad, sir," said the meteorologist, a young lieutenant wearing thick glasses and brandishing a pile of weather reports.

"What do you recommend, Commander Fellows?" the admiral said.

"Run, sir. Get the hell out of its way... sir!"

"If we can," the grizzled chief of staff answered.

"Where?"

"I recommend getting out of the Med. Run for the open ocean to the west." Commander Fellows said.

"I see another alternative," the chief of staff said. "The leeward side of Gibraltar is our closest protection, sir. That way, when the storm passes we can carry on our mission and get the mids ashore on time."

"The problem is that the paths of these devastating storms are very unpredictable, sir," The meteorologist stated. "Without seeming to be facetious, sir, they curve to starboard when they don't curve to port."

"Hmm. We already have diplomatic clearance, don't we?" the Admiral asked calmly. "When are the mids due in the ports?"

"Day after tomorrow, sir."

A bewildered fleet received the admiral's orders to turn toward Gibraltar and make best speed to the western side, the side protected from the wind. On arrival, the admiral ordered the ships to anchor in the deep water to wait out the storm, which now was predicted to pass on the eastern side.

The water in the open anchorage on the western side of the island was as flat as a kitchen table. Blake watched as the destroyers maneuvered to anchor in nests of two and three. The battleship anchored further to sea, but within sight of land. In the morning, after the storm passed, the fleet would raise anchor and split up to take the midshipmen to liberty ports such as Barcelona, Cannes, and Marseilles. Part of their training was to gain firsthand understanding of another culture.

The fleet turned in for a quiet evening of rest after three grueling days of battle exercises. But during the night the quiet sea became a boiling caldron.

The wind grew to frightening speeds. Gusting to fifty knots and more, it bombarded the ships with sheets rain. The storm changed direction. Blake was on the bridge when the admiral was wakened. He came into the flag bridge and quickly looked around. Messages were already flying back and forth. Ships were reporting their anchors dragging. They were experiencing damage to masts and other equipment. Captains were taking matters into their own hands, untangling themselves from their nests, heaving in anchors, getting underway. While still at anchor, some ships smashed into and holed other ships. There were several collisions while getting underway.

The admiral ordered the fleet to immediately head west, more from a fear of his ships going aground on one of the islands than escaping from the direction of the storm. There was no escaping it. They were in its way, but moving was better than staying.

Blake had been in storms before, but this one acted like a bully. It beat them, chased them, then left them to lick their wounds. Two days later Admiral Alexander ordered the ships to make for their liberty ports, deposit the midshipmen ashore for their leaves, and make repairs.

CHAPTER 29

SPAIN

The next day brought an uneasy truce from the weather, a respite from the rain and high winds. Yet dark skies and clouds lingered following the pounding, rolling, and horrible smells of seasickness that were part of riding out the ocean storm.

Midshipmen were ready for liberty -- any place; after the storm, just getting their feet on dry land would be enough.

Barcelona, with one of the few good harbors in Spain, was the port for the *New Jersey* and a few of the smaller ships. Situated on the northeastern coast of the Iberian Peninsula, it is Spain's second largest city. Tradition had it that Christopher Columbus announced his discovery of the New World in the Plaza del Rey, a courtyard in the city surrounded by medieval towers.

Only Madrid had more people, and it was to that city Blake, Erie, and other midshipmen were off on that Friday afternoon. Dressed in service dress khaki, neckties, and blouses, they assembled to be bused to the Barcelona train station early on the day after their arrival. They boarded a European-style train with compartments holding six passengers each. Opening onto a corridor that ran the length of the car, each compartment had a door and window with curtains on the corridor side.

They made it into Madrid in the late afternoon -- hot, dirty, sweaty, and thankful it was all over. They dressed, and from the train, boarded buses that took them to their hotel rooms, where they again stripped off dirty uniforms. After quick baths and a fresh change of clothes, Blake and Erie were ready to hit the beach. Because of their late arrival due to the storm, they only had two days of liberty in Madrid, and so they wanted to make the most of it. It was already about 7:30 p.m. As they walked through the city they saw that all the restaurants and bars were closed. They turned a corner and saw a nice-looking restaurant with the doors open. All the lights were on. They hurried in, but the place was empty except for the waiters standing around. Convinced that everybody had already finished eating and the place was about to close, the mids asked, in their best broken-Español, if they were still serving dinner.

The waiter replied in excellent English, "Si, señor. The longer you are here, the more people show up. Dinner hour for Madrilènes begins about 10:30 p.m. and they serve as late as one o'clock in the morning. Madrid is known for having better restaurants than Paris, particularly the seafood."

"Gracias, senior." Erie said.

"De nada."

They placed their orders and relaxed with a beer. By the time they finished and stepped out of the restaurant, lights filled the entire street. Stars flooded the cloudless night. Hundreds of people came out of nowhere going into stores, restaurants, and bars. Smells of charcoal fires filled the air.

With their early start, Blake and Erie decided to begin what they expected to be a long and very enjoyable evening of bar hopping. In each bar they bought a beer, and practiced their Spanish by chatting with the barmen, and observed the clientele. Blake, who was not good with his alcohol, was already a bit dizzy. The earliest civilian arrivals were families with young children, but as the night drew on, the young people began to circulate through the town. By 11 p.m., music radiated from every bar. Young men and women roamed the streets, dancing and singing as they went. Blake and Erie stood outside deciding whether to go into one particularly loud and popular place named "Texas Bar" that displayed a neon sign of cowboy wearing a hat. Inside the sound of castanets kept time with the music.

As they were still deciding, a small, four-seated European sports car pulled up, swinging into a parking place directly in front of the bar. Its convertible top lay rolled across the shoulder of the back seat. The bouncers, who normally guarded the good parking places, said nothing. In the car were three girls about Blake's age, and driver driven by a man in his thirties. Giggling and laughing, the girls jumped to the pavement next to Erie.

"Hi ho, girls!" Erie said. "Going into the bar? Need some company?" Already a bit tipsy, he doffed his midshipman cap and swept it across his waist in knightly fashion.

"An American! What a find! Who are you and what are you doing here?" Extending her hand, the girl with a ready laugh said, "My name's Abigail, Abigail Cass. They call me Abby."

"I'm Berry," said a dark-eyed, dark-haired beauty in a spangled miniskirt and go-go boots.

"And I'm Jackie," said an equally pretty blonde dressed in a cowboy hat, electric-blue mini-dress, four turquoise bracelets, and open-toed shoes. She had ten glossy, red-painted toenails.

Blake, who had his eyes on Abby, whispered into Erie's ear. "Bingo! We just won the lottery." He showed a look of great pleasure.

"Rascal. Thought you were in love with Viva or Beverly. Can't keep up with your love life."

Blake grabbed Abby's extended hand. "My name is Blake Lawrence and this is Larry Tallman. We're off ships in Barcelona -- a midshipman cruise."

"What's a midshipman cruise?" Abby, dressed in the most conservative clothes of the three, asked.

"A cruise is our practical Naval Academy training program."

"What's the Naval Academy?" Abby had high cheekbones, a slight indentation in her rather pointy chin and large oval green eyes that both smiled and searched in a teasing way. Her face was that of an angel, but her eyes had the mark of ornery devilment -- a smile sat easily in the corner of her mouth. "Kidding. Just kidding. We all know about Annapolis. We're studying at Barnard -- over here on vacation."

"Barnard? What's Barnard?" He smiled back. "Kidding. Just kidding -- Columbia University."

"How long are you in Madrid?" Abby asked.

"Just two days -- tomorrow and one more."

Erie shouted, "Follow me!" He grabbed the other two girls by the arms and bolted into the bar -- leaving the driver and Abby on the street with Blake.

"How is it you always end up with two girls?" Blake yelled to Erie.

"You want to go in *there,* miss? It's not one of Madrid's best bars. A bit low life."

"Hell, yes! I wouldn't have had you stop here if I didn't!" She grabbed Blake's arm. "Esteban Franco is a race car driver who works for my father's company. Oh shit! He never wants us to have any fun -- my father, that is. He's paying Esteban to chaperone us."

Inside they were taken to a table near the stage where a woman wearing lots of beads, a long skirt, and heavy leather shoes with large heels stood snapping castanets to the beat of the band's Spanish music.

Abby leaned over and whispered in Blake's ear," Esteban is a relative of General Francisco Franco. He knows everyone and everyone knows him. He can get anything. Nice table, don't you think?"

The music was so loud that Blake had to lean close to talk in her ear. "You mean the dictator?"

"Shhh. Don't say "dictator." Say 'ruler of Spain.' Sounds better."

Better or not, Blake knew that since the end of the Spanish Civil War in 1939, Franco, the dictator/ruler of Spain, had established his own political party and outlawed all others.

Huddled together drinking beer at a small circular table, they tried to sing along with the Spanish songs. From time to time, the woman got up and danced flamenco style, snapping her heels, turning and twisting as she kept time with the castanets.

Above the music, Blake asked Abby, "Where's home?"

"Saginaw, Michigan," she responded after slugging down the rest of her beer. "Esteban. Order another round. This time, make it brandy."

"Miss Abby. Your father would not like that."

"Oh shit! My father again... Piss on him! If you knew my father -- stodgy, old Michigan. Brandy! All around."

"What are you studying at Barnard?" Blake asked the very attractive woman whose heart shaped face looked like a painting of an angel.

"Liberal arts. You know, Shakespeare and all that."

Leaning across Erie, Berry said, "Ask her about her favorite play."

"Well, what is it?" Blake said.

"Oh, that's easy. *The Taming of the Shrew*, of course."

"Why?"

"Oh, it has to do with the lead character, Kate. I played her in a performance we did last spring."

"So, why is it your favorite?"

"Well, there's some confusion about what Shakespeare was trying to do. I happen to believe he was foreshadowing changing times for women. I believe Kate's final speech of submission is missing the real thesis."

"I certainly do. Kate is certainly not 'a graceless traitor to her loving lord!' The Bard never intended it that way." Suddenly the music changed, and the band began playing such American songs as "Rags to Riches," "Lady of Spain," and "Moments to Remember."

They sang along, and when the band began playing "Three Coins in The Fountain," Blake turned to Abby and asked, "Dance?"

"I'd love to," her voice purred.

On the small dance floor, now occupied by many young couples holding each other as if each might fly away, Blake and Abby swayed to the rhythms. Her body language encouraged him to dance even closer. They didn't talk, but the roaming of her hands at the base of his neck let him know that she enjoyed the romance of the music and his body against hers. They had only known each other a few hours, but they began to kiss. He guessed she was at least twenty years old and reminded Blake of an older Flame, passionate and bold. As soon as that song stopped and the next, "Perfidia," was beginning, Abby said, "I love your blonde hair. It's hard to find blonde-haired men."

Blake said, "Less blonde and more tarnished brown."

"Let's get out of here," she said.

Sensing an opportunity he hadn't counted on, he agreed to leave. "Where to?"

Abby walked over to Esteban. "I'm going for a ride. Keys, please."

"My pleasure, señorita."

"No. I want the keys. I'm going for a ride -- alone." She turned to the others. "We're going for a ride. We'll be back."

On the street, Abby slid into the driver's seat. "Esteban taught me how to race this car. Didn't you?" Esteban was standing at the curb.

"Señorita, you should let me drive tonight."

Realizing what she was about to do and how much brandy she had drunk, Blake agreed with Esteban. But she would have none of it. "Nonsense, Esteban. Hang on, Blake."

"Wait! We're coming too!" it was Erie, Berry, and Jackie. They climbed in and sat on the back of the back seat, their feet dangling on the seat itself.

"Hang on!" Abby screeched tires as she pulled out into the empty street. Blake, in the passenger seat, was jolted backward. They all grabbed the roll bar and hung on. She changed gears as if she had been racing all her life. The sound of the engine echoed into the night as she fast along the wide, tree-lined boulevard.

"I know this town!" she shouted. "This plaza is called the Puerta del Sol or Gate of the Sun. It marks the center of downtown Madrid. We're on Calle de Alcala, one of the city's main streets."

Abby laughed as she skidded the small car into and around large circles where, during daylight hours, streams of cars made their way. But at 4:00 a.m. there was no traffic and became Abby's race course. Faster and faster she drove, braking as she approached each oval with its central statue of one of Spain's national heroes, then changing gears to keep the car at a screeching speed -- just on the verge of rolling.

"Easy does it, Abby. Don't lose this baby on the turns." Blake's knuckles were white as he held tight to anything available.

In the back, Erie and the other girls were laughing and screaming as if they were enjoying a roller coaster ride at Coney Island.

At the end of the long thoroughfare, she shouted above the noise, "The bullfights are held at the Plaza de Toros --- over there." She pointed. "We'll go there tomorrow. I'll pick you up at your hotel. We'll also go to the University of Madrid and the Prado. It's one of the world's outstanding art museums. Houses a collection of more than 2,000 paintings by the masters: El Greco, Francisco Goya, Diego Velazquez and Las Meninas. We have to hurry. We have only two days for your education."

Hmm, I don't know what to make of this wild woman, at times overbearing, ultra strong -- more a tomboy than a lady.

She turned the car in a tight circle and reversed her direction, again racing at the highest speed she could get out of the car. Screeching to a halt in front of Texas Bar, they all let out a yell.

"Weeee! Wasn't that fun!"

Esteban was still standing on the curb with a frustrated look on his face. "Here are the keys, Esteban. You can drive us home now."

"Was that all you wanted to do? Race around in that car?" Blake asked.

"Of course."

Abby leaned over and kissed Blake. She ran her tongue into his mouth, when his hands started to move toward her breasts she pushed him out to the curb and Estaban got in.

"Silly boy. I'll pick you up tomorrow."

Blake and Erie stood on the sidewalk watching. As they drove away, Erie said, "She's the daughter of a big-time Michigan industrialist. Her family has more money than dirt and she's going to Yale Law when she finishes Barnard."

"How do you know all that?"

"Berry and Jackie. They know everything about her. She's also their class president, a feminist, and studies finance at Columbia."

*****

The next morning, Blake was awakened by a knock on his hotel door. "Señor Lawrence, Miss Abigail sent me. You are to come with me to have breakfast."

"What time is it?"

"Ten o'clock, señor."

Blake, hung over from the night before, dressed and went next door to Erie's room. "I'm going off with Abby. Her car's here."

"What am I going to do?"

"Oh, you'll think of something. You can go to the museums," Blake said.

"That'll be the day. Maybe the bullfights."

Esteban drove him to a small outdoor café where Abby sat drinking coffee. She got up and, without asking if he slept well or how he felt, kissed him full on the mouth.

"Give me a chance to get my eyes open – no, forget that." He reached to take her in his arms and kiss her.

"Oh, no! She again eluded his embrace. "There's so much for you to learn. Here, drink this." She poured dark coffee into a small cup. "Spaniards like to sit for hours, like we're doing, visiting at sidewalk cafes or in town or village squares. On weekends, city people often drive into the Spanish countryside for picnics or overnight trips. One of the best-known celebrations is the fiesta or festival of San Fermin, which is celebrated each July in Pamplona. Bulls are turned loose in the streets as part of the festivities. People run ahead of the animals to the bull ring, where they hold amateur bullfights. We don't have time to go there, but maybe some day we can."

Blake looked at her more closely. In the daylight she had the same angelic features he had noted the evening before. But now he could see an air of grace that he had missed. Her reddish hair was brushed tightly back and tied in Spanish style. It reminded him, except for the color, of Viva, but this woman didn't have to make a rehearsal. She sat carefully exposing an inch of knee, no more. She already had begun her tease. It wouldn't take much to own him.

She passed the plate of fruit to him, then took a sip of coffee. Didn't you say you were returning to Barcelona? Maybe I'll come there and visit you."

"I won't be there very long. We get underway the day after I get back."

"Enough time." She picked some cheese from a plate and tasted it.

He drank his coffee and said, "Enough! Let's get out of here!"

They were inseparable for the next two days, making the rounds of the bullfights, museums, and art shows. They spent both evenings at the Texas Bar where they danced until three or four in the morning, later walking in the chilled nights along wide streets where they pointed out the tails of comets to each other. In the pale lemon mornings when the high young sun broke over the mountains, they touched and kissed passionately as if it were their last chance to ever kiss again.

When it was time to go, the sun had risen full, glowing red like the blood of a bull they had seen killed the day before. Abby came to the train station to see him off, but she would not come to Barcelona. He told her not to because there wasn't enough time and he would be too busy.

"Will I see you again?" Blake asked.

"Will you?"

"Meet me in Paris!" He blurted.

"When?"

"In two weeks."

"I kiss you and love you with all my heart," she said. "But no promises. I will try to be there."

He drew her to him. "If I miss you, I'll call. Will you answer?"

"Only if you call."

They kissed again and he climbed aboard the train, still questioning why he liked her so much. In many respects she was like Viva and Beverly – they all know where they're going.

Maybe that's the kind of woman I'm captivated by. On the other hand, she does like to kiss.

CHAPTER 30

SUBMARINE AT SEA

Aboard the returning train, the other midshipmen, between laughs and jokes and the telling of their conquests, caught up on their sleep. Erie bragged that he had met a Spanish socialite. Her name was Señorita Margarita Garcia Cortez, and she showed him the better places of Madrid, including a room on the top floor of the tallest hotel.

But Blake's mind remained in Madrid, where he once again had fallen in love. He couldn't sleep. Now he had a real dilemma. Before Abby, he knew he loved Viva. He also liked Beverly very much. The only thing for him to do was get them off his mind, but his work had dried up. He was no longer the senior midshipman on the *New Jersey*. After Barcelona he became just an ordinary firstie. Another high-grease classmate took over as midshipman navigator for the remainder of the cruise.

Until the ship got underway he was still a member of the admiral's staff. He hung around the flag bridge.

The admiral stormed back and forth from his cabin to the staff briefing room to flag plot his battle control room. Agitated -- no longer the calm, affable, story-teller, and friendly fatherly figure to midshipmen - he barely noticed Blake was still around. Like a cranky high school principal, he bullied about the bridge barking for this information and that. "What will the weather be like when we get underway? Is every ship topped off on fuel? Is the training plan complete?"

Standing near a meeting of staff officers, Blake overheard the chief of staff say, "The reason he's so grouchy is Washington is on his butt for a decision about the storm damage. He's read all the reports and recommendations. Now he must decide. A lot of skippers could hang."

At lunch that day, Blake's last in the flag mess, the admiral took his seat and immediately began chatting with the visiting midshipmen. From the other end of the table, where he now sat, having been reduced in rank, Blake detected a change in the admiral's manner. He had returned to his normal take-it-as you-find-it attitude. As a result, Blake thought that after lunch would be the time to approach him with an idea he had already discussed with the chief of staff.

"Gentlemen," the admiral said as he held his water glass high. "A toast. To tough decisions."

"Tough decisions," came the unison response.

"After lunch I will announce the results of the investigation about the storm damage we experienced lst week to our task force and to the Navy. Then we'll see what happens."

We'll see what happens? Obviously, heads would roll. Pity the commanding officers who didn't protect their ships during that storm.

"But before the messages go on the air, I want you to know what action I've chosen. I have decided to accept complete responsibility for everything. No commanding officer will suffer as a result of my poor judgment. I ordered the ships to that anchorage, and I alone must accept the results."

The mess sat in stunned silence.

Blake's throat felt like there were a large stone stuck in it.

Had he heard the admiral correctly? Accepting full responsibility for thousands and thousands of dollars of damage? Exonerating every one but himself? Like Jesus on the cross? Wouldn't that mean the end of a promising career? It was the most noble thing Blake had experienced -- except when Greenfield spooned him plebe year. More than a few CO's will find relief in his decision.

"Please pass the twins," the admiral said with a grin. A mess man standing nearby jumped to hand Admiral Alexander the salt and pepper. "Mister Lawrence, the chief of staff tells me you wish to complete the cruise on a submarine. Excellent idea. Broaden your understanding of the Navy. Wish we could send every midshipman, but there are too many mids and too few subs."

The idea had come to Blake as he was walking down the pier with Erie after their return from Madrid. An attack submarine was tied up near *New Jersey*. The dark, quiet ship stirred Blake's curiosity.

"Wonder if I could get aboard to look around?"

"Go ahead and try," Erie said, continuing on his way toward his destroyer. "If it doesn't have wings, I'm not interested. See you back at the Academy."

"See ya later." Blake responded as he walked over to the small gangway. A seaman wearing dungarees lounged out of the sun.

"Is it possible for me to get a tour of the ship?"

The sailor shouted back, "Doubt it, but I'll call the duty officer and ask. What are you? One of those *New Jersey* midshipmen?"

"Yeah."

A few minutes later a lieutenant came on deck. "You want a tour of the boat?"

"If it's okay. Never been aboard one -- yet," Blake replied.

"What the heck. Come aboard, I'll show you around." The officer introduced himself simply as Bob. It struck Blake that he had never heard an officer offer that kind of informality before. "I'll show you the conning tower, control room, and a few other places. Can't show you the whole boat though, not cleared."

Blake followed Bob as he climbed down the ladder into the room, then through a tight passageway to a small mess deck, and then an engine room. On the way out, Blake asked, "When do you go to sea next?"

"We're underway before the rest of the task force. We'll play with the midshipman training cruise for a few days, giving the destroyers some anti-sub work."

The lieutenant wore an academy class ring so Blake, thinking there would be some sympathy there, asked him, "Any chance of my going to sea with you?"

"Don't know. Wait here. I'll ask the skipper."

He was back in a few minutes. "It's okay with him. But we're under the Opcon of your training group. You'll have to get an okay from the admiral and some orders. Follow me. He wants to meet you."

Sitting a room only a little bigger than a telephone booth was a short stocky commander wearing only a T-shirt and khaki trousers. He rose and shook Blake's hand. "Name's Ben Claggett. Understand you want to cruise with us. Couple of things. If you do get permission, bring only a few sets of clothes, nothing fancy. We'll make every effort to get you back to the *Jersey*, but I don't know how. Still want to come?"

*****

Blake agreed to Commander Claggett's terms and now, with the blessing of Admiral Alexander, he stood on the pier with a small duffel bag of clothes and approached his next adventure -- a long, dark cigar-shaped body enabled by its form to move swiftly underwater. The tall, thin structure called the sail, with its periscopes, radar, and radio antennas, sat in the middle of the submarine's deck like a chimney.

Thus far in his training, he had nothing to do with the silent service. Others in his class had gone to sea for a week during second-class summer but he was busy with his dad's change of command and other matters. However, he knew a lot about the history of submarines; Greenfield had made sure of that.

Now he crossed the gangway. He saluted the American flag, then a chief who was waiting on the boat. "Reporting for a training cruise, sir."

"Come aboard, Mr. Lawrence."

Blake was surprised that the chief already knew his name.

"Take him below and show him his bunk," the chief said to a sailor standing next to him. As Blake was passing to follow the sailor, the chief caught his arm and said, "Don't remember me, do you?"

Blake stopped and took a better look at the stocky, thick-jawed man. "Willowby? You're a chief! How'd you get aboard a sub?"

"I transferred from destroyers. Wanted subs all along but kept screwing up. I kept trying, and they finally sent me to sub school. Made chief, thanks to you, while I was there and here I am aboard the good boat SS-426 -- better known as *Tusk*."

As if he was demonstrating his knowledge of the boat Willowby said, "'Tusk' is alternate name for the cusk, a large edible saltwater fish related to the cod."

"Well I'll be damned. What about McMichaels, Jones, and Barber?"

"Lost touch after I left *Ingraham*. My guess is they went home when their enlistment was up. See you when I get off watch."

To the sailor he said, "Put him in a bunk near mine."

"Okay, Chief Willowby." The sailor motioned to Blake. "Follow me."

Blake hadn't previously noticed the diesel smell in the sub, but as soon as he put his gear on his rack, the odor seemed to seep into his nostrils. The mattress was covered with a plastic cover zipped tight to keep out the dampness caused by condensation, which looked to Blake to be on everything: pipes, stations, lockers.

"Diesel smell is sure strong, isn't it?" Blake said to the sailor.

"You'll get used to it -- it's in the air and soon will be on your clothes, skin, and hair. Then you won't even know. It's the trademark of a submariner. We call it our 'Eau de Diesel' perfume."

"Got to get back on deck," the sailor said. "You're welcome to go into the mess. Cookie'll fix you something. Food's good."

In the small mess deck, Blake sat on a round seat bolted to the deck. The cook asked, "Want something?" He looked different than any other Navy cook Blake had seen. Cookie was skinny and his uniform was squared away, not grease covered like those worn by cooks aboard *New Jersey*.

"Nope, not hungry."

"You the midshipman whose gonna sail with us?"

"Yep."

"Skipper told us to tell you everything about *Tusk*."

"Good."

"What do you want to know?" Cookie asked.

"Everything."

"Everything? Okay. Here goes. Displacement: Surfaced: 1,570 tons, Submerged: 2,415 tons. Length: 311'8"; Beam: 27'3"; Draft: 16'5"; Speed: Surfaced: 20.25 knots; Submerged: 8.5 knots; Complement: 81; Armament: 1- 5"; 1- 40mm; 1- 20mm; 2 -.50 cal. MG; 10 - 21" torpedo tubes; Class: BALAO."

It sounded very mechanistic, engineer-like.

"How come you memorized all that stuff? You're the cook!"

"Everyone has to qualify." His voice had a spark of pride in it.

Other sailors came in, took something to eat, and left. After about an hour, Chief Willowby came down through the conning tower. "You get a bunk?"

"Yep. But it stinks."

"This boat is a piece of junk. Tusk is old -- and beat up. She's a good ship, er, boat. I keep forgetting I'm in the submarine Navy now. Wait until you take a shower, in rust-colored salt water."

"How old is she?"

He sounded like Cookie, even worse. He had memorized the whole spiel. "*Tusk*'s not quite as old as *Ingraham*... but almost. SS-426 was laid down on 23 August 1943 at Philadelphia, by the Cramp Shipbuilding Co. then launched 8 July 1945, and commissioned on 11 April 1946."

The skipper came out of his cabin followed by the XO of the boat. "They're headed up to the bridge," Willowby said. "The top of the sail also serves as the bridge, from there the captain conns the submarine when on the surface.

"We're getting underway. Probably best if you went up to the sail and observed from there. The skipper might have a surprise for you," Willowby said. "I have to get up on deck and take care of the lines. You don't do that any more." He winked impishly.

The CO stepped toward Blake and said, "How would you like to get her underway and conn the boat out of port?"

Blake realized then that this could be the training period of his lifetime. He had sailed small boats back at the Academy and had a few days on board the yard YPs, the midshipman training boats, but he had never handled a ship. He was only a youngster aboard *Ingraham* and no one less than a commander conned the *New Jersey*.

"Yes, sir. I would!"

Commander Claggett spent a few minutes describing the boat. "The sail stands only about 20 feet high so you have a very low perspective compared to most ships. We have two propellers in the stern to drive the submarine. To steer the boat we have rudders mounted below the propellers. Any questions?"

"No, sir. Not yet."

"Okay, Mr. Lawrence, get her underway."

"Aye, aye, sir." Blake looked the length of the ship from stem to stern, then his eyes took in the entire harbor. She was moored portside to the pier. He would have to take in the lines and get her moving astern into the open seaway, then turn her for the open sea. He ordered, "Test the engines!"

From somewhere came an immediate response, "Engines tested satisfactorily, sir."

Hmm, just like at school.

328 CARL A. NELSON

"Single up all lines!"

"All lines singled up, sir." This time Blake turned his head to see where the responses were coming from. It was a sailor on a sound-powered headset.

"Take in all lines!"

The lines came in smartly and the deck crew lined up just like in the destroyer Navy.

Maybe this is Willowby's doing.

"All lines -- I mean all engines back one-third." He looked quickly at the CO and XO, who were standing right behind him, to see if they heard his mistake. They smiled.

The submarine slowly picked up movement astern.

"Give her a bit of right rudder, Mr. Lawrence. About ten degrees will do," the skipper said.

Blake thought. Right rudder will cause the stern to turn to starboard when backing. He ordered, "Right ten degrees rudder!"

"Sir, the rudder is right ten," the talker said.

Blake looked at the compass. "Steady as she goes." It was an order he had only heard in a classroom. It meant for the steersman to note the heading at the time the order was given, report it in degrees, and steer that heading.

"Steady as she goes, steering 180 astern, sir." came the response.

"Submarines don't back well at all," Commander Claggett said softly. "It's very hard to hold a steady compass heading. Better to just give rudder orders, Mr. Lawrence."

"Yes, sir. Rudder amidships."

"Rudder is amidships, sir," the talker responded.

No longer feeling the adrenaline, Blake was comfortable. With a few quiet remarks from the skipper he turned the boat and headed for the open sea. It was not long after they cleared the harbor that the skipper said, "Okay, Mr. Lawrence. Not bad. Actually, very professional. I'll take over now."

"Aye, aye, sir."

"This is the captain. I have the conn. Rig for dive."

"Rig for dive, aye."

A few minutes later everyone topside had disappeared into the control room. Only Blake and the CO were left topside.

Not long after, the officer of the deck reported, "Rigged for dive, sir."

"Take her down!" the captain ordered. He took one last look around and pointed toward the hatch. Blake and the skipper were soon in the control room and Chief Willowby was standing behind the man on the diving planes.

Blake stood off to one side as the skipper ordered, "Take her down to 100 feet."

Chief Willowby explained to Blake, "Steel fins called diving planes stick out from both sides of the bow and from the stern. They guide the ship to different depths."

Blake nodded, meaning he understood.

Soon the submarine was at its cruising depth and speed and after the skipper ordered the regular watch to relieve the maneuvering watch, Blake and Chief Willowby went back to the mess deck to get a cup of coffee.

It seemed that Willowby wanted to show Blake how much he knew about submarines and *Tusk* in particular. Blake figured it was because of his conversion and that he had recently been to sub school.

"How do we get back up?" Blake smiled.

"Two ways: just the opposite of diving," Willowby said. "Water is blown out of the ballast tanks by compressed air, or the diving planes are tilted so the boat angles up."

"What do you want me to do while I'm aboard?"

"Just relax and enjoy. We have a library, motion pictures, and games to help ease the monotony."

"Well, that's a bunch of crap. You know me, chief. I won't just sit around. Give me something to do," Blake countered.

"I'll talk to the XO. But the crew works a four-hour watch; you know, four on, eight off. I don't know what you could do -- you're not a submariner. There's some maintenance work you could do, but mostly you're free to observe, relax, or study until we return to port."

After supper, Blake went to his rack and turned in. He slept through the night and was in the mess hall when Chief Willowby came to get him. "Skipper said it's okay for you to stand some watches under instruction. You have the noon-to-four diving plane watch."

For the next two days, under the careful eye of Chief Willowby, Blake got the hang of maneuvering the boat's planes. He also took turns working the steering. In addition to his watches, he spent time in the control room just off the conning tower, watching how the skipper and his ODs moved in close to the formation by day using the number one periscope and antennas. They moved out 20-30 miles from the formation at night to charge their batteries. Occasionally he would be invited to take a look through number two periscope, which would go up for no more than a thirty-second spin around the horizon and focus quickly on the ships. For Blake it was right out of a World War II movie.

It was on one those occasions when Blake had the watch as planesman that the OD shouted, "A destroyer is turning in our direction, skipper."

"Quick, let me take a look." He swung his arms over resting bars. "Got her. Range?"

"Ten thousand yards, sir."

"No sweat. Skimmers in this water can't hold us. But let's take no chances. We'll play it for real. Down scope. Sound battle stations."

"Where's the layer?" the skipper asked.

"At about 200 feet," came a report from sonar.

"Take her to 300 feet."

"Battle stations. Three hundred feet, aye, skipper."

"Battle stations, battle stations."

Blake watched as everyone began running all at once, out of the mess where they were watching movies, squeezing past each other in skinny passageways.

The battle station planesman took over from Blake and, measuring the depth gauges, took her down and held her there.

Chief Willowby stood beside Blake. "The skipper will want us to stay quietly submerged to avoid detection. But if they get us, he will try to slip away. He's pretty damn good at this."

"What's a layer?" Blake asked.

"A temperature layer happens when a mass of cold water meets warmer water. If there is a layer -- and there isn't one always -- we can hide under it because the layer reflects back to the surface any sonar pings. The Med has horrible sonar conditions -- salt water meets fresh, warm meets cold. We can almost call our own shots."

"Okay, knock it off, you two. No more talking."

"Aye, aye, skipper," Willowby whispered.

After a while the pinging became louder. The XO said, "More than one, skipper. I think they have us."

For the next eight hours, *Tusk* lay at depth. Never moving. Pretending it was not a submarine. All non-essential equipment was shut down. Ice machines, lights, fans, blowers were turned off. Men were sent to their bunks to conserve oxygen. The pinging was incessant and irritating. Some men put pillows over their heads to muffle the sound.

After several more hours, the skipper tried a maneuver using battery power. He tried slowly reversing the course to go under the menacing destroyers circling above occasionally dropping hand grenades. Another time he put on a burst of speed and tried to outrun them. But despite the layer and his maneuvers, the surface ships hung on. At the end of the day, *Tusk*'s batteries became low and the air became foul. Carbon dioxide levels rose. To absorb the carbon dioxide, Commander Claggett ordered the use of canisters of lithium hydroxide crystals.

Then came a report from sonar. "Sir, I think there's another sub nearby. I can hear its signature."

"Commander Williams, put on the headset and listen."

"Hear that subtle noise under the loud pinging from topside? That's another sub. I think I know the reason the tin cans have us, sir. There's two of us here; another sub is tailing us."

"Can you classify it?" Commander Claggett said.

"Soviet."

*****

Blake listened to the tense, gripping discussions between Commander Claggett, his executive officer, and Bob, the lieutenant who took Blake on his tour of the boat and was now the OOD. Bob occasionally slipped in remarks like, "Battery is damn low, and the air is getting really foul."

Commander Claggett shook his head. "You think it's a Zulu class? They have to recharge on the surface or snorkel. Sonar: How long you think she's been trailing us?"

A sonarman said, "Well, they're probably snooping our anti-submarine ops. Maybe as much as eight hours; as few as three, sir. I never saw her until we made that slow turn. So she could have slipped in several hours before that."

"Their battery will be down -- lower than ours," the skipper said, his hands gripping the plotting table. "They'll have to surface before us."

Chief Willowby, in dungaree trousers and a bare chest that showed tattoos of a winged horse, an American flag, an anchor, a chain, and the word "mother," stood off to one side. He whispered to Blake, "This is strategy time. Way out of my league."

"We could surface and report it to Admiral Alexander," the XO said.

"True. We could," the skipper agreed. "Of course it is peacetime. But wouldn't it be better if we forced a Russian to surface? What if we team with our surface buddies and turn the tables?"

Commander Claggett scratched his head. "Wasn't it *Gudgeon* that the Soviets forced to surface?"

"Yeah, it was *Gudgeon*." the XO confirmed.

"We owe 'em one," the skipper said as he slapped the table. "Damn! And right here in our laps we have an opportunity to repay the bastards. Let the world know they're also doing some spying."

"One thing we could do -- a fast reverse. Leave Charlie in our dust," the XO suggested.

"What about some noisemakers? Put out a bubble of air. Maybe a burst over Gertrude?"

"If the reverse works we could tail him for a while," the XO added.

Blake was reminded of the time two years before aboard *Ingraham* when Commander Andriso thought he had caught a Soviet sub.

He almost unloaded on her that time. Commander Claggett better watch out -- one of those trigger-happy destroyer skippers could become confused about what's going on down here.

What happened next was a blur to Blake. The skipper gave orders and the crew jumped to it, but Blake in his infancy as a submariner was lost in a nomenclature he didn't understand. The thought processes seemed more like chess than poker. He suspected that maneuvering in the blind against another submarine risked collision. All he could do was watch and listen.

What he saw was a Navy commander sweating. profusely, a crew lit up like a team of sled dogs, and a chief, who always relished a fight, rubbing his hands together as if he were about to enter a barroom brawl.

"Mr. Lawrence, your orders only specified secret clearance. This stuff is even higher than top secret. Sorry, but we'll have to kill you before we get back to port." Commander Claggett held a serious look before breaking into a wide smile. "Just kidding. However this is highly classified stuff. Your lips are sealed."

"Sealed, sir," Blake responded in a serious tone.

"You're probably going to miss your next liberty port. Hope you didn't have a date waiting."

"No sweat, sir." Blake replied to the skipper, but he was thinking about Abby and their date in Paris.

What is it about the Med... Every time I come here I miss a date. First it was with Viva in Cannes and now Abby.

It was some time after that sonar reported that they held the Soviet directly ahead on passive sonar. "You want me to ping him, skipper?"

Blake looked at Willowby. "Ping him?"

"Send out one ping and get a range."

"Yes. Let's make him sweat a little."

"Done, sir. Range 2,500 yards."

For two days *Tusk* tracked the Soviet. They released a noisemaker occasionally to make sure the fleet above knew where they were. But the fleet had a midshipman training schedule to keep and soon went away. However, several destroyers seemed to appear out of nowhere. Commander Claggett said they would be units of the U.S. Sixth Fleet.

It was like holding formation. The Soviet tried a few tactics, even attempting to reverse on *Tusk,* but Claggett was too clever.

The air became terribly foul and the heat in the sub escalated. Nerves came to a razor edge until one evening sonar reported, "She's surfacing, sir."

"Got the S.O.B. We did it! Turned the tables! We're even! Hazzah!"

Tusk followed her to the surface but remained at snorkel depth.

"Up scope," Commander Claggett ordered. He ducked his head and, spinning the periscope as it raised, circled the horizon. "Destroyer on the port bow -- Soviet sub directly ahead. Right full rudder. Let's get out of here. Stay at snorkel depth -- charge our batteries and... OD, let the destroyers know who we are. We don't need to confuse our own boys."

CHAPTER 31

FIRST CLASS YEAR

By the time *Tusk* was recharged and made its way to the port of Naples, Italy, Blake had missed the remainder of his training cruise aboard *New Jersey,* including the port visit to Cherbourg and his Paris liberty with Abby. He was so late that the training group had already sailed for the States.

He was given transportation orders and flown home aboard a military aircraft. The plane landed in Washington, D.C., but before he left the airport, he inquired if there were any space available flights to anywhere near Los Angeles. He was told one was leaving that night, but he needed orders.

At the Academy, he showered and changed from the same uniform he had worn for several weeks. He collected his leave papers and headed back to Bolling Air Force Base. Before he left, he put in a call to Abby in Michigan. He would have gone to see her, mainly to sort out his confused love life -- did he care more for Viva or Abby? But he learned she was still out of the country. He left a message explaining that the reason he missed her in Paris was because the Navy unavoidably detained him at sea.

Then he called Viva in Los Angeles. He asked her if she would be back East during his leave period. She said she could not; she was working in her first movie and couldn't get away. She asked if he might get out to the coast. He lied when he said, "No money, honey."

Finally he called his mother in Pittsburgh. He told her that he was going to California for a few weeks and would stop in Pittsburgh before returning to the Academy. She asked, "What shall I tell Beverly?"

"Tell her I'm visiting a friend in Santa Barbara." He felt stupid balancing two girls with lies. He didn't feel good about either. One was to surprise Viva and the other to cover his tracks.

The plane, a new Air Force B-52 stopped in Ohio and Utah before touching down at March Air Force Base near Riverside, California. From there Blake hitched a ride with an Air Force major who had an appointment with a lawyer in downtown L.A. From city center he took a bus to Beverly Hills and booked into an inexpensive hotel.

The next morning he went searching for Viva. He traced her to MGM studios, and after a half-hour trip by bus, approached the gate.

"You got a pass, buddy?" the gate guard asked.

"Nope. But I was hoping you would make an exception."

"What are those anchors for? You in the Navy or somth'n?"

"Midshipman."

"Midshipman? What's that?"

"Student at Annapolis."

"Oh, I know that place. I was in the Navy -- WW II. Who you looking for?"

"A girl."

"Why am I not surprised? What's her name?"

"Her real name is Kathy Velenochi."

The guard searched the bottom of the list. "Nobody by that name."

"My guess is she goes by Viva. Try that."

"Viva. Hmm." His finger again traced the list to its bottom. "Viva Voce. On sound stage three at building 200. Now don't let anyone know I broke the rules. Here, put on this badge, sailor. And good luck."

Blake wound his way through the maze of buildings, halls, and rooms asking people as he went the direction to sound stage three. "Just around the corner," he was told.

She stood among a cluster of eight or nine girls apparently waiting their turn to go before the cameras. In costume she looked like just another of the many troopers Blake saw walking the lot preparing to do their parts to make movie magic. But when the director called for the shoot, it was Viva who bounced out front. Despite the fact that she looked like just one of the cast, she really lit up in front of the camera. Tall, leggy, and blonde again, she had the lead. She had the lead!! She was the star!! Viva could always sing. Her voice was beautiful -- from the time he first heard her at Sam's home in Philadelphia after the Army-Navy game, plebe year. In New York she could get good singing parts but she apparently didn't want that even though it was her strong suit. She wanted to be an actress, but in her acting parts she had been amateurish. But now she could act -- a gesture here, a powerfully spoken word there -- she seemed free and natural. All eyes were focused on her – like there was no one else on stage. It was a brilliant scene, and the director knew it when he said, "Cut! In the can! Beautiful, Viva. Just beautiful!"

Blake stayed out of sight, dodging the many people who rushed around in the making of a film. After the final take, he nudged his way through the several well-wishers. Standing behind, he waved over the crowd. "Hello, hello! Have a coke with a sailor?"

"Blake! How...? Where...? You're here! Another surprise! First it was me surprising you in Cannes, then you coming to New York, and now this! What a delight. Everyone! Everyone! This is my man from Annapolis -- you know, the place back east where they make the real John Waynes."

She took his arm and guided him away from the others.

She had changed. Blake sensed it in the way she spoke, the tone of her voice, and her body language. He shook his head and smiled. "You're a star!"

"Am not. At least not yet. But I'm working on it. Where are you staying?"

"A flea-bag over on Sunset Boulevard."

"That's not far from my flea bag apartment. Blake, I'm so busy. I haven't done anything. Let's see this town together. I'll fit you in. Will you be patient?"

"Wasn't I patient in New York last summer?"

"It wasn't last summer," Viva said. "It was the summer before. We've known each other now for more than three years."

"This may be getting serious," Blake said. He grasped her shoulders, then kissed her.

"Oh, I'm happy to see you," she said.

"I am too, very happy."

For the next week, they wove a path around her schedule. Between shoots they had sandwiches at the Hollywood Hilton on the way to Santa Barbara in her old Mercedes to spend a few hours with Blake's roommate Pete and his parents. They walked around Grauman's Chinese Theatre where Viva declared she would some day have her foot and handprints placed in concrete next to Fred Astaire and Rosalind Russell's. She told him about her good reviews in New York and Broadway, that she tested for Hollywood and signed a five-year contract. They attended an opening of a new release that her studio gave for one of its movies. The tickets were given to her cast as a reward for being under cost and ahead of schedule, a rarity in Hollywood. They danced and got tipsy together. He noticed that she got drunk easily, and that she liked it. In fact she drank too much -- she liked martinis too much and he told her so. She grabbed his hand and they ran up a street and played hop scotch, skip, and jump at the chalk marks left by kids earlier in the day. In kaleidoscope evenings, they held hands and walked on the Santa Monica beach. They even skinny dipped at a secluded section near Malibu.

Blake marveled at how casual their relationship became. It was new to him, but he loved the touch of her body, which was at least a ten.

On the chilly mornings they watched the sun sprint across translucent waves rolling in from Pacific seas. She reminded him that he was breaking what she called silly Naval Academy rules: "Conduct unbecoming. Ha!" He never thought of Beverly or Abby. Viva continued to capture his heart, but mostly his soul. He adored her.

At the end of that week Blake received a call from his mother. "They're trying to get you, son. Call the commandant's office. Something about the fall striper list. You will be home before you go back to school, won't you?'

"Of course, Mom."

He made the call. "Midshipman First Class Lawrence calling the commandant's office. Can you put me through?" He asked the operator.

Time lapsed before he heard, "Mr. Lawrence?"

"Yes, sir."

"This is Commander Baldridge, operations officer, Bancroft Hall. Your dad's out of town, on vacation in Europe. I have some good news. The commandant's Striper Board composed of the six battalion officers and myself have selected you to be the fall set six-striper."

Silence.

"You hear what I just said?" Commander Baldridge asked.

"Y… Yes. Yes, sir. I think... Did you say six-striper? Me?"

"You'll have to cut your leave a bit short. We need you here at least a week before academic year begins. Maybe the beginning of the week after next? Can you make it?"

He hadn't thought about it. The submarine trip, leave, Abby, Viva; his mind hadn't gotten around to first class year yet. He thought he would be a striper; everyone was, sooner or later, but six-striper?

That night they sat petting in her Mercedes parked high in the Hollywood Hills. Looking out through the windshield at the lights of Los Angeles, they talked about their futures. She said she would become a big movie star but also do plays and musicals on Broadway and even in Europe. His vision was less certain and much shorter in span. Sometime during his last year he would have to make his choice to become a pilot, submariner, or surface ship sailor. He told her he leaned toward going to sea on a destroyer.

"Why not fly?" she asked.

"Don't know. Haven't ruled it out. By the way, I got a call from Mom. She told me to call the Academy and I did. I have good news."

"What?"

"I'm going to be the first set six-striper."

Viva took her head off his shoulder, sat up, and looked at him. "That's good?"

"Well, part of our training first class year includes running the brigade. Don't you remember my telling you about the stripes on firsties' sleeves? At the football game, remember?"

"Oh, that."

"Remember I said the midshipman organization shadows the commandant's organization. The idea is to let the midshipmen manage themselves. Well, the six-striper heads the midshipman organization. It's a big deal."

"Will you have to work with your dad? You told me you two don't get along."

"Yeah. But -- anyway, I have to go back early."

"Early? How soon?"

"Tomorrow."

"Tomorrow?"

Her eyes dropped and he saw tears. "I'll miss you. This was going so well."

"I know. I feel the same way."

He held her for a few moments then said, "I'm flying back by way of Pittsburgh, commercial – to see my mom. Can you get me to the Los Angeles airport by noon?"

Blake and Viva parted at the entrance to the airport. She couldn't go in with him because she had to get back to another shoot. They kissed hungrily and squeezed each other like neither wanted to part.

"Try to get back east," he said. "We can go to another dance."

"And I can be a 'drag' again -- whoopee." Her cynical tone could have been from an old Rosalind Russell movie.

"Come on, it wasn't that bad."

"No, but I think I'll stay in a hotel. I'm beyond the drag house routine."

After he was on the plane, Blake thought about how close he came to asking her to become engaged, like he almost did at West Point the year before. But this time something told him that it wasn't right. Maybe he'd ask her next spring, after he knew what he would be doing in the Navy.

*****

During his short stay in Pittsburgh, Blake hung around the house with his mom. She told him that Charlie, after lying around Pittsburgh for a month or so after being found at West Point, had enlisted in the Army -- he vowed to recoup. He learned that Beverly no longer worked for Jack. She now worked for a department store as their merchandising manager. He called and took her out for lunch. She told him it was what she had studied in college and that she preferred sales to taxes. The length of his leave now seemed just right, even though it had been cut short by a submarine situation he couldn't talk about. He had gotten to the West Coast to see Viva and fulfilled his responsibility to visit his mother.

It happened the night before he was to leave. Sitting in the kitchen while eating cookies with milk, his mom said, "You know I like Jack a lot."

"Yeah."

"He asked me to marry him."

"You should, if you want to – if he makes you happy."

"I didn't want you to be surprised. I've already decided to marry him,"

"When?"

"In the near future."

He got up and went to his mom and hugged her. "It's a good move, mom. Good move."

*****

Blake kissed his mother good-bye and caught the bus to Annapolis. As he walked through the yard, a new feeling came over him. The trees seemed taller, the grass greener, and the late summer sun touched his skin with the comfort of a place he had grown to love. Soon he would be leaving to take on the real world. He was told to move into the room close to the commandant's office, which was reserved for the brigade captain and his deputy. After he unpacked he strolled into the main office and looked at the penciled-in names on the striper lists. Each place on the list was filed in with his classmates' names; everyone got a chance to show their stuff during the fall and winter. The best would make up the spring, or third, set list. He discovered that Lee Locke, his high grease competitor, would relieve him as the second or winter set six-striper. In the meantime Lee would play 150-pound football. Blake's basketball team didn't begin practice until later in the fall.

On the first morning of the new academic year, Blake stood at the lectern in the mess hall and looked out at the blur of 3,600 students extending from one end of the giant room to the other. The noise of upper classmen shouting at the new plebe class filled the air.

"How's the cow, mister? Eyes in the boat! You don't know the menu? Come around! What's the first law of the Navy, dufus?"

On Blake's left he heard plebes singing, "The Goat is Old and Gnarly." On his right a plebe stood on a mess hall table slapping two serving spoons together over his head and shouting again and again at the top of his lungs, "I didn't say 'sir,' sir."

"More balls, mister!" the firstie shouted.

"I didn't say 'sir,' sir." the plebe bellowed louder.

Blake listened as one fatherly classmate explained in detail to all the plebes at his table how to mix the goo, a midshipman-made condiment sauce used on hamburgers and other select foods. "Mustard, redeye, salt, pepper, and a bit of lemon. Mix it to a consistency of baby poop. You now are all goo strikers," he told them. "After you've proven your technical prowess, you may be promoted to apprentice goo maker."

His mind slipped back three years to his first days in the mess hall with the upper class. Nothing had changed. The cycle had begun again. The upper classman he remembered most vividly was Greenfield, the biggest prick in the brigade. He vaguely remembered a few other upper classmen, now a colorless blur. He remembered Tom Gladmore, who helped him plebe summer and who achieved his dream to become a Marine. Dale Thompson, the six-striper was quiet, thoughtful, and polite -- even to plebes. Dan Sloan, his own firstie, was a zero who was just putting in his time reciting IHTFP.

"Brigaaaaaade!" Blake waited for the din to subside. A hush came over the 3,600 hungry midshipmen as they came to attention. "Seats!" he said crisply in his newly authoritative voice.

Chairs scraped the floor, voices resumed, and first class year jumped into high gear for Blake and his classmates.

His seat was next to the officer of the day, a battalion officer named Jones who had just arrived from the fleet and command of a destroyer. Commander Jones leaned over to Blake and in a confidential tone said, "Your father wants a meeting with you right after breakfast."

"Aye, aye, sir."

*****

He stood outside the commandant's office undecided about his first encounter. He knew his father had been away on leave with Rose-Ann. They had no children so were free to travel to exotic places like the Caribbean or Paris.

He knocked.

"Come in."

"Midshipman Captain Lawrence reporting, sir."

"Blake. Congratulations." His dad got up from his desk, shook his hand, and motioned him to take a seat. "I learned of your selection while I was away. The striper board made the proposal and I approved. Left the whole thing up to them -- don't think they were powder-puffing me just because you're my son. You had the top grease and you're the class president. Your grandfather would be as proud as I am. However, there was one thing that the senior member brought to my attention after I had approved the fall list. The officer who reviewed your enlisted record discovered you did brig time. You never told me about that."

"I'm not proud of it."

"Well, the battalion officer and I were surprised to learn that. He did comment on how much you've changed, though. I would agree. Your grandfather would be proud of your turnaround. He had a few scrapes in his time."

Blake didn't say anything.

"Now," Captain Lawrence continued, "Rose-Ann and I are beginning a round of at-homes for the first set stripers. I want you to organize it. You'll be in the first bunch, of course. Now, let's talk about this year. I don't want any goof-ups from your class. You're president and the brigade captain so at least I don't have to talk to two people. I expect your class to run this outfit with an iron hand. Get the underclass to work hard on their academics, look good at P-rades, and bring the plebe class along smartly."

Blake got up from his chair. He bristled. "Our class is a damn good one, sir. You won't have to worry."

"Of course they are. I didn't mean that," His father said. "Look, you and I have had a strained relationship, but we should try to get past that this year. Maybe you'll see me differently after we work together."

Blake turned to go then turned back. "Ah, sir?"

"You don't have to 'sir' me when we're alone."

"Okay. I am asking our class about rates and privileges. You took a lot away from last year's firsties. I'd like to go over that with you as soon as I have the results of their input." Blake didn't know why he said it or where it came from, but he knew it would push his father's button.

"Rates and privileges?" His hand slammed down on his desk top. "They have too many already!"

"Permission to leave, sir?"

"Of course, son."

This is going to be interesting. I only suggested we look at rates and he blows up; this may not work. Of course it's a first for the Academy – a commandant working with his brigade captain son.

*****

Blake opened the door to his room and there sat Erie, feet up on the desk, smoking a cigarette. "So... big six-striper! Congratulations, old buddy. You've come a long way from a brig rat sailor to top of our class as president and brigade captain." He reached out and shook Blake's hand. "Anyway, we got this far." Erie continued. "Only one more year to go. Remember back in boot camp when we first started this shit? You didn't even want to try for the academy, then you wanted to quit. How you gonna get along with Super-P?"

"Thought you were gonna stop smoking. Get your feet off my desk."

"Frig you, buddy."

"And you were gonna stop cussing."

"Hey, you gonna get our car privileges back?"

"First thing out of your mouth. I was just talking to my dad -- the commandant -- about that. I'm already on his shit list for bringing up the phrase 'rates and privileges.'"

"You know what we have to study this year? Listen to this." Erie read from a list. "Naval organization, seamanship, AA fire control, naval construction, air operations, electronics, naval history, international law, guided missiles, internal combustion engines, meteorology, more electronics and last but not least -- we each have to write a big frigging research paper. This is bullshit. First class year is supposed to be fruit. I've got to have time to play some football."

"When did you guys start practice?" Blake said as he continued to stow the gear he'd brought over in his cruise box from his company area.

"As soon as we got back from cruise. While you were gallivanting around Hollywood. By the way, how is Miss Viva Voce? What a name. And what happened to you on that submarine? And what about Miss Abby? You bird!"

"She's good. Didn't see Abby on leave. But Viva, you know she actually changed her name to Viva Voce last year. No more Cathy Velenochi. The submarine -- we took a detour, that's all. How's the team this year? Gonna beat Army?"

"Pretty good. Gonna give 'em hell. Stone'll be a big star. You seen him yet? Been pumping iron. Gone is the skinny stick we knew when he was a plebe. And fast! Now if we can just get the ball to him. We're weak in the passing department. But, there's a plebe who looks good. When you start basketball practice?"

"Not until October. I may not make the team this year."

"You say that every year," Erie said.

There was a knock on the door. Blake continued to arrange his socks in his locker. Over his shoulder he said, "Come in."

"Midshipman Fourth Class Hunt Thomas, sir."

"Well?"

"I'm your plebe, sir."

Erie swung his feet off Blake's desk and got up. He walked over to the skinny kid with red hair and freckled face who was standing at rigid attention. The plebe's hat with a blue wing around the top was crushed against his leg.

"Well, if you're the brigade captain's plebe," Erie said, "Why is your chin stuck out, mister?"

"No excuse, sir."

"Damn right, no excuse, mister! Excuses are like assholes and noses -- everybody has one. Rig it in, mister. The brigade captain's plebe has to have more chins than anyone else in your class. Rig it in, shitbird!" His face was less than an inch from the plebe's. "Why are you smiling, mister?"

"No excuse, sir."

"Wipe it off!"

One hand crossed Hunt's lips. He made a motion like he was throwing the smile on the floor, then stomped on it. "Hell on the Hudson, class of '03, sir.'

"Why '03, mister?"

"For the three letters in 'cat,' sir."

"Cat? Why cat?"

"Met your mother in a cat house, sir."

"See ya, Blake. You've got a wise guy on your hands," Erie said as he went out the door. "Let's go ashore soon. A beer would taste good."

Left alone, Blake sized up the newcomer. "Thomas," he said.

"Yes, sir?"

"Well, tell me about you. At ease."

The plebe came to parade rest and began to talk. "I'm from Decatur, Illinois, sir, and I went to Decatur High School, sir."

"Yeah, but what else? Tell me about your family, why you came to the Academy. More, Mr. Thomas. By the way, what's you first name?"

"Hunt. Huntington, sir."

"Huntington Thomas. What do they call you? Nickname?"

"Just 'Hunt,' sir."

"Hmm. Why didn't I think of that? Well, Hunt, go on. What does your dad do?"

"Works in a paper mill. Mom works in a pharmacy."

"Why the Naval Academy?"

"Don't really know, sir. Ah, ah -- I once heard the Great Lakes Naval Training Center band play."

"That's all? That's your only connection to the Navy?"

"Well, the Academy has a good reputation. My uncle told me. He served as a sailor in World War II."

"Okay, Hunt. Here's the deal. Don't ever use the old "but I'm the six-striper's plebe" crap with any upper classmen 'cause it'll probably get you a whole lot of grief. They'll find out soon enough. I expect to see you every day until Christmas and I want to know how you're doing. You have any problem, you come and tell me. Academics, conduct, or plebe stuff -- you got that?"

"Yes, sir."

"Not Yes, sir. 'Aye, aye, sir.'"

"Aye, aye, sir."

You know what 'Aye, aye' means?"

"Yes, sir. It means 'I understand and will carry out the order.'"

"Okay. Good plebe summer! Now beat it. I've got work to do."

*****

Classes, fall P-rades, and football games filled the midshipman fall calendar. Blake's duties kept him so busy he hardly had time to write to his mom and Viva, let alone Abby and Beverly. He continued to attend endless meetings of such matters as the long-range planning of June Week festivities and Army–Navy game with transportation to Philadelphia and march-on details. The president of the United States would attend the game, so everything had to be perfect.

His own agenda included addressing the return of first class rates and privileges that had been lost the initial year of his father's tenure.

After years of no contact, Blake now saw his father on a daily basis. Although they were they were poles apart on matters of first class rates and privileges, he did agree with most of his dad's policies related to keeping a taut ship.

It was at the reception at the commandant's quarters that his father cornered him for a private moment. "You know they call me 'Super P' don't you?"

"They do? Who are 'they'?" Blake said with a straight face.

"That's what I want to know, Blake. Oh, I don't mean I want to know them by name, but I want it stopped. It demeans the office of the commandant."

"Come on, Dad. It's all in good fun. Every officer in the executive department has a nickname. You stir it up and it'll just get worse." It was the first time Blake had addressed his father as 'Dad' since his parents' separation and divorce.

"Well, it's gotten out of hand. Did you see the cartoon in last month's *Log*? It had a caricature of me with the sub-title 'Shazaam.' Disgraceful. I'm thinking about doing away with those magazines."

"You're what? Er -- sir."

"Don't use that tone of voice to me. Son or not!"

"I'm sorry. But *The Log* and *Splinter* have been around for a long time. The cartoons are harmless. They're the only way mids have a chance to be a bit irreverent about the place. Let off some steam and get a laugh -- even if it is at the expense of the faculty."

"Nevertheless, if the cartoons don't become more civil in their tone, I'm shutting them down -- and that's that."

"Does the superintendent agree with you on that, sir?"

"That's my business, Blake."

CHAPTER 32

HEROES

Three a.m., and the halls of Mother B were black except for a dull light near the MOW table. Blake, in his b-robe and slippers, walked toward the head. His mind had wakened before his eyes. He had to relieve himself and then of greater urgency he had to resolve his conflict. How could the son of an unpopular commandant settle the rates and privilege problems that had his classmates up in arms? Sure, he saw his class through rose-colored glasses. Like any class, a few were solemn with an IHTFP attitude, but the vast numbers of the brigade were enthusiastic. His class was even more so. But, after the bitterness of the previous year, there were many more than usual who were expressing negative attitudes. It was not unusual to hear mids saying, "A $200,000 education being shoved up our butts one nickel at a time."

His mind scanned the elements of his situation. Class company representatives had met. He had attended several of their heated preliminary meetings where some of his classmates accused his father of being a mean S.O.B. "Captain Super-P" was one of the nicer names he was called. Blake bristled at the name calling and told them he was sympathetic, but aside from their complaints, he needed some positive recommendations. Then, as he promised, he took their ideas to his father.

Blake never knew how to entreat, and he certainly screwed up his first effort. Bringing up rates and privilege first thing up to bat was dumb. He had to do better, but how? His relationship with his father didn't help. Captain Lawrence was adamant that the Academy had gotten soft, that midshipmen had to get back to the rugged ways of the past. Unrelenting in his decision of a year ago, he said, "Nothing new here. They just want the place to be like St. John's. Hell, this is a place to build warriors."

On return to his room, Blake crawled into bed but rolled and tossed. He couldn't sleep. An idea was on the edge of his mind.

Fubar! His mind finally closed down, but the reveille bell went off immediately. When he stood up, he had a headache. Two aspirin later, he made it across the yard to his first class, a discussion session about naval organizations. Even though he lived in an entirely different wing of Mother B, his classes were with his company mates. After class he pulled Sam aside. "You gonna be in your room later?"

"Not until about seven this evening. I'm up to my ass in stuff. How in the hell did I get so busy my first class year?"

"You always have your motor running full speed. I'll be over. Got things to talk about."

*****

After evening meal, Blake went over to Sam's room. Pete's blonde head rested on the back of his chair while the heels of his bare feet were on the edge of his bed. His lanky body was almost horizontal as he read *Playboy*.

"Attention on deck!"

Pete almost crashed to the floor in his effort to jump to attention and hide his magazine. "You shitbird, Blake. Scared the hell out of me!"

"You guys have to learn to snap to for the six-striper."

"Screw you."

"Peter, old boy. You'll get a hard on reading that stuff. Bad for your heart."

"Heart, my ass. What're you doing over here in peon country?"

"Came to see you and Sam. Where is he? Said he would be here about seven."

"You know him. He always has more on his plate than any reasonable person can ever get done -- and yet he gets it done. Don't know how."

Blake slid into Sam's chair and put his feet on the desk. "Want someth'n done, give it to a brilliant, busy man. How you do'n, Pete? Grades okay?"

"On the edge, as always, but I'll graduate. Conduct might get me though. It's a problem -- too many demerits."

"How many do you have?"

"A hundred twenty-five."

"A hundred twenty-five? How?"

"Got caught coming back from over the wall -- Class A."

"Pete, you dumb shit. I don't have to remind you that firsties are only allowed 150 for the year?"

Pete changed the subject. "Whatayahear from 'ol Viva? Boy, is she someth'n! Took my breath away when you brought her to Santa Barbara. My mom thought she was peaches and cream."

"She's mine now, Pete. You can't have her back. I almost asked her to marry me last summer. We've been writing occasionally. Can't get her to come back for a weekend. I might get out to L.A. over Christmas leave."

Sam pushed the door open with his back, wedged his stubby body in the space, and entered the room. The three company commander stripes on his sleeve were wrapped around an arm full of papers and books. "You slumming six-striper president! He said as he put everything on the desk next to Blake's feet.

"You forget? We talked this morning. You were going to be here by seven."

"Oh, yeah. Well, it's close to seven. Besides, you can wait for the man who made you famous. Saw you with your dad the other day. You two look alike. His hair isn't as blond -- and you're taller. Could be twins, but not in attitude. You see my Shazaam cartoon in *Salty*?"

"Yeah, didn't like it," Blake said as he swung his feet off the desk and walked to the window.

"Didn't like it? Why?"

"Goes too far."

"Since when did you start sticking up for your dad? You are, aren't you?" Pete said as he took out writing paper and a pen from his desk.

"Maybe," Blake said over his shoulder. "Things aren't going to get any better with that stuff out there."

"I think the cartoon was right on target," Sam said. "Sorry that he's your father, Blake, but he's really good material. Swab handle up his ass, aloof, hard. Makes for good cartoons."

"I know. His problem is that he stays in his office. I don't think he knows the mids. He knows the firsties don't like him, so he doesn't get out among the brigade."

"All the more reason to do him in *Salty*. Got another good one coming out this issue."

"Sam, I'm trying to think of a way to turn this thing around. He won't relent on first class rates and privileges. Gets overheated every time I bring it up. But I have an idea."

"What?" Sam asked.

"He likes anything that's old Navy. If we could get him out of the office and among us, I think we could convince him. How about we do a dining-in?"

"Dining-in? What's that?" Pete asked.

"I've been thinking about it for a while. My grand-dad told me they're done in the fleet all the time. It's a formal supper, military officer style. Bagpipes, beef, and gentlemanly discourse. In the fleet, they're great fun. I peeked in on one during my first cruise -- in the wardroom of *Ingraham*, where I wasn't allowed to go."

"What about it?" Sam asked.

"Well, what about our company having one? You're the company commander you could organize it. I'll help you. Invite me -- and my dad. Let him make a speech. We show him we're not a bunch of -- you know what. Maybe we can turn him around."

"Turn him around? From what? From a prick to an asshole?" Pete said.

"You try'n to piss me off, Pete?" Blake said angrily. "You say that again, I'll punch your lights out."

"I'm sorry. My criminal mind just couldn't resist."

*****

It took Sam and some of his company firsties about three weeks to put the event together. Blake accompanied Sam the afternoon when he invited the commandant to Mess Night. In a small room off the main dining hall, the men of Blake's company gathered. They wore their full dress uniforms; only a few had any medals, and those were from previous service as enlisted men. Alcoholic beverages were not permitted, so instead of a cocktail hour, they stood talking among themselves sipping soft drinks.

Blake escorted his father from his office to join the company. Captain Lawrence wore his evening dress uniform with the wings of a naval aviator and rows of World War II and Korean War combat medals splashed across his left breast. He stood awkwardly off to the side not mingling with the firsties, nor they with him. His body language told the story: stiff like a board, overly formal, even with Commander Blatton, the battalion officer and Army Major Lapressa, their company officer, who were also invited.

At exactly 1750, with Sam on one side and Blake on the other, the two escorted the commandant to the dining table, which was arranged in the shape of a U.

Sam, as President of the Mess, took his seat at the center of the top of the U with Captain Lawrence on his right and Blake on his left, the other officers outboard of them. At precisely 1800, a drummer, followed by a Scottish bagpiper, marched in ahead of a messman holding high above his head a tray that held the roast beef. They paraded once around the table. The president thanked them and they retreated to wait the serving.

After pledging allegiance to the flag, a small band played the National Anthem. They took their seats, and the many courses were served. During supper the men chatted among themselves but were occasionally reminded by the president that Pete acted as Mister Vice. He was sitting at the other end of table and was in charge of discipline. Anyone who wished to be excused for any reason had to have his permission. Mister Vice in turn stood to remind them of their manners and that no one was to break the rules of civility in this evening of gentlemanly conduct.

Following dessert, Sam stood and made a signal to the table servers who came and placed wine glasses·next to each firstie.

Sam looked sheepishly at Captain Lawrence and said, "Mister Vice, charge the glasses for a round of. toasts."

Before the commandant could object, Port wine was poured into each midshipman's glass, and still standing, Sam, as President of the Mess, began his opening speech. "Captain Lawrence, we are honored to have you with us tonight. And to even have the illustrious Brigade Captain is a pleasure." He waited until the chuckles died down. "We are gathered here to contemplate the theme: Whether a human can do ignoble things like make war and also be noble in other matters."

A few firsties made strange faces and wrinkled their brows, signifying they thought the theme all too hefty for this kind of evening. Sam continued, "Before we pursue this heavy subject, which, sir, we would be pleased if you would address," he said, looking at the commandant, "Let us rise for a round of toasts."

Sam held his glass high and said proudly, "To the Commander in Chief. Gentlemen, to the President!"

"To the Commander in Chief," the Vice said.

All responded, "To the President." The officers took a sip of their port, but the midshipmen, not permitted to drink, only kissed their glasses.

Blake next stood and said, "To the Chief of Naval Operations."

"To the Chief of Naval Operations." Port glasses were again kissed.

They then made toasts Commandant of the Marine Corps. the Superintendent of the Naval Academy, the Commandant of the Naval Academy and finally to our missing and lost comrades."

By the time the toasts were complete, the Vice gave permission to light the smoking lamp, and they began to laugh and joke among themselves. Sam tapped his water glass to get their attention. "Gentlemen, it is my pleasure to introduce my old roomie, who now lives in other exalted parts of Mother B. Our classmate, our class president, and our brigade captain, none other than his majesty Blake Lawrence III."

His company mates gave a rousing round of applause accompanied by a few irreverent remarks.

Blake stood. "Thanks, Sam. Well, you all know the story. Like the plot in a spaghetti western movie, I end up as brigade captain working for my father, the commandant. 'Nepotism!' they shout! Well, maybe, but only he can say. Nevertheless, I have the honor of introducing my father to you. I know his career inside and out. I'm not sure he knows that I know, but a son follows those things. He's a highly decorated pilot. He fought in two wars. He was a standout midshipman. He's the son of a man I idolized while growing up. And in truth, I think after we've had a chance to hear him tonight we will all know him better. Gentlemen, the commandant."

Captain Lawrence stood and shook Blake's hand and uncharacteristically, for their family, gave him a fatherly hug. The firsties applauded cautiously.

"Mister President, Mister Vice, Commander Blatton, Major Lapressa, Brigade Captain, gentlemen." He clipped his words as if he were irritated with some aspect of his surroundings. They had the sound of a man whose mind ran fast and who was impatient for others to catch up. "I'm delighted to have this opportunity." He frowned, then slowly smiled, showing his sense of humor. "Of course, Mister President, you have set a precedent here tonight. Port wine at the Naval Academy?"

That set off a round of applause, not for the wine, but for the fact that the commandant had approved of it.

He continued, "A sheet, as you all know, is a rope line that controls the tension on the down-wind side of a square sail. If, on a three-masted, fully-rigged ship, the sheets of the three lower course sails are loose, the sails will flap and flutter and are said to be 'in the wind'. A ship in this condition would stagger and wander aimlessly downwind. Thus came the Navy slang, 'Three sheets to the wind.' Which, I assume you will not be after this meal."

That set off another round of laughter and applause.

"Of course," he went on, the pace of his language slowing. "If a crewman is standing watch on the weather side of the bow, he will be subject to the constant beating of the sea and ocean spray. He will be 'under the weather,' which I also hope you will not be after this much port wine."

He held up his hand to calm their exuberance. "One more. You know where the phrase, 'Cold enough to freeze the balls off a brass monkey came from? In olden times of sailing ships and the like, between a ship's guns were lip-edged brass trays called 'monkeys.' A monkey held a pyramid stack of cannon balls. You engineers know that in cold weather, the brass tray would contract faster than the iron balls and the balls would go tumbling on the deck. And there you have it, how naval slang has permeated American life."

Another round of laughter and applause filled the room.

"That brings me to the theme of the evening." His tone turned serious. "The president has asked me to speak about whether a human can do ignoble things like make war and also be noble in other matters -- a very heavy topic. One which I might not be the best to address, but I'll try because it gives me an opportunity to explain myself, and maybe that was why I was invited." He glanced suspiciously at Sam and Blake. "I have one more Navy term I'd like to remind you of. When called to line up at attention, the ship's crew would form up with their toes touching a seam in the deck planking. Thus we have the slang, 'toeing the line,' which is also now in the general American vernacular.

"In a former geological era, when I was a boy --" A slight smile creased his lips. "While studying Latin, I had occasion to read one of Caesar's remarks. As nearly as I can remember, it read something like this, 'In the wintertime, Caesar so trained his legions in all that became soldiers. And so he habituated them in the proper performance of their duties, such that when in the spring he committed them to battle against the Gauls, it was not necessary to give them orders, for they knew what to do and how to do it.'

"In the defense of this nation we -- our Navy -- and others, like, and -- I choke on the word --" He put his fingers around his throat. "Army --

The midshipmen laughed.

He raised his hands to regain control and became serious again. "We sometimes do pursue a course of ignobleness in the name of achieving noble ends." He stopped and scratched his head, then smiled. "Not sure 'ignobleness' is a word. Where is an English prof when I need one?" Smiles came across midshipmen faces because he admitted his uncertainty.

"Permit me to meander a bit as I discuss this. It brings us to the question: What are the moral aspects of war? It is messy and always a hand-wringer. Many of our forefathers faced this issue. The framing of your question conveys the idea that waging war is ignoble. I would argue that if the cause of a nation is noble, then choosing to make war is not ignoble. It is bloody, terrible, tragic -- all of these -- but not ignoble. Some acts committed in war are awful, inhuman and should not be excused, even if the cause of war be just. Criminal acts should never be treated as ends to justify the means. Was the fight against Nazi tyranny ignoble? I think not! Was the armed struggle by our American patriots for freedom and independence ignoble? I think not! Perhaps the question should be better framed, although I don't want this to sound too academic, 'Can an officer act nobly in carrying out his wartime duties?' Or, 'Is there a contradiction between an officer's quest for nobleness and the violence of his actions in war? Or simply 'Is it possible to act nobly in war?'

"For instance, have you men ever wondered what happened to the 56 men who signed the Declaration of Independence? Five were captured by the British as traitors and tortured before they died. Twelve had their homes ransacked and burned. Two lost their sons serving in the Revolutionary Army. Another had two sons captured. Nine fought and died from wounds or hardships. What kind of men were they? Twenty-four were lawyers and jurists, eleven were merchants, nine were farmers and large plantation owners. All of these men signed the Declaration of Independence knowing full well that it would lead to, in their minds, the noble act of making war, and that they would be killed if they were captured.

"Yet their bravery ultimately brought about this very noble experiment called the United States of America. Some of us take our liberties, for which they bravely sacrificed, for granted -- but we shouldn't. Too often we take only a few minutes each Fourth of July to silently thank these patriots, but they deserve more. Remember, freedom is not free!"

Sam and Blake looked at each other. Sam's eyes widened and his lips mouthed the word 'WOW.' Blake had never heard this side of his father -- the lecturer, the philospher, the after-dinner speaker.

"We often think of the Academy as only a fraction war-training school, the major part college. My office is about the war-training component of it, at least the leadership attributes of being a naval officer: 'Mastery of the mind.' America is not always hospitable to military virtues, not always hospitable to even identifying those virtues, but let me tell you: You honor your country by being here, for joining the naval culture and going next where life will, I assure you, be tough. You will find yourselves in far-off places and, unlike your civilian counterparts, with no board of directors to give you guidance. You will find yourselves in isolated places where your activities will be known only to you, but you will be expected to live in that isolation with character. You will find yourself in the temporary overload of battle, where you will feel pressures likened to plebe year but more so. Yet you must have the will power, the moral courage to do the right thing, always. You learn that through the plebe process and by living the Spartan life of sacrifice and discipline. The Academy breaks plebes down, in part, so they get in the habit of following orders; a man will never be successful at giving orders if he can't first learn to follow them. We learn here, at the Academy, as the old prayer says, 'Keep me true to my best self, guarding me against dishonesty in purpose and in deed, and helping me so to live that I can stand unashamed and unafraid.' We are about the military profession, and we must avoid the dangers of a permissive civilian society that could drain the fiber needed to do the ignoble thing of war fighting, yet find it in ourselves to also be noble in other matters.

"It is not true that the armed services can only truly serve if they are a reflection of the current society. There is a healthy gap between what we do and what life in the American society is like at any given time. Mark me, in our democratic society it changes all the time. By its nature military life must be an exemplar of certain virtues that at times seem anachronistic, but it is the nature of the military to be exemplars. The ideal leader is one whom the sailors will follow -- even at risk of death -- because they believe in their leader.

"We live in a 'me, now' age and as our nation matures, it may become even more so. In a sometimes whiney, individualistic, self-absorbed, crybaby nation, the gap between the military and that society will widen -- all the more reason to hold the line. The naval service is unforgiving. We make no apologies for it -- and do not need to. It is not soft, it is hard. In an ever-increasingly litigious world, you will nevertheless be expected to take the high road. There is no room for snivelers, sea lawyers, and wimps. It's just not tolerated in the Navy. Hard is about vigilance, discipline, determination, and violence if needed. But soft is even harder than hard because it's about honor, forgiveness, reconciliation after the violence, gentlemanliness, and protection of the weak, particularly your sailor crews.

"George Orwell said, 'We sleep safe in our beds because rough men stand ready in the night to visit violence on those who would do us harm.' I add, it is those same men who permitted the Wright Brothers, Edison, and Henry Ford to develop science into products that have improved society, all very noble efforts.

"Gentlemen, you are here on the banks of the Severn because you are in training to become leaders, to learn to exercise judgment, and be like those who came before. You are not here for materialistic reasons; you are here to acquire moral superiority, and it takes years to achieve that. This is what sets us apart. As Lincoln said, 'God must have loved the common man, he made so many of them. But it is the uncommon man – who, when nations get in danger, as they invariably do, must come to the fore and lead.'" He paused. "Let there be no mistake, the military exists to engage in violence. At the end of four years -- which is a long time to train anyone -- will you be ready for your war? If you are, when your time comes, gentlemen, may you be just like them and live *your* few moments well."

Silence. The mess sat erect but mute for several moments before they broke out in cautious applause, which grew louder as they reflected on his words. After it died down, Sam stood and thanked the commandant for an inspiring and informative talk. Then he asked if he might take a few questions.

Captain Lawrence agreed and stood to accept them. The audience remained silent, so Sam said, "Thank you for your inspiring talk, sir."

"You are welcome."

"Sir --" Egg Butler, Blake's brilliant, quiet, tactless, technical classmate stood nervously. He asked, "Do you expect Midshipmen to live in some Zen-like simplicity? If so, what effect will it have on recruiting?"

The commandant cleared his voice. "Interesting question." He cleared his voice again as if seeking the appropriate answer. "Zen -- you challenge my memory -- A movement of Buddhism -- introduced into China in the sixth century A.D. and Japan in the twelfth century. It emphasizes enlightenment by means of meditation and intuitive insights. Now, I haven't seen many of you sitting around contemplating your navels -- not enough time. No -- to answer your question, I don't think we need that extreme, but what sets us apart is our ability to live with a certain level of simplicity -- less than society, without many of the trappings of a civilian college. I don't think it will have any effect on recruiting. In fact, it may be an incentive for the kind of person we want. Next question."

"Sir, do you think we will ever have women midshipmen?" Pete asked.

"Over my dead body! Never! Next question."

"Will our car privileges be restored to us?" Egg Butler asked.

"Car privileges?" The words were clipped and testy.

Blake had an embarrassed expression on his face when he looked at Sam and nudged his elbow. Sam stood and said, "Thank Captain Lawrence for an enlightening evening."

"Wait. Let me answer." The commandant smiled. "This has been a good evening; the stuff of old Navy, and I'm grateful you asked me. Tell you what: I will consider restoring your car and weekend privileges, but only if you take charge of a few things, such as cleaning up Goat Court. The empty bottles and water balloons have gotten out of hand, even worse than when I was a mid. And the Goat Court concert? You're driving the executive department officers up the wall. Can we knock off Bill Haley and the Comets -- there's only so much of "Rock Around the Clock" anyone can stand. And you must ease up on the tone of 'Salty Sam;' it's getting to be a little too much. Let's see if we can we work something out?"

CHAPTER 33

THOUGHTS OF MARRIAGE

The caption under Sam's cartoon in the very next "Salty Sam" column in *The Log* showed, ABRACADABRA AND SHAZAAM. SUPER-P IS GONE. **Replaced by a good guy after all! The asylum has been returned to the inmates! Let there by liberty!**

An article, secretly written by Blake, applauded the commandant's restoration of first class weekend and car privileges. It went on to discuss the cleanliness of the yard and especially Goat Court, which now had a daily plebe clean-up detail supervised by a firstie.

Blake's schedule was fuller now than during his plebe year. In addition to his brigade captain duties he had a multitude of chores that, as class president, he had to attend. The Army-Navy football game was right around the corner. His class hadn't won since plebe year, but had a chance this year with the addition of an excellent roll-out quarterback who could get the ball to Stone. Blake's job was to energize the brigade for the big event. Basketball practice started, but the coach had not yet decided on the team members. Blake was on the cut line again as he had been youngster and second class year. Being a firstie, a striper, and class officer meant nothing on the court. Every day he was tested by the younger and sometimes quicker players. Blake's strong suit was still his hustle.

He had to fit his homework around a schedule that kept him out of his room, except to sleep and catch an hour or so of study time, just enough for the next day's quiz.

Blake often lost track of time, and one afternoon a few weeks before the big game, he sat back in his chair and scratched his head. He looked across at Roland Smalzer, his five-striper deputy, and asked, "When was the last time Hunt was around?"

"Seems like a week or more," Roland responded between strokes of black polish on his spit shined formation shoes. "He used to hang out here, but I never see him anymore."

It turned out that, after they thought more about it, Blake's plebe hadn't come around for several weeks, so Blake went to Hunt's room. He rapped his class ring against the door and entered, the six stripes on the sleeve of his blue service uniform preceding him.

He was met by the sounds of scrapping chairs against the floor, books falling off tables, and the mad scramble of plebes trying to get to attention.

"Midshipmen Fourth Class Malcolm, sir."

"Midshipman Fourth Class Reilly, sir."

"Carry on," Blake said. "Where's Hunt?"

"Come-around, sir."

"Tell him his firsty was here. Send him over to my room as soon as he gets back."

"Aye, aye, sir."

Just before taps, Huntington Thomas knocked and entered Blake's room.

"Midshipman Fourth Class Thomas reporting as ordered, sir." His white hat came off his head, revealing short very red hair. Hunt came to parade rest.

"Knock that shit off, Hunt. Told you to carry on when you come in. Sit down. Where you been?"

"What do you mean, sir?" Hunt frowned. His freckles were covered with a light fuzz of facial hair.

"Come on. You know what I mean. I told you to come around every day until Christmas. You no longer come. Why?"

"No time, sir."

"How are your grades?" Blake knew that grades were the first thing to go when a plebe was in trouble.

"I'm on the tree in two subjects and the bush in one."

"Grade point average?"

"Two point four five, sir."

"How can a high school valedictorian be flunking three subjects and have a grade point average of only 2.45?" Blake already knew the answer because it had happened to him and lots of others.

"You shave today?" Blake asked.

Hunt shook his head. "No time, sir." His shoulders slumped forward; his chin rested on his chest; his eyes looked toward his belly.

Uncharacteristically, Blake shouted, "Sit up! Tall!"

Hunt jerked to a sitting attention. His eyes showed surprise. They shifted to look at Blake, his firstie who never yelled at anyone.

"Stand up!" Blake shouted again. "Look proud! Now get out of here and get back to your studies. Get to work! And shave -- first thing tomorrow morning."

Hunt left the room, and Blake went searching.

He asked Hunt's roommates, and after some prodding, found out that a second classman was on Hunt.

Blake then went to Hunt's company commander, an old pal from plebe summer days, and asked that he keep him posted on Hunt's progress. From there he went to the company commander of the second classman who was working Hunt over. "Don't want to overstate this but my plebe, Hunt Thomas, is on the tree. He seems like a good kid and I don't want to interfere. Maybe the secondo can ease back until after first-term finals."

"Why don't you tell him yourself, Blake?"

"Don't like to meddle in your company."

"Be my guest. He's an asshole anyway. Another Greenfield. Remember him? The biggest prick in his class! Serve him right if the six-striper paid him a call."

Blake had hoped for that exchange. He thanked his classmate and went around the corner to the second classman's room. He knocked his ring against the door.

"Come in."

Inside, Blake saw two strapping midshipmen, built like offensive linemen, pumping weights.

They stopped when Blake stood at the door in silence.

"Help you, Mr. Lawrence?"

"Yes. Which one of you is Seabeck?"

"That's me," the more muscular of the two answered.

"I need to talk to you about a plebe named Huntington Thomas."

"That skinny little shitbird. He's a screwup! What'd he do now?" Seabeck said.

"He's a screwup?" Blake questioned.

"Ahh -- why do you ask?" Seabeck's tone was defensive.

"Well, to be honest, he's my plebe and I'm worried about him."

"He's your plebe?"

"Yes, didn't you know?"

"No." Seabeck's face showed a bit of anxiety, maybe guilt.

Blake went into the room and sat on the edge of the desk. "I want to be careful here. Don't want you to think I'm intruding into the plebe process. But Hunt is failing academics. He probably didn't tell you that, either."

"No, sir. He didn't."

"Well, he seems to me to be a good guy. I wanted to know how you think he's progressing. In your opinion, do you think he'll make a good naval officer?"

Seabeck shook his head. "Mr. Lawrence, you know what he did? You know a week or so ago COMBEEFSTEW (nickname for officer in charge of the midshipman mess) served trout with their heads still on. No one except Norwegians and Swedes eat the damn things. Well, I suspect him of planting two of those fish on top of our overhead light. Talk about smelling bad! He's got grit and obviously he's not a sniveler or whiner, or I would have known you were his firstie."

"You know he put the fish there?"

"I don't know it, but I'm sure. Listen, Blake, I'll ease off. I didn't know about the academics."

"Appreciate it. Let me know if I can do anything for you two." Blake said. Then as he was leaving he added, "You could have checked his grades."

"Right, but I do know he's got a lot of demerits."

*****

She's coming back to Philadelphia for the game.

Blake's mind couldn't stay focused. He led the brigade through Wednesday afternoon P-rades like an automaton. From the shouting of, "Brigaaaaade, pass in review!" to leading the chapel service colors, his thoughts were always about seeing Viva again.

He had called her around Thanksgiving time and told her about how well Erie and Stone were playing and that Navy had a better chance to win the big game than even plebe year -- the last game she saw. To his surprise she said yes, she would come back. She said she hadn't seen her parents for a long time and had a break before she started her next movie.

"Who's singing the National Anthem?" Viva asked.

"National Anthem?"

"Yes, I remember when I attended the game your plebe year a civilian sang the National Anthem before the game."

"Well, I don't know."

"My agent thought I should ask you to throw my name in the hat. I'd love the chance, Blake."

"Well --"

"Couldn't you ask your dad?"

"Viva --"

"Blake, please?"

"Well -- I'll try."

*****

"She's a star. Her voice is like an angel. All I ask is that someone in the superintendent's office check it out. Someone has to sing the anthem. Why not Viva?"

Blake was standing in front of his dad's desk. Captain Lawrence sat with his hands on a file in which Blake had placed Viva's resume and other materials that her agent had mailed from Hollywood.

"This will be perceived as too much. A lot of people already think this business of your being the brigade captain is nepotism at its worst. No telling what they'll think if your girlfriend gets to sing the National Anthem at the big game." He shook his head. "I can't take this forward."

"Will you let me take it over to the supe's office? If I can get it in, will you at least be non-committal if they show interest?"

"Okay. But I didn't send you."

"Thanks, Dad."

*****

Blake went straight over to the superintendent's building. He knew Lieutenant Billings, an officer in the public affairs office.

"What do they call this?" Billings asked.

"Not sure. I think they call it a press or entertainer's kit. Could you call West Point and find out if they have any objection? Remember, this is a hometown Philadelphia girl. She's already famous there and her movies are making her well-known almost everywhere else."

Billings picked up the phone and called his counterpart at the Military Academy. After a few minutes of discussion he hung up.

"He said it sounded interesting. He thought we could make a great deal out of it: brigade captain's girl, prominent Hollywood star from Philly, sings at big game! Like the movie *Long Gray Line*. He'll get back to me. If they'll go along, I'll get a go from the admiral."

*****

Midshipmen jumped up and down, rubbed their gloved hands together, and stomped their feet. The temperature was near freezing as they waited to enter the stadium. Snow had been plowed to the sides of the road to make a path for the march-on of the corps and brigade. It seemed that the wait was hours, but in reality only about twenty minutes passed before the column of companies began to move onto the field.

The public address announcer's very professional voice declared, "And now entering the stadium is the brigade of midshipmen from Annapolis, Maryland, led by Brigade Captain Blake Lawrence III and his staff of midshipmen officers."

Once the brigade and corps had marched on and off the field and into their seats and the football teams were waiting to play, Blake walked with his counterpart the first captain of West Point, to escort Viva onto the field for her song. Blake hadn't seen her for half a year, and the change was overwhelming. Instead of the black-haired Italian girl he had met four years before, he saw a glamorous, leggy redhead. Her hair was done in a very sophisticated style. She wore a beautiful fur coat to ward off the freezing temperatures. He wanted to show some affection but the rules didn't permit it.

"You look good, Viva," Blake whispered as they approached. The cadet showed surprise; he didn't know Blake and Viva knew each other.

"What's with the red hair? You didn't tell me."

"You still like me?"

"I do. The hair will take some getting used to."

"Where will I meet you? You told me, but I forgot."

"Forget whatever I said before. I'm sitting where you are."

She waited until the announcer introduced her. "And to sing the National Anthem, a native of Philadelphia who now resides in Hollywood and is under contract to Metro Golden Mayer Studios. Here is the well-known actress, dancer, and singer, Viva Voce."

After a moment of applause and some cheers by Philadelphians for the hometown girl, the stadium quieted. Hats came off and were placed over hearts. Uniformed military saluted. She began. A pin could have been heard among the audience as her voice brought to new heights the patriotic emotions the people of America feel through their one great song. The TV cameras came in on a close-up as she finished "...the land of the free and the home of the brave." She held her final note to just the right moment as she turned to face the flag and pointed her hands in the direction of its fluttering presence.

A moment after she finished, the nearest spectator shouted "Beat Army!" The other side rang out "Beat Navy!" Blake escorted her to her seat down front where the admirals and other senior dignitaries were now focusing on the two teams lined up for the kick-off.

The game was on and Blake felt like a million dollars. He felt closer to Viva than ever before. She was not only beautiful; her voice set the people in stadium on fire. He wanted to put his arm around her, but too many people watch the brigade captain.

Running the ball always seemed to be Army's tactic; throwing the ball in a wide-open game was Navy's. Back and forth they rushed the ball, a great tackle here, a dash there. At half-time the Army team was ahead by two touchdowns, foreshadowing a dim life at Navy during the Dark Ages.

As the meager sun dipped toward the West, temperatures bottomed. The chill found its way under the heavy
overcoats worn by midshipmen and cadets alike. They
stomped their feet, and foggy air escaped their lips as
they tried to ward off the cold by a continuous
competition of cheers, one side trying to be louder than
the other.

The teams came back from their dressing rooms with
renewed energy. Each player wore a determined
expression. Blake and Viva could see Erie and Stone
talking to each other, each slapping the other on his
shoulder pads.

"We need a couple of quick scores to get back in this
game."

"Stone hasn't done much," Viva observed. "Thought
you said he was the team's big scorer."

"That was true during the early season, but not
lately."

The kick-off went to the Army team. They drove
near the middle of the field before they had to kick.
Navy took the ball near the 30-yard line and for two
plays nothing happened. With eight yards to go on third
down, the new plebe quarterback dropped back to pass.
Out of nowhere Stone raced around toward him and
took the hand-off. It was the old "Statue of Liberty
play," and he rounded the left side into a wide-open
field. He out-sprinted the nearest Army player and the
score was narrowed to Army up by only one touchdown.

On the kick-off, Army's best running back was
injured and was carried from the field. In the very next
play, Erie broke out of his linebacker's position to hit
the quarterback, who fumbled. A Navy player picked it
up and ran it in for another touchdown. The score was
tied. Navy plebes were still on the field doing their

push-ups from the first touch down of the half when the second one occurred. They flopped down again and counted out another fourteen push-ups.

A bewildered Army team took a time out and huddled near the sideline where their coach railed at them, arms flying in the air like an LSO waving off a bad carrier landing.

From that moment on, the two teams played back and forth near the center of the field, each struggling to be in position to put the winning score across the goal line. But, struggle as they could, neither would give in to the other. As the clock ticked off the time, the intensity in the stands heightened.

"Good. It's going to end in a tie," Viva said.

"A tie's like kiss'n your sister."

With but a few minutes left in the game, Navy got possession and marched to within field goal range.

The stadium went silent as the two teams lined up. Army called several times out to "ice" the kicker, a youngster from Oklahoma. The center delivered the ball, and it flew the thirty-odd yards straight and true.

Navy won. Pandemonium! On the Navy side, caps flew into the air and the boys shouted. On the Army side silence was equally deafening -- heads fell on chests, and tears were seen in the corners of the eyes of grown men.

Blake grabbed Viva and hugged her; then, after the singing of Navy Blue and Gold, he introduced her to his father and Rose-Ann. (Blake still could not bring himself to acknowledge her as a step-mother). They excused themselves and made a mad dash for their reservations at a stylish restaurant.

"I'm starving," Viva said as he helped her off with her fur coat.

Her eyes were still as dark as coal, and they still smiled when she talked. But now, like the movie star she was, she seemed more animated. The first thing she did when she arrived at the restaurant was ask, "How can we find out if anyone heard the reviews of my performance? Do you know if the TV announcers were kind to me? When will the newspapers be on the street? Maybe I should call my agent."

"Relax, Viva. Who knows? Papers won't be out until after midnight -- and who cares what sports announcers say,"

"Blake, be a darling, and order me a martini while I go to the little girl's room."

When she returned, she had an early edition of the newspaper. Between sips of her martini she read carefully aloud. "'A red-haired Philadelphia singer named Viva Voce gave a powerful rendition of the National Anthem, especially the ending.' That's nice." She emptied her drink and asked Blake for another before she said, "The head waiter heard from one of the other diners that they liked me."

"Of course they liked you. What's not to like?"

From the beginning, their relationship had been fun, lots of laughter, and a few tender moments. They had never gone very far -- a lot of petting. It was as if nothing would ever get serious even though Blake wanted that. But after supper, more drinks and dancing, Blake became quiet.

"Come on, Blake, get with it. One more martini, and you can take me back to my hotel. We have some lov'n time to get in." Her eyes gave an invitation to things Blake had long dreamed about. "But I have an early flight back to Hollywood in the morning."

He didn't want to spoil the gaiety of the moment, but he did want to do something he had attempted several times before.

"Ah -- Viva." He reached across the table and took her hand. His hands were sweating and shaking. Inside he felt excited. "This is my fourth try at this. Something always stopped me before. Viva, would you be my girl?" He took out a small box and slid it across the table toward her. "Here, open it."

Viva didn't pick it up. "Silly boy. You know I don't -- can't become engaged to be married right now."

"I'm not asking for your hand -- at least not now. But at least open it. It's my class pin. Will you wear it?"

She opened the box and took out the small replica of his class crest. Her eyes widened and glittered. "Of course. It's so different. Thank you," she purred. By now, Blake was unsure of that tone. What was real, what was acting? She put it on and extended her face across the table. They kissed.

"You are now officially pinned," Blake said.

"What does it mean?"

"We can say we're going steady."

"Does that mean we can't see other people?"

"Well, you must know how I feel about you. I won't," Blake said.

"I'm not sure I can live up to that. Hollywood is very far away from Annapolis."

"I'll take that chance."

"Come, sir," she said taking his hand and pulling him. "Take me to my hotel. Hurry."

CHAPTER 34

WINTER SET

Blake was relieved as brigade captain by his friend Lee Locke. Their meeting with Blake's father before the winter striper set kick-off was uneventful. The commandant mentioned that he hoped the basketball team would have as successful a season as the football team.

Now, without stripes and the responsibilities that went along with them, Blake moved back to his room with Pete and Sam. He filled his time with basketball practice, games, and thoughts of Viva.

She had sent only one letter since the Army-Navy game and that one was rather short. It did explain her new contract called for her to do at least one movie a year so she was constantly busy. She thanked him for helping her get the gig to sing the National Anthem; her agent had parlayed that into a better contract. She said she had a good time and now wore his pin constantly. She asked if he knew yet what he would do after graduation. "Will you be stationed near Hollywood?" She concluded her letter by reminding him that her new movie *House of Wonder* would soon be released. "Watch for me on the big screen. Love, Viva"

At her hotel room after the Army-Navy game he told her how much he cared for her and even went so a far as to indicate that at some future time he intended to ask her to marry him. She, in turn, thought that what they did in life separately would be too difficult to overcome. He would be away much of the time, and her acting and singing might keep her on the road. "It's no way to raise a family," she said. "I won't give up my career, and neither will you."

He argued that they should not close out the thought. "Things change. Now don't go marrying some Hollywood guy with a fifty-dollar haircut."

But he knew she was probably right. Viva wanted people to see her, to look at her, to admire her. He, on the other hand, felt adverse to public attention. It bothered him even when he was on the basketball court, or when he heard his name when passing in review at P-rades. He liked her better than any other woman he had ever met -- a free spirit with common sense. They found lots of things to laugh about and, even though their interests seemed as separate as art and science could possibly be, they listened to each other's point of view. If she did marry him, he knew it would not be boring. As a Navy wife, she would certainly bring excitement to their social setting.

Settling into his final Dark Ages, he found being with roommates Sam and Pete as lively as it had been plebe year. Pete continued to hang on the academic and conduct edge with a 2.65 average and 230 demerits. Sam, now that he was no longer the company commander, found time to run plebes and take his mysterious trips to Washington, D.C. on weekends. Blake accused him of having a new honey, but Sam insisted he was just doing special research for his advanced work in the language department.

Hunt Thomas was one of those Sam caught rounding corners and out of uniform.

"Midshipman Thomas Fourth Class, sir," the plebe reported. Sam kept him at attention instead of the carry-on their own plebes normally assumed.

"How long you been in the Navy, mister?"

"All me blooming life, sir! My mother was a mermaid, my father was King Neptune. I was born on the crest of a wave and rocked in the cradle of the deep. Seaweed and barnacles are my clothes. Every tooth in my head is a marlinspike; the hair on my head is hemp. Every bone in my body a spar, and when I spits, I spits tar! I'm hard, I am, I are! sir."

"How come you can quote that flawlessly and can't keep your uniform squared away and make proper corners?"

"I'll find out, sir."

Before the come-around was complete, Blake, who kept quiet during the grilling, found out that Hunt now had 300 demerits -- if he went over the 350 mark, he would get the boot.

"Where've you been? And why didn't you tell me?" Blake asked.

"No excuse, sir." Hunt's freckled face reddened, showing embarrassment Blake had never seen before.

"Well? At ease. Carry-on. What's happening?"

Sam went about his routine, leaving Hunt to his firstie.

Hunt's chin dropped forward. "Well, sir. I didn't want to bother you. You're high grease, a star man, a basketball letterman, and I'm not having an easy year. I'm thinking about dropping out."

"Now wait a minute. It wasn't always this way with me. I had a bad period too. And the first time *you* got in trouble here wasn't your fault. Get your chin up!" Blake barked.

Hunt jerked to an erect posture.

"Get over this sloppy stuff, no more immature games -- at least not this year. You can do this! Okay, back on the daily come-arounds to your firstie."

"Aye, aye, sir." A grin came over Hunt's face.

"Shove off," Sam said.

"Aye, aye, sir."

*****

Blake hung on the basketball team by the skin of his teeth. Except for a tall center, he was the only firstie on the team. Younger players with more talent had eventually replaced everyone who had made it up to the varsity from Blake's plebe team. The coach had expanded his recruiting sphere to as far away as the west coast and brought in the best high school talent who could pass the entrance requirements. They were bigger and faster, but younger than the team of last year. Blake was elected team captain, but during most games he sat quietly on the end of the bench, applauding the good plays. He always raced to the referee's table whenever he was called as a substitute, which was only in those games when Navy was very far ahead or when, at the end of the game, a loss was a certainty. Enthusiasm remained his strong suit.

As the season came closer to its end, Blake gathered a following, mostly of classmates who knew his situation. Led by Sam, the group even had a special cheer.

> Lawrence, Lawrence, he can play,
> Put him in any day
> Lawrence, Lawrence, he can play,
> Put him in some day!

When he did get in, the mids raised holy hell with their shouting and cheering. The coach soon became well aware of the increase in noise level and began to take advantage of it in games where he had to instill zest in the team. He would put Blake in the game for a minute or so, just enough to get the fans interested in the game. This in turn seemed to spark the rest of the team. Attendance at basketball games soared to the highest in Naval Academy history, not just because the team was doing well, but for the cause celebre engendered by Sam's fertile mind.

Sam even went so far as to create a cartoon character he alternately called "Bench Boy" or "Captain Bench." He wrote a short supporting article for *The LOG* titled "The Rise and Fall of a Class President and Brigade Captain." In it he described Blake's fate of being Bench Boy, maybe forever.

Blake took it all in stride even though it was a bit embarrassing. He felt his value to the team was more important than his loss of luster.

Fortunately, the Army-Navy game was played at Annapolis that year. For that Saturday game, even the faithful townies had a difficult time getting tickets to the game. Both teams had winning seasons going into the big game. People came from as far as New York and the surrounding area to witness what would be one of the best contests to be played in the East that year. Army's star forward led the nation in field goal percentage; their point guard led in assists. Navy, on the other hand, had an All-American center whose long, looping hook shot seldom missed, and a pair of outside shooters who spread out the offensive game so the big man could score at will.

Blake had never felt more excited. This was his last Army-Navy game. He had played in two others but would graduate without an N-star on his sweater unless the team won this year.

The game began with Navy getting the tip-off, but the score see-sawed to a half-time score of Navy 32, Army 34.

During the break, the coach chewed ass. He thought that talent-wise, Navy should be ahead by 50, but that Army wanted it more. Unless they played better in the second half, Navy would lose again.

Blake waited in the background until the coach completed his talk, then stepped forward. "Everyone knows my nickname: 'Bench Boy,' he said to his teammates. "But, frankly you all look like Bench Boys. Don't you care? This is the big one -- no tomorrow. What do you want to read in tomorrow's newspaper? You, Kyle." He pointed to the team's high-scoring youngster. "What do you want to read?" Kyle's head was tilted toward his knees. "Kyle! Get your head up!" Blake barked. Kyle's eyes jerked upward and he responded to Blake: "That the Bench Boys won."

"Robert, what about you?" Blake asked. "What do you want to read?"

The strong defensive player, said, "That Navy Bench Boys won!"

"All right, bring it in here." Blake put his hands out and the team put theirs on his. "Together now. Bench Boys, Bench Boys. We can win. Win! Win! Win!"

*****

Lead article Washington Post newspaper

ANNAPOLIS, Md. – Navy used the defense of Robert Williams and the offense of Kyle Reider and Chris Ball to defeat Army yesterday 80 – 74. Reider and Ball each scored 23 points with Williams matching his career high for the midshipmen. They combined for 35 points in a 12-minute span late in the game, shortly after the appearance of Blake Lawrence, the midshipman known as "Bench Boy" or "Captain Bench." Lawrence, who literally ran on and off the court in a matter of three minutes, sparked an otherwise lethargic first-half team. While he was in the game, Bench Boy, who is a senior and the team captain, managed 0 points, 0 assists and 3 fouls, but succeeded in rousing the student body. From the time Lawrence entered the game until the final whistle, the midshipmen went wild. One local spectator commented, "Never before heard that much noise. No wonder Army lost." It was Navy's first win over Army in five years.

*****

With Viva on the West Coast, Blake's love life during the Dark Ages stagnated. He spent much of his time writing her letters but received few in return. He felt unsure of their relationship, so a couple times a month he used his paltry midshipman pay to call her. She had given him several phone numbers. Often he was told by roommates or managers that she was not available, to call back later.

He had promised her that he would not drag anyone else, but had an uneasy feeling that he was getting the run-around.

After several tries they connected.

"How have you been," Blake said, trying hard to develop a conversation.

"Very busy. My agent has me running all over this town auditioning for parts in movies, TV, and modeling."

"Modeling? Thought you were a singer."

"Of course, but they see me a multi-talent. Got to make a buck."

"I miss you – you miss me?" Blake said.

"Of course I miss you too."

"I've been staying close to home – haven't been dating – you're missing a lot of dances."

"Oh, Blake. Please don't do that."

"Do what?"

"Not date others, miss your dances. You should be dating. I am. I occasionally go out – you should too."

Silence.

He knew.

She had told me, but in my naiveté, I didn't want to believe her.

"I really don't want to. I was hoping we could – would –"

"Blake," she cut him off. "I love the pin but I'm not ready."

He stuttered his way to close the telephone call and returned to his room feeling as low as a groundhog in the winter.

The next week he invited Beverly for a weekend. She now was heavily involved with merchandising for a big department store and could get away only occasionally. The only other girl he was interested in, Abigail Cass, had returned to Barnard. He called her several times and finally convinced her to come down for a spring dance, but she seemed preoccupied with her father's corporation and mentioned that one day she wanted to run it.

Service Selection, the time when each firstie had to decide what he would do during the initial few years after graduation, was held near spring break. Blake, Pete, and Sam discussed their options and came up with tentative decisions. Each had alternatives if their lottery numbers did not permit their first choices. Pete, who always wanted to go into the Air Force, added another reason. He could easily get back to California and his new girlfriend. Sam wanted the Marine Corps because that's where his dad had served during WWII. But Blake wasn't sure. He was stuck between naval air and naval surface. He leaned toward going to a destroyer for his first duty assignment. He ruled out submarines because he didn't like the thought of dying in a tube at 300 feet under water.

The numbers and schedule for selection were posted. In a block of about twenty numbers, each midshipman had fifteen minutes to race to the rotunda and make his choice. Pete had the best number, near the top, so he got his first choice. Blake's was in the middle, and after some hand wringing, he selected a destroyer out of Long Beach, mostly to be with sailors like those who touched him most on his midshipmen cruises. He could also be near Viva. Sam's number was near the bottom, and he had to wait out the Marine quota, which was limited to only a small number, about 10 percent out of a class that had lost more than a third of its original plebe summer size.

"What time do you have to be in the rotunda?" Blake asked from his perch on the radiator under the window.

"Twenty-two hundred -- but it won't matter if all the slots for the Marine Corps are taken. It'll be Navy line for Sambo. Lee Locke is watching the numbers for me."

Pete, who was reading a Micky Spillane novel, dog-eared a page corner before putting it down on his desk. "Lee's sure got it knocked. He made the Rhode's Scholar list. He's off to London for a couple of years."

Blake had a bad thought. He and Lee had knocked heads in everything, academics, sports, and grease. They were friends, but they followed the other's successes with a competitive eye. The six-striper job for the final set was up for grabs, and usually one or the other of the two previous brigade captains was selected for the last set. Being chosen to study in the prestigious Rhode's Scholar program gave Lee the edge.

At about 2130, a messenger knocked and entered their room. "Rig it in, mister!" Pete said to the plebe standing just inside the door.

"Aye, aye, sir."

"What's up?" Blake asked.

"Sir, Mr. Locke sent me to tell Mr. Tallau that there are two slots left for the Marine Corps. That he should come up to the Rotunda and stand guard."

"What the hell's he mean by that -- stand guard?" Pete asked.

"Probably means take your sword with you and kill the first sonofabitch who even looks like he's taking the last slot," Blake said. "Better do what he says, Sam. Go!"

Sam grabbed a white hat and rushed by the plebe. He was gone for the entire half-hour and returned grinning from ear to ear.

"You got it."
"Yeah, how'd you know?"
"You silly bastard."

*****

It was several weeks after Service Selection when Blake found a note on his desk to report to his company officer, an Army officer on exchange from West Point for a year before returning to an operational unit. Captain Armando Lepresa, an infantry ranger, paratroop, Special Forces trained Mexican-American from Los Angeles, looked every bit the image of his training. Slender, sallow, hardened cheeks, crew cut he wore an immaculate uniform over a hardened body that got plenty of exercise every day. He motioned Blake to sit.

"How ya do'n, Blake?" Lapresa asked.

"Not bad, sir."

"Hear you decided on Navy line -- a ship out of Long Beach. Your girl in Hollywood will be pleased to know that. Tell her yet?"

Captain Lapresa knew everything about his midshipmen. Of course his dope about Blake was extracted during the winter set, after Blake's return to the company from his six-striper room near the Rotunda.

"Yes, sir. Called her right away."

"Blake, we have a problem."

"Yes, sir?"

"Your dad has decided to make Lee Locke the final set six-striper. You know it was a difficult decision for him to make, you being his son and all that. But the politics of it made it impossible for you to have the job. Now we have to figure out what's best for you. I'm new here and thought you should have a say in the matter. I can negotiate any striper position you want. You know you are one of the top five grease men in your class. Frankly, the commandant thought you might like to be a regimental commander or deputy brigade commander. What do you think? As far as I know it never happened at the Point. For that matter, I don't think we ever had a commandant and son there at the same time, either. What do you think? You could be my company commander; I'd like that. We could have a chance to win the colors. What do you think?"

Blake listened respectfully as this obviously hyper-competitive officer rattled on about the midshipman chain-of-command. Not being the six-striper was inevitable, he had anticipated it, particularly after Lee won the Rhode's scholarship. He hadn't really thought too much about the other posts. Almost any other position in the chain would do. He didn't actually care. Inside he felt a bit like he did when he thought Viva was dating a Hollywood hunk or a West Pointer.

"If I were company commander, what would happen to Sam? He had it fall set and is the natural selection for the job."

"Well, we could work that out."

"Could I have a few hours before I decide, sir?"

"Sure, take some time, Blake. But I need an answer before the end of the day. Keep in mind we could win the colors with you in command."

CHAPTER 35

WIN THE COLORS, LOSE THE GIRL

March. The first hint of spring brought sky with shades of blue splashes between puffy white clouds. The bay lay like splinters of glass, sparkling, reflecting. Worden Field, green from end to end, stretched from Balch Road to Rodgers Road. It was bounded on the long side by the old brick homes called Captain's Row that lined Upshur Road and ran parallel to the long line of the march. The earth tones of the playing fields spread lazy brown, matching the dull colors of the nearby academic buildings.

The smell of freshly cut grass filled Blake's nostrils as they made the short turn onto Balch from Decatur Road, the other long side dimension, to enter the field. It wasn't the first time he'd led the march. When he was brigade captain, he was way out in front of the long line of troops in company formation. Then he had a "V" shaped staff of midshipmen officers trailing him, and his destination was a position centered on the company formations opposite the reviewing stand. From there he ordered the manual of arms demonstration and led the pass-in-review.

Now he was with the troops, the leader of about 150 midshipmen of all classes. The number of firsties in the company was now down to 25 from about 45 at the beginning of plebe year. They were headed for their last

P-rade of the competition for the colors, and he felt excited because they had a chance to win. In truth he had felt a bit elitist as the six-stiper. He was always uncomfortable with that. His grandmother, a native of Sweden, was the one who implanted his notions of being a street American. She often told him about the European elitists who searched for place and rank before substance, and suggested he always seek to align himself to the sailor and to think of the common people in all his decisions.

*****

After his discussion with Major Lepresa about which striper job he wanted, Blake returned to his room. His thoughts were on the reasons why he wasn't selected to be top striper and why the commandant, his own father, would have his company officer tell him. At first it bothered him that he'd lost out to Lee. Even though they were good friends and Lee deserved the job, Blake felt like he had lost a fight. It wasn't something one lobbied for, but there was some behind the scenes politicking. Company and battalion officers wanted their own men to hold the better slots in the shadow command structure. The commandant and the superintendent saw the top jobs as an extension of the Academy's image. Only the square jawed, handsome, and tall should apply.

Blake rationalized that even though he knew his grease was a touch higher than Lee's, it was the subjective stuff that got him. The discovery of his captain's mast and brig time when he was an enlisted man might have been a factor, but he doubted it. After all, how long would that dumb stunt haunt him? He was just a kid. He had done a lot of good things since then.

He wasn't the only brigade captain in the history of the Academy who had served brig time. The old Reina Mecedes had housed a few mids in its time. On the positive side, Blake had received a letter of commendation from the skipper of *Ingraham*. Both he and Lee had won N-stars in the their sports -- Lee was a star on the 150 pound team -- Blake had been captain of the basketball team. They were both involved in many extracurricular activities. But it was Lee's selection as a Rhode's scholar that got him the job. Blake never even thought to apply. His grades were as good, but he just wanted to get to the fleet and feel the deck of a ship under his feet.

He was still sitting in his room pondering his options when Sam and Pete returned from class. Pete threw his books on the desk and lit a his cigarette. Sam slammed his books down and cursed, "IHTFP! Goddamn pukes over in the juice department. No way I got only a 3.0 on that electronics quiz. They're still grading on a curve. Shit."

"Glad I caught you in a good mood," Blake said, sitting with his feet on the radiator and facing the window. He spun around. "Got something serious to talk about, Sam, after you've cooled down."

"Piss on 'em!" Sam yelled, waving his hands in the air. "I'm never going to cool down. I'll be glad when I'm a Marine and away from this place."

"Yeah, good luck at Camp Lejeune. That'll be easy," Pete said. "I don't know what you're crying about; I'm the one about to bilge out if I don't pass the next exam. You're bellyaching because your grade point might slip a tenth of a point."

"Whataya have to talk about?" Sam asked in a grouchy voice.

"Never mind. You're too pissed off," Blake said.

"I'm over that," Sam groused.

Blake shook his head.

"What?" Sam asked.

"Nah, it's the wrong time." Blake stood up and walked to his locker.

"You've pushed my curiosity button," Pete said.

Blake spun around holding a set of clean underwear like he was getting ready to take a shower.

"Well, Ranger Major called me in today."

"So?"

"So. I'm not getting the final set six-striper job."

"Bullshit!" Sam said, throwing his blue-banded white Dixie cup across the room and onto a small table that held a few reference books. "That's why IHTFP."

"Who's getting it?"

"Lee," Blake said.

Sam raised his hands toward the ceiling. "All praise. At least they're giving it to a good guy, not some nerdy. Ranger Major give a reason?"

"No, but --"

"It's goddamn politics" Pete said. "You got better grease than Lee."

"You don't know that," Blake said.

"No, but you do. You've never had less than 4.0 from your peers. The upper class and officers always love you."

"Well, it's a done deal."

"So, whataya gonna get? Deputy brigade? Regiment?" Pete asked after taking a big draw and blowing out a ring of smoke from his cigarette.

"He gave me my choice."

"Choice?" Sam exploded. "No one ever gives me a damn choice!"

"Well, this one involves you. I can have the deputy, regiment or the battalion – or -- the company."

"No brainer. Take the regiment," Pete said.

"Actually, I'm leaning toward the company. What do you think, Sam?"

Pete blurted, "I thought Sam would get the company again. I don't get shit with my grease."

Sam sat quietly for a few minutes as if he was mulling a strategy or having one of what he called his "hard-thinks." Finally he said, "Actually, you'd be good at any one of them, Blake. But you'd make the best company commander. With you we could win the colors."

"I don't want to screw you."

"Hey, we need somebody who looks pretty out in front so we can win the marching competition. We got lousy grades in the fall because I'm such a stump."

"You sure?" Blake asked.

"Only if I can be your sub-commander," Sam said. "I'll be your hammer."

"Of course. You sure?" Blake asked.

"That way we get the best of both worlds: pretty boy and the brains."

*****

"Right turn -- march!" Blake ordered. He was guiding the line of other companies as they made their way to their assigned blocks, facing the grandstand and meticulously aligned on the company to their right. Once in their position, each midshipman listened intently for the orders to present arms for the playing of the National Anthem and then the manual-at-arms demonstration. Unbeknownst to the watching civilians, each of these were a graded exercise, a major part of the color company competition. Blake's company was in the hunt. The calculation weighted company academic averages, sports, professional signal flag and flashing light competition, and extracurricular as well as the marching. In the end, one company would be best. Some companies took the competition lightly; others, like Blake's, worked hard at it. The reward was the opportunity to be singled out at the June Week parade and, in the fall, to carry the national colors onto the field at the Army-Navy football game. In addition, the winning company commander's girl became the Color Girl of Annapolis. With that came photographs on covers of magazines and newspapers around the country.

Behind him, Blake heard Sam reminding everyone within earshot of the importance of straight lines and precise hand movements. Sam had gracefully decided to accept company sub-commander, even though Pete thought he was getting screwed. As such he handled the administrative matters and organized the color company training, activities for which he was an exact fit. Now his organizational baby was about to be born. He told Blake that, unless he screwed up, they would cake walk home with the colors. "Just one more P-rade; I'll be right behind you and won't let you screw it up."

Sam marched one step to the left and the rear of Blake's left shoulder. On Blake's other side, Del Butler carried the company guide-on. Pete, one of the tallest men, served as the right guide and marched at the extreme forward right corner of the company. His job was to keep aligned with the company ahead.

"Present arms!" cracked the order from the field in front of them.

The hard clap of gloved hands slapping rifles in unison could be heard all across Worden Field.

The band played the National Anthem then "Ruffles and Flourishes" for the senior officer present.

One of the second classmen, from his front row position said, "Hey, check out the honey in the red dress. Nice tits."

Sam growled, "Save it, dumb shit. We're in competition."

"Right shoulderrrr... arms!" The manual of arms drill began.

Without moving his lips, Sam shouted, "Slap those guns together, goddamn it!"

That complete, they waited for the order to move out and pass in review.

"Pass... in... review!" Lee Locke, the brigade commander shouted.

As they waited their turn, Sam reminded Blake, "Okay, it'll be a crisp eyes right and hold your head tall. Look like a Nazi elite guard without the goose step."

Out of the corner of his eye, Blake could see the tail end of the company on his right peel off and catch up with the line. At the precise moment he ordered, "Right turn – March!" His company followed the one in front as they made two left turns and began their approach to the reviewing stand where the graders stood with clipboards in their hands marking down the subjective relative scores as they passed by.

"Get ready," Sam said.

"Shut up, Sam. I got it," Blake said without moving his lips.

Marching had become automatic; they had practiced it for four years. All Blake heard was a solitary stick beating the cadence on the edge of a drum. But just before they were pass in review, the band launched into the march music of "Something About a Sailor." Although the beat was the same and despite the miserable heat and sweat, when the band began the new song, it lifted the spirit a notch. Chests swelled and they walked with a prouder gate.

"Eyes..." He waited to hit the exact mark. "Right." Blake's sword handle came up to his mouth, the tip pointing momentarily toward the sunlit sky, then smartly to his side, where the tip swung parallel to the ground. His eyes caught sight of the admiral; his dad stood to the supe's right. At the same time every face in the company snapped right, eyes staring at the reviewing officer.

The public address system bellowed: "Now passing in review is one of the companies leading in the competition for Color Company. It is led by Midshipman Blake Lawrence III of Pittsburgh, Pennsylvania."

At the next mark, he ordered, "Ready -- front!" The sword and eyes snapped back.

"Perfect, Blake," Sam said. "We hit it!"

Soon they were off the field and making their way back to Mother B. The men in the back rows began to talk about girls; those in the front wondered if they had done well enough to win.

In their rooms, Blake, Sam, and Pete ripped off their full dress uniforms and released the Worden Field heat. They drained sodas brought them by one of the plebes next door.

"How soon will we know?" Pete asked.

Sam slid out of his pants and hung them in the closet. "Ranger Major will be the first to know. He'll come shouting."

They showered for supper and changed their uniforms. The formation bell rang, and they still didn't know. In the passageway, the company lined up in platoon formation for the march to the mess hall. Blake was just about to order the march when Major Lepresa came around the corner. He was wearing a toothy grin.

"Blake. Hold up. Let me say a few words."

"Company, at ease!" Blake shouted.

"Men. You did it. You won the colors!"

Laughing and shouting sprang from the mids.

"Hold it down," Blake said.

Major Lepresa continued, "Congratulations! You won by fifty points. Now we find a color girl for Mister Lawrence and march in the front of the brigade to receive the color company banner at the graduation p-rade. Congratulations again. Well done!"

*****

Early the next day, Blake was in Major Lepresa's office. "You gonna ask the girl in Hollywood, Blake?"

"Yes, sir. Thought I'd call tonight. She'll make a beautiful color girl."

"Won't do the Academy any harm to have publicity photos of a pretty actress. Let me know what she says and I'll get the ball rolling with Mrs. Harris, the social and protocol director."

*****

Blake dialed the number. It rang. It was for this very moment that he had decided to take company commander instead of a bigger staff job. And it worked out. Practically nothing he planned ever worked out the way he wanted it. Most of his life had been just responding to opportunities, things that just turned up. But in this, for the first time, he had envisioned the future, and it had come true. He had won the colors and he was calling Viva to ask her to be his color girl.

It rang again. No answer. He let it ring. Finally a female voice said, "Hello."

"May I speak to Viva?"

"No Viva here. Wrong number." The phone line went dead.

Blake looked around then shook his head.

What the heck? Should I call back? Did I dial the wrong number?

He dialed again. Again it rang for a long time. Again the female voice. "Hello."

"Is this 310-289-3435?"

"Yes."

"Good, may I speak to Viva Voce -- or maybe... Kathy Velenochi?"

"Nobody here by that name." The sound of plastic slammed on plastic jarred his ear.

Blake stepped back from the phone.

This isn't happening to me.

He took out his list of telephone numbers and found Kathy's mother's number and dialed.

"Yes?" an elderly sounding voice said.

"Mrs. Velenochi?"

"Yes."

"This is Blake Lawrence. I'm trying to get in touch with Viva. I must have the wrong number. Can you let me have it again?"

"Oh, the boy from Annapolis. Sure. You're Sammy's friend." Her voice had an Italian accent. "But I don't know if right." There was a space of time while she searched. "She move. Try 310-289-4000 or 310-289-3990. She move."

"Thanks, Mrs. Velenochi. How you do'n, by the way?"

"Oh, not so good. Kidney problems. Dialysis. Go every other day..."

"I'm sorry to hear that, Mrs. Velenochi. I hope you feel better. Want to call Viva right away. Good-bye."

"Wait, I no finish telling you about dialysis --"

"Thanks, Mrs. Velenochi. If Viva calls, tell her I'm trying to get a hold of her. Bye."

He hung up and dialed the new number. This time the phone was answered on the first ring. "Metro."

"Can you put me in touch with Viva Voce, please. A phone number will do."

"We don't give out phone numbers."

"Well, can you verify that she works there?"

"She does," the bored voice answered.

"Can you take a message? Have her call me, immediately?"

"Okay... what's the number?"

Blake gave the Naval Academy number and hung up. The excitement he felt when he first called had now faded like dry spaghetti in boiling water. He thought of going back to his room and preparing for class the next day, but he needed to tell her. So he dialed the other number.

A man's voice answered. "Kent's residence."

"May I speak to Viva, please?"

"Who is this?"

"This is Blake Lawrence calling."

"Does she know you?"

"Well, yes. Who is this?"

"I'm her husband."

CHAPTER 36

GRADUATION

Blake didn't believe, so he re-dialed the number, the one given him by Kathy's mother. "Ah – excuse me, is the right number for Viva Voce -- Kathy Velenochi?"

"Viva did change her name from Kathy, but -- yes, this is the right number. Can I help you?" There was a touch of irritation to the sound of the male voice.

"Did you say you're Viva Voce's husband?"

Blake's heart rested on a knife-edge prepared to explode if it was a mistake; his stomach was poised to vomit.

"That's what I said."

"Ah --" Blake took a deep breath. "Oh, well -- I'm an old friend -- Blake Lawrence is the name. Could you ask her to call me? It's important."

"Number?"

"She has my number."

*****

When Blake returned to his room, Pete immediately asked, "Well? You tell her? She com'n back?"

Blake couldn't answer. At first he felt devastated, hurt, empty. Then the pain turned to anger. He felt offended, insulted, indignant, damaged. He ached so badly that he choked up, but he held back any tears. Instead he kicked the desk and then a chair. He picked up his pillow and threw it across the room. It hit the window and fell to the floor. Then he picked up her photograph from his desk and slammed it upside down. The glass shattered.

He swallowed hard then said aloud, "I should have seen it coming. Man, am I a nut case!"

Sam swung his feet off the desk. "That bad? She moved to China?" He tried to be funny but Blake wasn't buying.

"Would you believe she got married?" Blake said. "Damn!"

"Getoutahere!" Sam said. "Viva married? The papers and magazines would have been full of it if she was. You'd have known before this. She's a star, for christsakes. I'd at least have heard from our neighborhood. Well, don't say I didn't warn you."

"She tell you?" Pete asked.

"No, her husband."

"Something's wrong," Sam scratched his head. "She's always been a stand-up gal."

"Yeah, before Hollywood," Blake said.

*****

Blake sat in Ranger Major Lepresa's office. The Army officer scratched his head. "We've got to come up with something, Blake. Out of three girlfriends, can't one of them come here and be the color girl?"

Blake wore a frown on his face. His blonde hair had almost totally turned a tarnished brown. A few early grays mingled among the longer strands. He shook his head. "Tried them all -- Viva's married, Abby has her own graduation on the same date, and Beverly will be in Europe on a buying tour."

"Mrs. Harris is on the telephone with me practically every fifteen minutes. She wants hat size, background, everything. I keep putting her off but she says, 'There has always been a color girl.'"

Blake sat in silence.

"You have a sister?" the major asked. "Maybe she could do it. It's only for a weekend."

"No sister," Blake said.

"What about a cousin?"

"Nope."

The telephone rang.

"Major Lepresa."

"Yes, ma'am. No. Not yet. Working on it. Wants to see us? Okay, right away. Thanks."

He turned to Blake, "Mrs. Harris is on my butt, Blake. Commandant wants to see us both. Right now."

They marched through the maze of Bancroft Hall corridors arriving in the Rotunda just as a meeting was breaking up. Blake and the major were ushered into Captain Lawrence's office.

"Sit down, gentlemen. I understand we haven't solved the color girl problem yet. Sorry about Viva, Blake -- heard she got married. Now what do we do?"

"Don't know, sir."

"Well, I have an idea. It's a bit bizarre, I'll admit, but it could work. Here's what I propose. I'll call one of my classmates at the Pentagon and have him run a competition for color girl."

"That really is bizarre, sir." Major Lepresa said.

"Well, we've got to have a color girl. The Naval Academy has never been without one, and it won't start on my watch. What do you say, Blake? All you have to do is date her for the weekend. What happens after that is up to the two of you. If I guarantee she won't be a brick, will you do it?"

Blake smiled when his dad used that term because that was what he was already thinking. Neither of his three no-shows were bricks, but an image appeared immediately. He visualized a long line of plebes and underclass marching down the passageway rattling and smacking their wooden shower shoes together as a prelude to the presentation of a red brick for the ugliest drag. It happened after every weekend, but never for the color girl.

Blake nodded his agreement. "Please, no bricks."

However, he knew that even if she was a raving beauty who exuded personality, it would be a downer weekend. Not because of anything the girl would do, but because of his lousy attitude, the bad taste Viva had left.

*****

Two weeks passed. Nothing was heard from either the commandant's office or the pentagon. Mrs. Harris wrung her hands and ran back and forth between her office near the Rotunda and the superintendent's reassuring everyone that a color girl would soon emerge.

In the meantime Blake had other problems to solve. His plebe Hunt Thomas, who came around before every meal for a uniform check, had accumulated 355 demerits, five more than the limit for a plebe. Blake and Major Lepresa had argued for probation, and the superintendent's board approved, but with the understanding that any more would mean dismissal. Pete was the other problem. His demerit total had stayed the same, but he was flunking Skinny. He had dug himself a hole so deep that if he didn't pass the final, he wouldn't graduate.

In Hunt's case, Blake called the firsties in his company together. They talked about Hunt and agreed that he was a screw-up, but a risk-taking screw-up -- the kind who would probably make a hell of a war fighter some day. They all agreed to lay off him and help him avoid any more demerits. However, about two weeks before the semester was complete, a second classman caught Hunt goosing his roommate as they chopped up a ladder between classes. It looked like he was a goner until Sam talked the segundo into tearing up the report. Days inched by, with Hunt on the edge. He finally made it to the cut day surviving by a whisker.

Sam's solution for Pete was to make him memorize the formulas and re-take the daily quizzes over and over again, hoping enough would stick for the final.

*****

The telephone call came one week before the color parade. Major and Mrs. Lepresa were to meet the winner of the Pentagon's beauty contest and bring her for introduction to Blake. They were to meet in the parking lot near Dahlgren Hall.

Blake was stunned by the girl's appearance. Medium height, long black hair to her waist, light completion, and eyes as blue as hot smoke. She looked like she came off the cover of *Vogue*. Her name was Hope Twain and she was beautiful, the perfect color girl. She had been selected by the mysterious doings inside the Pentagon, where obviously everything was not about bullets and bombs.

Blake liked her immediately.

He asked Major and Mrs. Lepresa, "Are we permitted to be alone? To get acquainted?"

"Of course," Mrs. Lepresa said, without consulting her husband. "It's most appropriate. Don't you agree, dear?"

Blake took Hope to dinner that evening before the dress rehearsal.

"Are you comfortable with this?" Blake asked.

"You mean being with you or the contest?"

"Either."

"I'm quite open about the beauty contest. Lots of the E-ring secretaries thought it would be fun."

"What happened?"

"Well, the winner, me, was chosen from an assortment of about thirty entrants, all of whom had to pass the test of questions in front of five Navy captains. That was the only shabby part of the process – standing there, but we girls went along with it. We wanted the prize: color girl."

"You know I tried several of my girl friends. None could come."

"It doesn't make any difference to me. This is an adventure – fun. I just hope I measure up to the job."

"Oh, don't worry. You're just right."

Blake found that he was not repelled by a blind drag Color Girl. In fact, he warmed to her. She was so open about the whole thing. They laughed when he told her, "You'll have to kiss me in front of the entire Academy, and make it seem real."

The color parade went like clockwork. Blake's company led the brigade and was positioned front and center. Hope looked elegant in her flowing gown and billowing white hat. She transferred the flags to the color guard for the next year. Blake presented her with a bouquet of flowers, and the kiss she gave him was held more than the moment he expected.

The best company trophy was presented. Then to the music of "Anchors Away," Blake led his company to pass-in-review.

Afterward, in careful dignity, Blake and Hope attended the superintendent's garden party, a setting for a reception of the graduating class and their parents. That evening they attended the dance featuring the big band music of Claude Thornhill, after which Hope was chauffeured home to Falls Church, Virginia; she had another date the next day. Besides, she told Blake, "I have to be back at my secretary job at the Pentagon on Monday morning." They did agree that the fun and romance they experienced on that strange weekend might extend beyond his graduation.

Tecumseh had been painted for the occasion. A flight of Navy jets screamed by in an air salute to the new grads. Herndon Monument had been greased with 200 pounds of solid shortening, and a blue-rimmed plebe cover had been placed on top waiting to be replaced with a combination cap.

Graduation day was an attempt at prolonging the garden party dignity, but the day began with breakfast in the mess hall for graduates, parents, and friends where the dignity collapsed quickly because everyone was in a rush. There were uniform changes, packing for vacations before new duty stations, or honeymoons with the sweethearts who survived the sanction of not being married while the young man was a midshipman.

To the solemn strains of "Pomp and Circumstance," the grads marched in to Thompson Stadium and took their seats. Next entered the faculty, the superintendent, the commandant, and the commencement speaker, who was none other than the secretary of defense.

Blake expected the secretary to give a traditional commencement address, the same kind that at that very moment all over the world was being given where ever young people were graduating from high school or college, the kind of talk that challenges and gives benign encouragement to charge into the race to the top.

At first, Blake just heard a few of the words. "There are two kinds of graduates who emerge from this institution. One is the war fighter. The others are those who will develop equipment and train the war fighters for the next war."

But most of the speakers words were lost in a sea of Blake's thoughts about his own future.

I'm off to be a sailor and I think I now know what it is -- sailoring. It's the ocean experience, foreign ports, excitement, the wonder, classmates, shipmates, and war fighting.

The secretary, a tall, slender Naval Academy graduate of great reputation, a man not born of privilege but a gentleman to his fingertips, continued, "You have been trained to serve a great Navy. But would it be great without the graduates of this institution? Maybe, but unlikely. Graduates of the Naval Academy have been involved in every aspect of the growth of this nation and its Navy."

My grandad told me, "It's for the land and our way of life -- the ideals, built on a short national history based on one document, which is actually no more than a concept."

"Will the training stick with each of you the same way? We know it will not. Some of you have been spouting IHTFP every day you have been here." He smiled. "But you will someday learn the meaning of your training and be proud of your accomplishments. What are the rewards for staying? Actually the midshipman life is much like a naval career: hard work, competition, an interesting life of variety, but a life of tough schedules and high standards. The career is about staying power. The reward will only be your achievement of assigned tasks. If it's riches you want -- not here. But if it's satisfaction, that's another story."

The ocean experience -- with few exceptions it was totally new to my classmates, the men who entered four years ago. Much like the cowboy experience must have been for people not born to the range. It's like the sky experience -- seeing the sky when there is no reflected light, just pure stars. And you realize you are just a speck, less than a grain of sand.

"The value of this school to the nation is complex. Most people live their lives based on instinct. They do what feels good for them. They just want to be left alone to live their lives without hassle. Some others, a fewer number, do their duty. You have been trained to be in this group. We teach duty, honor, country. It is the motto of your football adversary to the north. But -- even a smaller group of you have a sense of nobleness. You are the ones who feel the spirit for the country and the Navy. None of you were born to noble birth. You are not knights in silver armor, but you will feel that way..."

When I started here I wasn't sure I could live up to the oath. Now can I live up to what is expected of a naval officer?

"From your training you should have gathered a set of values that will remain with you until your death. Honor, integrity, truthfulness, duty. You know the Navy likes industrious people, but more important, we value cleverness, brains -- discovery over industry. Above all, we value noble character. You will determine this over time. What I say this moment will be lost in the exuberance and excitement of this day. But the values are deep set; you will never forget them. Good luck in your new lives. Remember that war is not just for the brave, but also the smart. Should the necessity arise, go in harm's way, but always serve with courage and grace."

The speech was over. One by one the graduates walked to the beat of somber symphonic music across the temporary stage, shook an extended hand, and grasped the coiled parchment that represented the gateway to opportunity.

Finally the "anchor man," the last man academically, received his diploma and was hoisted on the shoulders of his classmates. When all students had returned to their seats they were sworn into their respective services as ensigns and second lieutenants.

They had to repeat the exact oath they took four years earlier. This time Blake repeated the words willingly.

They returned the brigade's cheer: "Hip, hip, hoorah for the graduating class!"

It was over.

The crescendo, the climactic ending, came when Blake and his classmates threw their caps high in the air.

For many the curtain had finally come down on childhood.

The graduates swept past the dignitaries as they went to greet loved ones. Blake strolled with dignity until he was near his family; then he let out a war whoop that blended with 600 others. "Yahoo!"

They were all there. His plebe Hunt Thomas was the first to salute him. He received a silver dollar for the effort. His mother, with her new husband, Jack, was there with Charlie. His brother was now a warrant officer in the army. Blake's father came late, after his duties were finished. His wife stayed home to prepare for the after-graduation party. Blake's bitterness about his father had long since dissipated. He had his own life to live.

Only one person was missing -- Viva. The woman he still cared about. He missed her laugh, the little side giggle when she caught him saying something naive or dumb. She always said his secret charm was his innocence. She had finally dropped him a short note -- but never called. It just said that her career was on hold because her baby would be born in late summer.

I'm sorry I didn't tell you earlier. I was a coward. But, nothing covers words on paper. I betrayed you, Blake. I'll always admire your honesty and forthrightness. You deserve better. Do you want your pin back? If not, I will keep it always as a memory of our times together. Someday we will meet again. Maybe in New York or Cannes?

Erie, Stone, Pete, Lee, and Sam came by on the way to their own happy gatherings.

"Hey, Pittsburgh!" Erie said. "Good thing we took that exam in boots. Can you see Chief Bellychecker right now if he knew we made it? Hey, I'm gonna be a jet pilot."

"I'm off to the Air Force," Pete said. "After I see my new honey in Santa Monica. See ya, Blake."

Stone shook Blake's hand and he introduced his parents he said, "I'm going to a ship, just like my dad!"

Sam didn't go off to the Marines. The strangest thing happened. He received his diploma, but his commission was held up. It was disclosed that he spent his mysterious weekends in Washington, D.C. talking to some Russians at their embassy. The FBI, CIA, and the Marine Corps wanted to know more about what he was doing. Blake knew it would be resolved and he would see his friend again, soon. The Marine Corps would be all the better with a man like Sam Talau.

It was over. They spread to the four winds -- a class with things to do and places to go. Some would be jet pilots, others seagoing deck officers while others would seek the deepness of the ocean in submarines. They were a class, and somewhere, sometime, as they all say, "Where two or three shall meet ..." their paths would cross, and it would be as if they had never left the academy.

EPILOGUE

First he prowled the few rooms of Bancroft Hall, that is, those that alumni were permitted to enter. Then he left and walked slowly to a seat on a bench across from Mother B and watched the activities of the yard as he remembered the days and his classmates.

His shoulders and head were bent forward as if he were peering into a distant horizon looking for a landfall. A fedora sat forward shading hair grown silver from his years of service. The blue blazer he wore over gray slacks showed travel wrinkles. His right foot tapped to the beat of the marching music that vibrated across the yard.

She, on the other hand, was in a hurry, approaching from the opposite direction, maybe Rickover Hall.

He turned his head to size her up as he would any other officer-to-be. Short and slender, the woman midshipman looked squared away in her smartly tailored blue service uniform. Her sleeve showed four stripes, the rank of a class leader.

He observed the air of confidence his Granddaughter showed as she advanced toward their meeting.

As she came closer, her smile grew into a grin, "Hi, granddad. Did you visit Mother B?" she pointed. "It's still there. Where we all live – 3,600 strong – in the largest dormitory in the world."

Midshipman First Class Mary Talau sat on the stone bench opposite her grandfather. Her legs were crossed at the ankles. Her body posture remained tall, as if she were on parade.

"Sure did." Sam Talau's voice quivered with age. He swallowed hard to clear what appeared to be a slight cold. "You sure you have time for this? I suppose you're busy with your studies and all that -- don't want to interfere."

"No sweat, granddad. My next event isn't for more than an hour. Bet you remember that statue over there." She pointed. "Tecumseh. It's still there. We still throw pennies at him on the way to our P-works and finals."

"Some things never change," he said.

"The place has changed since you were a mid in the '60's, though, lots of women now," she said.

"True, but the Academy's like a moving target, constantly keeping up with war fighting of the times." Then, for a moment his head bent and his eyes focused from his granddaughter to the ground as he spoke. "If your grandmother was alive, she would be as proud of you as I am."

She smiled. "Thanks, granddad. I miss her, too."

"Well, dear, I don't want to take too much of your time. Better get to it. You've heard my story, now it's your turn." Sam said, pulling the collar of his coat a bit tighter around his neck to ward off the chill of an Annapolis fall. "Is the Academy the same or different? You were going to explain for me if you think the backbone of this place is the same as in my day or not? You know what most old grads believe, don't you?"

"That it's not as tough as when they were mids."

"Well -- is it?"

"I've always liked your story; you guys had some fun and some rough times, but you know what, sir? Mine are just as good. In fact, the stories we women tell are better."

"Like what?"

"Like, for the first class of women – they came in the summer of 1976 -- most of the men didn't want them. They left dead mice and rats in some women's mail boxes. They even succeeded in loosening the elastic on their underwear. Even so, of the 81 women in the original class, 45 graduated -- a higher percentage than the men. I'm told that a girl in a later class was cuff-linked or tied, whatever, to a urinal. There were all kinds of pranks that have occurred. Some mids moved a female company officer's office -- furniture, pictures, and all -- into a men's head. They filled one company officer's office to the ceiling with newspaper. Others stole the Army mules and brought them to Annapolis during Army week. We still have food fights."

"Sounds like something mids might do. They have women company officers?" Sam asked.

"Yes, sir, and they're darn good. Actually, I think there's less hazing than in your day -- that's because of the heavier academic workload; the curriculum is no longer lock-step. We study the same basic engineering program you studied, but do the work for a specific major on top of it. And I never heard of a plebe taking on a firstie, but I guess it could happen. His dad being commandant at the same time he was brigade captain seemed damn far-fetched, but I guess it could happen."

Sam shrugged his shoulders and smiled, the smile of experience. "You're not answering my question, Mary."

"Granddad ..." she said in the tone of her age. "I'm getting around to it."

Sam tugged on his hat, sat back against the bench, and folded his arms.

"Sounds like Blake Lawrence III had three girl-friends at once," She said.

"Ah ha, you remembered the girlfriend part of my story. But he lost the one he really cared about. You're still not answering my question, dear."

"Sir, with due respect to an old grad, I did listen patiently to your story."

"Okay. You got me. I'm afraid I've never been known for my patience."

"Of course things have changed. For every class it begins the same -- with the oath -- that hasn't changed. And, I think the four years in the yard remains the same timeless rite of passage you went through. The difference is that we have to be ready for our war, and ours will be more technical and possibly more human. The ships and planes and submarines you described in your story are obsolete -- probably been ground up for scrap by now. Like, in every period the technology drives what we have to learn. The period from about 1960 until 1978 was the period of biggest change here. The major thing that happened was in 1975. That was when the law was passed to permit women to attend. I believe the school did change after women were admitted. In my opinion women are treated better now than in your day. I believe that perhaps some of the language improved and women as a whole are given more respect -- not just the mids, but the girlfriends, too. I think there's more compassion in dealing with problems without giving up the hard shell that was called for at other times. Midshipmen now learn to deal with diversity, differing opinions, and differing solutions. Those who believe women don't belong in the military get practice in dealing with the realities before entering the fleet."

"Mary, what I want to know, is, is the same sense of nobleness Blake Lawrence spoke of engendered in the graduates of today?"

"Well, the iconoclasts would say 'no -- and good riddance.' But I know better. We spend as much or more time thinking about such conceptual things as *you* did, maybe more. Today we have courses in philosophy. We are still expected to take the high road. Yes, I think there is a sense of nobleness instilled today. Some would call it 'duty,' but it's still about honor and country -- and we know it. We may not totally adhere to 'Ours is not to reason why, ours is to do or die,' but we sense that sacrifice to country is noble, and that does exist."

"What's it like to be a woman midshipman? Did you have a good plebe year?"

"For me, a good plebe year is one in which each mid learns a lot about themselves. They have to answer the question: Is the ocean experience for me? I believe plebe year should be difficult, so that by the time it is over, each midshipman can have a personal sense of accomplishment.

Sam reflected on how professional his granddaughter seemed.

Were we this squared away? She uses the same language I do, none of that "like" and "you know" stuff she used in high school.

"Was your plebe year just like the men?"

"I think so. It was very similar -- at least in my company. On the other hand I didn't expect any special treatment. Some women thought they shouldn't have to meet the tough physical standards. Those women were treated more harshly or with less respect. Plebe year taught me that it was okay not to be the best at everything as long as I always did the best I could. I believed in not lying, cheating, or stealing no matter how difficult the situation. I also developed a much deeper sense of pride and patriotism."

"Did you ever consider quitting, like Lawrence did?"

"No, not really. I never had any hand-wringing because I never thought I would leave. But lots of others did."

"Do you date?"

"Granddad???"

"Okay, none of my business -- but -- you were going to explain for me if the backbone of this place is the same as my day or not. You still haven't."

"Okay, okay, Granddad. Yes, I believe the core values are still in place. I believe that the Academy is still strong and capable of producing solid leaders. Based on the hero of your story -- Blake Lawrence was a very good one at that -- I'd say we measure up very well. The core values are still there and probably won't, and can't, change.

"It's the Mother B experience -- things that happen in here that can't be replicated anywhere else. No college can do the same thing. And one other thing -- the ocean experience -- that hasn't changed either."

"Well, it took long enough. As if you're unsure."

"I'm not -- it's a good place for what we must do. But... Well, Granddad, what do you think? Do I have values?"

"Mary, you're my granddaughter. You know the answer to that question. But, we really won't know, will we? Not until you're under fire. I don't mean bullets, although that, too. I mean under the pressure of leadership -- command. Then you'll know."

"Granddad, can I ask you a few questions about your story?

"Sure. What?"

"You always tell it with Blake Lawrence as the main character. Why not you?"

"His story was more spectacular."

"Where is Lawrence now?"

"Still in the fleet -- commanding big things -- fighting wars -- building the Navy."

"What about Lee Locke?"

"He's doing big things, too."

"Do they still call you 'Napoleon?"

"Some do."

"Granddad, you have my curiosity. What was the most significant thing you did in your intelligence career?"

"I wish I could tell you, dear. But I can't." He smiled. "I'd have to kill my only granddaughter."

LETTER FROM A GRAD

Carl,

Sorry it has taken me so long to respond, but here's the answers to the questions you asked.

1. I had a fairly good plebe year. I had no military background and was not good at rote memorization, so the professional material was extremely difficult for me to grasp. Academics were challenging (largely due to the time constraints and having validated quite a bit), but the teachers were fair and helpful. Overall it was a huge learning experience for me. Having been the typical mid at the top of my high school class, it was a big adjustment for me to learn that I no longer could accomplish everything to perfection - there just weren't enough hours in the day to get it all done. I participated in sports and glee club so I had an outlet from all the work, and I think extracurriculars are very important to developing a well-rounded individual with a greater variety of experiences to draw from.

2. To me, a good plebe year is one in which each mid learns a lot about themselves, the Naval Academy and military life. The foundations of teamwork, courage and personal integrity need to be formed from the beginning. Plebe year should be difficult, so that by the time it is over each midshipman can have a personal sense of accomplishment. Navy life requires that you work hard, even when there are other things you would rather be

doing. I think you need to learn discipline, how to function under pressure, and how to meet deadlines. Formations, inspections, chow calls, come arounds, sports and academics help develop this. There also needs to be some relief valves in place though. My company was very close and there were opportunities to have a little fun with all the classes throughout the year without losing respect for the upper classes.

3. I believe my experience was similar to the men in my company. I did not feel that I was any different then the men, I didn't expect any different treatment and I do not think that I was treated any differently. There were women who expected to be treated differently - some thought they shouldn't have to meet such tough physical standards, or that they could flirt a little and these women were treated more harshly or with less respect.

4. Plebe year taught me to work hard, to work together, and gave me greater self-confidence. It also taught me that it was OK not to be the best at everything as long as I always did the best I could. I believed in not lying, cheating, or stealing no matter how difficult the situation I faced was. I also developed a great deal of trust in and respect for fellow midshipmen and the chain of command. If I was having trouble in anyway, I knew I could count on a fellow mid no matter what, even if we did not know each other.

5. One of the biggest lessons I came away with was "Do the right thing because it is the right thing to do." I learned to take care of the people who work for you. They are your greatest asset. As a leader you really need to listen to their concerns and find ways to help them

improve themselves. Professionally I learned to stand up and take charge. When you are in a position of leadership those below you are looking for you to make your best judgement and take charge, not sit back and be wishy-washy. I learned how to analyze data quickly, form an opinion and make a plan. I also learned how to identify the most important items to be accomplished since not everything could always get done. I also developed a much deeper sense of pride and patriotism.

6. I never had a hand wringing because I never thought I would leave.

7. I believe the school did change after women were admitted. I believe that perhaps some of the language improved and women as a whole were given more respect - not just the mids, but the girlfriends too. There may be more compassion in dealing with problems when needed without giving up the hard shell that is called for at other times. Midshipmen learn to deal with diversity, differing opinions, and differing solutions to the same problems and those who believe women don't belong in the military get practice at dealing with the realities before entering the fleet.

8. I did not see anything that I would consider hazing, although the girl who made headlines with the urinal incident during Army-Navy week was a classmate of mine. My personal opinion is that she brought most of the upperclass actions on herself not because she was female but because of how she acted. I didn't know her well, though and I don't have any specifics.

9. There were all kinds of pranks that occured while I was there. Some examples are moving a female company officer's office (furniture, pictures, and all in to a men's head), filling the company officer's office to the ceiling with newspaper, stealing the Army mules and bringing them to Annapolis during Army week, starting food fights.

10. I thought the academics were challenging. I was a chemistry major who was not nearly as bright as all those planning to attend medical school. Within my major, however, everyone worked together so very few dropped out after the beginning of youngster year. I spent most nights as an upper class studying until midnight and studied every weekend to succeed. As long as the instructors taught well you could get good grades if you worked hard enough. However, I did have several poor instructors - both military and civilian.

11. My intention as a plebe was to get well started in a career before ever thinking about dating. I was very focused and did not date during my first two years there. I had many male friends with whom I am still very close today. However, during the fall of my second class year I started dating a firstie. We kept the relationship very low profile and very professional around the hall. We never went out together in Annapolis. In fact, most of my classmates did not even know we were dating until after he graduated. We got engaged in February of my first class year and have now been married almost 9 years.

12. I do not think that boy-girl stuff is a problem if everyone behaves maturely. There will always be those

few that bad apples to tarnish the reputation. In fact, I felt like I had so many big brothers it was amazing. If I even thought about dating someone, my "brothers" had to give the approval first. Also, there were many times when fellow mids would ask for advice. Sometimes it was better too to have a member of the opposite sex for a sounding board when you were struggling with a problem.

13. We had several dining-ins while I was there including one I attended while playing sports in Canada at one of their military academies. I thought the events were great for instiling some of the great traditions of the Navy. We never started food fights then like they do in the fleet.

14. I went on several cruises, and I think they really helped me to decide which career path I wanted to follow. My elective cruises (2 sailing cruises and Plebe Summer Detail) helped me develop leadership while having some fun. My gray hull cruises gave me an view of Navy life outside the shelter of the Academy. As a younster I went on a Destroyer Tender and worked mostly with the Snipes. My running mate, a huge BT2 who didn't think women belonged in the Navy and wouldn't even speak to me at first, gave me a real appreciation for what the enlisted personnel really think. Living in enlisted berthing was a good educational experience. As a second class we went to Quantico, Pensacola, and Kings Bay to experience those career paths. As a first class I flew with a CH-46 squadron. After my aviation cruise I no longer wanted to fly and instead chose the Supply Corps. At that time women could still choose Supply since combatants weren't open

to women yet. I am happy that it was an option, because Supply Corps has been the perfect community for me, and I've still spent plenty of time at sea - much more than my aviator husband.

15. I believe the root values are still in place. For a time I believe the midshipmen were given too much liberty (weekdays, excessive weekends) and freedom and this allowed them to become unfocused and undisciplined. However, that has changed again and I believe that the Academy is still strong and capable of producing solid leaders.

I hope this information helps you. If you need clarification on anything please let me know.

Katie Edwards '92

BOOKS ABOUT ANNAPOLIS

Letters From Annapolis: Midshipmen Write Home 1848-1969, Anne Marie Drew, Naval Institute Press, 2000.

Blind Man's Bluff: The Untold Story of American Submarine Espionage, Shery Sontag and Christopher Drew, Public Affairs, NY, 1998.

The U.S. Naval Academy, Jack Sweetman, Naval Institute Press, 1979.

Plebe, Hank Turowski,'71, Paradigm Press, 1994.

Return of Philo T. Mcgiffin, David Poyer,'71,

A Sense of Honor, James Webb, Prentice Hall, 1981.

✳*The Nightingale's Song,* <u>Robert Timberg,</u> Simon & Schuster, 1996.

A Civil War: Army Vs. Navy, John Feinstein, Little Brown and company, 1996.

An Annapolis Plebe, Edward L. Beach, Class of 1888.

Annapolis Plebe, John H. Keatley, New York: Duell and Sloan, 1957.

The Story of the Naval Academy, Felix Riesenberg, Jr., Naval Institute Press, 1958. Forward by W.R. Smedberg, III, Superintendent USNA.

The three volume Midshipman Robert Drake books are:

An Annapolis Youngster, Philadelphia: Penn Publishing, Co., 1908.

An Annapolis Second Classman, Penn Publishing, Co., 1924.

An Annapolis First Classman, Penn Publishing, Co., 1923.

Buck Jones at Annapolis, Two editions, Capt. Richmond Pearson Hobson, Class of 1889, published in New York and London by D. Appleton, one in 1907 and one in 1910.

H. Irving (Harrie Irving) Hancock (1868-1922), who did not attend the Naval Academy, wrote the Midshipman Dave Darrin books, which also feature Midshipman Dan Dalzell. They are:

Dave Darrin's First Year at Annapolis, Akron, Ohio & New York: The Gaalfield Publishing Co., 1910.

Dave Darrin's Second Year at Annapolis, The Gaalfield Publishing Co., 1911.

Dave Darrin's Third Year at Annapolis, The Gaalfield Publishing Co., 1911.

Dave Darrin's Fourth Year at Annapolis, The Gaalfield Publishing Co., 1911.

Brigade, Seats! The Naval Academy Cookbook, Karen Gibson, Naval Institute Press, 1993.

Folklore & the Sea, Horace Beck, Wesleyan University Press, 1973.

The Amphibians Came to Conquer: the Story of Admiral Richmond Kelly Turner, Volumes I and II, George C. Dyer, Department of the Navy, Library of Congress Catalog No. 71-603853, 1969.

The United States Navy in World War II, S. E. Smith, Editor, William Morrow & Company, Inc, 1966.

Bridges at Toko Ri, James Michener, Ballantine, NY, 1957.

OTHER BOOKS BY CARL NELSON

Published Novels

Madam President and the Admiral, New Century Press, 2008. Sequel to *Secret Players.* Nominated for Pulitzer.
Secret Players, New Century Press. 2003. Winner of the 2003 "best thriller" award by the prestigious San Diego Book Awards Association.
The Advisor (Cô-Vân), Turner, 1999. Won "best fiction" as judged by Southern California Writers Conference. Endorsed by Elmo R. Zumwalt, Jr., Admiral, U.S. Navy (Ret/Dec) and Robert S. Salzer, Vice Admiral, U.S. Navy (Ret/Dec).

Published Non-fiction Books

The Message of the puzzle Ring: *(A true story that can change your life (and the world), NCP, 2011.*
Import/Export: How to Take Your Business Across Borders, 4rd Edition, McGraw-Hill, Inc., **2009**.
International Business: A Manager's Guide to Strategy in the Age of Globalism, International Thomson Business Press, ITBP, 1999.
Exporting: A Manager's Guide to World Markets, ITBP, 1999.
Protocol For Profit: A Manager's Guide to Competing Worldwide, ITBP, 1998
Managing Globally: A Complete Guide to Competing Worldwide, Irwin, 1994.
Global Success: International Business Tactics for the 1990s, TAB-McGraw-Hill, 1989.
Your Own import-Export Business: Winning the Trade Game, Global Business and Trade Communications, 1988

Read Carl Nelson's other books by placing your order at his website: www.carlanelson.us